D1493233

Stroganov in Company

Collected Stories by

CARYL BRAHMS

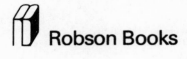 Robson Books

FIRST PUBLISHED IN GREAT BRITAIN IN 1980 BY
ROBSON BOOKS LTD., 28 POLAND STREET,
LONDON W1V 3DB. COPYRIGHT © 1980 CARYL
BRAHMS.

Brahms, Caryl
    Stroganov in company.
    I. Title
    823'.9'1FS   PR6001.B6
    ISBN 0-86051-103-0

Printed and bound in Great Britain by
Redwood Burn Limited, Trowbridge & Esher

To Alan Coren, the finest humorist of his day writing in this country, with gratitude and affection.

The Author would like to thank that great lover of words and Dean of Drama Critics, J. C. Trewin, for a foreword any writer must envy her. Miss Elizabeth Rose and all who work at Robson Books, her much tried publishers; and to *Punch* and the *Guardian* in which journals some of these stories first appeared. To Ned Sherrin, for reading the stories aloud to her when she was in the throes of selecting them, in the most appropriate of his seven voices; and to the memory of S. J. Simon who created the character, Stroganov, with her.

Contents

Introduction

I am sure Caryl Brahms rises early. Certainly she and the White Queen share at least one gift: they can believe as many as six impossible things before breakfast. The White Queen, dear soul, stops there; but Caryl Brahms, hypnotic at any time of the day, goes on to persuade her readers. Often, after an hour or two with our least orthodox historian, I have wished that she had the official re-shaping of the centuries; facts and people are so much more cheerful as she rearranges and juxtaposes them on the page.

That is the full-length Brahms. But in her shorter stories, though as a rule without the same blending and blurring – the juxtapositions are always there – she still uses her period sense to animate a scene in the fewest possible words. Take this (from *Yesterday, Last Night*):

> Caroline and Lorna were bowling along St James's in a hansom-cab – two English roses, their stems tucked under the apron, wearing boaters and veils, nid-nodding in time with the clipper-clopper, clash and jingle, on their way to the offices of the family laywer.

Or, earlier in the same story, turn-of-the-century:

> Down in the village it was bedtime. Paraffin lamps were being twiddled; candle wicks snuffed out between

moistened rural finger and moistened rural thumb. Up at
The House they were at dinner.

Lady Elinor (up at The House) 'patted her pearls. Five rows –
most reassuring'. We know everything about Lady Elinor. But
so at once we do about any of Caryl Brahms's people. Whatever
their affairs, they reveal themselves in a witty rhythm, in a prose
of precisely-planned pause-and-effect – if you will, choreo-
graphed – where every detail, every repetition (and observe the
Brahms way with repetitions) is exactly in key.

In these stories Caryl Brahms can be both delightedly a
participant and, as in the first sentence of *Just Another Party*,
coolly an observer: 'The Palazzo, when at length it was located,
proved to be a vast pile of a proud but needy grandeur, pink in
parts.' The last three words are true Brahms. But then so is this
passage from *Cotillions and Ices*, tale of two little girls, a Queen
and Princess (and future Queen) at a Children's Ball at Buckingham Palace on a May evening in 1829:

> And in this dream of flying ribbons and satin dancing
> slippers, the evening whisked away. They were wearing
> Bombazine and Algérine, Barège and Voluto, Mull and
> Alpaque, Peau d'Ange and Pekin, and Satin Esmeralda
> with Passementerie; Taffetas and Leno Lawn, Mous-
> seline and Poplin, Piqué, Foulard, Benzaline and
> Balzarine, Challis and Tarlatan, Calamanco, Carmeline,
> Clementine, Chiffon Gros-des-Indes, Paduasoy, and
> Looking-glass Silk and La Sylphide, and many, many
> other tissues with enchanting names.

It is the kind of run – like Caryl Brahms, I find it irresistible –
that reminds me of what Ivor Brown called the 'glorious word-
waterfall' in one of Edward Thompson's poems (they should be
better known) that begins 'Tramboon and cinnamon: Myrrh
and Myrabalon', and goes on from there.

Caryl Brahms, as happy with an orchestrated sway of
language as with a sequence of swift short-cuts, is a romantic
and an ironist; she is as sensitive as sympathetic. She likes to

discover names (Lady Mcgilliefleur, for instance, and Mrs Multifarious); and you never know where you are going to be next. Possibly with Stroganov (now what can you say of him? his creator says it all), or the little Queen who slipped and fell, or balloons in an Edwardian sky, or Lady Postern (who is 'Mum' in the wry little miracle of that name). Maybe, too, an ancient holding on the marshes of the East Coast (festival time), or Chekhovian vignettes that show Caryl Brahms's love for the man of whom she has always written acutely, or home life with the crimson lady who 'whipped through the wall and wafted unhurriedly to keep tryst with the Cardinal on the West Wing staircase', or the narative of a Daimler limousine which ends simply: 'This story of a car and its price for sale happens to be quite true: and yet how few believe me when I say so.'

Not at all. I repeat: she makes us believe. We began with the White Queen. Let me end with the Dickensian lady in the wig, from *Martin Chuzzlewit:* 'Mind and matter [she said] glide swift into the vortex of immensity. Howls the sublime, and softly sleeps the calm Ideal, in the whispering chambers of imagination.' Somehow I think that Dickens, when he wrote that, had been borrowing from Caryl Brahms who – with a gleam in her eye – would have handed it to him in his dream, very early in the morning. That done, and nearly 140 years on, she would have settled down wittily to her own pre-breakfast pleasures: probably the story of Christmas, Cherry the housemaid, the third footman, and that environing society of ghosts.

Hampstead, 1980   J. C. TREWIN

STROGANOV

A Bishop in the Ballet

Evening in Santa Fé, with the distant snow mountains rose-tipped in the sunset and the Ballet Stroganov guesting at the Opera House. It was the off-season.

Vladimir Stroganov was sitting in the Presidential Box, a carnation resplendent in his buttonhole, his bald dome shining with enthusiasm, beaming at the spectacle his company was presenting. Beside him sat the Bishop of Chi-hua-hua, an unlikely companion, all things considered.

On stage a gaggle of straggle-tailed swans were doing their somewhat bleary best. In the wings an assortment of mothers were crossing themselves Holy Russianwise, or shaking dubious heads, according to whose daughter was about to embark on a technically perilous pas-de-deux or variation – her own peerless little genius or some less fortunate mamoushka's clodhopper.

On the other side of the auditorium in the Stage Box, Madame Arenskaya, the Ballet Stroganov's spirited Maîtresse-de-Ballet, was being restrained with difficulty from hurling a shoe at the simpering Prince, currently a young – well, middle-aged Master Eyelashes with a receding hairline, who had bought himself into the Stroganov company and bribed his way into a few leading rôles, though he was in no way ready for the honour in Madame Arenskaya's frequently-expressed opinion.

Stroganov glowed at the Bishop: 'My Company is perfect, no?'

'No,' said the Bishop, deciding for once not to hide the truth under a biretta.

Fortunately the headlong Stroganov had not stopped talking

to listen to him. 'Wait only till you see our *Giselle* – the mad scene,' he specified, and ticked it off on one podgy finger, 'our *Boutique Fantasque*,' he continued ticking off should-be masterpieces, 'our *Oiseau de Feu*,' he ticked, 'our *Sylphides*,' he ticked, 'our . . . our . . .' he sought for a ballet to clinch his argument, 'our *No Holds Barred*, a Nevajno work, *bien moderne*, the scene it is a boxing ring, in,' he paused for dramatic effect, 'Outer Space.'

'You have run out of fingers,' observed the Bishop, coldly.

'Me,' announced Stroganov, 'I envy you who are seeing the fabled Ballet Stroganov for the first time. What rapture awaits you!'

'This a rapture?' The Bishop of Chi-hua-hua did not sound convinced. He gazed disbelieving at the middle-aged young Master Eyelashes who at that moment was surrounded by, but alas! not lost in, a group of depressed swans.

'That one,' said Stroganov dispassionately, 'is a geese. But he is rich, so each time Arenskaya give him sack, he give me bribe,' he rubbed his hands, 'so me I say, Poof! and I take him back.'

In the Stage Box Arenskaya was turning to her companion, an antique General who had attached himself to the company, in what capacity no-one could say.

'General,' she ordered, 'oblige me, *mon cher*, go to my dressing-room and bring me my pearls I have borrowed – Sheherazade,' she explained all – 'without my pearls I am non-stop nude.'

'Aie!' said the General, alarmed, and creaked away..

Freed from his restraining presence Arenskaya removed a shoe in readiness.

The curtain fell but rose again immediately lest the audience should take it seriously. The ballet itself was at an end. But it had been merely the hors d'oeuvres before the banquet. Now the real business of the evening began. The bows and the bouquets. First the corps de ballet scampered on with not an hibiscus among them. Then four soloists lined up and advanced to what the great Fokine once designated 'The Tootsies'. Each soloist clasping to her non-existent bosom the flowers sent by mamoushka, husband, or self. Hardly time to bow gracefully. From the crimson and gold splendours of the Presidential Box, Stroganov applauded vigorously. 'You do not clap for my children?' he asked the Bishop incredulously. 'The poor ones will think they have not pleased you.'

The Bishop, recalled from whatever holy theme he had been pondering, clapped obediently; but Stroganov could tell that the episcopal heart was not in it. And he was right. The Bishop had been thinking how to get a receptacle full of white heroin tablets through the inquisitive British Customs. He was no common or garden bishop. He was a common or garden pusher.

Now it was the turn of the Swan Princess – gin would not melt in her mouth, but a great many carbohydrates had. She stepped forward clasping her flowers to her stomach of which, currently, there was no lack. 'All of it muscle,' her mamoushka declared to the whispering and pointing fingers in the wings where the usual bunch of eyebrow-raising mamoushkas raised their eyebrows. They smiled pityingly.

The Bishop answered to his cue and clapped loudly. Stroganov grabbed the holy hands.

'Me, I do not applaud this one,' he protested. 'She has the mamoushka money-conscious! Already now she has eye on Presidential Box – this Box,' he could not resist boasting. 'So me, I sit on the hands,' he demonstrated, 'lest she demand of me the wages I owe the fat little daughter.'

By now it was the turn of the middle-aged young Master Eyelashes with the receding hairline to bound on boyishly. He bowed to the Presidential Box, he bowed to the audience, he bounded off into the wings. 'That one,' said Stroganov admiringly,' is a bounder. The pity is, he does not dance so good, Arenskaya is right; but do not tell her so for it is bad for her character.'

'Ah!' said the Bishop. He placed his fingertips together and surveyed the stage, gazing over the tops of his rimless spectacles, as the bounder bounded back on-stage. Once again, he bowed to the Gallery, to the Family Circle, to the Grand Tier, to the stalls, and finally, a grave mistake, to the Stage Box.

'Now,' breathed Madame Arenskaya. She hurled.

The brouhaha had all but subsided. Vladimir Stroganov, mopping his brow, bobbed up from behind the Bishop, where he had been hiding from the wrath, which, born optimist that he was, he hoped was not to come.

'Quick, little Father,' he implored, 'we make the getaway damnquick and lock ourselves in my office before they start the cry and hue. The tequila and soda awaits us there: we have the little sozzle before the rich one with the eyelashes comes to demand his bribes back. And later, when all is over and the little mothers are marching their little daughters straight back to their little hotels, for the morals in my company are very strict, you understand, we risk backstage together, where there will be waiting Zoë Zeitlinger, your little chou-chou.' The Bishop blinked. 'She has the figure tempting,' Stroganov outlined the curves with two podgy hands, 'and I caution her to be kind to you. Also she have no mamoushka, only the husband for the work permit, and he will not interest himself. And after, we take her and the Rich One with the big bum and the tide-out hairline to supper to console him. Arenskaya we do not take; always she demand the gipsy music and always it end in tears.'

'But,' said the Bishop . . . he fumbled for his indigestion capsules.

'You go pale, little Father, but do not have the fears financial. The Rich One will pay. I offer him another spectacular rôle so he pays now and later I take the rôle away and he give me spectacular bribe to get it back again. There are,' said Stroganov happily, 'always ways.'

'Ho-hum!' said the Bishop.

'But for now it is the tip-toe through the tulips – you get me?'

The Bishop did. The tip-toe was mother's milk to a pusher, but Stroganov could not know this. Together the ill-assorted couple crept out. The corridor gained, a shrill voice brought them to a halt. It was Arenskaya, one shoe on and one shoe in the incensed grasp of the middle-aged young Master Eyelashes. 'Vladimir,' she shrilled, 'you go at once to the dressing-room of the Eyelash One and you demand back my shoe I have borrowed from Dyrakova who is away and do not know she lend – she dance *La Folle de Chaillot, chez* the Beryl Grey, a long woman. But she come back to us tomorrow.'

'*La Folle de Chaillot* will not have the look-in when Dyrakova find out,' opined Stroganov, 'when Dyrakova go mad she have a *grandeur* unmatchable.'

'Me, I am no joke at going mad,' Arenskaya boasted to the unintroduced Bishop. '*Tiens*! I like your shirt – purple suit you.' She turned her back on Stroganov. '*Alors?*' she urged. She placed her hands on her hips (Zizi Jeanmaire in *Carmen*). She tossed her bright red head. She waited. Stroganov read the signs.

'Why throw, my darlink?' he pointed to the slipper. 'Why you not think first?'

'But this I do,' said the aggrieved Arenskaya, 'I think there is the dancer world-wide-worst. I think I throw Dyrakova's shoe at him, and then, *mon cher*, I throw.' She turned for sympathy to the unintroduced Bishop. ''E 'as big bum,' she explained, pointing to it. The middle-aged young Master Eyelashes flinched. Arenskaya jerked her crimson curls in the direction of the pass door. 'Go, Vladimir, go at once – at once – or else . . .' She propped herself against the Bishop to take off Dyrakova's other shoe. She shook it at Stroganov, 'or else . . .'

'Do not impatient yourself, my darlink. We go at once, my new chum and me. Hand in foot we go together.'

'Ah, *bon*!' Arenskaya said. She relaxed.

Up in his office Stroganov was his own man again. He motioned the Bishop to the armchair – the only armchair. He poured tequila with a lavish hand. He himself sat on the revolving chair behind the desk. He spun round on it – sheer swank – and when he had come to rest the pair of them toasted each other. 'Should auld acquaintance be forgot,' intoned the Bishop.

'This the old chum will never let you do,' Stroganov shook a realistic head: 'Or they are after you for the free seat, or they are after you for the money you owe them.'

'Then,' the Bishop suggested, 'we will drink to new friends.'

'New friends,' said Stroganov enthusiastically. They drank.

'There is a little matter I would like to discuss,' the Bishop looked round him furtively – for a bishop, that is.

'You can confide in me,' said Stroganov. 'My office it is sacrosanct. No-one comes here and if they do I kick them out damnquick.'

'Ho-hum!' said the Bishop. He polished his rimless spectacles.

Should any reader ask himself how Stroganov and the Bishop
became 'the chums bosom' the answer is easy.

Both had been gazing wistfully at the windows of the local
Tiffany's. Stroganov was attracted immediately by the bright
shade of pink that passes for purple in a Bishop. Remember
that it is out of season at Santa Fé. Barons and bishops are hard
to come by. If only he could capture this one and seat him
beside himself in the Presidential Box it would dress his house
which badly needed it. Before everything he was an impresario,
the Stroganov One reminded himself. As to the pusher, he was
looking for a credulous individual to carry his heroin through
the customs for him. Stroganov fitted the bill. Were not his eyes
a child-like blue, and his despatch case much labelled with the
names of far-away lands?

The next two hours the enstomached gentlemen wasted
cautiously stalking one another. Finally thirst put an end to
caution, and they found themselves sitting side by side at a little
table outside the Taverna in the Plaza.

For a time they conversed amiably – the cost of living. The
cost of lemon tea. The cost of politicians. The cost. Then
Stroganov popped the question – 'You come to my box at the
Ballet tonight? I give you card.' He scribbled.

The pusher whistled a happy tune. Heroin was as good as in
the Chelsea fixer's bag.

Back at the office the Bishop was putting his head as close to
Stroganov's bald dome as the latter's revolving chair permitted.
Next to his ballet, his revolving chair was the pride of
Stroganov's life. He travelled it everywhere with him.

'My friend,' the Bishop was intoning, 'I have not known you
long as time goes, but there is something about you that ins-
pires confidence.'

'My chair?' Stroganov gave it a twirl. 'In me,' he announced
when it came to rest, 'you can have the confidence absolute.'

'You see,' the Bishop lowered his voice, 'it is – ah! – a family
affair, and in my position . . .'

'*Mon ami*,' Stroganov answered him, 'I comprehend to
perfection. All families have the skeleton in the cupboard, *n'est-
ce pas?* But me, I am the soul of discretion. Mamoushka is the
word!'

'It is?' asked the Bishop dazedly.

'Me,' said Stroganov virtuously. 'I do not even tell the Eyelash One with the bum *énorme*, and,' he beamed, 'the money to make the mouth water in the letter from his aged wife with the oil-well in Texas – which remind me,' he leapt up from his seat and studied the calendar on the wall. 'This month she is late already. But no matter; he has much jewellery she give him to tempt him that he shall return to her. With this he can raise the hurricane.' The Bishop blinked. 'And so, little Father, you can count on the secrecy absolute. We are cosy here, no? No-one dare to come to my sanctum to disturb me.' He twirled.

'Sit still like a good chap,' said the Bishop, 'and listen attentively.'

'I am the alert.'

'Back home in Chelsea, England, I have an aged grandmother,' the Bishop confided.

'No kidding?' asked Stroganov, looking pointedly at his white locks.

'See this wet, see this dry?' said the forgetful pusher. He blushed.

'And this aged one, she is in the trouble financial?' asked Stroganov from out of a wealth of experience.

'The trouble physical,' said the pusher. Stroganov's misplaced English was getting to him. 'If my old grandmother does not get her fix – I mean the medicament I shall give you for her...'

'She gerfut?'

'She gerfut,' agreed the Bishop.

'Then why you not take it to her damnquick?' Stroganov demanded, reasonably enough.

'I have duties – ecclesiastical duties – to perform in Mexico,' his new friend explained. 'You will be in England before me. So, I tell myself, "Perhaps you would be a..."' the pusher bethought himself. From out of his small store of Bible stories learnt at the Borstal chaplain's knee, he produced '"Good Samaritan" and take this package to Chelsea. And there a – mm – colleague of mine will relieve you of your trust and convey it to my ancient grandmother.'

'*Bien sûr*,' Stroganov beamed. 'Before everything me I am impresario, and after that the Samaritan good – for the moment,' he added with unusual caution.

'Then it is understood?'

'It is understood.' The Bishop had recourse to his indigestion tablet. You come to my box – the Presidential Box,' urged Stroganov, 'tomorrow night and you give me your little grandmother's medicaments.'

'And you do not tell a living soul?'

'Not a syllable to a sturgeon,' swore Stroganov. He took off in his revolving chair.

The door burst open. It was Arenskaya.

'Sit still, Vladimir,' she commanded.

Stroganov frowned. 'What you do in my sanctum, old chum?'

'I . . . I . . . I . . .' Arenskaya stuttered. She reared her head like a good Russian goose.

'You . . . you . . . you . . .' greatly daring, Stroganov mimicked her. 'In future, you knock. Then I call out go away, and you vamoose damnquick. You must understand I am busy here with my new chum and the matter confidential about his ancient grandmother.'

'Ho-hum!' coughed the Bishop, and cast a warning look at Stroganov. But on that one it was lost for already he was in full if broken spate.

'The little Father entrust me with the medicaments for his ancient grandmamoushka, and I have give my word – the word of a Stroganov, woman – not to tell a living creature, and not you, it is certain, that I take the packet to England and give it to . . . and give it to... to whom do I give it?' he enquired of the sweating Bishop, who was quite bereft of words.

There was a sharp knock at the door. 'Go away,' called Stroganov. He twirled. Relentlessly the door opened and in came an irate mamoushka trailing her hesitant daughter, that night's Swan Princess.

'Sit still, Stroganov,' she said. 'We have come to plead our stomach.' She pointed to her daughter's protruding abdomen and patted her own for emphasis. 'We are *enceinte*,' she added unnecessarily.

Arenskaya took in the stomach at a glance. 'She is right, Vladimir,' she concurred, 'she is *enceinte*, and this is why she keep leaving my *Classe de Perfection* and lock herself in the loo, where she bring up.'

'We need money,' said the mamoushka.

Stroganov looked at his new friend. 'Poof!' he said. He shrugged.

'The back months already you owe us.'

'And the advance generous,' suggested Arenskaya, evilly paying Stroganov out for some ancient injury – she had forgotten which.

'On whose side you are?' he asked her hotly. Then at bay, he turned on mamoushka and daughter. 'You go away. It is out of hours, and me, I am busy with the Bishop. I have to write myself a note to remind me what to do with the medicament for his little grandmother. It is the errand of mercy, you understand, and also the matter confidential, so me I don't tell no-one.' He looked at the apoplectic pusher. He winked.

There was a knock at the door. It was the middle-aged young Master Eyelashes. But the assembled company could not know this.

'Stay out!' they called as one man. 'Go away,' they added. 'And don't come back no more,' screeched Arenskaya solo.

The Eyelash One blinked. He decided to bivouac outside Stroganov's office, if necessary for the night. 'We Eyelashes,' he reminded himself, 'We Eyelashes hang on by ourselves.'

For the next week the little grandmother of the Bishop was the name on the lips of everyone remotely concerned with the Stroganov Company and even some quite unconnected with it. But it was not until after the Bishop called at the Box Office to collect the pass to Stroganov's box ('The Presidential Box,' pointed out the Box Office Manager, bowing with touching respect. 'And how, my Lord, is the health of the little grandmother these days?') that he remonstrated with Stroganov again.

Up in his office Stroganov was in full spate. 'But I tell you,' he was shouting into ththe telephone, 'I pay the creditors all, all, all – but not my tailor. The ancient little grandmum of my new chum, the Bishop, has for me the gratitude immense, or will have, when I give the fellow in Chelsea the capsules which keep her ticking.'

'Vladimir,' said the Bishop, shocked, for the friendship had flowered into Christian names. 'You gave me your word that you would not tell a soul.'

Stroganov nodded violently. 'It is the matter undisclosable,' he told the telephone. 'My lips are sealed and you must say nothing to no-one, and specially not to my tailor – *entendu? Eh bien, mon cher Esteban, au revoir.*' He put down the phone. He gave his chair a twirl. 'And now, old chum,' he said, 'what is new?'

'You promised, Vladimir. You promised you would not disclose a syllable.'

'To a sturgeon. This, Francesco, I remember. And I have only told a fat little pigeon in the second row, who is my new love personal, and the Gipsy in *Petroushka*, who is my love old – soon I give that one the sack – and the Master Eyelash One, instead of the rise he covet; and still the wife in Texas does not send the money urgent – you do not think she know all?' Stroganov turned a stricken face on the Bishop.

'All, no, the merciful heaven forbid,' said the Bishop, shocked.

'And the Manager Bank, him I tell for sure, that one has no *joie de vivre* and the company physiotherapist,' he recollected – 'that one he pommel it out of me!'

The phone rang. Stroganov applied himself to it and in a babble of Bishops, new chums, grandmamoushkas, capsules and gerfuts told the disembodied enquirer all – or as near all as made no difference.

The Bishop looked at the ceiling. It remained oblivious.

'But who were you telling on the telephone, Vladimir?'

'Poof!' Stroganov dismissed the disembodied voice, 'That one was my very old friend from the British Customs, so we have nothing to fear.'

The Bishop seemed to be having breathing trouble. He clutched his throat. But Stroganov appeared not to notice this. From his desk he picked up a bill. It was one of many. He glared at it. 'My tailor,' he observed, 'is the disgust. He demand small fortune and besides his suit it do not fit, for the food in the Americas South it is very rich with oil and olives, and me, I like good blow-out very much and . . . and . . well, see for yourself, Francesco – the suit across the estomach do not meet.'

He breathed out. A button popped.

On the following afternoon no-one in Madame Arenskaya's somehat optimistically named *Classe de Perfectionnement* was at the very height of high spirits. The one and only daily paper that rated among the ballet-goers of Sante Fé had been less that ecstatic about the Stroganov ensemble. It seemed that their unanimity was insufficiently unanimous, as 'Ajax', their fussy little ballet critic, had not failed to note; their solo variations, dangerously chancy with all the odds against their finishing face to the audience, their Musical Director richly deserved to be fired out of hand, or should it be band? – Ajax was quite a wit, as ballet critics go – and as to their two leading dancers, they resembled two plum pigeons getting together, mating and walking away in opposite directions, each unimpresed by the other's performance.

Was the Stroganov artistic direction slipping? Emphatically, Ajax warned his readers.

Only the Regulation Soviet Defector – they were increasingly to be found world-wide in ballet companies – was bounding hopefully about the Opera House Ballet Room, limbering up with coltish grace combined with soaring ambition. Boris Bashkirtsov, a mere sixteen going on seventen, already had his *entrechats* at his toe-tips. Was he not the Definitive Defector? Nureyev, poof! Barishnikov, tcha! or so he told himself and tried to believe it.

Bashkirtsov had the makings of a *danseur noble,* as Ajax had not failed to indicate in his notice. Why must his Arts Page Editor always blast his bedtime prospects by fiendishly cutting any praise from his copy?

Arenskaya's *Classe de Perfectionnement* trundled on. The Definitive Defector essayed six tumbeld-into turns, achieved two and a half, from which classroom disaster he ended up, not facing the mirrored wall, but facing the pianist, a lady with large hat and a perpetual cold. Confidence ebbed. Had there not been that all too brief season with an ad hoc off-Broadway company at at time when the great Barishnikov was appearing at the Met? 'I can do that,' the sixteen-year-old told himself, erroneously, for already some of the New Yorker's attitude to the prowess of other people had rubbed off. 'I can do that,' he told himself again, and tried. He could not. This morning he watched the middle-aged young Master Eyelashes with, and understandably, the hangover from Stroganov and the Bishop of Chi-hua-hua's roistering last night, demonstrating his second act *enchaînement* from *Giselle* to a limp-wristed group of would-be Princes. They couldn't do that and they damn-well knew it!

Soon a well-known voice cut through the lassitude. The limp wrists stiffened. The class's collective stomach turned over. Madame Arenskaya, a schooner doom-laden, had sailed into her *classe de perfectionnement*, the General, a bemused tug, in her wake. She dropped anchor in the doorway, filling her arch like a sallow Sarah Siddons. Her eyes searched for an erring object on which to unleash a tirade: it was child's play. 'You,' she screamed, 'the growing-bald one with the behind *énorme,* you vacate the centre of stage and Boris show you 'ow it is done, or should be, should be, while I address myself to the posture of *la petite* Miranda, who 'ave the hips small and the boobies none-at-all.'

She turned to the General, swaying her own curved hips and cupping her own lustrous bosom. The General flushed. The pianist sneezed and emitted a timorous arpeggio or two. Arenskaya shot her a murderous glance. '*Assez de chi-chi*! You play valse from *Coppélia* and mark well the beats.'

The pianist sniffed, pulled down her hat and thump, thump, thumped. The assembled company, exhausted in all but its ambition, toppled from one predicament to another. Madame Arenskaya's *Classe de Perfectionnement* was on its long, long way.

Halfway through the morning the Bishop of Chi-hua-hua dropped in. He looked around. He fished in his robe for an indigestion capsule. No Stroganov. How could there be since at this very moment that one was up in his office telephoning his man-of-law, Sir Arbuthnot Chiddingfold, continent to continent, as he boasted to the uninterested operator:

''Allo . . . 'allo . . . 'Allo . . . 'allo – 'allo!' Stroganov was jiggling the instrument so no croak from the other end could thread its way among the crackles to him. 'Is that you, *mon cher?* I wish you to write the villain Ajax that me, I 'ave crossed through his name on the free list many, many times – in violet ink' – he clinched it – 'and to the manager of my London bank in

Cheapside – cheap, I ask you? – to say if he do not stop pursuing me with his boring demands I will cancel my overdraft. And to my tailor that I cannot be bothered with his silly bills and . . . and . . . to the little grandmother of the Bishop of Chi-hua-hua . . .'

At this point Sir Arbuthnot slammed down the receiver causing Stroganov to erupt into a storm of 'Allo, 'Allos and jiggering at the end of which he took a refreshing twirl in his chair. The enemies had been silenced, or soon would be. He had won the day. All was mooch better in the best of all possible worlds.

Meanwhile, down in the classroom, Arenskaya had undulated across to the Bishop. 'You slept well, my friend? *Bon*! And 'ow is the *estomac* of the little grandmamoushka to whom we take the pillules?' She patted her own. A glazed look passed over the Bishop's eyes. It was just such a look that might be found in a cod's eye on the fishmonger's cold marble slab. Should he kill off his little grandmamoushka forthwith and scotch the danger that surely must be lurking in the future? And yet . . . the pusher thought of the money there was in the capsules. The Bishop thought of the Sante Féan jail. Beneath the petunia robe that they were sporting both Bishop and pusher engaged in a man-to-man struggle. Greed won the day.

'Pretty,' said Arenskaya, oblivious, fingering a petunia fold.

And where was the middle-aged Master Eyelashes, who, offended, had flounced out of class? Well, actually he was on the osteopath's couch. The osteopath, no mean judge of ballet, was pommelling.

'That's for your *Prince Igor* . . .'

'Ouch!'

'And that's for your *Florizel*.'

'Ouch!'

'And *this* is for *Sylphides*.'

'Ouch!'

The balleto-osteopath executed an involved and particularly painful joint-shaker.

'And this?' asked the victim, 'it is for *Giselle*, no doubt?'

'No doubt at all,' said the balleto-osteopath. He went on thumping.

Time passed.

'Now,' ordained Arenskaya, 'we take the doubles. You Boris and the little Miranda, *au devant.*'

Bashkirtsov and the little Miranda took up their positions in front of two lines of furious partners. It wasn't fair. Always the Definitive Defector and the boobless Miranda were put in front of them.

'First, my darlinks, the Fish Dive,' Arenskaya said fiendishly, and waved her pupils on to their catastrophes.

Boris and the little Miranda went to it.

'There now,' said the suddenly materialised Stroganov, 'there you see the future saviour of the Ballet Stroganov.' He pointed to Baskirtsov, 'If 'e stay,' Stroganov reminded himself.

That night the Company seemed inspired – at least to its titular head, Stroganov. 'They 'ave dedicated this performance to the little grandmum,' he explained to the dozing Bishop. 'See 'ow the legs of the Bashkirtsov one twinkle.'

From swan to swan, gosling to gosling, soloist to soloist, and even the semi-dormant Benno, the Prince's friend, the word was whispered. 'The tablets for the antique grandmamoushka. How happy she will be when she has them safe in her hands. Nothing shall befall it, we have sworn,' vowed the swans, 'to the last drake.'

There was a thud. The semi-dormant Benno had failed to catch that night's ballerina, a Yugoslavian dancer. She picked herself up from the stage. She could be seen to be swearing in good round Armenian oaths.

The ballet went on.

Nothing out of the ordinary at Heathrow Airport, that after-noon. Just the usual mix of overheated travellers, Japanese, American, Indian, Blacks and the po-white British, plus a racing-round of everyone's kids. No, nothing out of the ordinary.

Yet what was this bald-headed old buffer at the Customs Bench using his arms like a protesting windmill, trying to snatch back a tin from the customs officer who had opened it.

'But it is the medicaments for the Bishop's grandmamoushka, like I say,' Stroganov was shouting.

'This is so,' said his whole company and one elderly Russian General, grouped round him.

'Without her medicaments she gerfut,' Stroganov persisted.

'She gerfut,' agreed his indignant company.

'So you oblige us, and tell no-one,' Stroganov urged, 'for the Bishop he not forgive you if it transpires.'

But the Customs were adamant.

'*Non*! *Non*! I tell you, *Non*! I do not smuggle for the money. I have no need. Or shall have when the pocket-money for the Eyelash One shall arrive from the rich wife in Dallas.'

'Nonetheless,' said the Customs – they could be adamantine, too.

Somewhere unbeknown to Stroganov sweating in the held-up and cursing about it queue, a Bishop was feeling very, very sick. He fumbled for his tin of indigestion tablets. He swallowed one. It had the most extraordinary effect. He could have sworn that he was floating.

Three hours had passed. 'But you do not understand,' Stroganov was shouting to the plainclothes detective at Bow Street Police Station, 'first I demand my man-of-law. He is for the moment in New York, so you get on the telephone damn-quick!

'But,' said Inspector Lawless, paling, 'New York – that's in America.'

'*Précisément*,' Stroganov agreed. 'We will speak continent to continent – at expense of police.' He pounced. He jiggled, ''Allo, 'allo, 'allo, 'allo,' he began expectantly.

But this time Detective Lawless pounced and attempted to snatch. 'Oh, no, you don't.' The detective tugged. Stroganov held on. Deadlock.

Suddenly Stroganov bethought him of another ploy, and let go. 'Get me Inspective Detector Quill,' he commanded.

Detective Inspector Lawless blanched again. 'Quill? Adam Quill?'

'Damnquick,' said Stroganov purposefully.

Detective Lawless mopped his brow. Clearly he was out of

his depth. 'But Mr Quill – I mean, he's the Assistant Commissioner.'

'Ah, *bon*,' Stroganov beamed. 'Then he assist me, you will
see.'

At that moment a Presence made itself felt. Commissioner
Quill, suitably be-buttoned, and tailor-made, had emerged
from some glorious inner office to see what the brouhaha
outside was about.

Overjoyed, Stroganov threw his arms around him and kissed
him on both cheeks.

Inspector Lawless could scarcely believe the evidence of his
eyes.

'Monsieur Quill,' cried Stroganov, 'my old chum Inspective
Detector!' He hugged the aggrandized but unresisting Quill.
'You tell this policeman it is all fault of the little grandmum of
the Bishop One.'

'You heard, Lawless,' the Assistant Commissioner barked.
'Release Stroggy – Mister Stroganov.'

'Damnquick,' said Stroganov.

'Exactly,' said Commissioner Quill.

'And we go at once to your office and have the whisky-and-
soda, and the smoke-salmon sandwiches appetising, while I tell
you about the antique grandmamoushka, the Bishop, and the
capsules entrusted to me. Without them our grandmamoushka
she gerfut.'

And that is how certain clients in Chelsea paid an all-time
high price for bicarbonate of soda.

A Brabble in the Ballet

'Brabble: A clamorous Contest.
A Squabble. A Broil'
Dr Johnson's Dictionary

It was twelve o'clock noon and therefore the hour of Madame Arenskaya's company class for the Ballet Stroganov. It could have been taking place in London or in Paris or in New York or, of course, in Topeka, Santa Fé or San Francisco, the sights and sounds would have been much the same. The screeches of disgust (Arenskaya). The thumping of the stick (again Arenskaya – who else?). The pounding on the out-of-tune piano.

And then, of course, there would be the excitable fringe of Ballet hangers-on who were nothing if not partisan. The even more partisan curdling of Ballet-Mamoushkas. The odd ballet critic – and ballet critics can be very odd. There would be Fernando, the sardonic, interested Barman-Balletomane from the station buffet where the Company could chalk up their one meal of the day. And, finally, we must not forget the dancers straining away at the barre in preparation for the forever out-of-reach mastery of limb and balance when, the barre abandoned, they proceed to centre-practices and, inevitably, from one catastrophe to another. Here they pose, preen and peer at themselves in the long mirrors that line one wall – oh, that they need never move – but move they must, gliding and unfolding – hoping, poor lambs, for the poetry of a perfected technique, but perpetually abandoned in the hop . . . hop . . . hop stage.

Of course the scene would have been much the same at twelve noon the world over. It just so happened that today and for the next fourteen days, it was taking place in the rehearsal hall at the Opera at Monte Carlo where the Ballet Stroganov was temporarily becalmed, and where Arenskaya was exercising her well-known screech and beating out rhythms with her alignment stick on whatever surface was nearest to cane.

Up in the office in the Dome of the Opera, two Puppa Stomaches were chatting amiably across an opulent desk.

'For the moment,' the bald man with his back to the light was emphasizing, 'for the moment I am the broke.' He was a Russian Puppa Stomache.

'I congratulate you, Mr Stroganov, on your candour,' said the visiting, and incidentally British, Puppa Stomache.

'*V'la!* We are the bloody brothers!' he announced. 'I have the best Ballet world-wide. You,' he pointed a chubby finger, 'come to me with the money for an important investment, and Allez-Hoop! we are in business.'

'We are?' asked the British Puppa Stomache just a shade dubiously.

Stroganov jumped up from his desk and shook his new blood brother enthusiastically by the hand.

'Come,' he commanded. 'We go together to Arenskaya's Company Class where you shall select for yourself the little Ballerina luscious,' and he sketched her inviting shapes in the air.

'I say!' said his bloody brother, blushing again.

Down in the rehearsal hall a well-matched pair of dancers, slender, supple, musical, were executing a doubles routine with seeming ease and style, which put the envious class, by now crowding the imaginary wings, to shame.

The little Serafina was partnered by B. Bashkirtsov, the Definitive Defector from the Maryinski Ballet, so she went sailing through the air like a bird on the angled wing with B. Bashkirtsov supporting her, lifting her, turning her and returning her.

B. Bashkirtsov was the secret pride and joy of Madame Arenskaya, as was well-known to the Stroganov Company, since she was as ready to tell her own secrets as she was to impart those of other people.

'B. Bashkirtsov, my darlink,' she was cooing, 'you are the British Prince Charles of Dancers, or will be when I have finish you off.'

'The British Prince Charles of Dancers – Oh! He is – He is!' breathed the little Serafina fervently.

'Stay silent, you,' snapped Arenskaya. 'Is it not enough that I, Arenskaya, his teacher, approve?'

'But he's such a wonderful cavalier, Madame. Me, I am sure no-one in the world can partner as well as the British Prince Charles, I mean,' she explained, confused, 'B. Bashkirtsov.'

'The British Prince Charles,' muttered a Mamoushka, optimistically, 'high time he is married, that one.'

'You will not listen to Serafina,' Arenskaya was screaming at B. Bashkirtsov. 'She is a stupid struck-star little girl and will only swell you the head. Besides,' she played her finishing stroke, 'she 'ave no boobs.'

It was at this point that Stroganov erupted into the rehearsal hall with his prospective backer in tow, like the tail of a well-upholstered comet.

'Good mornings, my Angel. You have slept well, no?' His angle glared.

'Go away, Vladimir, and,' she switched glares, 'take your fat friend with you.' The well-upholstered comet's tail had been feasting his eyes on the pair in the centre, B. Bashkirtsov and the little Serafina. He tugged at Stroganov's sleeve. 'Introduce me,' he hissed passionately, indicating the elegant partner.

'But,' Stroganov misunderstood, 'she is flat like a boy.'

'Introduce me like you promised, or else . . .'

Stroganov beckoned urgently, 'I keep my word, the word of a

Stroganov.' He threw back his shoulders. 'This,' he indicated, 'is the little Serafina. And this,' he pointed to his prospective backer, 'is my bloody brother.'

That evening two *tables-à-deux* had been reserved at *Le Sporting*. Fortunately, they were at opposite ends of the restaurant, for at one Vladimir Stroganov was at supper with his Ballet Mistress, while at the other his potential Backer was supping not with the little Serafina but with B. Bashkirtsov.

'Have some more caviar,' he was urging, 'it is delicious.'

At the end Stroganov was attempting to soften up Arenskaya.

'More caviar, my darlink,' he was pressing on her. 'It is not at all bad.' Arenskaya was wary. When Vladimir offered her caviar, something fishy was sure to be afoot.

At the other table B. Baskirtsov was gazing intently at his opposite number.

'Did you say a Company?' he asked.

'I did,' said the British Puppa Stomache.

'Of my own?' B. Bashkirtsov was determined to put this all-important matter on the line.

'Of your own,' the Puppa Stomache endorsed.

'Les Ballets B. Bashkirtsov,' breathed B. Bashkirtsov.

'Exactly,' said his host, happily.

'And I can have the little Serafina to star in it?'

'Well . . .' said the British Puppa Stomache, a lot less happily.

'So you see, my darlink, you have only to give the little Serafina the advice *bien maternelle* . . .' Stroganov gazed with his eyes full of sentimental tears, but the pitying expresssion on Arenskaya's face could not be ignored; so he hurried on. 'My backer prospective, he demanded the little Serafina.'

'But, Vladimir,' the pitying expression remained on Arenskaya's face. 'Look only,' she besought, 'at table at end of room.' Stroganov looked. *'Mon Dieu!'* he slapped his brow. *'Mon* backer providential! And me, I never suspect my new blood brother is, too, the lib gay!'

'Innocent one,' said Arenskaya, almost lovingly. Stroganov changed the subject.

'This British Prince Charles – the royal one – I think I invite him to draw the Tombola prizes at the Gala we shall hold for

Les Petits Lits Blancs. What say you?'

What Arenskaya said was strictly unenthusiastic. Stroganov ignored her. 'A pity, only, he makes all the time little chokes . . .' He had another try at the difficult British word. 'Yokes. Like his father. No matter, I 'ave already invite 'im to my Tombola.'

'And you think he come?'

'*Bien sûr,*' said Stroganov, the optimist, 'after all, he is not Benôis himself. *Tiens!*' he bethought him, 'that one ought to marry.'

'And if he do not come?' Arenskaya asked.

'Doubtless he send the younger brother, the British Prince Andrew – he, too, love the little yoke.'

Next noon, after class, Arenskaya beckoned B. Bashkirtsov over. 'We go to the station buffet empty, where no-one listen, and we have the little talk *maternelle,* and me, I pay.' She clinched it.

So together they walked down the steeply sloping hill to the station.

Seclusion achieved, save for the acutely listening ears of Fernando, the Barman-Balletomane, Arenskaya opened fire.

'My darlink, I have been thinking of your future.'

'Me also,' said B. Bashkirtsov, 'I am meaning, I am thinking of *your* future.'

'This,' said Arenskaya, 'is kind but *pas nécessaire.* Me, I have no future – only,' she winked, 'a past. But for the present – I teach.' She drained her *fine* to the lees – if a brandy, however indifferent, can be said to have lees; B. Bashkirtov quaffed from his can of Pepsi-Cola.

'You teach, Madame,' he said, 'your class is superb!' He kissed his finger-tips. 'But where?'

'You should know; you are late for my Company class every day at noon.'

'Where?' B. Bashkirtsov repeated intently.

'B. Bashkirtov, it is my opinion considered that you are mad. Me, I am the greatest teacher world-wide.'

'*Entendu, entendu,* 'her pupil bowed to her. 'But where?'

The needle seemed to be stuck in the groove.

'But in the Ballet Stroganov, idiot. Some day I make it the greatest Ballet world-wide. But for the moment it is only great, *tout court.*'

'But some day,' said the Definitive Defector, slyly, 'when I have Ballet of my own . . . which is already promised . . .'

'Some day,' said the great Arenskaya, not hearing, 'when I have scolded you into a great, a very great *Danseur Noble;* some day, when I have taught you to hold in reserve a little something so that public think you pause in the air when you lengthen your leap; some day, when I have exile from your face the schoolboy grin like the British Prince Charles – *tiens!* That one ought to marry – and replaced it with the expression haughty as becomes the *Danseur Noble;* some day . . .'

'Some day,' echoed the Definitive Defector. He pulled himself together. 'You and I shall drink to the Art of the little Serafina.' Arenskaya did not want to lose her favourite pupil. 'If,' she admitted, 'this little sparrow with the windmill arms, make happy . . .'

'Oh, she does! She does! Moreover she dance with so much *abandon . . . .*!'

'She dance *pas trop mal,* the little Serafina, or will do when I have scream at her and hit her with my stick sufficient. But is it the dance only that she do with passion?' asked Arenskaya acutely.

'So far,' admitted B. Bashkirtsov. He frowned. 'We must together learn this sex thing,' he admitted. He blushed.

'Oho!' said the overhearing Barman-Balletomane. He had brought over a saucer of bullet-hard, unripe olives, such as abound in the South of France.

'Aha!' said Arenskaya, delighted. 'Sex I do not teach my Ballerinas. Sex is like bortsch – good Russian bortsch. A woman must be born knowing how to make the bortsch, and the sex.'

'She must?' B. Bashkirtsov made a mental note. He decided that this was the ideal moment to lay his trump card on the table.

'I am to have my own company,' he said, 'the Ballet B. Bashkirtsov. In lights. This is promise.'

'Who promise?' Arenskaya's eyes were two slits. Someone was out to steal the pride of her leaps, beats and turns.

'Stroganov's bloody brother,' said the barman who prided himself on being the first with the news – any news.

'Is this thing true?' Arenskaya asked B. Bashkirtsov.

'It is true,' he told her, 'and already I engage the little Serafina. Together we dance on to Glory.'

'Tell me more,' said Arenskaya grimly.

'And you are to be engaged as teacher to the Company B. Bashkirtsov,' said the Barman.

'I am to be the what?' Arenskaya was outraged.

'There will be much money,' B. Bashkirtsov told her. 'Money for you, money for dancers, money for new ballets, the classics, everything. We commence in the New Year, and till then I have much to plan. Cigar,' he ordered.

'Oh, no you don't. The smoking is bad for the dancer – not so bad as the sodomy, which enlarge the behind, but bad for the breathing.'

'But,' B. Bashkirtsov started to object, 'I do not know what Stroganov pay you?'

Arenskaya sniffed.

'Not much,' chipped in the Barman.

'I double this,' said B. Bashkirtsov, grandly.

'The deal big!' said Arenskaya. 'Now, listen to me, Big Boy. Me, I have had many such offers, for my Method it is unsurpassed. Me, I teach Ballet Stroganov for the peanuts and teach good because I love this company. Not nothing nor no-one can bribe me away from Ballet Stroganov. I never would desert Vladimir Stroganov.'

Into the silence, a tribute to Arenskaya's eloquence, a human projectile burst. It was a bald-headed, big stomached projectile and already it was in full spate, both arms in play to back up mere speech. Vladimir Stroganov had arrived at the Monte Carlo station buffet.

'Villain! Villain! You,' he pointed a pudgy finger at the Definitive Defector, 'you are the wolf in snake's clothing who catch my Bloody Brother and Prospective Backer *énormément riche,* you . . . you . . . you . . .' Words failed him as he towered over B. Bashkirtsov, who had leapt to his feet and took refuge behind the hovering Barman. Arenskaya had been visibly swelling with the need to utter. Words had not failed her. They never would. She addresssed herself to the flailing arms.

'Vladimir,' she screeched, 'only I, his teacher, may scream at him. Is this understood?'

'You,' said the boiling-over Stroganov, 'are the feeble old woman who is fit only to dry the sunflower pips for sensible people to nibble.'

Arenskaya rose to her feet, the better to deal with this heresy. 'Did you say feeble?'

'Silence, woman!' Stroganov thundered – at least he meant to thunder, but since rage invariably sent his voice up into the treble clef, the words came out in a ventriloquist's squeak. Meanwhile B. Bashkirtov had crept behind the bar to serve himself a large *fine* and an equally large cigar. Now he emerged to face Stroganov in a cloud of smoke. He took an uncertain step in roughly the right direction.

'Have the big cigar,' he offered from out of his newly-cushioned *richesse*.

Absently Stroganov nodded, selected the choicest and stowed it away in his breast pocket.

'Have a *fine*,' the Barman invited, 'a double,' he specified, 'on him,' he pointed. 'Impresario to impresario.'

Arenskaya, who had not forgotten the deadly insult of the sunflower seeds, had been biding her time. 'I Arenskaya, am leaving you also to teach the Ballet B. Bashkirtsov, so put that in your cigar and smoke it.'

Stroganov turned a reproachful look on her; and if ever a gaze said 'Et Tu, Arenskaya,' his was it.

The discordant party was now joined by the little Serafina. B. Bashkirtsov, who had been downing the *fine*, rocked to his feet. 'Before everything,' he promised her, 'I am the great lover – or will be, when we have sorted this sex thing.'

The little Serafina smiled her Portuguese seraph's smile.

'My angel,' he swayed towards the little Serafina, 'were you born in the Bortsch?'

'B. Bashkirtsov,' said Arenskaya, 'if you not stop babbling, I do not teach your low class company.'

'*Bon,*' said Stroganov.

'I do not teach at all.' The threat was terrible. 'I retire.'

The gun in the fortress at Monaco broke the incredulous silence of all present. The Stroganov Company pulled itself together. The gun had spoken. It was four o'clock, time to go back and rehearse. Stroganov and Arenskaya were the last to leave.

'*Eh bien,* old woman,' he said.

'I will never desert you, Vladimir, this you know; but also I will never, never give in to you, when you are in the wrong; and this,' said Arenskaya, 'is the always.' But she took his arm as he puffed up the steep unavoidable hill.

A busy day at Bow Street police station which in itself is in no way out of the ordinary. The usual unkempt rabble of morning-after-riotously-drunken-night-before. The usual marches of demonstrators demonstrating, to be protected from the usual marches of anti-demonstrators anti-demonstrating. The usual house-breakers, car-stealers, rapists, kidnappers, black-mailers. Trouble at t'Airport, 'and so on and so forth,' thought Assistant Commissioner Adam Quill – not an original mind. And, of course, the Irish, and this was without counting the continual movement of The Royals. Herself enjoying one of those 'walkabouts' so popular with the populace, so hair-raising for the police. His Nibs chairing a debate on UFO's. Princess Anne, Mark Phillips and horses driving down to Hick-stead. Princess Margaret due over-the-way (and a very narrow way at that) at the Floral Street Entrance to the Royal Opera House for the Royal Ballet, Princess Alexandra tasting the produce with every appearance of relish at an ice-cream factory, and Roddy Llewellyn – Oh, well!

And only this morning an unofficial but urgent call from Greenland that Prince Charles was pondering an invitation to a Gala Night at Monte Carlo – time he got married, of course, but that would only mean more work for the police; and then there'd be the two of them to keep an eye on at the Winter Slopes, and the good lord knew where not! And one has only to think of burly Sergeant Banner on a ski-slope to see that he would figure on the crowded list of Quill's catastrophes.

But what was this envelope, insufficiently stamped, from . . . he scanned the postmark . . . Monte Carlo? A coincidence? In spite of the murder-hunt which should have been on his mind, Quill ripped open the envelope. Good old Stroganov – he never forgot 'Inspective Detector' Quill. What was it this time? A late

Christmas card? An early Easter card? A highly coloured view of Rio de Janeiro?

It was a letter, written in Stroganov's usual compulsive English, headed *'Urgent*. Not to be read by no-one – and special Arenskaya,' and inserted in his letter, a note in a more spidery hand. 'This letter I steam open – it is bore. Arenskaya.'

Stroganov's missive ran: 'You come quick, Monsieur Quill. We give the *Scheherazade Im*-peccable. It is a pity only she have no boobies. Vladimir. PS. I have invite the British Prince Charles who have no wife – why, I ask myself? – to the *Bal de Petits Lits Blancs*, where my Ballet dance – B. Bashkirtsov, he dance *magnifique;* but there is one who would steal him from me. So you come instant, and see he don't. Vladimir Stroganov, Impresario and Businessman.'

Quill was definitely tempted. He could do with some sparkling sunshine. He was due some leave. And only the day before he had received word that a particularly slippery British confidence-trickster, wanted internationally, had touched down in the Principality. He could do worse than drop in on Stroggy and his Ballet Company – quite like old times.

A slack day at the Monte Carlo station buffet, but things were to look up, for here came Stroganov, out for his early morning jog – a new activity.

'Good mornings,' he greeted the yawning Barman between gasps and puffs.

Hardly had he settled at his marble-top when in jogged – to be honest it resembled less a jog more a stalk, which was the way Nicholas Nevajno the intellectual modern choreographer, usually progressed, and already he had produced a cheque book. 'You schange schmall scheque?' he suggested optimistically.

'No,' said the Barman. Nevajno was in no way perturbed. He did not even waste time simulating surprise.

The sound of heavy breathing wafted over to them. A presence made itself felt. It was an enstomached British presence. It had not been so much jogging as pounding up-hill, trying to track down Stroganov. Now that its search was brought to a triumphant conclusion it produced a cheque-book. 'Vladimir,' it puffed, doing its breathless best to sound confident, 'you might change a cheque for me.'

'Me,' said the astounded Stroganov, determined to settle this thing beyond reasonable doubt, 'schange scheque for you?'

'Got it in one,' said his estranged, but ignoring this, blood brother.

'But your Bank Obliging?'

'*Fermeture Annuelle,*' said his Backer Prospective errant. He lowered his weight gingerly onto a spidery seat at Stroganov's marble-top to an accompaniment of creaks. It was beginning to dawn on Stroganov that maybe his Backer Prospective was less your heaven-sent, more customer slippery.

'But,' said Stroganov hotly, 'you have steal from me my Defector Definitive and give him a company with your money multitudinous which you promise to me – to me.' Stroganov's voice mounted to the treble.

'Come, come, Vladimir. I do not give B. Bashkirtsov his Ballet – I only promise . . . on certain conditions. Which,' the large pink face looked a little bleak, 'he has by no means met as yet.'

'The little Serafina attend to that,' said the all-knowing Barman, 'or will do when they learn the sex thing.'

'Go a-way!' said Stroganov. He scanned his blood brother's candid countenance – or was it? It was an innocent at large in the jungle of the ballet world. In need of guidance from a more sophisticated fellow.

'Come, old chum, let us jog together to my office where there are no ears flapping to overhear, and where we shall see,' caution came back, 'what we shall see!'

Together the two enstomached gentlemen jogged congenially away.

What they saw, Stroganov's office reached, was Assistant Commissioner Adam Quill. True, he was not in uniform, but there was no mistaking his orthodox black shoes and the firm set of his chin, or the keen glance as he recognised Stroganov's companion. Quill knew his Rogue's Gallery. He had seen that face before.

'My old chum, Inspective Detector, it is good to see you here, in time for the British Prince Charles, who no doubt have the little choke with you.'

'No doubt,' said Quill glumly.

'Why he do not marry, like his father, who can say?' Quill affected not to hear. 'And now, my old chum, I present to you my new bloody brother.' He looked round. *'Tiens!* He is not here. Where can he be?' Stroganov peered under the table fruitlessly. 'Can he have done the bunk? I ask myself. But I tell myself "No", for I was just about to ask Box Office to schange him scheque.'

'Oh, well,' said Quill, 'we'll pick him up at Nice Airport.'

In the mornings, from ten till noon, Arenskaya gave private lessons. This morning she was late.

Meanwhile, B. Bashkirtsov awaited her with the pianist who was stroking a few of his favourite chords. They supplied the right ambiance for confidences. B. Bashkirtov was in a mood to make them.

'Me, I do not believe this backer who promise me my company because he admires my Art. It is queer, this . . .'

'It is very queer,' said the pianist, somewhere between a high-pitched giggle and a stroked chord.

'Somesing he says and somesing he looks – but never will I . . . will I . . .'

'Disappoint the little Serafina?' suggested the pianist helpfully.

'Never!' B. Bashkirtsov swore. 'Only unfortunate is I slate up big monies at station buffet and I schange Nevajno schmall scheque and . . . and all on my . . . on my . . .'

'Great expectations?'

The Definitive Defector bowed his blond head. 'Queer,' he mused.

A Kidnap in the Ballet

La Bazouche is by no means Cannes. It is not even Menton or Monte Carlo, being smaller than either. But it can boast a Casino Municipal. Moreover it can rely upon its alert and energetic Sûreté.

'Ballet Company,' the officer was saying, 'called after some Rousski dish.'

'Piroshki?' suggested the new man, keen as French mustard.

'Stroganov,' his superior remembered. 'Last time he was here there was trouble.'

'What kind of trouble?' the new man asked.

'Troublesome trouble,' said his superior severely. 'So you cut down to the Casino and – mark me well – no Boules'

'Boules?' The new man sounded deeply shocked. He was hopeful of creating the impression that butter wouldn't melt – at least for the next few weeks.

'Cut along then and keep an eye on the suspect,' the new man was instructed. 'Draw your own conclusions and keep out of sight.' The new man dashed away. His second day only and already a suspect! Indeed, a whole Ballet of them!

'Mesdames et Messieurs': the plump man with the bald dome mopped it. 'It is for me the pleasure inexpressible – so why I try to express it, you ask yourselves? And me, I tell you. It is because the gentleman with the indigestion chronic from the Press Department of your Casino hospitable demand it of me. Now where was I?' Vladimir Stroganov gazed questioningly at the dual microphones, but answer came there none.

'Inexpressible,' prompted little Louis Legrand in a hiss. He produced a heart-shaped box – his Marie-France had embroidered it with her own plump hands – and from it took another peppermint cachou. '*In*-expressible!' Stroganov beamed at the busy little pigeon of a man from the Press Department; he it was who had insisted on the dual microphones to lend the somewhat sparse occasion dignity; for little Legrand was hand-in-glove – or rather, pocket – with the local T.S.F., although whose hand was in whose pocket was always an arguable point among less successful journalists. For little Legrand was also 'Vigilante' of the Friday Column in the *Bazouche Reveille* and *Homme le Nôtre* of the *Marseilles Meridienne*. But it was high time for Stroganov to press on.

'Last time I am here at La Bazouche – I remember it well – not only do I lose the shirt at your roulette – that croupier was no true Balletomane,' he complained. 'It was all his fault I have no money left to pay my hotel – l'Hôtel de la Gare et de L'Univers,' he swanked, 'but all end well, for I do the flit-clair-de-lune . . .' he leafed frenziedly through his notes. 'ah, oui! We have no ballerina suitable for our gala *Giselle* so Arenskaya tell Dourakova we are the Ballet Beryl Grey – a long directrice – who have engaged her and,' he chuckled, 'paid her fare out, and as one *Giselle* is much like any other, we kidnap Dourakova and she dance with us. It is a pity, only, that she hit the Duke with sword in the Mad Scene – an old friend,' he explained.

A potted palm rocked perilously. The new man from the Sûreté, having dropped by at the Salle de Boules just to see how the numbers were running for his system, had arrived behind it in time to hear the word 'kidnap'. Phew! and only his second day at the Sûreté. But wait a bit. Now where had he stowed away his obligatory carnet? The one that would accompany him on oath at the hôtel de ville. His uniform had many pockets; he felt hastily in all of them. *Vide!* Nothing for it but to return to the Salle de Boules. In spite of the pickle he was in, the new man's face brightened, only to cloud over again. The skies and all they held forbid that he had left his carnet on the marble ledge on which to note 'openly confesses to kidnapping'. He tried to write it on his thumb-nail . . ,. too damn small. *Merde alors!* Soberly he retraced his steps.

That day only the costumes for the one ballet, and that, *Coppélia,* and some of its décor had torn itself from the clutches of Stroganov's creditors, but *'V'là!'* said the bald impresario, 'We are in business!'

The next night they gave, *faute de mieux,* that glorious masterpiece or old warhorse, which description depended on whether the speaker was the optimistic impresario, or his modern choreographer, Nevajno. The new man from the Sûreté was there – or would be when his new combination came up in the Salle de Boules. From his box – the Burgomaster's since that functionary was abroad in Britain learning how to run a strike for bigger Burgomasterly bribes, Stroganov scowled at his audience. Whoever invented the tickets complimentary should be made to sit on them – behind pillar, he observed, not for the first time.

Coppélia had ambled itself to the point where the old mechanical toy-doctor, Coppelius, was having trouble in losing the key to his attic workship. It should have dropped from his pocket when he pulled out his handkerchief, but the Puppa Ivanov, all false nose and shaggy eyebrows with an eye-patch, and a leer for real, had been bereft of his bandana by the Boss's creditors, together with sundry other props.

Arenskaya, the company's formidable *Maître-de-ballet* as she was wont to describe herself, *'Maîtresse, c'est autre chose'* – was sitting weeping into his snowy handkerchief which she had purloined. 'If only my dear husband P. Puthyk were dancing – never did I allow him to forget a prop.' She rounded on Stroganov: 'Why you let them lock him up in that pretty mental home in Surrey? Everyone in every ballet company is mad, it is well known, so why my Puthyk?' But Stroganov was leaning from the Burgomastrolian box at a dangeous angle, casing the house.

'Tiens!' he exclaimed as he spotted a thin man concentrating on the goings-on upon the stage, 'Is that my antique good friend, Dr Kalmanski, the Impresario from New York? What he do here?' Arenskaya's voice had an edge to it. She, too, leant dangerously from the box.

'What he do?' she repeated. 'Do not tell me. I know. He is here to sing the song of the siren to charm our Ballet away to New York where Clive Barnes kill us! You,' her elbow dug

Stroganov in the ribs, which nearly shot him diving into the stalls, 'you will forbid him our Casino, or he come every night!'

'He pay,' said Stroganov judiciously. She gave him another shove.

'You listen to me, Stroganov.'

'I listen,' said Stroganov, striving to wriggle himself back into the box, 'but I am a man of business. I must hear what his offer is, then debate the matter with myself, then I say No and he bid again.'

'Vladimir,' said Arenskaya, 'you are the Disgust Artistic. What has our Ballet to do with money?'

'Often I ask myself,' said Stroganov sadly, 'but until tonight myself cannot answer.'

The first act curtain came cracking down. Stroganov applauded heartily. Not so his antique good friend, the Impresario from New York.

'Why he not applaud my children, the Kalminski one?' he asked wrathfully. 'Is not my Ballet good enough for him?'

'Maybe no,' said Arenskaya, 'if only your antique good friend could take a fancy to Nevajno and take that one to New York,' she sighed. She did not see eye to eye with Stroganov's modern choreographer.

Next morning, a thin figure with a thinly rolled umbrella was to be seen pacing the corridor outside Stroganov's office. Soon a tall and melancholy figure arrived – definitely not Stroganov and in fact Nevajno – to pace in the opposite direction. Round the corner, as though glued to the wall, the new man from the Sûreté, a sturdy type, was, as he told himself, all ears. No-one spoke.

Then Arenskaya arrived to break the silence. She addressed herself to the thin man.

'You here long? It is a boring place.'

'I stay,' said Kalminski, 'for the gala.'

'When I danced, every night was gala night,' Arenskaya swanked. The thin man bowed. *'Sans doute, Madame.'*

The sturdy man round the corner made a note. But like the prunus that blooms in the spring – Tra-la! – it had nothing to do with the case. It dealt rather with a new, exciting and triumphant use of the number seven when next he found himself in the Salle de Boules.

The figures outside Stroganov's office continued to pace. Finally the great man himself appeared, a mere three-quarters of an hour late. The new man at the Sûreté made a note.

'Good mornings, good mornings, good mornings, my friends. Mais entrez, donc! Entrez! We will take the glass refreshing of lemon tea.'

'No lemon,' said Arenskaya, who had purloined the last one for her own use the evening before. It failed to deflate Stroganov. 'Nevajno, be a good chum and run out for lemons.'

Nevajno looked infinitely offended. 'And maybe – maybe – I ask my antique good friend to schange you schmall scheque,' blandished. Dr Kalminski blanched. Nevajno sped away.

'It bounce,' said Arenskaya, a prophetess of gloom.

'I say only maybe,' said Stroganov. 'This does not commit. I am clever, no, my antique chum?'

His antique chum looked glummer than ever. 'An Impresario's word is his bond, I guess. Impresario's Honour,' he reminded Stroganov without much hope.

'Impresario's Honour?' This was a concept new to Stroganov. He waved it away with a podgy hand. 'Oho! But do I not say "I don't think" under my breath, and does this not make all kosher, as my little grandpapoushka used to explain to the customers if they found out he had cheated them!'

Understandably Stroganov's antique chum looked, if anything, glummer than before. Stroganov made a big concession: 'If Nevajno's schmall scheque bounsch I myself introduce you to Box Office where they will schange *my* scheque and I replace to you.'

'Impresario's Honour?' asked Doctor Kalminski, cautious as ever.

'Impresario's Honour,' declared Stroganov joyously.

'And when *your* schmall scheque bounsch, Vladimir?' asked a clairvoyant Arenskaya.

'Go away, woman, and teach someone something,' said Stroganov, furious.

'No, Vladimir. I will not go, though I wish not to stay. I remain and make the combat for my Ballet. My Ballet mean more to me than my dignity personal!'

'Since when,' Stroganov demanded of the ceiling, 'does she have dignity?'

The thin Impresario sought to throw oil on the troubled waters. 'I come,' he announced, 'to ask my old friend Vladimir a schmall favour – Impresario to Impresario.'

'Beware, Vladimir! It is the Roll-Mop to catch the Sturgeon,' warned Arenskaya.

'She mean,' Stroganov explained the difficult English metaphor, 'the Shrimp incautious to trap the Salmon wily.' He leant back and beamed at his own linguistic cleverness.

'I spit myself of your Salmon!' Arenskaya suited the action to the word. 'You can put your Salmon in your pipe and smoke it!'

It was at this somewhat sensitive moment that little Legrand, a pigeon in a hurry, shot into Stroganov's office, propelled by the need to still his heartburn with another of his mother-in-law chérie's peppermint cachoux so lovingly popped in by his even more – much more – cherished Marie-France. He slipped one in his mouth before addressing the assembled company and the heavy window-drapes behind which the new man from the Sûreté, who had entered the room via the fire escape, was lurking.

'Monsieur Stroganov,' said the pigeon of doom, as clearly as peppermint cachou permitted, 'I bring bad news for you.'

'Oh, dear!' said Dr Kalminski, a quick thinker if ever there was one.

'Monsieur le Directeur has told me in total confidence that if the Box Office figures do not improve by the end of the week he will kick you out,' he illustrated, 'and present instead, The David Frost Follies.'

'Pouf!' said Stroganov – but his heart was not in it.

'Do not despair. All is not lost. I,' said little Legrand, tapping his temple, 'I have in my head the plan to put the Ballet Stroganov in the headlines.'

'Oho!' said the ebullient Stroganov, instantly euphoric. Even Dr Kalminski looked a shade less grey. Little Legrand addressed himself directly to the principal in the affair. 'I will arrange for you to be kidnapped.'

That word again – the window-drapes rustled. Note was being taken.

'Me?' said Stroganov. He tasted the idea. A romantic at heart, a kidnapping appealed to him – so did the headlines. 'Ah, *bon*! When we start?'

'No, me,' said Arenskaya. She hipped a hip at little Legrand. A spasm passed over his face – but it was not desire. He fumbled with the lid of his cherished mother-in-law's cachoux.

'I don't suppose I would fit the bill?' said Dr Kalminski, a counter-tenor who had no hope of being asked back at an audition, and at the word bill, he shuddered. 'These world-wide headlines tempting that you dangle before us, *mon cher*, you are sure they will work?'

'They worked for the British Mrs,' said little Legrand, pained that his conception should be questioned.

'The British Mrs who?' asked Dr Kalminski, a stickler.

Stroganov waved Agatha Christie away. 'Oho!' he crowed, 'my friend, you have a measure of genius! I see your headlines world-wide and they are mouth-watering, "Impresario Celebrated Vanish",' he improvised. 'And under this "Ballet Company Grieve", and under this, "Can it be the kidnap?"'

But Arenskaya could improvise too. 'And under this "The Impresario not so young and very fat",' she corrected.

'Non, non, mon ami,' said Stroganov but Arenskaya was still improvising.

'Famous Ballerina who now teach bad-paid company kidnapped.'

'*Tiens!*' said the smarting Stroganov. 'Maybe she have the right idea!' They glanced at each other.

'Famous Ballerina *et femme amoureuse,*' Arenskaya amended.

'Ballerina look more romantic than not so young, fat Impresario,' mused little Legrand.

'And bald,' said Arenskaya, hoping to clinch it.

But Stroganov was looking to far, far away. It was clear that he was in the throes of composition. 'Impresario-Business man kidnapped for his riches,' he visualised. 'The great Vladimir Stroganov held to ransom . . .'

'Now remember,' warned the dyspeptic pigeon, 'not a word to a single living soul or I shall call the whole thing off and get fired by the Direction.'

'Not a syllable to a sylph,' vowed Stroganov.

'Impresario's Honour!' swore Kalminski.

'Ballerina's honour,' Arenskaya topped it.

'Whatever that may be,' observed Nevajno loftily, to the ceiling.

Arenskaya glared at him but already her mind was running on another track. 'And certainly not to the Mamoushka who owe me twenty pounds English monies for private lessons for her untalented daughter, all feet and teeth.' She remembered something. 'And bum,' she added.

'Bum,' noted the new man at the Sûreté behind the window-drapes. No-one could say he missed out anything essential, he assured himself.

'Trust us,' said Stroganov, 'your kidnap is safe with us. We will be the shtum!' and he laid a plump finger to his lips.

'Shtum!' they swore!

And yet, a few hours later, sounds of the Battle over who should be kidnapped and make the headlines were to be heard floating through many a latticed window at most hours of the day and certainly all through the night, in little La Bazouche, known affectionately to the entire Stroganov company as Bazouchka, complete with a counterpoint of sworn silence on the subject, in spite of which the determination to be the sacrificial swan spread like wildfire, though quite how the secret was breached was a mystery known only to every Ballet company hemisphere to hemisphere. Ballerinas and their cavaliers grew shrill and imprecatory, soloists were increasingly insistent, coryphées could be heard pleading and all of them, whatever their status, were of course offering so that little Legrand, faithful to his Marie-France (save for his Tuesdays) was tempted to arrange to kidnap himself. Mamoushkas grouped themselves in pecking order and hissed. Only one girl – back row corps-de-ballet – affectionately nick-named Little Big Bum by the entire company, a soubriquet she more than justified, did not join in the clamour to be kidnapped and went on solidly practising her flailing fouetté. Her Mamoushka was bent in two, the better to apply her ear to the keyhole of Stroganov's vociferous office, which posture was hardly worth the backache when straighten-ing up, since the entire Casino Municipal was locked in battle. In the first place she had taken up her position outside

Stroggy's sanctum with the intention of demanding some other Mamoushka's hard-fought rôle for her own unrecognised genius-child.

'Or we dance the Finger-Variation at the matinées,' she had been rehearsing herself, 'or we go, my Little Big Bum and me!' which desperate threat was to be backed up with 'What is more we go owing Madame Arenskaya twenty pounds for private lessons.' This, she had felt, would clinch it.

Meanwhile her Little Big Bum was scandalising all in the rehearsal room: 'Me, I do not wish to be kidnapped,' she announced between fouettés. 'I snap my fingers at headlines.' She endeavoured to illustrate this but only came abruptly off-pointe. She was no Pavlova and she knew it. But she had her reasons. Her reasons being the Chief Electrician. His lighting wasn't all it should be, but he operated the spotlight at matinées and Little Big Bum was well aware which side her follow-light was buttered. 'I do not wish to be kidnapped,' she repeated.

'Little Big Bum, you are out of your mind! We will see what your Mamoushka has to say about this. She will settle the matter before you can say *"les femmes de bonnes humeurs".'*

The Battle went on. Never had beds been put to better use in Bazouchka. 'Now I have given you my all, you pass the big bribe to little Legrand.'

'But you have been giving me your all for the last six months.'

The new man at the Sûreté was beginning to feel quite an old hand. It was time, he told himself, to ask a few masterly questions of Monsieur le Directeur du Casino Municipal, system to system, for this one was a distinguished gambler.

But Monsieur le Directeur, when bearded in his office, was in a daze. He was reading and re-reading a bomb which had arrived not five minutes ago in the form of a *petit bleu* from Frostie:

'Cancel personal appearance stop unable fit you in this year stop tried Marcia stop too busy stop tried Harold stop writing volume twenty stop tried George stop publishing volume twenty stop.'

It was clear that Monsieur le Directeur would have to make do with the Stroganov disaster however often the Box Office

threatened to walk out. Next year he promised it, the Richard
Nixon One!

And that is how Nevajno arrived to find Stroganov and Dr
Kalminski drinking little Legrand's champagne ('Never touch
the stuff myself' and he produced his cherished Marie-France's
box of his mother-in-law's peppermint cachoux) at the station
buffet at La Bazouche.

'. . . And what, my ancient chum, is this favour which you
beseech of me?'

'It is like this,' said Dr Kalminski nervously – for a Ballet
Impresario, that is. 'I am stretched financially for the moment,
you understand?'

Stroganov understood only too well.

'And I am in need of a loan – just to tide me over, y'know.'

Stroganov knew.

'And I thought if you would change me a cheque post-dated
to the year after next . . .'

'That,' said Nevajno before Stroganov could shake his head,
a look of fury on his face, 'is my exclusive material.'

It was at this emotion-charged moment that the new man
from the Sûreté came panting in. He flung himself at the dapper
feet of the startled little Legrand.

'Kidnap me, I entreat you,' begged the man in charge of the
Sûreté's case. Subsequently it emerged from a babble of
disasters punctuated by pleadings, that not only could the new
man not solve his first case, but he had totally lost the *carnet* with
all his suspicions written in it *en clair,* which by now had become
merely academic, since he had, in addition, added to his short-
fallings by dipping into the Widows and Orphans Policier
Fund to finance his infallible system at Boules, which pre-
dictably turned out not to be infallible. What was there for him
but to lie low until the combination unassailable turned up?'

'Meantime,' he allowed the suggestion to float on the air, 'you
allow me small capital outlay?' Stunned silence. 'You,' he
looked pointedly at little Legrand. Little Legrand looked at Dr
Kalminski. Dr Kalminski looked at Stroganov. And Stroganov
remembered he was a man of business.

'This new system infallible,' he said. 'How mooch you ask to
sell?'

A Contract in the Ballet

Co-written with S. J. Simon

The ambitious author, sitting timidly on the edge of a chair (borrowed from *Spectre de la Rose*), gazed in awe at the froth of curls jiggling to the jerky rhythm of a typewriter. What luck! To think that he had just walked through the stage door of the Mausoleum Theatre, New York without even as much as a visiting card, and here he was in the presence of the confidential secretary of the great Vladimir Stroganov. Practically the father of the Russian Ballet — that is if you did not count Diaghilev, De Basil, and Blum.

And the great man was due in this very room at any moment. The secretary had kept assuring him of this for the last hour. She seemed a friendly creature.

'What sort of a man is Mr Stroganov?' he asked, taking his courage in both hands.

The typewriter stopped. The froth of curls swung round. The blue eyes lit up.

'He's wonderful,' said Galybchik. 'Galybchik' in Russian means 'little darling'. Back in England she had quite an ordinary name, but this had got mislaid when she joined the Stroganov Ballet. 'He's got such energy, such optimism. And his gift for organisation . . . Why, do you know he got his whole ballet to Bolivia on credit?'

Just then the energetic organiser bustled in, sat down at his desk, mopped his bald dome, and beamed happily around him.

'I have arrange it,' he announced triumphantly.

Galybchik was eager. 'The programme for tomorrow's opening?'

'*Non.*'

'The electricians' strike?'

'*Pas encore.*'

'Credit for the dresses?'

'*Mais non.*' Stroganov waved these trifles aside. 'It is my Russian tea. At last I find the warehouse that sell the brand I desire. I had to buy maybe too much,' he confessed, 'but what would you? The crate it come at any moment.' He turned to the author. 'It is a terrible place, your America,' he complained. 'Everywhere I go they bring me the orange juice. Even for my breakfast!' He shuddered.

'He's an Englishman,' explained Galybchik, 'and he wants to write about the Ballet.'

Light dawned on Stroganov. This man he had been addressing must be a stranger. Doubtless an important stranger. He extended both hands in welcome. 'It is with much pleasure that I meet you. You are from the *London Daily Post* – no?'

'Er . . . ?' said the author.

'You tell your editor,' said Stroganov, 'that he is wise to make for me the big publicity. New York shall see that in London at least I am the appreciate. The publicity here is the disgust.'

'We've been rehearsing for a week,' said Galybchik hotly, 'and they've only printed his photograph once.'

'A small photograph,' added Stroganov peevishly, 'and not in my admiral's uniform.' He delved into a drawer and produced a batch. '*Tiens!* Here are a few of our voyage for the London papers.' He shuffled. '*Voilà* – me with the deck tennis. Me with the *Capitaine*. Me with the whiskyansoda.' He thrust them on the author and returned to the drawer to emerge with a cabinet-size reproduction.

'This,' he announced, 'I give to you personally. *Tiens!* I sign it. You have the pen.' He reached over, plucked one from the author's waistcoat, signed with a flourish, passed over the portrait, and flung the pen into a drawer.

'Er . . . my pen,' said the author.

'*Pardon,*' said Stroganov, passing him an ashtray. 'Today I am *distrait*. I have the so many troubles. Our opening it is tomorrow . . .'

'I am going to it,' put in the author.

'You come to my box,' said Stroganov automatically. 'And still,' he continued, 'nothing is settle. It is not even arrange what ballets we present. *Sylphides – bien entendu, mais après?*' He turned to Galybchik. 'You have spoken to Nicolas?'

The author pricked up his ears. Were they talking about Nicolas Nevajno, the advanced choreographer, the mere mention of whose name had broken up innumerable balletomane parties from Bloomsbury to Baltimore.

They were. Nicolas, it appeared, was adamant. There could be no opening night without a minimum of at least one Nevajno ballet. It was in his contract.

'But New York is not ready for Nevajno,' Stroganov argued. 'Here they know only Balanchine and him they find too modern. We must lead them gently. First a little Fokine, then a little Massine – the early Massine – and only then dare we burst on them the *Gare du Nord.*' He turned to the author for support. 'Am I not right?'

The author was flattered. Here was Stroganov actually asking his advice. He was not to know that Stroganov always asked everybody's advice and never listened to the end of it.

'Well,' he began weightily, 'I saw it in London and candidly . . .'

'I fear as much,' groaned Stroganov. 'You see it is impossible. So,' he turned to Galybchik, 'you must speak to Nicolas again.'

'He will be very angry,' said Galybchik.

'Poof!' said Stroganov. 'There will be other angry ones tomorrow. I have decided,' he announced, 'that tomorrow we dance *Boutique*. They rehearse it downstairs now.'

Galybchik was bewildered. 'But the doll in the can-can dance?'

Stroganov shrugged. 'Mimi shall dance it. Or Dyra.'

Mimi Vanillova and Dyra Dyrakova, thought the author ecstatically.

'Yes,' wailed Galybchik. 'But which one?'

'Why you pester me now?' said Stroganov crossly. 'Tomorrow is another day.'

'But we're opening tomorrow,' Galybchik moaned. 'Why, oh why, did you give them both a contract that allowed them to select any role they wanted?'

'What would you?' said Stroganov. 'Unless I agreed to this,

Dyra, she would not come to America. And Mimi, she had it in her contract already. It is not fair that you blame me,' he complained. 'How could I foretell that they would both desire the same part. They are foolish too, for little Olga she dance the can-can better than both.'

A new thought struck Galybchik. 'Who is dancing it at the rehearsal?'

'But both,' said Stroganov blandly. 'I have arranged it with much cunning. I take Mimi aside and I tell her that she dance the first night and Dyra the second. But I plead with her not to tell Dyra for already I have told Dyra that she dance the first and Mimi the second. Now they are both happy and each one she pities the other. And tomorrow I make my decision.' Suddenly apprehensive, he turned to the author. 'Of course, I tell you this in confidence as a friend of ballet. You do not print it in your *London Daily Post*.'

The author's conscience was pricking him. Was he gaining the confidence of these people under false pretences?

'As a matter of fact,' he said boyishly, 'I'm not a journalist. I'm an author. I just came here to collect a little atmosphere for my novel about the ballet. It is my first novel,' he said blushing slightly, 'and I wondered if you'd mind frightfully . . .'

'I, too, am the writer eloquent,' interrupted Stroganov, on whose consciousness only the word 'novel' had penetrated. 'Already I begin the second volume of my memoirs. *Tiens* – I read you some.' He rummaged furiously.

There was a knock at the door.

'My tea,' said Stroganov.

A shock of black hair surmounting a grey polo-neck sweater, one gold slipper and one blue, strode furiously into the room. It was already talking.

'Tomorrow,' Nevajno was announcing, 'I leave the Ballet Stroganov for ever.'

Galybchik paled. 'Oh, Nicolas – not again.'

'Again,' said Nevajno firmly. 'A first night without a Nevajno ballet is the insult I cannot overlook. I leave at once.'

He sat down and lit a cigarette. 'You will regret this,' he announced darkly, 'for I have just conceived the idea superb for a ballet.'

Stroganov started apprehensively.

'Your ideas they are expensive.'

'This,' said Nevajno, 'is the simplicity itself. I have made it so specially for America. All that it calls for is a bull and a bear. The bull he lift the ballerina and the bear he drop her quick. It will be called *Wall Street*. The idea it come to me in the subway as I read the paper over the shoulder of man who concentrate all the time on a column of figures that are of no importance. It appears that many people in New York do this.'

'It has the possibilities,' mused Stroganov. 'Olright, I produce it.' He turned graciously to the author. 'You may announce it in your *London Daily Post*.'

'*Bon*,' said Nevajno. 'It is agreed. So I overlook that you break my contract and there is no Nevajno ballet tomorrow. But to console me you schange me small scheque?'

Stroganov looked at Galybchik. Galybchik nodded emphatically. Reluctantly Stroganov produced his wallet.

'*Bon*,' said Nevajno and went.

Stroganov beamed at the author. 'You see how we are all here one happy family. We have the little difficulty but always with tact we arrange it. They look on me as a father and each other as brother and sister.'

There was a knock at the door.

'My tea,' said Stroganov.

'You come at once,' shrilled a hideous, dark woman in a purple practice costume. 'Mimi and Dyra they kill each other.'

'*Pardon*,' said Stroganov. They raced off together.

'That,' said Galybchik, 'was Arenskaya, our ballet mistress.'

'A character,' said the author, playing safe.

'They'll soon quieten them down,' prophesied Galybchik.

An unholy clamour came from downstairs.

'I think,' said Galybchik nervously, 'I'll go and see what is happening.' She darted away.

The author followed thoughtfully. Somehow none of this fitted in with the plan for his book.

The life of the ballet dancer is composed of classes, applause and conflict. The enthusiasm of the public, the stacks of flowers at the end of a performance, the comfortable pay envelopes – these are the trimmings of the profession. But it is the lifelong rivalries that keep a ballerina going – possibly to the betterment of her technique. To hoodwink a critic, that – as Arenskaya put it – was the chicken feed. But to put one over on a rival ballerina – ah, what satisfaction!

Now, even the conflict between Dyra Dyrakova and Mimi Vanillova had got too keen to be comfortable. It had been more or less all right so long as they worked for different companies, for then they were limited to exchanging press notices and distasteful kisses. But since both had joined the Ballet Stroganov, each with the title of *Ballerina Assoluta* and each with a contract confirming this, matters had reached seething point. Even the quarrels of the mamoushkas who swarm round the Russian Ballet like maternal bees, even the rows between Arenskaya and the pianist, Nevajno and the conductor, Stroganov and his backers – all faded into insignificance when Mimi and Dyra decided simultaneously that they wished to dance the can-can in Massine's *Boutique Fantasque*. The little Olga, whose role it was, was swept aside with the entirety of a wild violet in a stampede of elephants, and deposited, a weeping flower, in the arms of her boyfriend, David Dovolno.

Right across Bolivia, Stroganov had managed to keep the feud over the New York opening at bay. After all, so often it had looked as though there would be no New York opening. The Metropolitan was already booked and every other theatre seemed to want a large cash deposit in advance. The ballerinas were not going to waste time quarrelling over the vague future when there were so many good bonfires ready to hand.

But once New York was reached, the theatre miraculously secured, and the first night definitely fixed – then it was different. The role that would reap the most applause in the ballet that even Bolivia had liked – this was something worth fighting for. Stroganov was never left for a moment. No sooner had he got rid of one ballerina with bland promises that she bragged of it to the other, who in turn burst in to bully, cajole, wheedle, weep, or throw hysterics as the occasion demanded. At times Stroganov was almost tempted to abandon *Boutique* and put on *Prince Igor*, in which there was no role for either, but always the thought of the new dresses he had ordered, on which he had actually paid the first deposit, renewed his determination. Which of them danced it he did not care – but *Boutique* must go into the opening night.

A further lavishness of promises had shelved the problem for the moment, but tomorrow a definite decision would have to be taken. At the moment there was the new problem of the rehearsal. Neither of the ballerinas wanted to run through the part for the benefit of the band. The false security of Stroganov's latest promise had lent to each an inward glow.

'You do it,' said Mimi kindly. 'You need the practice.'

'You do it, darlink,' said Dyra magnanimously. 'It is the only chance you get this season.'

The band struck up. Neither moved.

A few yards away David Dovolno stood disconsolately awaiting their decision. He would have much preferred to partner the little Olga. She was not so heavy to lift. And he loved the girl.

A few yards farther on the little Olga watched wistfully.

'You do it,' said Mimi. 'I know the part well.'

'You do it,' said Dyra. 'And I enjoy myself watching you.'

The purple frock of Arenskaya bore down on the combatants.

'*Alors* – still you squabble? *Bon* – you enjoy yourselves but me I waste the time no longer.' She clapped her hands. 'Olga!'

Olga ran eagerly to the trolley and took her pose beside Dovolno. Simultaneously, both ballerinas ran forward and pushed her off it. Then they both climbed up.

'You go away,' said Mimi. 'I do this dance now.'

'Get you out,' said Dyra. 'I get here first.'

They pushed. A terrified Dovolno legged it into the wings. Arenskaya legged it for Stroganov. The corps-de-ballet shivered deliciously. What fun it must be to be an *Assoluta*. Absorbed, the conductor went on playing.

'*Alors*,' said Stroganov, 'it is settled. Mimi she dance *Boutique*.'

'It is settled,' agreed Arenskaya. 'Dyra she dance it.'

Stroganov yawned, pushed aside the glass of the inferior but costly brand of tea he was making do with, pending the arrival of the crate, got up and pulled apart the curtains. A skyscraper peered at him; Stroganov shuddered. Dawn in New York was no more invigorating than in Bolivia. He drew the curtains hurriedly and returned to the combat. It had been waging since

midnight after a strenuous dress rehearsal at which none of the
dresses had arrived and the disputed role had remained
undanced.

'But, darlink,' pleaded Stroganov, '*Soyez raisonnable*. Dyra
maybe she dance the role better, but Mimi she give me the
'otter 'ell.'

'Me,' said Arenskaya magnificently, 'I am the artist. It is you
who are the businessman and have to listen.'

'I am artist, too,' pleaded Stroganov. 'That Dyra she dance
Boutique better it weigh much with me. But never do I forget that
it was Mimi who hit me on the head with hard-block ballet
shoe.' He rubbed his bald dome tenderly.

'When Dyra is angry,' said Arenskaya ruthlessly, 'she throw
the samovar at General Dymka. It is well known.'

'There are no samovars in America,' said Stroganov bitterly.
'And my tea it has not arrived.'

The old combatants gazed at each other mournfully. Their
silence was laden with the heaviness of a thousand such all-
night sessions.

'*Ma cherie*,' pleaded Stroganov. '*Soyez sympathique*. Whichever
dances, I am in the *purée* anyway. It is in their contracts. It is
only that I seek that the *purée* it be a little dilute. I am old and
tired.' He sagged in his chair.

'All would be simple,' said Arenskaya, 'if Mimi should get
her migraine.'

Inspiration came suddenly. A rejuvenated Stroganov leaped
to his feet.

'But I am the idiot. Always I worry myself which will be the
angry most. But that is stupid. For if it chance that one of them
should be late for the theatre then it is me who is angry. It is in
the contract.'

'But they are both of the habit punctual.'

'Poof!' said Stroganov. 'The accident it can happen. Me – I
look after that.'

Arenskaya was thoughtful. 'So if Mimi she is late
tomorrow . . .'

'If Dyra is late,' corrected Stroganov.

They toasted each other in second-best tea.

'*Alors*,' said Arenskaya, 'it is settled at last. Dyra she dances.'

'It is settled,' beamed Stroganov. 'The dancer it is Mimi.'

Eleven o'clock that morning saw the young author striding jauntily past the stage-door keeper. He had come to watch class, to steep himself in that atmosphere of tradition, concentration, and quiet discipline which had so inexplicably eluded him yesterday. Here, in class, where a dancer may be found at her daily devotions – that ritual which no earthquake, nor revolution, nor transatlantic crossing can dislodge . . .

He entered hopefully.

'When I say tar-ra-ra,' Arenskaya was screaming at the pianist, 'I mean tar-ra-ra, and not tum-titty-tum-titty-tum. You, you play tootle-ootle-oo all the time.'

The pianist snorted and banged down the loud pedal. Dolefully the ballerinas applied themselves to the barre.

With a certain amount of misgiving, the author settled himself in the quietest corner he could find and took in the scene. His misgivings increased.

Arenskaya, a small, vindictive figure in a scarlet practice costume, stood in the centre of the bare room thumping the floor with a stick. Another minute, thought the author apprehensively, and she would be thumping the ballerinas – those ethereal creatures he had worshipped from the stalls, who at close quarters had consolidated alarmingly into a battery of thighs and drab pullovers. Not a face that was not bedewed with sweat, not an arm that was not red and straining, and not an instep that did not end in a pair of old, and probably odd, ballet shoes. And not a glimpse of glamour among the lot of them.

Leading the barre at one end was the great Dyrakova. Leading the barre at the other was the famous Vanillova. They were not on speaking terms.

In the centre, the little Olga strained and stretched at the barre. She was utterly without Dyrakova's famous développé. Her arabesque in no way compared with that of Vanillova. Bu she had a freshness and an eagerness that both would have given their life-seared souls to possess. Also she had a boyfriend, David Davolno, working like a demon beside her. He followed her about almost as insistently as her mother.

'Battements,' announced Arenskaya.

The thick thighs rose and fell . . . rose and fell.

Determined to keep what few illusions he had left, the author

produced the podgy notebook in which he conscientiously
jotted down each gem of thought as it occurred to him.

Upstairs Stroganov was wrestling with the telephone.

'*Non!*' he was saying violently. 'Not the bump-off. Not even
the beat-up. Only abduction. And you bring her back
tomorrow in good time for *Femmes de Bonne Humeur.*'

'Ya,' said the voice at the other end of the line. It added something . . .

'Si, si!' said Stroganov hastily. 'Have the confidence in me.
The advance I pay you afterwards . . .'

'The grace of a gazelle,' the author was writing ecstatically,
'and the sinuousness of a snake . . .'

'Ah,' beamed Stroganov, materialising unfairly at his elbow
and breathing hard over his shoulder, 'doubtless you record
already your impressions of tonight's performance for your
London Daily Post?'

'Er . . . ?' said the author.

'That is olright,' smiled Stroganov, 'you finish later. For now
I have arrange for you the little treat. The hour has come when
you shall meet my Dyra.'

The author glowed.

'And also,' continued Stroganov, 'you should take her to
lunch.'

The author's hand stole towards his pocket.

'In this,' continued Stroganov, 'you do me the turn immense,
and also,' he added cunningly, 'you are the good friend to the
ballet.' He had not been dealing with balletomanes all his life
without learning something of their mentality.

Pleasure, pride and penury fought their bewildered way
across the author's countenance.

'Do not worry, *mon cher*,' said Stroganov understandingly.
'Already I have prepared the invitation irresistible. I will do the
talking for you and you shall nod. Dyra will not refuse. You will
see . . .'

'But . . .' said the author.

'Later, later,' said Stroganov. 'Dyra!' he called. 'Dyrushka,
my darlink, come you here!'

The great Dyrakova detached herself from the barre and
undulated over to join the two men.

'*Ma chérie,*' began Stroganov, 'I have the pleasure to present to you the British Lord Streatham, who is also the editor of the *London Daily Post.*'

The great Dyrakova melted at once. Graciously she extended her hand – just too high for it to be shaken. The British Lord Streatham looked appealingly at Stroganov. 'Kiss it,' hissed the impresario urgently.

'The good lord,' said Stroganov, 'has been for many years the fervent admirer of your exquisite art.'

'*Entendu,*' said the great Dyrakova.

'Always he has want to meet you.'

'Why he wait so long?' asked the ballerina, puzzled.

'He has the shyness British,' explained Stroganov. 'But today he has overcome it. Nod,' he hissed to the author.

The author nodded.

'He has for you the idea magnificent for the poof,' continued Stroganov. 'He is seized with the desire to write the story of your life in his *London Daily Post.* Nod!' he hissed.

Delighted, Dyrakova turned to the author. 'Tonight I dance for you alone, and after we have the little supper *intime.*' She turned away.

Beads of sweat bedewed Stroganov's dome.

'Wait,' he besought the ballerina. 'The good lord he cannot eat the supper. He has for then a conference of the most important.'

The ballerina stiffened.

'But', said Stroganov hastily, 'he pleads that you take the luncheon *ravissante* at his costly country club. He drive you there in his Royce-Rolls.'

The author started visibly.

'You have the drive luxurious,' urged Stroganov, 'the lunch gourmet in the air beneficial. And afterwards you rest, and you dictate to him your memories.'

'But,' said the ballerina, 'I have the fitting for this afternoon.'

'Poof!' said Stroganov, 'the dresses they have not yet come. And neither,' he added crossly, 'has my tea. But do not distress yourself. Americans are efficient – it is well known. Both will arrive in God's good time. The British Lord Streatham will look to it that you are not late.'

The author nodded without being hissed at.

'*Eh bien,*' assented the great Dyrakova, 'you wait ten little minutes while I change my frock . . .'

The British Lord Streatham spent the next hour following busy Stroganov all around the theatre, vainly pressing for some reasonable explanation for his sudden burst into Debrett's. The ease which Stroganov skated over every question was almost unethical. He was still no wiser when Dyrakova, mysterious, perfumed, and in black, came down the stairs. Stroganov propelled them quickly through the doors.

A magnificent Rolls-Royce waited disdainfully outside the shabby walls of the Mausoleum stage door. Waving the chauffeur aside, Stroganov himself flung open the door with a flourish. Dyrakova settled herself luxuriously. The British Lord Streatham turned an anguished gaze on Stroganov. But the impresario took no notice. A sudden thought had struck him.

'You do not neglect to buy my Dyra the orchids,' he hissed.

'But I've only got seven dollars,' hissed back the despairing Lord Streatham.

Stroganov gulped but manfully pulled out his wallet.

'You pay me back later,' he said magnanimously.

As the car drove away, the British Lord Streatham turned an anxious eye towards his battered Ford standing by the curb in silent reproach. He was wondering how many tickets it would have collected by the time he got back.

Rubbing his hands, Stroganov turned round to face a pathetic Mimi.

'Why,' she demanded, 'you give the British Lord Streatham to Dyra? Is she not two years less young than me?'

Stroganov chuckled: 'It was the genius irrefutable. Now it is assured that you will dance *Boutique* tonight. Dyra she will not be back till the many hours after your curtains.'

'Her car it break down?'

'*Mais non,*' Stroganov said furtively. 'You not tell anyone if I put you wise. *Eh bien,* it is the abduction.'

At a quarter past five the Rolls-Royce reluctantly abandoned the main highway in favour of an asphalt track.

'And so,' the great Dyrakova was saying, 'I arrive at Nijni-Novgorod. The reception I still remember it. The snow was cold but they lay down the carpet for me all the way from the station to the theatre.'

The young author fidgeted uneasily. His conscience was troubling him. Here he was, winning the confidences of the great ballerina under false pretences. Really he ought to tell her that he was neither the British Lord Streatham nor the editor of the *London Daily Post*. All along the outward journey, right through lunch, and all the way back, he had been steeling himself to make the revelation but his attempts had always been stemmed by a St Petersburg gala, a conquest of Europe, or a triumphant tour to Tokyo.

'There's something,' he said diffidently, 'that I must tell you.'

'You tell me later,' said Dyra, not interested. 'But first I tell you how at the Scala Toscanini he . . .'

The Rolls-Royce abandoned the asphalt in favour of the grass and Toscanini faded out in the ensuing bump.

'What is it?' asked Dyrakova, sitting up and noticing her surroundings for the first time. 'I do not remember these bumpings before.' Her umbrella rapped against the window behind the stolid back. The stolid back ignored her.

'You stop him at once.' commanded Dyrakova. 'He lose us the way.' She rapped again.

The stolid back turned, waved a reassuring hand and plodded on. Dyrakova relaxed.

'Doubtless,' she said, 'it is the cut short.'

The Rolls-Royce quivered all over and drew up before a tumbledown shack with boarded windows and heavy doors.

'*Mais – qu'est-ce que c'est que ça?*' demanded Dyrakova.

But the broad back had alighted from its perch and was holding open the door. The other hand held a revolver.

'Out!' said the chauffeur briefly. He was a large man with fierce features and wistful eyes.

The British Lord Streatham drew himself up. 'What, sir, is the meaning of this outrage?'

'Call me Al,' said the fierce features cordially. He jerked his thumb towards the shack and waved his revolver. 'In there.'

Many things had happened to the great Dyrakova during her coloured career but no one had yet tried to get her into a broken-down shack at the end of a gun. There was nothing in her technique to cope with it. Bewildered, she alighted from the car and went through the heavy door that Al had opened.

'Radio,' motioned Al's thumb. 'Bourbon. Bed. Back tomorrow.'

'You leave me here,' wailed Dyrakova, only understanding half of it.

'Ya,' said Al. 'Orders. Back tomorrow. Come on.' He stuck his revolver in the author's back.

'I'll stay where I am,' declared the author heroically.

Al shook his head. 'You gotta be back. Orders. Something about a notice in a *London Daily Post*.'

'Mistaire Al,' appealed Dyrakova. 'You cannot be so cruel as to leave me here alone.'

'Not alone,' said Al, pointing to a hefty figure working in a field. 'Shem.' He turned back to the author. 'Get going.'

With the gun fitting snugly in his left lung, the British Lord Streatham returned to the Rolls-Royce.

At half-past six a large crate was delivered at the stage door of the Mausoleum Theatre. With one accord the corps-de-ballet left Prince Igor to his own devices on the middle of the stage and clustered round. The dresses at last!

Beaming with relief, Stroganov pushed his way through the clutter and planted his foot on the crate.

'Did I not tell you,' he said, 'to have in me the confidence unmentionable. *Voilà*, the dresses I have promised and there is still time for the alterations. We examine.'

A stage carpenter, chisel in hand, got busy. The wardrobe mistress came hurrying over. You could almost feel her rows of irons sizzling in readiness for the creases.

Slowly the lid was prised off. The corps-de-ballet pressed near. A murmur ran through the throng. Simultaneously Arenskaya and Stroganov peered down into the box.

'*Imbécile*,' screamed Arenskaya. 'What is this that you have done?'

Luxuriously Stroganov straightened himself. Delight shone on his face. 'My tea,' he said in evident self-satisfaction, 'it have arrive at last.'

Pandemonium broke loose.

Ten vociferous minutes later, during which the actual dresses arrived unnoticed, a battered Stroganov was summoned to a telephone booth. The message was reassuring.

'*Bon*,' he beamed. 'The abduction it is safely over. *Très bon. Merci mille fois.* You come to my box tonight,' he added generously. Gloating, he bounced from the booth to meet Arenskaya stepping out from the booth next door. Curiously enough Arenskaya seemed to be gloating too.

They addressed each other.

'I have fix it,' said Arenskaya. 'There will be no trouble. Dyra she dance tonight.'

'All is well,' said Stroganov. 'I have arrange it. Mimi, she dance.'

Two beams died simultaneously.

'*Comment?*' said Arenskaya.

'*Quoi?*' said Stroganov.

They looked at each other.

'I have fix,' said Arenskaya clearly, 'that Mimi she will not be at the theatre till too late.'

'I have arranged it,' said Stroganov with emphasis, 'that Dyra she will not be at the theatre at all.'

They looked at each other again.

'Let us be calm,' yelped Stroganov, striding up and down and waving his arms furiously. 'It is not the moment to lose the head. Let us discuss without the passion.'

'How can I be calm,' screamed Arenskaya, 'when you act the imbecile and do not tell me? My poor Mimi!' She burst into tears.

'You have kill her,' said Stroganov, horrified.

'*Non*,' sobbed Arenskaya. 'I send her to street One Twenty-five which is long way off, so she do not get back to theatre till too late.'

Stroganov was puzzled. 'But why she go?'

'I tell her,' explained Arenskaya, 'that we are kick out of here because we no pay the rent, and that you find new theatre in street One Twenty-five where they give you the credit.'

'And she believe you?'

'*Naturellement* she believe me,' said Arenskaya. 'She is a stupid woman. It is well known.'

'It was clever.' In spite of the critical situation Stroganov was impressed. 'And cheaper much than what I do to Dyra.'

When Al emerged from the roadside telephone booth he was smiling. But you had to know him very well to realise it.

'Asked to his box,' he announced, climbing back into the driver's seat. 'Me,' he added, explaining everything.

The author examined the fierce features incredulously.

'Do you like ballet?'

'Ya.' Al nodded. 'Gets me.'

'But how did it get you in the first place?'

'Dad was doorkeeper at the Maryinsky,' explained Al. 'Art in my blood.'

'But,' said the author bitterly, 'you put your business before your art.'

Al was hurt. 'Me?'

'You,' said the author. 'Kidnapping Dyra Dyrakova.'

The car stopped dead.

'Was that Dyrakova?'

'Ya,' said the author, catching the habit.

'But she's dancing tonight,' argued Al unconvinced. 'In the papers.'

'She's locked in a shack twenty miles back,' said the author.

Al's face puckered. 'But I want to see her dance. I've never seen her famous développé.' Fiercely he turned on the author.

'Why didn't you tell me?'

The author swallowed. 'I thought you knew.'

'How could I know?' demanded Al. 'Took orders. Asked no questions. What's the time?'

The author swallowed again. 'About seven.'

'Might just make it.'

The Rolls-Royce swivelled round and headed for the shack.

'*Mais, mon enfant,*' pleaded Stroganov, '*soyez raisonnable.* There is no need for the nerves. You know the part well.'

'But,' said the little Olga, 'Mimi and Dyra will scratch my eyes out.'

'You dance it,' ordered Arenskaya, 'and I will be nice to you in class tomorrow.'

'You have the success *fou,*' prophesied Stroganov, 'and maybe the small rise in salary.'

'But Mimi and Dyra . . .'

'We send you the wreath magnificent,' said Stroganov. 'Not

wreath,' he amended hastily as Olga shrank back. 'The bouquet. And afterwards we take you to the champagne supper.'

'We take Dovolno too,' blandished Arenskaya.

A boyfriend, a bouquet and a New York début. What more could a ballerina ask? But still the little Olga hesitated.

Stroganov had an inspiration. He hurried off and came back with Olga's mother.

'What's this?' The mother took charge. 'Nonsense. Of course you'll dance. Let Mimi and Dyra scratch out my eyes if they can!'

Stroganov beamed at her. It was aost the first time in his experience that he had had occasion to beam at a mother.

'*Alors*, it is settled. I hurry now to rub up my first-night speech. It is difficult, this American.'

Desperate Olga played her last card. 'But who'll dance the tarantella?'

'I will dance it,' said Arenskaya promptly.

'Ah!' said Stroganov.

Arenskaya looked at him.

New York is very keen on ballet. Obviously. Much to the box office manager's surprise, the opening night was a sell-out.

At a quarter to nine when the conductor mounted his rostrum and shot his cuffs the better to evoke the moonlit mood for *Les Sylphides*, the theatre was packed.

Stroganov was in his box, his bald dome almost blotted out by the number of people he had invited to it. Arenskaya was in the wings, terrifying the corps-de-ballet with last-minute instructions. The little Olga was in her dressing-room, holding David Dovolno's hand and trying to take courage from her mother's rosy prophesies. Mimi and her resigned taxi-driver were wandering round One Twenty-fifth Street searching for a theatre which did not appear to exist. Dyrakova was on her way back to New York. Al had returned to the shack, collected her in a couple of sentences and started off. Simultaneously she was demanding explanations, apologies and more speed, interspersed with occasional threats of suing the British Lord Streatham for his entire fortune.

At eight-forty-eight the moonlit sylphs stirred to life, rose like white startled birds on their pink satin points and filled the stage with beauty.

'Terrible,' said Arenskaya, making a mental note of exactly what she was going to say to the fat girl in the second row of the corps-de-ballet.

At nine o'clock there was an interval at the Mausoleum Theatre. There was no interval for the British Lord Streatham. He had given up attempting to explain that he was not the editor of the *London Daily Post*. Mimi having changed three 'stoopid' taxi drivers in rapid succession, had abandoned all hope of finding the new theatre and was hurrying back to the old. That she was already much too late mattered little to her. If necessary she would dance without her make-up.

At twenty past nine Stroganov appeared in front of the curtain to announce that by a coincidence regrettable both his ballerinas had been unavoidably taken ill. However he had the good news. He had arranged the substitution masterly. The little Olga Ostorojno would assuredly win all their hearts. Her technique was maybe not yet so strong and her fouettées were admittedly . . .

At this point Arenskaya managed to tug him off.

The little Olga was in the wings clutching at Dovolno. Mimi, Dyra, and tomorrow's scratched eyes had faded into insignificance. She was just terrified.

Dyra was in a traffic block turning the full power of her personality on to a red light.

Mimi had decided that it had now become necessary for her to dance in her street clothes.

At nine-thirty the ballet was half-way through. Olga and Dovolno mounted the trolley. Her mother hovered around thinking up last-minute encouragements. She might have been seeing her off to Australia.

The Rolls-Royce and the taxi drew up outside the Mausoleum stage door together.

'*Toi*,' said Vanillova.

'*Toi*,' said Dyrakova.

Two ballerinas raced past the stage-door keeper.

'Hey!' said the taxi-driver to the British Lord Streatham.

Two ballerinas arrived in the wings just in time to see Olga and her partner sail into the white lights. An encouraging sound of clapping came from Stroganov's box.

'Pom-pom, pom-pom,' went the big drum. The can-can dance was on.

The two ballerinas moved closer to each other, the better to watch the performance of the future threat to their joint throne. They looked at each other; they smiled.

'She is light, the little one,' said Dyra, 'but she has not your school.'

'Her costume looks nice,' said Mimi, 'but she has not your développé.'

The lifelong enemies had struck up a temporary truce.

Flushed with excitement the little Olga ran into the wings but backed, alarmed, at the sight of the two ballerinas.

They patted her kindly on the back.

'You did very well,' said Mimi, 'but your turns they do not finish in the fifth. You watch me next time – you shall see.'

'You did very well,' said Dyra, 'but your pointes they are not yet strong. You watch me in the *Pizzicato* and . . .'

But the little Olga had fled into the white lights again.

'The next time,' said Dyra, 'I dance it.'

'The dancer will be me,' said Mimi. 'It is in my contract.'

The two ballerinas looked at each other. The truce was at an end. With one accord they darted for Stroganov's box.

'My children,' pleaded Stroganov, '*soyez raisonnables*. We do not discuss the family matters in the presence of the guests distinguished that are in my box.'

'Me, I discuss nothing,' said Dyra. 'I demand that the next time I dance the role. It is in my contract.'

'If I do not dance it,' declared Mimi, 'I speak to my advocate.'

'Have the confidence in me,' urged Stroganov. 'I settle everything. The next time, Mimi, you shall dance.' He winked at Dyra. 'The next time, Dyra, you shall have the part. I promise.' He nudged Mimi.

A dazed young author floundered over to the bar. He had decided to write about Hollywood.

IN COMPANY AT HOME

Yesterday, Last Night

Down in the village it was bedtime. Paraffin lamps were being twiddled; candle wicks snuffed out between moistened rural finger and moistened rural thumb. Up at the House they were still at dinner. Two clearly demarcated ways of country life, lived each according to its code and station, for it was the turn of the century.

'Pudding, M'Lady?'

'Thank you, Partridge.' Lady Elinor scooped out a goodly wedge of bread-and-butter pudding.

'Pudding, M'Lord?'

Lord Ampleworth looked sad. It could have been the green in the gaslight. Or the Government. In fact it was the bread-and-butter pudding. He prodded it.

'I'm worried about the children,' she told her husband. 'Caroline and Lorna are dear girls, good girls. But have they any idea of the value of money?'

Butler coughed. He was almost as bored with the value of money as His Lordship was with bread-and-butter pudding. Butler had been with The Family longer than Her Ladyship and came under the heading of fixtures, like the Raeburns; held in trust and naturally taken for granted. Butler rattled the coffee cups. Lady Elinor dared not neglect her butler's signal.

'We can manage for ourselves now, Partridge, thank you.' Butler withdrew. But there was no polite code of conversational protection for a husband. 'Caroline and Lorna have discovered our charge accounts. They have been buying clothes at the stores and charging them to us.'

'Isn't that what accounts are for?' asked Lord Ampleworth, 'for you and the girls to charge your purchases so that I may discharge the bill on the tenth of the month along with my other obligations?'

'That is beside the point, John, and you know it. When I was a girl there was Madame Mackintosh. There still is. But will the girls go to Madame Mackintosh? They are dear girls, good girls, but they're both stock size, and that's fatal. And as for Vivian . . .'

'Vivian; what's he discovered?'

'Paris,' said his mother tersely.

'Ah,' said Lord Ampleworth. 'Broaden his mind. *La Ville Lumière.*' He sounded wistful. 'And, incidentally, must we have this,' he prodded, 'this mish-mush every night?'

'It's bread-and-butter pudding, John; and we don't. And it's very good for you. And an economy. And with Caroline and Lorna positively encouraged to acquire expensive tastes, and Vivian in Paris – broadening his mind . . . and India already on the horizon . . .' And Lady Elinor patted her pearls. Five rows – most reassuring.

The clock over the stables struck nine. Thomas Tompion had built it for the Ampleworths in 1636 for twenty guineas – Her current Ladyship had complained about the cost at the time. Still, as the maker had assured her, it had been builded to last.

In London the girls, Caroline and Lorna, were dressing for a ball. They were dear girls, good girls but they still believed in fairies and that money was for spending.

Lorna, a pale blue cloud, drifted back from the long looking-glass. 'I'm tired of tulle,' she said.

'But you can't wear that old rag again,' squealed Caroline, a pale pink cloud, 'I mean you've worn it already. Haven't you anything else – your lavender muslin? . . . or your Bridesmaid?'

The pale blue cloud brooded. 'Archie spilt champagne all down my Bridesmaid's front.'

'Oh well, you'll just have to manage in the one you've got on,' said the pale pink cloud. 'It's sweetly pretty, really. Like . . . like a pale blue cloud.'

'You said that last time. And the time before.' The pale blue cloud's face clouded. 'And Tuesday's the Canfields' coming-out dance.'

'Tomorrow,' said the pale pink cloud purposefully, 'we will go to the store and choose a new dress – two new dresses – each.'

'And shoes to match!'

'And everything to match . . . each.'

'And charge it?'

'Certainly.'

This much decided, the two clouds floated radiantly down the staircase and off to the ball.

'We all of us have our allowances,' Lady Elinor was saying. 'Goodness knows I do my best to remain within mine. I shall take the children to the family lawyer. Rubinstein can put our financial position to them dispassionately.'

'No doubt,' said Lord Ampleworth.

'I shall make an appointment as soon as Vivian returns from Paris and before we leave for the tiger shoot. Rubinstein,' said Lady Elinor, 'will make the children understand the value of money.'

And so, one bright sun-splashed day in early summer, Caroline and Lorna were bowling along St James's in a hansom cab – two English roses, their stems tucked under the apron, wearing boaters and veils, nid-nodding in time with the clipper-clopper, clash and jingle, on their way to the offices of the family lawyer. Their mother was on her way there too but she, of course, was travelling by omnibus – tiring but cheaper.

'I wonder what it's all about?' said Lorna for perhaps the fifth time. Her boater sported a band of turquoise coloured ribbon in ribbed silk.

'Goodness only knows,' said Caroline. Her ribbed ribbon was cerise and rather daring. 'We're ruined, I expect.'

'Or else we've come into a fortune!'

Turquoise ribbon and cerise nid-nodded at one another. A fortune . . .

And that, in fact, was exactly how they interpreted the situation when later, after they had been joined, first by their brother, who had sauntered over from his club at the last moment, and, sometime later and a little breathlessly, by their mother, the family lawyer went into the financial facts of their life.

'Now let me get this clear,' Vivian was the first to cope with the good news. 'We have each of us a private income?'

'That is so,' said the lawyer. He had a voice of dry parchment. It crackled. 'A yearly sum of a settled amount.'

'Mother and father and the girls and me – each?'

'Each,' confirmed the dry parchment crackle.

'Each,' breathed the Cerise and the Turquoise.

'And that is all,' their mother pointed out. They disregarded her. Three hundred and fifty pounds for spending. Added together that made . . . more than one thousand pounds. Laid end to end it would reach straight to Bond Street.

'Let's go,' hissed Lorna urgently. She was a dear girl, a good girl, but she was impulsive.

Outside as the cab clip-cloppered over the cobbles she was the first to break the starry silence. (Their mother was proceeding to the station on foot – slower, but it did save a bus fare and it was a lot less bumpy.)

'Let's have a spree and spend it – splosh!'

The cab spanked smartly round a bend. And there, in the sky, as though punctuating her sentence in mid-air, hung a beautiful, shining, silver, bulbous exclamation mark – a balloon!

Three pairs of starry eyes gazed up at it.

Effortlessly, triumphantly, the silver circle and its pendant golden basket climbed the cloudless sky.

That night, when dinner was done (hot-pot may or may not be delicious but it uses up all sorts of left-overs) Lady Elinor took up the lighted storm-lamp Butler had brought in with the coffee. The Tompion clock was striking nine pm.

'I must go now, and say good morning to Mama,' said Lady Elinor brightly.

Lord Ampleworth de-sleeped a somewhat wizened pear. 'Do,' he said.

And so, lantern in hand and galoshes on feet, Lady Elinor

went out into the night and down to the Dower House where her mother, Conradine, Lady Margaretting, pursued a third way of living in the country – a way uniquely her own. For at the age of seventy-six Lady Conradine, an otherwise sensible woman, lived every minute of her day – why not? But the point is that she lived it, consistently, sanely – according to her own way of thinking – and all through the night.

Lady Conradine was always called betimes with early morning tea each evening at seven pm. And since in girlhood she had been taught that a gentlewoman sets aside an hour a day for writing in her diary and attending to her correspondence, she had dealt with letters and diary and was down for breakfast and the morning paper by nine pm.

At ten, having ordered her household and quarrelled with Cook, she would take her trowel, a pair of secateurs, the wide flat trog, and her gardening hat, and go into the garden with a storm-lamp. In the winter gardening was very properly confined to the conservatory. At a quarter to twelve she would pull off her gloves, and come in for her 'Midnight Tonic' – a glass of champagne into which a raw egg had been beaten. 'With a silver fork, dear, Doctor's orders.' From midnight until one am her household claimed her. Then luncheon – a cutlet and a glass of claret – and her after-dinner nap – till four am. At a quarter past four in the morning they brought round the carriage and a well-wrapped-up Lady Conradine drove out to call on her sleeping friends. 'No answer,' she would say incredulously to her coachman. 'Dear me! They must still be abroad. People don't seem to like their homes these days!' And off on her rounds she'd go, at starlings, as they say, still marvelling.

Dinner at eight am: a pleasant hour with her embroidery, and so to bed, just as the world got into its troublesome stride.

Lady Elinor, then, arrived at seven minutes past nine that night to find her mother at the breakfast table.

'Kipper?' said Lady Conradine. 'No? Slimming again? No? Then there's something up. I can tell by the look on your face. Come on – out with it!'

Lady Elinor settled down to share her load with her mother.

'. . . They're dear girls, good girls, young Lorna and old Caroline, and I think that Rubinstein has at last taught them the value of money.'

'Money,' Lady Conradine considered it. 'Money – I don't know what you people do with it. Wages – and an occasional load of manure for the garden – that's enough for me. Years since I've paid a visit to the stores in person.'

'Yes, it would be, of course.'

'Books for boys and knick-knacks for gals at Christmas. Deal with reliable firms and order by catalogue.' That, then, accounted for the patent potato-peeler last Christmas and the patent fire-lighter the Christmas before last.

'Rubinstein,' said Lady Elinor, 'was very lucid – for him. "Take care of the pennies," he said . . .'

The oblong building with the big glass roof looked like an airship itself; an airship moored to the green fields of North London. In fact it was the largest balloon factory in England – in the world, they boasted locally.

Two would-be aeronauts stood looking rather lost before it – human packages bundled up in brand new ulster capes, flat cloth pancake caps tied to their fly-away heads by yards and yards of motoring veil. Caroline and Lorna had just been decanted from the comparative safety of Vivian's new and dashing horseless carriage. It had quivered, snorted, honked and trundled them all through London; only actually exploding once – in the Holloway Road.

Vivian had rushed off and bought the gleaming yellow automobile on the day he'd learned the value of money.

It was the busy season for balloons – the bright and blue-skied busy season – and the Ampleworths could hardly hear their own hearts thumping for the hammering and whirring and pump-pump-pumping that was going on inside.

'Come on,' said Vivian, in a fever to be back with his bright yellow beauty, abandoned rather crookedly in the curb, 'let's buy one and get it over!'

And in they went.

In addition to various balloons in various stages of manufacture there were several veterans in for repair, spread ignominiously on the floor, deflated of pride.

Three would-be aeronauts gazed somewhat dazedly at the fascinating scene.

Lining the walls, some nimble-fingered women were stitching and tugging at their thread. In the centre equally nimble-fingered men were knotting, testing, examining, inflating, and varnishing.

'Are all these gentlemen aeronauts?' asked Vivian keenly.

'In a manner of speaking,' said the Managing Director. 'You see, they're all old sailors – what I call Jack Tars – they're used to clambering up and clinging on.'

'Ah' said Vivian, as one aeronaut to another.

'Oh!' said Caroline.

Lorna giggled.

'Here we have the gores of a new balloon on what I call the production line. We cut them out with what I call a razor. We shall have her up there sailing the skies within the fortnight,' said the Managing Director confidently.

'Ah!' said Vivian.

'Oh!' said Lorna.

'I suppose,' said Caroline, 'it wouldn't be for sale . . . ?'

. . . And up at the House Lady Elinor looked up from the label she was writing.

'Not wanted on the voy . . .'

'India,' she said. 'It's very far away, John.' It was clear that she was feeling dreadfully homesick already.

'This time tomorrow we'll be on the boat,' said her husband. It was clear that he was not. 'You know, m'dear, I'm looking forward to the food on the boat.'

'They're dear girls, good girls – if only they would keep their feet on the ground . . .'

Down at the Dower House the clock on the breakfast room chimney-piece was energetically chiming the evening away. It was, in fact, that time of night when Lady Conradine habitually tackled her morning's mail.

'. . . Receipt . . . receipt . . . bill – impertinence! . . . ha! a penny stamp at last – from Anastasia Hobbs and about time, too.' Lady Conradine would have known that spider dipped in purple ink, those inverted 'M's anywhere! – sheer affectation! She ripped open the long heliotrope envelope. She read on. She frowned . . .' Of course I know it's none of my business but I do hope that those girls of Elinor's are not as flighty as some ill-natured folk have been saying . . .'

Flighty! . . .

. . . 'And this,' the Managing Director of the Highgate Balloon Factory was saying, 'this is going to be what I call the parachute!'

The morning of Lord and Lady Ampleworth's departure for India, young Lorna and old Caroline were down early for breakfast and even Vivian was hardly late at all.

'Now remember, darlings, no entertaining until I get back. Your father and I have to make this very expensive trip and we must keep the tradesmen's books down. Mrs Manifold will pay the household bills as usual – and see that they are kept to the usual level. And Butler has a sum in hand for Eventualities. Visit your grandmother first thing at night and remember your father and me in your prayers.'

Vivian nodded. Caroline nodded. And Lorna wept a little.

They stood in a group in the front porch and waved as the brougham trundled off with their parents safe inside.

They stood at the back porch half an hour later and waved to a silver ball and its basket, growing rounder and bigger every minute. It came down in the home paddock. A jaunty young aeronaut stepped from the basket while the under-gardeners made the ropes secure under Vivian's instructions.

'I am the test pilot,' he said. 'Mr Roper – *young* Mr Roper,' he explained. 'The Head Test Pilot,' he emphasised. 'My instructions are to take you for a spin and teach you how to sail her for yourselves – she's a peacherino,' he announced.

'We've christened her,' said Caroline, 'Silver Orb.'

'You'll stay to luncheon, won't you?' said Lorna.

And as he thanked her the Head Test Pilot thought he'd

never seen a pair of eyes so blue – like the colour of a sky in ballooning weather.

They had planned their first flight carefully The girls and their pilot cast off after tea as soon as the wind dropped, and Vivian was to follow below in his beloved yellow automobile to bring his sisters back by road should it prove impossible for them to return by air, for, as young Mr Roper said, you never knew where you were with a balloon except that it was likely to be several miles from anywhere you wanted to be.

It was a great moment when the restraining ropes were finally cast off and two excited girls helped young Mr Roper to drop bag after bag of ballast with a thud onto the turf. And then, with a rush of air in their ears they were off in their very own balloon. Away they sailed, over the elms and into the sunset and as the earth grew purple and the sky dark and the lights of London twinkled out, the aeronauts quite lost track of time and also Vivian, in his yellow car, which was less surprising.

'Behind that low belt of murky haze on the horizon,' said the pilot, 'is the greatest city in the world, the hub of Empire – London.'

They seemed to be making for it.

'The mother of cities slumbers not nor sleeps,' said young Mr Roper, indicating the dome of St Paul's, a pearly white mushroom in the moonlight as they floated past. 'A balloon, dipping near the roof-tops, can skim low enough to catch a fleeting view of the city that only the pigeons usually enjoy!'

'Whatever would Mummy say,' shouted Lorna into the wind.

At sea the Cunarder was making her way past Southend pier – a chain of lights reaching out to them from the shore. The Ampleworths had come on deck after dinner.

'I wonder what young Lorna and old Caroline are doing?' mused Ma.

'The hors d'oeuvres weren't what they'd led us to believe,' said Pa, a disappointed man.

'They're good girls, dear girls, but, oh, if only they hadn't got
their heads in the clouds!' Ma sighed.

Winds can be fickle up there in the changing blues of night; and
the flight of a balloon must alter with them, and indeed it was a
great many chill but blissful hours later that the Silver Orb
finally sailed through the aura of haze – part smoke, part
moonlight – that was sleeping London, bound, as all aboard
supposed for home, although as young Mr Roper said again,
you never knew with a balloon.

'You'll spend the night, of course,' said Lorna.

'What's left of it,' said Caroline.

It was that hour of the night when Lady Conradine would be
carrying in the storm-lamp, her gardening done, ready for her
post-prandial siesta, prior to driving out to leave cards on
deeply sleeping, infinitely unheeding friends. But London is
never quite deserted at night, as Caroline and Lorna were soon
to learn. By now the balloon had left St Paul's, a pearl-domed
mushroom, behind and, strangely, on the slant. The Silver Orb
was drifting above Trafalgar Square where Nelson, a grey stone
admiral, stood on his grey stone column, looking, as in life, little
and alone.

But even as they gazed the moment of recognition passed, for
in that flash of time when a balloonist can identify an object, he
has already been wafted on his way. The high speed that a
balloon can travel – sometimes twenty miles an hour – came as
a great surprise to the two girls. London lay not far below them,
with St James's Park looking stricter and narrower than usual
and most unwelcoming to nesting aeronauts. The gardens of
Buckingham Palace, though, formed a plush pin-cushion that
was highly tempting so no doubt it was as well that the balloon
had already sailed over them before you could say 'turn of the
century'.

The town seemed quite still. Yet now and again the clop-
clopping of a horse and cab bringing home some late party-goer
rose faintly to their ears; and here and there two pools of amber
light proclaimed the passing of a carriage in the quiet streets.
When they were floating over Pimlico, young Mr Roper
produced a megaphone – purely for statistical purposes, as he
explained.

'Hi there below!' he shouted to the sleeping roofs, 'This is the Silver Orb, balloon-ship, making a signal from the sky. Can any of you hear us down there?'

Silence.

Now and then a gaslight flickered up where only a darkened doll's house had been before. This encouraged young Mr Roper to repeat the signal.

'Ahoy there!' he bawled.

'Ahoy!' came back an answering signal from the world below. 'Bet yer can't bring 'er down in Battersea Park!' yelled a cockney voice. 'Bet yer can't bring 'er down at all! Bet she comes down of 'erself in the river! Bet yer can't . . .!' and on and on. The taunting voice seemed to be following the course of the Silver Orb, which was a puzzle, and also dreadfully undignified.

Young Mr Roper noted this in the log-book.

Then Lorna, leaning dizzily over the rim of the golden basket, a blanched silver in the moonlight, solved the problem. It was some errand boy on a bicycle on his way early to work or late home from a night-shift.

She grabbed the megaphone.

'Shut up,' she shouted, 'you down there on the bike – shut up.'

It may have looked unladylike in the log, but it worked. Or would have, but for another, more imposing voice

'Quiet up there!' it boomed, a deeper, slower, richer bass. 'There's folks down 'ere as wishes to get their sleep.'

'That,' said young Mr Roper, 'will be a Guardian of the Peace.'

'A policeman!' said Caroline, horrified. 'Oh, Lorna!'

Unthinkingly, Lorna flung herself upon a bag of ballast. Fear lent her strength. Out of the balloon she toppled it. It fell to earth she knew not where.

'I say!' said the appalled Mr Roper. Nothing for it but to fling out more ballast and ascend, swaying wildly, out of reach of the arm of the law.

'Down there – look – the river!' gasped Caroline. They peered down. Everywhere purposeful craft were taking advantage of the tide, and lights, red, green and apricot, were chugging along or else just bobbing silent at their moorings, small as swans.

'You were quite right, Mr Roper,' said Lorna. 'London never does sleep entirely.'

Young Mr Roper smiled – an avuncular smile – and did his best to see to it that it shouldn't : 'Ahoy! down there – this is the balloon-ship Silver Orb, making a signal from the sky!'

Soon though the balloon was off on another course. Higher and higher it soared. Eastward, again, the town stretched out below them utterly without limit, threaded by fanning-out ribbons of rail and tram ways. Dolls' houses clustered and clung together on both sides of the broader silver of the Thames in lines that merged and dwindled on the sight. London was fading out in an irregular fringe leading to other, more distant, clusters of lights. Chatham, Rochester, Maidstone even, until it seemed that Kent itself, like London, slumbered not nor ever slept. Their last sight of London was a broad distant track studded with faint points of light. 'As though the Milky Way had fallen on the earth,' said Mr Roper, his head in the stars.

At last the lights below sprayed over the open country. Only the fields, the early morning's haze and the glassy light thrown back to the sky from the ponds.

It was four-thirty am. Lady Conradine's carriage was at the door. Lady Conradine stood on the steps, visiting-card in hand.

'We're late starting off today, Coachman. Never get our calls done at this rate. We'll start with Lower Lapwing, the Dower House.'

Coachman yawned. He gave his sleepy horse a flick. Her Ladyship was on her way to have a straight talk to Anastasia Hobbs.

Flighty, indeed!

'Look, there's our village!' The balloon swooped dangerously.

'Look, there's the Tompion Clock!'

'Hope we don't come down on the stables!'

Young Mr Roper twiddled. The Silver Orb deflated, hissing gently. The golden basket swung lower and lower and all the time gently towards the earth. It avoided the stables, hung hesitantly over the elms, lurched perilously and came to a floating halt in mid-air; and there it swung slung by its ropes from a telegraph pole, until, with a rending of silk and a creaking of wicker and a cracking and crashing of wood in its wake, it subsided onto the village green bringing the wires and telegraph pole and also an ancient and overhanging branch of an elm, and half the tree, down with it as it slithered to rest in, of course, the pond.

'Are you all right, Lorna?'

'Yes, are you?'

'Yes. Are you all right, Mr Roper?'

'Brought her down within a stone's throw of the objective,' crowed the happy aeronaut, coming up from a sea of silver silk. 'Of course there'll be quite a lot of repairs to be carried out before she'll be airworthy again. There'll be some repairs to the telegraph system, too.'

'Oh dear!' said Lorna.

'Oh dear!' said Caroline. 'And we've all of us spent our allowances for the whole year.' Frantically, she tried to wring the water out of her coat.

From the front door Butler, in his night cap, looked affronted. It was clear to him that this was going to be an Eventuality.

Round the bend of the road came a sorry sight. A yellow horseless carriage that should have been travelling under its own steam was being towed home ingloriously by a horse-drawn brougham. Lady Conradine, driving along a lane in her old-fashioned equipage had come to the rescue of her deeply humiliated grandson.

Dutifully the Tompion clock struck seven.

'Back in good time to change for dinner,' said Lady Conradine, well pleased.

'You'll stay to breakfast?' said Lorna to her jaunty aeronaut.

And after all does it really matter which way round the clock one lives one's day?

Cotillions and Ices

On the evening of May 27th, 1829 two little girls were looking forward to the marvels of a Children's Ball.

At Kensington Palace, plain, plump, little Drina (the future Queen Victoria), safe among familiar faces, places and possessions, was secure in the love and care of her *dear* Mamma and her governess, dear, *dear* Lehzen; idolized by her nurses and her mother's ladies. It was her first Ball, due to take place this time tomorrow at Buckingham Palace in the august if profusely sweating presence of 'Uncle King'. She had been nine years old for four days now, and she was wondering which of the good but simple party dresses in her wardrobe she would be allowed to wear.

The other child was thinking of this time tomorrow with more mixed feelings. She was little Maria da Gloria, the Queen of Portugal, and the Ball was being given in her honour. It was a heavy responsibility. She was nine years old too – a few weeks older than the future Queen of England, but she had no mother and indeed no fixed home as she stood on tiptoe before the cupboard in which her jewelled gowns of ceremony were hanging. Maria da Gloria had been staying for some weeks now in a country cottage at Laleham. Dom Felisberto Caldeira Brant Pontes, Marquis of Barbacena, had brought her from Brazil to England where he was bent on collecting a faction to regain the crown of Portugal from her uncle, fiancé, and, until a few weeks ago when he had grabbed the crown (an action which put an end to the unnatural 'engagement' with some finality), her Regent, Don Miguel of Braganza. At the same time the foppish and dissolute old Marquis was seeking a bride for that gay widower, Maria da Gloria's father, Don Pedro,

Emperor of Brazil, from among the Princesses of Europe. So the Princess be pretty and alluring the balance of power in Europe might go hang was the Emperor of Brazil's understandable attitude. But so far there had been no rush of royal ladies, pretty or otherwise, to be his Empress, and no doubt the constant presence of the Emperor's permanently close companion, the Marqueza da Santos, mother of Maria da Gloria's half-sister, Maria Isabel, the black sheep of her distant nursery, had much to do with this reluctance.

Though the Ball was to be held in her honour, the little Queen of Portugal had been kept hanging around in London at the Hotel Crillon week after week without being granted an audience by 'Sir, my brother and cousin', as his 'good sister and cousin' addressed King George IV. And there she had been established in encrusted grandeur waiting on His Majesty's pleasure, while her store of money flowed through the Marquis of Barbacena's lavish fingers. 'Dona Maria da Gloria's table alone costs £96 per day,' he wrote. 'This is the place where the King of France recently stopped which is the custom of this court because there are not enough palaces,' he further reported.

The reason for the King of England's delay in receiving the Queen of Portugal was the embarrassing trick played upon the child by history. When she had set sail for Europe from Brazil in the British steamer *Red Pole*, the crown of Portugal had appeared to be in the Brazilian bag. Impoverished Portugal was deeply in debt to England and the creditor country knew that the only hope of getting back their loan was through the wealth of the rebellious and now independent Brazil. Assistance to the Queen of Portugal who was at the same time a Princess of Brazil looked like a politician's short cut to reimbursement. But in the meantime Maria da Gloria's uncle, erstwhile fiancé, former Regent and now usurper, had persuaded the Duke of Wellington that the people of Portugal preferred a king to government by crinoline.

So George IV deemed it expedient to be unavailable.

He was ill. He was having the Palace redecorated. It was only after Barbacena had pointed out that if the decorations were not soon completed British interests in Brazil might suffer, that an audience was granted. Maria da Gloria was able to leave the

near vicinity of St James's and Barbacena could write to the
Emperor:

'Today the visit took place between the Queen . . . although
the King can hardly stand on his enormous legs (he perspires in
bucketfuls and tires at the slightest effort to move) he absolutely
insisted on walking to the first stair-landing in order to receive
the Queen and to lead her from salon to salon.'

Maria da Gloria was in!

And so on May 28th the Children's Ball took place, and the
palace became a dream of polished parquet, and Waldteufel
Waltzes, and the two little royal nine-year-olds, both in their
best, were whirled away by their noble partners.

The Duke of Argyll has left a record of these fortunate
partners and so we know that the Princess Victoria at her first
ball danced with Lord Fitzalan, the future Duke of Norfolk,
Prince William of Saxe-Weimar, the young Prince Esterhazy
and the sons of Lords De La Warr and Jersey. Maria da Gloria
danced the first Quadrille with the son of the Prince of Lieven;
the second with the son of the Prince of Polignac; the third with
the son of the Marquess of Palmella, and The English Lancers
with the nephew of the Marquess of Londonderry. 'And though
the performance of Dona Maria was greatly admired,' writes
the Duke of Argyll, 'all persons of refined taste gave the preference to the modest graces of the English-bred Princess.'

A dream, then, of gliding, turning, chasséing. The Queen's
own Dancing Master directed the ball and the two young royal
ladies danced in the same Quadrille.

Maria da Gloria, Barbacena tells us, looked very splendid,
'her dress was encrusted with jewels.' And we can imagine the
flashing of the Brazilian diamonds, the deep blue sapphires and
shallow aquamarines, the rubies and the purple amethysts of
Brazil shining against the stiff gold damask of Spain as the
Queen of Portugal went spinning round beneath the massive
chandeliers.

'The Queen was finely dressed,' noted Mr Greville, the
Wicked Uncle of the diarists, for once in a kindly mood, 'she sat
by the King. She has a sensible Asturian countenance.' But His
Grace of Argyll informs us that 'the heiress formed a strong
contrast to the glare and glitter around the precocious Queen.'
Mr Greville, however, has it that 'our little Princess is a short,

plain-looking child and not near so good-looking as the
Portuguese. However,' he points out, 'if Nature has not done so
much, Fortune is likely to do a great deal more for her.'

The King looked very well and stayed at the Ball till two.

And in this dream of flying ribbons and satin dancing
slippers, the evening whirled away. They were wearing Bom-
bazine and Algérine, Barège and Veluto, Mull and Alpaque,
Peau d'Ange and Pekin, and Satin Esmeralda with Passe-
menterie; Taffetas and Leno Lawn, Mousseline and Poplin,
Piqué, Foulard, Benzaline and Balzarine, Challis and
Tarlatan, Calamanco, Carmeline, Clementine, Chiffon Gros-
des-Indes, Paduasoy, and Looking-glass Silk and La Sylphide,
and many, many other tissues with enchanting names.

But silken dreams can turn to nightmares, and polished
parquet floors can have their perils, and before the Ball was
over that hybrid blossom Queen Maria da Gloria had slipped
and fallen down and dissolved into scalding tears like any over-
excited nine-year-old from a common or garden nursery. Oh,
the hot-cheeked shame of it! They carried her carefully off the
floor and the Monarch himself consoled his discomforted guest
of honour, and the dance went on.

The Princess Victoria, a kind little girl, showed great concern
over her cousin's mishap. Was she, one wonders, reminded of
the day, not so long ago, when she herself had had the
mortification of falling in the street, on which upsetting occasion her own first words had been, 'Does dear Mamma know
that I am not hurt?'

Still in a dream, by now of a soft May dawn, two little girls
were driving home through Knightsbridge in two grand
carriages. One, the little, lucky, 'Drina' to be kissed goodnight
by her well-pleased Mamma (did the feathers of the Duchess of
Kent's head-dress tickle the pink ear of her daughter as she
inclined her head in the maternal embrace?) to be put to sleep
with a glass of warm milk. The other to drive on and on through
the awakening countryside to Laleham, upheld by the
knowledge that she had done her country – both her countries –
credit. Was it a dream that she had tumbled down and cried
like a little girl? Oh, almost certainly it had been just another
dream inside a dream of cotillions and ices.

No Minstrels

'I believe, tho' they may not find Art enough in the Builder to make them Admire the Beauty of the Fabrick, they will find Wonder enough in the Story to make 'em pleas'd with the Sight of it.'
    Sir John Banburgh writing of Blenheim Palace

1

The lady in the crimson farthingale was sitting at the kidney table in the Elizabethan Room, dressing her hair. It had taken an unconscionable time a-doing. But then, it was Christmas Eve at Lyttletoun, as indeed it was the world over, not counting the Holy Russias, where they would not be getting around to celebrating the season of peace and goodwill till some time later, and no doubt the poor soul was anxious to look her best.

Soon now, she arose, put off the loose holland powdering-robe, and drifted, in all her glory, over to the long mirror. From its grey-green depths, tarnished as time, a crimson figure looked back at her. There they both were, the lady and her reflection, large as life and twice as handsome by candle-light; their hair curled and powdered, with gay little galleons sailing through their beautifully-arranged waves, their grey eyes round as the pearls on their index fingers, their patches in place on bosom and chin and one hundred and seventy-five yards of crimson paduasoy abut the hem.

And yet the crimson ladies were scowling at each other:
'I'm sick to death of red,' observed the one.
The other nodded complete agreement with this.
The clock in the stable gable struck the three-quarters. Far

away in the servants' hall the booming of a great gong rever-
berated from the underworld. The Steward of Lyttletoun was
about to be served, and served with all the pomp and
circumstance of life below the salt in the greatest of the great
houses of England. From attics undreamed, through grand,
dim corridors, the scuttle of the little maids began, like the
rallying of all the mice in Gloucestershire on an earlier occasion.

The crimson lady whipped through the wall and wafted
unhurriedly to her tryst with the Cardinal on the West Wing
staircase – for the ghost of the Fourth Marchioness had been
doomed to keep the apparition of His Eminence waiting
nightly, down the centuries, and this was how it always
happened.

There, at the other end of the Gainsborough Gallery, His
Eminence was pacing, and a close observer could not fail to
have noticed a certain thinness about the lips set in that bland
pond of urbanity, the Cardinal's countenance. For though, of
course, it was no new thing for His Eminence to be kept
hanging about the draughty corridor by the Lady Lavinia Linneage, this endearing feminine shortcoming had failed to
endear the corridor to the Cardinal.

'Your humble child fears that she has kept you waiting here
alone, Lord Cardinal.'

'Not alone, daughter, for I waited with pleasure.'

So much tradition required. So much it was accorded. But
obeisance and bow tossed off, 'C'mon,' said the Marchioness,
and swept down the State Apartment Staircase straight past
the toiling-up nun who was bearing her head on the Com-
munion Plate, quaint girl!

On the Traitor's Landing a housemaid in a hurry, trim as a
little yacht in her Afternoon Black, passed, with her starched
white cap-pennants flying straght through the pair of them
with never a by-your-leave or bob. For they were only Lavinia
the Lethal and the Bloody Cardinal, who always walked the
West Wing at this time of night. The little maid had been at
Lyttletoun for two years now, and it would have given her quite
a turn if she had not met with the visitants round the bend as
she hurried the steaming copper wash-can up to the Dowager's
Row ready for M'Lady's final ministrations.

At ten o'clock the House Steward of Lyttletoun was served.
Already the visiting servants had taken their sherry with the
resident upper servants in the Steward's room. Now they were
handed in, in strict order of precedence. The English have a
genius for impressive ceremonial in palace, cathedral and the
perfect service of a stately household. The visitors took on the
rank and name of the ladies and gentlemen they served. Miss
Dullwater, personal maid to the Duchess of Dullwater, went in
to dinner on the arm of the Steward of Lyttletoun while Mrs
Multifarious, the housekeeper, was armed in by Mr Dullwater,
His Grace's man, and so on, through Lords, Ladies and merely
Honourables to the discreetly titled but well-bred squires and
mistresses of mid-Edwardian high society below stairs. Or
rather, and nearly so on; for right at the bottom of the snow and
silver table, beside Captain the Honourable Gwylliam
Vulliamy-William's valet was a glaring blank. Mrs Multifarious noticed it the minute she sat down. From it should
have blinked the pinkly overawed countenance of Charity
Callender? known down in the village as Our Cherry because
there might have gone any one of the inhabitants of Christmas
Meagrefold, but for the grace of, etc.

What could have come over Charity Callender? asked Mrs
Multifarious's left eyebrow. She had been up at The House for
a year now, quite long enough to have learned that Punctuality
was the Politeness of Princes' Personal Attendants and that
Marchionesses' Maids must be ready to be handed in to their
place (which they were expected to keep) at longest three
minutes after the last reverberation.

But all she said was, 'Indeed, Mr Dullwater, the weather is
extremely seasonable for the time of year.'

As though impelled by this same news, one of the age-old
oaken doors creaked open. But not to admit Charity Callender.
Our ghostly visitants were doomed to pass through the
servants' hall on their haunt from the gun-room where Lavinia
the Lethal was due to snatch up a stiletto and hide it in her
bosom there to be concealed until she should find a convenient
opportunity to raise a portion of the one hundred and seventy-
five yards of hem-line and tuck it in the pleached plush garter,
and thus equipped, on and down to the still-room where the
Cardinal would come upon the flask of malmsey into which he

had every intention of voiding the poison behind the archi-episcopal ring.

Nobody looked up from the turtle soup. Only Lady Mandragon's French maid shivered a little. *Mon Dieu, ces revenants anglais!* She drew her marabou more firmly about her shapely French shoulders.

Her Ghostly Ladyship took in the Christmas decorations at a glance, the ton of holly brought in by the head gardener, the mistletoe coyly placed by the Steward himself, the laurels about the portrait of the Dowager, this latter being Mrs Multi-farious's spirited contribution to the festive scene, and the strings of paper chains made in the Linneage nurseries and thoughtfully sent down by Her Ladyship herself.

Now they were bearing away the great tureens and still Charity Callender had not put in an appearance, yet Their Babyships had been bustled into bed at the earliest possible moment, ready for tomorrow's over-excitements, and there was nothing to keep the resident nursery-maid from her place beside Mr Vulliamy-Williams, but rape or sudden death. Mrs Multifarious naturally preferred to envisage the latter. But scarcely had her mind's eye smothered the holly in crape, when the door opened again and Charity Callender, pink and pop-eyed as even Mrs Multifarious could have hoped and looking as though saddle of mutton wouldn't melt in her mouth, slipped into the vacant seat.

'Charity Callender, come to my room after coffee,' signalled Mrs Multifarious's right eyebrow to the foot of the snow and silver. The other was busily engaged raising itself at His Grace's gentleman's account of a visiting gentle-man's gentleman whom, Mrs Multifarious gathered, was no gentleman.

'Quite so, Mr Dullwater, service is not what it used to be!' she observed feelingly.

What could Our Cherry have been up to at this time of night of a Christmas Eve, with her charges, the nannies, relieved of their charges, the little Lordships and Ladyships and the visit-ing Honourables, and nothing left washable under the pantry ceiling of the Schoolroom Wing?

Lavinia the Lethal, hovering around, could have told Mrs Multifarious, had not the worthy housekeeper offended her deeply, when only a brash young still-room maid, by publicly disbelieving in her.

For what the Lady Lavinia had learned about Our Cherry had been imparted by the Spectre of the Buttress Tower, a headstrong lass who had hurled herself off the turret and into the moat for lack of a lover in the fifteenth century.

'There'll be another of us soon, you'll see,' she moaned, 'y-o-o-l s-e-e-e!' and disappeared from the conversation head foremost.

'Not if I can help it,' muttered the Lady Lavinia, and forthwith went into the matter for herself.

And what she found entirely failed to reassure her. For Our Cherry was lovelorn as ever a nursery-maid could be.

He was a footman. The third footman. He whose duty it was to carry up and serve the nursery dinner.

His little Lordship, Gervaise, Thirteenth Lord Mullibeare, loved the third footman dearly and would stand behind his sister's chair comparatively still for minutes on end in imitation of his powdered hero. And hero-worship being catching, Our Cherry had fallen mortally in love with Mr Horridge, so that it had become both a pleasure and a pain to lend a hand with the nursery washing-up. A pleasure because this mundane exercise lit the world each day at waking for Our Cherry, and a pain because she never could think of anything to say when The Moment came. And the third footman? Well, to him Our Cherry was just another pair of hands about the place, fortunately not too high up in the relentless hierarchy of the servants' hall to lend him one.

And since the third footman had a way with women which generally led to his having his way with women, it follows that Charity Callender was a natural for the next hauntship. Or so Lavinia the Lethal read the writing on the nursery pantry wall.

In the still-room she said as much to the Cardinal:

'Our Cherry,' she observed, 'has been wasting too much time embroidering a pair of slippers for the third footman's Christmas present.'

'Time,' said His Eminence. He sounded envious.

'That was what made her late for dinner,' said the Lady Lavinia. 'She was putting the last cross-stitch in the final pansy.'

'Indeed,' said the Cardinal, 'but then, no doubt the choice of flower was – um – fortuitous?'

The Cardinal came upon his flask of malmsey and did something pretty practised with the archi-episcopal cabochon. Not that the Fourth Marchioness perceived this. She was far too busy whipping up a hundred and seventy-five yards of crimson paduasoy the better to secure a neat stiletto.

'All the same,' she confided, perpendicular regained, 'I wouldn't like anything to happen to the girl – I'm inclined to think that the Eighth Marquess was at fault there.'

'You bet your sweet death he was,' said His Eminence. He chuckled.

'She's got the blue, blue eyes of the Linneages,' the Fourth Marchioness pointed out.

'But not their red, red noses,' said the Cardinal coarsely. He chuckled.

'Seriously, Cardinal,' said the Lady Lavinia, 'don't you think Our Cherry has a strong look of me about her?'

'A trace, no doubt,' said His Eminence obligingly, 'but she lacks your haunting quality.'

He picked up the Fatal Flask and whisked through the wall.

Meanwhile, since as Mrs Multifarious had observed, mutton wouldn't melt in Charity Callender's open mouth (not even though it came from one of three famous Christmas Meagrefold herds, from which three sheep of different breeds were butchered every week for the needs of Lyttletoun alone: one Southdown, one Westmoreland and one Brittany, the last being set aside solely for its succulent cutlets), Our Cherry had both time and occasion to stare at her footman to her faithful heart's content.

Or rather to its distinct uneasiness; a heavy kind of heartbeat entirely unknown to its owner in all her going-on seventeen years, safely cradled, as they had been within easy earshot of Our Gran'mum in the village of Christmas Meagrefold.

For the third footman had taken in Lady Mandragon's personal maid and was in his turn being taken in by that French hussy.

By the time the upper servants had adjourned for their coffee and the glass of cherry brandy traditionally served in the housekeeper's room – which was just about a nursery-maid's lifetime after Charity Callender had discovered that strawberry ice-cream wouldn't melt in her mouth either (and this, too, had not happened to Our Cherry before) – the girl had gone and got herself into a rare old state.

With half an hour to go before delivering herself up to Mrs Multifarious for her well-earned wigging ('Charity Callender, you have brought shame on Lyttletoun . . .'), Our Cherry was hanging about outside the green baize door of the house-keeper's room listening to the laughter of the upper servants and their visitors; laughter nicely graded from the fruity boom of Mr Plumwick, the butler, with reciprocal roulades from the visiting Lords and Ladies on the housekeeper's hearth-rug, well within the immobile orbit of the Dowager Lady Linneage in oils, to the titters of the mere Honourables standing about in the draughts. Loitering this side of paradise, Our Cherry had no great difficulty in unskeining the general babble and follow-ing the shrill strand of Mam'selle Mandragon's nasal laughter, which, as the cherry brandy continued to circulate, had taken on a penetrating hiss together with many an Oo-la-la; which didn't mean nowt and sounded downright daft to the pink ears of Charity Callender, and yet, in a terrifying way, seemed doubly to fascinate the gentlemen's gentlemen.

Then, as the aristocracy behind the baize door showed no sign of going about its business, Our Cherry trailed herself disconsolately up to her attic to take a quiet gawk at the moon. This solitary occupation fitted in nicely with the growing melancholy of her mood. And indeed, of late, and for no reason she could lay her surprisingly shapely finger on, Our Cherry had felt fair down-in-the-dumps, but at the same time, strangely uplifted. So tonight, with an undignified discourage-ment heavy on her, the little nursery-maid did not bother to stop to light the paraffin lamp on the wicker-work chest, but instead drew back the curtains (their wooden rings rattled like a cupboardful of skeletons) to flood the attic with wan, cold light, so that the iron ribs of her high bedstead were thrown like the bars of a man's cell against her bedroom wall. There, on the quilted counterpane, lay the precious embroidered slippers, worked on with some pretty hard breathing when it came to the motif of the heart's-ease and forget-me-nots, not to mention being laid aside for many a day-dream, and obligingly soled by Mr Farthingwick, the estate cobbler. And beautiful they looked too, with their scarlet ground and dear little pansy faces and all done in cross-stitch. Our Cherry picked her slippers up and held them against her cheek. They were soft as swansdown, or well-nigh. She did not herself know what she hoped might come of her Christmas present to Mr Horridge – Albert. She only knew the making of them had meant a lot to her.

With great care, and with a truly touching tenderness, she wrapped them in the special Christmas gift-paper she'd managed to get at while Our Gran'mum was serving young Mrs Lovelock of Coronation Cottages with a packet of tea and picture-given-away of Her Majesty Queen Alexandra in Crown and Ermine and as pretty as a picture even though they did say that the Queen spoke the King's English with a foreign accent. Then, still with loving care, she licked the label addressed in her best ink printing and only one blot, to Mr Albert Horridge, and clutching her present to the well-developed bosom she strapped in as tightly as her modesty dictated (though with something less concealment than her niceness could wish, for you could still see the swell of them if you looked for it, which so far, one somehow sensed, Mr Horridge hadn't), and speeded by love and fear of Mrs Multifarious, swift as the winter's wind, Our Cherry went back to the servants' hall where the great Christmas tree had been standing all day long.

There it stood, dark and ample and receptive against the crimson twill folds of the curtains in the great window embrasure, and ever so much bigger than Her Ladyship's own; the one in the William Kent or Garden Ballroom; which while it was big enough to hold the entire village at the coming-of-age of younger sons, was still more intimate than the Antioch Ballroom in the State Apartments, used for the coming-of-age of the heir, and the officially unofficial visits of the Sovereign.

And this time tomorrow there would be a twinkle of little lights from the coloured Christmas candles set among those spreading branches, and a sparkle of diamond-frost, and a gleam of red, blue, pink, green, lustre-glass baubles and little toys, and all to be counted on Twelfth Night by Mrs Multifarious, and packed carefully away under her supervision till next year's glory.

And at the foot of the Christmas tree (Our Cherry hadn't been up at The House at Christmas-time before, but this was a custom she knew well, for it was legend in the village), at the foot of the tree in the servants' hall were laid all the presents for the staff – indoor workers and outdoor workers – and there they had to be left and not fingered till half past six of a Christmas Day night, when Her Ladyship herself came down with all her noble guests and graciously distributed them just like prize day at the village school, only this time everyone, no matter how new and humble and snubbed, but just like in Heaven, everyone would be going up without exception, all blushes and pleased expressions, to receive a gift.

So here, the very first of the many, many packages to be deposited, Our Cherry laid her Christmas offering, breathless as the moment before a summer rain falls on the waiting earth. And was about to straighten up when a pinch on her bent behind made her rudely aware that she was not alone.

She flicked up and spun round and found herself face to face with him for whom it was intended. For the third footman was on his way, and none too early at that, to take up Her Ladyship the Old'un's last-thing herbal. And my! but he had a lively shine in his Irish eyes tonight! For there could be no doubt but that Mr Albert Horridge had been looking on the cherry brandy when it was red. And on that Mam'selle Mandragon.

And one thing leading to another, 'Hullo,' says he, and picks up the parcel spry as a silver trout – and as slippery – and Our Cherry in a panic, made to catch it.

'Here's a thing.' He waved it just above her frantic reach.

'And a very pretty thing.' He felt it with inquisitive thumbs.

'And who is the owner of this pretty thing?' And he whirled around and bent to read the label.

'Oh, stop it! Give it to me! You mustn't – really you mustn't . . .' bleated Our Cherry, but to no avail.

'For why,' says he, 'if it isn't for m'self, whatever it may be – well, well, well! Who'd have thought it!' and Mr Albert Horridge looked fair staggered.

Just then a witch came scudding into the hall, turned herself hurriedly into a weasel and disappeared through the wainscot. She was Harriet Simple, accused of stealing the wits of an innocent by black magic in the reign of James the First, which charge she denied to the end strenuously and, no doubt, with truth.

'Put that parcel back at once!'

What with embarrassment and fear of bringing shame on Lyttletoun and this reason and the next, Our Cherry was well nigh blubbing – a big girl like her – when, 'Well, well, well,' says he, 'I must give you a kiss for this,' and did.

And the next thing, mercy on us if he wasn't looking for the swell of her bosom.

Wildly Our Cherry broke from him and ran.

'Charity Callender, you have brought shame on Lyttletoun . . .'

Our Cherry dropped her starry eyes before the accusing gaze of Mrs Multifarious, but even in the face of the housekeeper's practised eloquence, her countenance was of one who had seen the glory.

2

By the time Mr Plumwick, the butler, had laid aside the golden fountain pen which was engraved with His Majesty King Edward the Seventh's own cypher and with which he had been engaged on his nightly task of writing up his diary, that somewhat ponderously-phrased record on which he was some day to base his book of memoirs, *Longleat to Lyttletoun – Being Some Leaves From A Butler's Laurels,* to the distinct annoyance of the Dowager who had been on the point of writing something on much the same lines herself; and long before Our Cherry had gloried herself to sleep, the clock in the stable gable sounded the twelfth stroke of midnight and the Mechanicalle Mirracle of Prince Rupert's Folly saluted the happy morn with a ting-tang topline of *Christians, Awake!* delivered with a great deal of wheel grinding and cogging as ancient hammers hit age-old bronze. It was the signal.

Up at The House despairing ladies, with or without heads, flung themselves off battlements with gay abandon; gentlemen duelled in the tilt-yard; poisoners pressed their dire drams on victims in boudoirs or libraries, abundantly supplied with secret panels; corridors were a-clank with the dragging of chains. The cold air was iced with groans and moans, and draughty passages were all the draughtier for the rush of unpunctual spectres wafting along them.

For it was Haunting Hour, that time of night when Lyttletoun was given over to the revenants of the centuries, doomed to enact their violent ends till time became a word without a meaning. Among them, Lavinia the Lethal and her Bloody Cardinal. They, for the suddenness of their cutting-off, were doomed to go through the fateful moves that led to it, in the Cardinal's Suite, which, at the time to which we are looking back over envious shoulders, had been allocated to the Captain the Honourable Gwylliam Vulliamy-Williams.

Halfway through the midnight stroke the Fourth Marchioness tugged at His Eminence's sleeve.

'Have you got your ring on?' she said, quite unnecessarily, but then she always had been one to fall into a fuss on first nights.

However, as the last note of midnight rotunded into the past, with heightened colour and a brightness of eye which merely portended that a professional was about to do a job of work, and, being a good professional, was anxious to get the best possible result; her head held high and her ribands flying, the Lady Lavinia led the way through the wall.

'At last, Lord Cardinal, we are alone!' The voice was the vibrant voice of the Fourth Marchioness, up an octave with first night nerves, but the line, though traditional, was something of an understatement. For there, on Queane Eleanoure's Bedde, sleeping like a childe, lay Captain the Honourable Gwylliam Vulliamy-Williams, with nary a shiver nor shake.

'You have brought the secret document,' intoned the Cardinal with an anxiety that seven centuries of affirmations had done nothing to allay.

'Assuredly.' The Lady Lavinia rummaged. His Eminence suppressed a smile. Long though the run had been, Lavinia always fumbled with the props on first night.

'La!' she said at last, and flung him the plans of the fortifications.

Captain the Honourable Gwylliam Vulliamy-Williams moaned gently in his sleep. The Lady Lavinia looked affronted.

'Come, daughter.' From the purple depths of his sleeve his

his Eminence produced the flask of malmsey.

'But the pardon,' panted the lady. 'Milord Cardinal will not forget his promise to his obedient daughter – the life and freedom of Lord Lackday is the price that you are sworn to pay me.'

'By phosphorus! Woman, do you doubt mine honour?' And, black as magic, the Cardinal produced a parchment.

The Lady Lavinia snatched it from him. She did someting very dexterous with a hundred and seventy-five yards of paduasoy. When the dust had subsided the fold of parchment was nearly tucked into the pleached plush garter and a dagger nestled in the paduasoy, its handle t'wards her hand.

But the Cardinal was too busy to observe this. From out of his other sleeve materialised two goblets. He filled both. He passed one. He raised the other. 'To the Day,' he toasted the fair informer. 'To the Night,' corrected the Fourth Marchioness. She drained the draught. Not so the wily Cardinal.

From the Queane's Bedde Captain the Honourable Gwylliam Vulliamy-Williams burrowed his head deeply into the pillows.

'More malmsey,' said the lady hoarsely. She passed up her goblet.

His Eminence smiled his secret, thin-lipped smile. But even as he turned to the flask, Lavinia the Lethal had sped his life with a thrust of her Spanish dagger in his back.

The Cardinal gave a great cry. It was loud enough to awaken the dead. But not, it seemed, Captain the Honourable Gwylliam Vulliamy-Williams. Blood gushed from his wound. And with his latest breath he gasped; 'Repent you, daughter, for the wine you drank is poisoned and you have scarce an hour to live.' And his time having come, the Bloody Cardinal gave up the ghost.

With a wild and eldritch shriek, the Lady Lavinia swounded.

Captain the Honourable Gwylliam Vulliamy-Williams passed his tongue over his lips.

'Ham,' he muttered drowsily. 'I have been dreaming of ham,' and fell to sleeping like a child once more.

3

For the indoor staff at Lyttletoun, that army of well-trained underpaid specialists in rubbing, scrubbing, stoking, polishing, cleaning, scouring and other reiterative lifelong occupations, Christmas Day in the morning started at four am being an hour earlier than usual when His Nibs was at home. Even the Christmas stocking-conscious little Lords and Ladyships did not blink a peeper in the Linneage night nurseries till a quarter to five, praise the Lord!

But then, these were the good old days, when all the Charity Callenders and third footmen (out of a population of which one in forty was in domestic service) were expected to earn their pretty handsome keep; and in the case of Our Cherry, twelve pounds per annum, and two uniforms found, two morning prints and one black alpaca for afternoons.

So, with the hot, strong, sweet tea still stinging her throat, her slice of bread-and-dripping scarce bitten into, Our Cherry scurried down the dark passages to lend a hand with the William Kent or Garden Ballroom, a task in which all Lyttletoun personnel not otherwise employed had been co-opted.

Already Mr Brotherly and Mr Trance had been at it. It being their sole duty to pick the flowers and arrange them to the best possible advantage in the great Dresden urns and in the various halls and drawing-rooms, the one hundred and fifteen bedrooms in use, not to speak of nooks, crannies, window embrasures and the flower arrangement for the dinner-table. This latter complicated the lives of Mr Brotherly and perhaps a little more especially of Mr Trance by reason of the large gold plate figure of the Eleventh Marquess baring his breast to the battle-axe of a Menacing Fuzzy-Wuzzy which, remarkable though it may have been for reasons of sheer circumference and verisimilitude, was an undeniable thorn in the flower decorations on ceremonial occasions at Lyttletoun.

By the time their little Ladyships, bless their bright eyes and pretty manners, had done with their oohing and cooing over the Dutch dolls, discovered stark naked in Christmas stockings no longer hanging at the foots of beds, and were busily engaged in tearing them limb from solid wooden limb, you could see your face in any portion of the William Kent or Garden Ballroom (save in its saucy ceiling) and in a great many parts of a great many other apartments, halls, wings, drawing-rooms, sitting-rooms, and several solid marble staircases. For under the eagle-eyed deployment of Mrs Multifarious, the indoor staff of Lyttletoun was pretty practised in polishing.

But the hands of the third footman had found employment other than that of giving Lyttletoun its Christmas Morning shine; though not so closely connected with the recumbent form of Mam'selle Mandragon as no doubt the audacious fellow could have wished.

For these were the days when footmen wore their powder, a form of coiffure seriously ruffled by their duties when out with the carriage. For their high cockaded hats disturbed the iron smoothness of their chevelure and your footman had to powder every day, in any service worthy of the name of service.

Now we need have no fear but that the footmen of Lyttletoun were gloriously attired, all six-foot and over of them, in their mulberry plush breeches, mulberry face-cloth coats with silver frogs, their rich cerise satin waistcoats, their pink silk stockings and their shoes with silver buckles on them.

Small wonder, then, that our third footman, a royalist if ever there was one, was whistling *Good King Wenceslas* contentedly enough as he mixed the violet powder he obtained from Runciball's, the chemist shop in Fairingsford (or 'Town' as it was always called in the village of Christmas Meagrefold) with some of the chef's fine flour, for although he had a powdering allowance of two guineas a year, it never saw the third footman through. And so, to the daily routine of a footman's hairdoing. The washing of it with soap. The combing of it all out. The getting it set in its waves. The powdering of them. For in those days a footman did not dry his hair, but left it to set firmly like cement. Which process had to be achieved in good time to carry up the Dowager Marchioness's early morning tea.

For among the earlier risers on this crisp and sparkling Christmas Morning, as indeed on any other day of the year, Sundays regretfully excepted, was the Dowager Marchioness, who, summer or autumn, winter or spring, was already engaged upon a work of encyclopaedic dimensions, entitled *How to Be a Good Tenant,* with entries on anything that happened to pop into or out of the author's capacious, lively and needle-quick seventy-six-year-old mind. Upon completion the book would be privately printed and distributed, with red flannel petticoat or fretwork letter-holder according to sex, to all the workers on the estate.

'Walnuts,' her ladyship was writing when her morning tea arrived, 'Don't waste 'em – pickle 'em.'

Next on the third footman's early morning tea list were the nurseries.

And on this bright and early Christmas Morning, Miss McKindlecandle, the head nannie, had not only her rightful little Lordships and Ladyships to disentangle from their own and one another's Christmas booty before morning prayers in the Lyttletoun chapel, but all their little visitors had to be weaned from fascinating toys and pastimes, too.

The third footman, stepping agog-like over the tracks of a clockwork engine which was running round and round the rails to the delight of a small boy whose fascinated head was circling with the engine, deposited his tray on the nursery table, but received only the curtest of thank-you's from the four flights-up nannie, who clearly thought nothing of such-like attentions.

In fact Miss McKindlecandle was trying to put a point of view to the rapt and rotating head of His Little Lordship's guest.

'Come away from that railway engine now, Master Emmet, or we'll never have you washed, dressed, and apple-eaten in time for morning prayers . . .'

At eight o'clock of the stable gable, sixty trays of morning tea had been carried in smilingly to as many bedrooms, where curtains were rattled apart and blinds pulled, compliments of the seasons paid and returned with varying degrees of good will and fervour, and, in the case of those rooms in the South Wing, windows flung ruthlessly open to admit the tin-tang topline of the Mechnicalle Mirracle whirring itself erratically through *Oh, Come, All Ye Faithful*.

For Christmas had come to Lyttletoun in full measure.

Morning prayers took place in the Chapel which had been a pious afterthought added to Lyttletoun in the reign of the late Queen, in memory of Boadicea, the Ninth Marchioness.

The Chapel, then, was a jumped-up affair in comparison to the battlements. In fact, the ghosts of Lyttletoun ignored it. Not a grave to gape at the midnight toll! Indeed, the only candidate for hauntship since the place had been built was Lady Lettice

Linneage, the Tenth Marquess's elder sister, who had died at
the age of eighty-two of her habit of eating out-of-doors; and
woe betide the guest who shivered when the snow-flakes fell
into the soup!

At twenty-five minutes past eight the maids betook
themselves to the attics from which they emerged, a bare two
minutes later, in black bonnets with velvet ribbons tied under
the chin and cramming the cold chapped fingers into black
cotton gloves, they scuttled, sped, almost hurried, or made their
way, according to the precedence of the servants' hall, to the
doors of the Domestic Chapel. At a minute to the half-past, His
Nibs, Her Ladyship, their little Lordships and Ladyships and
all the visitors entered the Chapel for morning prayers. The
servants filed in after them. And on the very stroke from the
stable gable, the Domestic Chaplain, a holy man for all the
bottle of claret that went up on his tray every night, appeared to
conduct the household through its morning prayers.

Now Lyttletoun applied itself to its devotions.

Or did it?

For the children had their presents on their mind, and the
nannies had their charges on their mind, and the housekeeper
had the maids on her mind, and as for the housemaids . . . well,
Our Cherry, for one, was concerned with the smile on the face
of the third footman. For that one gazed impenitently out of the
Chapel window – the one where the stained glass wasn't, all
ready for Her Ladyship the Old'Un to pass away, and whatever
his thoughts, they were mighty pleasing to him.

And Our Cherry, poor chick, try as she might to fix her
thoughts on George, Prince of Wales, the Princess May, and all
the Royal Family, could only think that in two hours from now,
she would be lending a hand with the washing-up in the
nursery pantry, up there alone with the porringers and Him,
and her warm little heart beat fit to bust out of her bodice.

But breakfast at Lyttletoun on Christmas Morning was an
ample function endlessly prolonged. Brawn was the time-
honoured Christmas breakfast dish at Lyttletoun. This dish
had come down from great antiquity and was obtained from a
vast distance. It was prepared from the flesh of boars which had
been allowed to run the woods half-wild, and then placed in the
fattening pen fast-trussed to make the flesh more dense. But

bacon and eggs were also served as usual. Places had been piled high with presents from His Nibs and Her Ladyship to all the family and guests, and from the guests and family to Her Ladyship and His Nibs, and by the time the ribbons had been undone, the wrappings removed, and their contents exclaimed over ('Another tea-cosy from Cousin Jane – how kind! The very thing we needed!'), and the table had been cleared, it was time for the maids to stand in line outside Her Ladyship's sitting-room, under the strict supervision of Mrs Multifarious, there to state their names and length of service to Her Ladyship who would then smilingly present the traditional length of dress material, which for centuries had been bestowed at Yuletide on the maids of Lyttletoun by the Marchioness herself – the men-servants got a groat from the hand of His Nibs, who generously translated this into modern coinage in the shape of a newly-minted golden sovereign, and a shining shilling. So this morning Our Cherry's hand would not be available for being lent to wash up in the nursery pantry, after all. And today of all days! Our Cherry could have fair cried her eyes out!

And at the end of all that standing about in the cold corridor with the other maids, when she should have been up in the nice warm steam of the nursery pantry, it was all for a length of morning print, not the dress-length that Our Cherry had dreamed of Mr Albert Horridge taking her to the Flower Show in . . .

'. . . But the Queen of the Flower Show is you, Miss Callender, if I may make so bold!'

'Oh, Mr Horridge, the things you do say!'

At eleven o'clock the household could breathe again. For His Nibs and Her Ladyship, the children and the guests, and thank goodness, the visiting servants, all went to service at St Jude's, the Norman church down in the village of Christmas Meagrefold. But the third footman, always on call for the carriages, was needed on the box of the barouche that took Her Ladyship the Old'Un to the lych gate. And that meant having to powder all over again, for the high hat with the ribbon cockade would be sure to disarrange his hair. And that meant, Christmas or no, Mr Albert Horridge would be in one of his sulks, and like as not decide to dry up for himself. Oh dear!

So what with lack of sleep, and the emotions of the morning, it was a wan little Charity Callender who stepped carefully over the frosty cobbles of the kitchen courtyard and stopped to gawk at the fish-pond, where the carp from the river River Lytte were lying in fresh water to rid them of the taste of mud; and so to the kitchens to lend a hand where most needed, on mandate to Chef from Mrs Multifarious.

The kitchen at Lyttletoun was a realm unto itself – a hot, clattering kingdom, much given to hysterical outbursts; with its two great hearths, one for roasting whole beasts over the open fire, the other for the monster oven in which the Lyttletoun baking was done, besides the battery of fires and stoves and heating apparatus, such as the bricked-in grill-grid, the various gas ovens in the pantry, the vegetable stove, the water-heater, and the hot-plates, and all of them blazing away and been at it since long before daybreak, to prepare the Christmas Dinner – turkey and plum pudding and mince pies – and the seven-course meal this evening, and both in duplicate for dining room and servants' hall, and this in addition to the elaborate breakfasts, elaborate teas, elaborate snacks and such-like.

Clearly Providence had taken the matter of the Lyttletoun daily bread to heart! Moreover M'sieur Soidisant, King of the Lyttletoun kitchens, was a close friend of the pastry chef at Sandringham House, and many were the recipes which passed between Norfolk and Paddockshire.

On her way to the vegetable kitchen to help peel the eight hundred potatoes that went to a midday meal at Lyttletoun she stood fascinated before the open fire over which two whole sucking pigs were slowly turning on their spits and sizzling sweetly as they turned – the faintly larger pig was for the servants' hall.

Naturally.

Cherry stared at the icing-sugar glory of the giant Christmas cake (A Merry Christmas To All At Lyttletoun), which was destined for the staff, and the faintly smaller frosty giant for the family.

Of course.

She looked longingly at the twin plum puddings, sure to be borne to respective tables in a sea of blue-green flames. The lesser one with the silver lucky charms went to the dining room. But the Christmas pudding for the servants' hall had twenty-

seven newly-minted five shilling pieces well stirred into its
plummy interior, according to Lyttletoun tradition, and Our
Cherry came near to praying that her slice might contain one of
the precious silver bits, now that her Christmas Length had
turned out to be the morning print she'd a right to, anyway; so
that her frock for the Flower Show, had, after all, to come out of
her bit of pocket money.

Noticing Our Cherry standing there, regarding the great
Christmas pudding with the rapt face of an angel gazing on
glory, Mr Chef himself stopped in the middle of his sprint from
the tasting of the apricot filling for the Lyttletoun Merrie-
Mould ('Mm– ? Ça va!') to the tasting of the brandy-cream
('Mais qu'est-ce que c'est, cette atrocité? Pfui!') to beam at the
neophyte:

    'On mangera bien ce soir, n'est-ce pas, ma petite?'

4

The Cardinal was pacing the Garland Hall, waiting for the
Fourth Marchioness to join him till death. His Eminence, who
had been pacing there for quite a time (three hundred years, in
point of fact), was bored. Each evening at the selfsame hour His
Eminence paced this measly stretch of marble, stepping on the
black squares only, and feeling utterly and unutterably bored.

If only he had known he was about to die violently, before his
time had come, he would have seen to it, in the very first
instance, that he gave up the ghost in a more cheerful frame of
mind.

At length the Fourth Marchioness appeared. In crimson
paduasoy, as usual! 'Late again,' snapped the Cardinal, their
customary greeting gabbled.

How right he was. For already they had been overtaken by
the green-blue nimbus of Selina the Saintly (who had lost her
hope of a halo by cutting ace high for the soul of the Bedevilled
Bishop, his bewitched Lordship having fiendishly produced the
joker provided by his familiar), which was bowling merrily
down the bannisters, punctual to its appointed hour.

'Don't scold,' said the Lady Lavinia. 'I'm worried to death.'

'A matter of grave concern, no doubt?' said His Eminence
wittily.

The Lady Lavinia looked at him. In silence they took up their haunt.

In the still-room the Marchioness relented. 'It's Our Cherry,' she explained.

'Again?' said the Cardinal. 'What's the matter with the girl? She's had her nice dress length, hasn't she?'

'And a slice of Christmas cake with her tea,' confirmed the Marchioness, 'and she's going to find a five shilling bit in her Christmas pudding tonight if I have to put it there myself!'

'Then what's wrong with the girl?'

'He hasn't spoken a word to her all day long – not so much as a Merrie Yuletide!'

'Sensible fellow. Steering clear of trouble, no doubt,' said His Eminence with strong approval. He did something singularly dexterous with the archi-episcopal cabochon. 'Did you say something?' he enquired blandly. Though he knew quite well that the Machioness had only smoothed down a hundred and seventy-five yards of paduasoy and sniffed.

All through the turtle soup, and through the turbot, all through the sparkling moselle (specially set aside for dinner in the servants' hall on Christmas Night by the two gentlemen who came down from London for two weeks a year to go over the Lyttletoun wine cellars, cataloguing and replenishing), Our Cherry gazed at the third footman gazing at Mlle Mandragon.

All through the turkey, all through the water-ice, all through the sucking pig, all through the claret (which Our Cherry had no need of Mrs Multifarious's restraining eyebrow not to touch, for indeed she had not taken sup nor bite, but just messed her victuals about like any fine lady), she did not take her eyes from Mr Albert Horridge who did not take his eyes from Mlle Mandragon.

All through the Merrie-Moulds, all through the Crystallizeds, all through the nice mince pies, her gaze did not falter.

And not so much as a word except 'No, thank you' passed the Christmas Dinner through between Miss Callender and Mr Vulliamy-Williams who had taken her in, and not even an 'After you' was vouchsafed Mr McGilliefleur, the coachman, on her other side.

'Must be in love,' thought Mr Vulliamy-Williams. 'But not with me. A pity.'

And, in fact, not until the dramatic darkening of the servants' hall, ready for the arrival of the Christmas pudding in its sea of flames, did her eyes forsake her hero and turn to what was on her plate.

But prod and plough the plummy chunk as she might, no glint of silver rewarded her seeking fork. The Queen of the Flower Show would have to abdicate!

And then . . . the lights went up, and there was the third footman pressing a five shilling piece into the hand of Mlle Mandragon.

And he needn't've! Oh, he needn't've!

And a wavering outline that might have been a left-behind brandy flame, tugged at another left-behind wavering sleeve.

'Quick,' it hissed.

And a draught passed through the servants' hall, bending the flames of the candles. And by the time it had subsided and the candles were burning sentinel-straight again, lo and behold! Our Cherry found she'd made a mistake and there lay a five shilling bit under a lump she must have forgotten to crumble. And Mille Mandragon was looking reproachfully at the third footman.

And then, suddenly, it was midnight. Time for all the servants to rush out into whatever weather there was in the courtyard and dance to the swirl of McGilliefleur's pipes, while from the windows warm-as-toast guests watched the pretty sight of the bobbing-about maidservants with snow-flakes in their hair.

All the guests save Captain the Honourable Gwylliam Vulliamy-Williams, that is. That one had retired early to bed.

And hardly had he fallen asleep, when the Cardinal's dying groan and the Marchioness's swounding shriek brought him smartly to his senses. The room was empty. It was also very chill. Captain the Honourable Gwylliam Vulliamy-Williams shivered.

'Corn,' he complained. 'I've been dreaming of corn.' And straight away fell to sleep again.

It was while Mr McGilliefleur was a'blawing and a'skirling 'em into the Eightsome, down in the courtyard, that Our

Cherry chose to flout the Lyttletoun tradition and slip away by herself into the house.

For the third footman, though as fine a fellow at the Valeta as you could wish to see, had absented himself for quite a while from this ould-fashioned kind of cavortin'; and Our Cherry knew just where to find himself!

And shame on her for an old Paul Pry, if she didn't go creeping up (hating herself for the act, and yet compelled to it) to listen outside Mlle Mandragon's door.

And there she crouched and heard for herself; and unmistakable it was and no mistake!

For, 'Please,' Mr Albert Horridge's voice was pleading, all hoarse and funny-like, 'Please!' and then, 'We must! . . . Sure, what harm can it do? . . . We must! . . . We've got to! Please! . . .'

And then the hated, high-pitched, foreign gibberish: 'Mais quoi donc? . . . Ah! Cela, alors! . . . Non! Non! No-o-n!'

And the last long-drawn word, part protest, but greater part invitation, died away and turned, a listener's lifetime later, into a gasp.

And bitter tears ran down Our Cherry's cheeks; for though they had not taught her botany at the village school, she had no manner of doubt of what it was the pair of them were up to in there.

5

Like many-coloured, soigné butterflies, the Eleventh Marchioness and her guests had descended to flutter about the servants' hall, to wait upon her staff at dinner. Her Ladyship and friends were enjoying themselves enormously.

Like moths, the poor-and-hating-it relations of their brilliant hosts, the staff, attired in made-over flung-away ball dresses, were seated at table for the one meal in the year no-one among them had the stomach for.

For it was Wassailing (or Boxing) Night at Lyttletoun, and this was a part of the Christmas Tradition of that great and hospitable establishment.

For centuries, on Wassailing Night, the Marquess and Marchioness of Lyttletoun and their Yuling guests had come

down to wait upon the serfs until, on the stroke of eleven by the
stable gable, the wassailers from the village would come carrying their lanthorns over the Maltravers Meadow, over the
Bridge of Lytte, and up and round the drive where the trees
were planted in battle formation after the fashion of 'Landskip
Plantacion' as practised by Capability Brown at that comparatively upstart establishment, Blenheim Palace, and came
to a stop at the great cookhouse door, there to call their
traditional greeting: 'God Rest You Mullie; Be Ye Wassail!'
And then on again and all around till they came to the
Queane's Plott, where they stood to sing their Christmas carols
accompanied on handbells. Then, at the stroke of midnight,
they would form a torchlight procession to march singing over
the bridge and all around and back again to pass the punch
bowl in the servants' hall.

But the Lyttletoun wassailing tradition was quite beyond
Our Cherry tonight, who did not rest her mullie, or in fact, at
all, and throughout the grandiose repast turned eye to plate
and once again would have nothing of it. For she had discovered
that life was not worth the attic candle, and fain would rid
herself of the burden. But how? Not, clearly, by starvation – for
to starve to death at Lyttletoun was next door to impossible,
and in any case would take a very long time indeed. And Our
Cherry would be gone at once. And so she sought around, and
around, while Her Ladyship and Guites laughed heartily at one
another's mishaps, and her young head fairly spun, and every
minute was an eternity.

Did not the River Lytte run through the grounds? They did
say weeds, in these parts, grew green and strong and binding
and would hold a body down. A body that had no kind of use
left for itself – no kind of use whatsoever.

And though, of course, Our Cherry did not speak this
thought aloud, the Fourth Marchioness, a wavering candle-
flame behind her chair, was as privy to Our Cherry's dreadful
purpose as though the dark thoughts had been born of the
shadows of her own mind.

She plucked now at the ghostly sleeve that hung wavering
beside her.

'What did I tell you!' she exclaimed, her triumph almost out-
weighing the supernatural anxiety in her moan.

'When?' asked His flame-like Eminence protectively.

'Mark my words, Our Cherry will make a sudden end on't!'

'How do you know?' The other wavering outline blinked dangerously.

'Because I was a young girl myself once,' snapped the wavering Fourth Marchioness.

'That,' flamed His Eminence, 'was centuries ago!'

Unwaveringly the Fourth Marchioness looked at him.

6

The quality had retreated to the Bow Room Window, there to rest them mullie and to be them wassail, while watching the subsequent proceedings from the big window.

Snow crowned the walls of the Queane's Plott where in the summer ripened peaches, lush progeny of a tree which had been planted by the Queane herself in the face of the sun-dial's warning, which went:

> . . . *Wan Lite sal fale*
> *Andd Tym is donn*
> *Whare den sal standd*
> *Grete Lyttletoun?* . . .

but your Wassailers are impervious to cold.

> '*O Lyttle Toun of Bethlehem*
> *How still we see thee lye.*'

they warbled, to the relaxed expressions in the Bow Room Window and one green-blue face looking out from the nursery wind. This latter the Wassailers ignored. For it was only, as any one of them could have recited backwards, the Ghastly Gouvernante, who haunted the Lyttletoun Schoolroom with intent to chalk up, in spiky, governess-like, luminous letters, the Legend:

> *Pittie dis*
> *Pore Soules*
> *Painnes*

till the Kingdom of Compassion Come, since the Fifth Lord
Mellibeare had shown her none in the bitter plight he had
plunged her in. And at his age, too!

And so, to a husking of carols and jangle of handbells, the
hour of Wassailing sped, punctuated by many a cheer of 'God
Rest You Mullie!'

'Rest!' moaned His ghostly Eminence, enviously.

'R-e-e-s-s-t!' Like the leaves of the forest lamenting the
autumn, with the desolation of waste paper blown about an
empty street, like the wind outside in winter, and like lost souls
sighing down the centuries, all the revenants of Lyttletoun took
up that blessed word.

'C'mon, Cardinal,' snapped the Lady Lavinia at length, 'this
is no time for self-pity. We've got a life to save. We've got to stay
that poor, chaste child from dying untimely, and we've next to
no time to do it in, so get a waft on!' And the Lady Lavinia
whipped up one hundred and seventy-five yards of crimson
paduasoy and whisked it through half a yard of solid stone wall.

The Cardinal whisked after her. And it was apparent to His
Eminence that the Lady Lavinia was about to have the time of
her death!

Now in Lyttletoun, on this same Wassailing Night, some-
body else beside Our Cherry did not Rest him Mullie. For
Captain the Honourable Gwylliam Vulliamy-Williams was not
feeling himself at all. He had a bump on his brow the size of a
melon. For, as Dr Johnson has discovered, 'Building is not at all
more convenient for being decorated with superfluous curved
wood.' He had retired to his room soon after Good King
Wenceslas looked out. By midnight he had fallen into a light
doze.

'At last, Lord Cardinal, we are alone!'   The voice was the
vibrant, and, indeed, by this time, familiar voice of Lavinia the
Lethal. And there was something quite uncanny about the
speed of its utterance.

'La!' the lady simply hurled the secret documents at the
Bloody Cardinal.

What's more, Captain the Honourable Gwylliam Vulliamy-
Williams could have sworn that she'd skipped something. And
the Old Boy was in such a hurry that he nearly dropped the
ghostly goblet.

'To the Day!' he toasted the Fair Informer hastily.

'To the Night!' she answered like a flash.

They drained their glasses at the double.

They fell a-choking.

From the Queane's Bedde Captain the Honourable Gwylliam Vulliamy-Williams opened a pained eyelid.

'I say,' he said reproachfully, 'you're gagging!'

7

Meantime Our dismal Cherry, who could not bear the Mullie Wassail an eternity longer, had stolen away from her fellow revellers and she ran, in nothing but her year-before-last's prize-giving cotton (with the sleeves cut off and the neck scooped out – a concession to custom up at The House, where the indoor staff were expected to wear evening dress for dinner) and with nary a cloak nor muffler flung about her shoulders, so soon now to be held down by the slimy weeds of the Lytte – along the path that led out by the foot of Monarch's Bridge.

And on the bridge, Our woebegone Cherry turned and looked down to Lyttletoun, to take her leave of all things lovely.

There it stood, the Quiet City, as it had stood throughout the ages, a dark shape in the surrounding snow – an ample human habitation, with warm light shining from the windows, just as in ancient days and times gone by.

And over to the Monarch's Bridge there floated, high and husky, in the snow-spiced air, the strains of *Holy Night,* accompanied on handbells.

And a lump come up into her throat; but still Our Cherry would be gone.

And even as she stood there shivering a great procession had formed itself and now could be seen weaving in and out among the trees – a friendly dragon breathing flames of torchlight. And somewhere towards the tail of it, she thought, would be approaching, with something less than his habitual energetic stride, Mr Albert Horridge, third footman.

Soon the torchlight procession must pass this way.

And now Our Cherry trembled in every limb. For she knew that she must go at once if she was to go at all.

With agitated, half-numbed hands and with knees grazed from the frenzied scrambling, she got herself on to the high parapet. Stood for a moment upright. Balanced – it must have been from force of habit – there on the broad stone ledge. Covered eyes with her hand that she might not see the dark waters. Cried, illogically enough, 'Forgive me, oh! forgive me, Mr Horridge!' And jumped.

8

Meanwhile something had come over Mr Albert Horridge, and you can call it being haunted by his conscience if you like, for I do.

For Lady Mandragon having to go to bed, for once, with a headache, her French maid had been sent for, halfway through the Wassailing. So the third footman had time for reflection. And what Mr Albert Horridge saw reflected, look where he might, this Wassailing Night, was the white, set face of Our Cherry, as last he had seen it, during dinner, though he hardly had been aware of this, haloed in candle-shine.

The window-pane, the smooth bright surface of the polished table, among the flames that were leaping and playing over the Yule log; even in the mirror where he stood, for a moment to smooth his parting – there was the mournful little face of herself.

Sure, and it must be his blessed conscience! For now he remembered that never a word had passed between them since Her Ladyship had handed him what turned out to be as fine a pair of flowery bedroom slippers as you could see in a forest of Christmas trees and worked, were they, by Miss Callender's own fair hand, as you could see for yourself if you looked at the bump on the join at the back of the heel!

And search as he might he could not find the dear little creature.

Sure, and likely it was she'd stepped out to take a breath of air, and a peak at the Wassailing.

Noel! Noel!

And, as though motivated by invisible hands, the third footman found himself stepping out to take a breath of air, too. And right cold and frosty he found it. And soon he was jigging about to keep himself warm. And then it was that certain invisible hands grew more urgent.

They pushed, they tugged, they dragged and bobbled, they butted and prodded, they beat and they pinched Mr Albert Horridge, till, will he, nill he, he found himself trotting at a right smart pace.

In fact, they were the invisible hands of the revenants of Lyttletoun, who no respecters of the centuries, had forsaken their private tragedies to come to the aid of a foolish lass who was seeking to make an untimely end, even as they had.

So, with Lavinia the Lethal strongly in the lead, the Lyttletoun spectres streamed about the third footman, moaning and groaning, sighing and crying, and, of course, hooting, according to the terms of their haunt.

There was Lavinia the Lethal and her Bloody Cardinal, the Nun without a Head, and the Ghastly Gouvernante, Saintly Selina and the Bedevilled Bishop, Headstrong Nell and the Naughty Knight, and a dozen or more other case-book entries, and all of them highly vocal.

Small wonder that Mr Albert Horridge broke first into a scramble, then into a scuttle, then into a spurt, then into a dash, then into a run, then into a sprint and thence to a gallop.

And did he try to turn round and run back, an embranglement of branches caught at him. Turned he off from the drive, and they tripped him up. On, on; thorough bush, thorough briar, the footman was hurried and scurried until there, round the bend, he could see Monarch's Bridge.

No need now, for unseen hands! And as the third footman, irrespective of his good black suit, plunged headlong into the dark, the ice-cold water, the revenants of Lyttletoun could scarce forbear to cheer.

9

By the Third Day of Christmas the Lyttletoun guests began to go. By train, by brake, by carriage and, in the case of Captain the Honourable Gwylliam Vulliamy-Williams, by automobile (de Dion Bouton), with their maids and their men following on with the baggage.

A regiment of sandwiches had been cut and bestowed. A battalion of flasks filled with soup, coffee or a discreet nip. Rugs had been arranged, re-arranged; farewells exchanged and coroneted handkerchiefs returned to handbags.

In short, the guests had gone.

By three o'clock by the stable gable (and ten past nine by the Mechanicalle Mirracale) Lyttletoun could allow itself a welcome breathing space. Tomorrow would see a mort o'scrubbing and scouring. But this afternoon Mrs Multifarious could allow her piled-up head to nod before her sitting-room fire and Chef would cover his with a bright bandana and frankly snore.

And the third footman slipped out by the little latch gate and took the short cut through the fields to the village.

He was carrying a small but choice bouquet of flowers that never would be missed from the urns and bowls at the foot of the South Wing Staircase (Inigo Jones). Nevertheless he looked nervously over his shoulders as he passed by the South Lodge for fear Mr Brotherley or (worse still) Mr Trance should catch him at it.

But safely arrived at Christmas Meagrefold, Mr Albert Horridge made straight for Our Gran'mum's cottage – fourth in a row of well-kept, sturdy red-brick villas, built in the last reign, called Jubilee Row.

And the six-foot-and-over of him needs must stoop as he entered the doorway that opened straight in to the dark little living-room, with its photograph of Her Ladyship the Old'un on the mantelpiece and her late Majesty looking down from the wall and very like a bulldog in a widow's cap.

And there, sitting in the armchair before the fire, looking almost pale in a bright pink flannelette dressing-gown, sat Our startled Cherry, with Our gratified Gran'mum, a bustling cottage loaf, in attendance, and not for one moment taken in by Mr Horridge's statement that he'd just happened to be passing that way!

And, 'What do you say to the kind gentleman who jumped in the river after you, when you had that fit of vertigy?' demanded our Gran'mum.

And, 'Thanks,' said Our Cherry, embarrassed by remembering her manners.

'Don't mention it!' said Mr Horridge, with all the polish of a gentleman's gentleman of the world!

'There now!' Our Gran'mum, for some reason known to

herself alone, sounded strangely gratified. And she bustled off to brew a nice cup of tea in defiance of Her Ladyship the Old'-un's entry to her privately distributed manual, *What to Eat and Why for Cottagers,* which read:

'TEA: taken strong this beverage is a drug. Don't drink it, drown it.'

And no sooner had Our Gran left the two of them alone when from behind his back the third footman produced his (and Mr Trance's) bouquet.

'For me?' said Our Cherry, and never can those much used words have held so much of wonder.

'Who else?' said himself. 'And I'll have you know that it's missed you are up at The House.'

'Me?' Our Cherry drank in this piece of information. Then she buried her nose in the flowers and from the depths of a choice carnation: 'Busy?' she asked.

'That'll be tomorrow,' said the third footman, know-ledgeably. 'It's scouring and scrubbing from morn to night we'll be.'

And she not there to lend a hand with the nursery washing-up. Our Cherry hid her face in her flowers again.

'But there now, cheer up,' said Mr Horridge. 'They're gone, the all of 'em, and good riddance, is what I say! A fellow can call his soul his own again now!'

'Can he?' said Our Cherry who appeared to have perked up suddenly. 'But there's . . . some . . . you'll be missing con-siderable, I'm thinking?'

How to breathe till he answered?

'Och, her!' The third footman decided against tactful con-cealment. His voice was cold with scorn. 'If it's herself you're meaning it's cheap she is an' scraggy as the ould scarecrow!' And his roving eyes slid down from the throat of her which was making a modest white V in the folds of the bright flannelette, till they rested on the swell of her.

So Our Cherry bent over her flowers again. And silence fell between the two – a strangely happy silence. Then Our Cherry thought o'summat to say.

'Them flowers,' she said, 'they're beautiful,' and buried the peaky face of her in a great curled chrysanthemum, the size of a sunflower. 'Beautiful,' she repeated.

And the third footman smiled his tenderest smile at Our Cherry and says he: 'Sure, it's lovely they are – and hard to come by – but the choicest flower of any I see is yourself, Miss Callender, if you'll pardon the liberty!'

And 'Oh, Mr Horridge, what things you do say!' said His Cherry. But she said it in a whisper.

On the Third Night of Christmas there was a certain lassitude about Lyttletoun; even the ghosts seemed to be affected by it. The Bloody Cardinal muffed a cue and Lavinia the Lethal yawned twice.

For the party was over, the Guites had gone their ways with God. The Cause had been fought and won. The Day had been saved. And there was nothing left remarkable under the visiting moon.

Yoohoo-o-o-o!

Now there would be no-one to frighten out of their wits – supposing they had any – until Easter at the earliest.

Yoohoo-o-o-o!

And once more in the Quiet City, as in all great houses, time was the word without a meaning.

And it had been such fun having to hasten for once in an eternity!

Yoohoo-o-o-o!

Nymphs and Shepherds Go Away

Cray Point is quite unspoilt – an ordinary English fishing village. An ancient holding on the marshes of the East Coast. A huddle of redbrick cottages in the teeth of the wind.

In the winter the parlour gets all silted up with sand. Or else the old harmonium is awash. In the summer they hold the Cray Point Music Festival. And all year round they fish the seas and hope for the best.

It was Cray Point's very sturdiness; its general air of minding its own lobster pots; the total unconcern with which their appearance was greeted in the bar of The Hoy or at The Fishing Smack that first attracted Sebastian and Heidi. Specially Heidi.

'Buster,' she said, 'I love this place – it's so unspoilt. Let's *live* here!'

So they did.

It was as simple as that.

For Sebastian Bradleigh could write his operas anywhere, and Heidi'd given up her fashion modelling when she married him. Being wife to England's most uncompromising composer had become her full-time job.

So they bought two cottages and knocked their heads together, and felt as though they'd lived at Cray Point all their lives, and were apt to behave as though they owned the place. Specially Heidi.

But where there is a prophet a cult will surely raise its head, and this is just what happened.

It began with house guests. Fellow musicians. A critic who

hoped that by proclaiming Buster's pre-eminence before he became pre-eminent he might come in for a share of the future glory – little can he have known human nature. A buddy or so of Heidi's, one or two people vaguely known as 'useful'.

And in the second year, when they'd got the garden properly going, the Duke.

The Duke had married an old school friend of Heidi's. It had been quite a Cinderella story at the time – but that aspect was pretty old hat by now – and it certainly had been a social godsend to Buster's Sinfonietta in B Sharp Minor.

It was while the Duke was staying with them that the idea of the Festival was born. The little Duchess suggested it.

'Down here?' said Buster doubtfully.

'Could be,' said Heidi quickly, good hostessmanship to the fore.

'A Festival,' said the besotted Duke, still besotted, though they'd been Duke and Duchess for all of two years now. 'The very thing. Let's make a Festival of Buster's music.'

'Not mine alone,' said Buster, overcome.

'I don't see why not,' said the Duke. 'After all, there's Salzburg, isn't there?'

'And Oberammergau,' said Buster. He laughed. So, but a shade less readily, did the Duke. The little Duchess took her cue from her husband.She screwed up her pretty pussy face and giggled deliciously.

'But do you think they'd come – I mean the public – Cray's right off the map,' said Buster guilelessly.

'Of course they'll come,' said Heidi, who could have killed him. It didn't do to pour cold water on people's plans – and specially ducal projects. 'If Tim and Natasha come,' she smiled maternally at the little Duchess. Everyone always did.

'They'll come if we come,' said the Duke, a social realist. 'I'll be your patron,' he proposed confidently. 'And Tash can open the bazaar – I mean the music jamboree.'

'Well, then, that's settled,' said Heidi, was it a shade too quickly?

'Sun's out,' said Buster. 'Who's for a swim before tea?'

'I hear,' said Mrs Tarrant to Mrs Wilkins, waiting to be served at Mineral Waters, Tea and Ices – it was only later that it was called The Cake Shoppe – 'I hear we're to have a kind of beanie-feast or summat.'

'You dew?' said Mrs Wilkins. 'Well, think of that, now! Can I give you a hand with your parcels, there's room in the pram?'

The doorbell jangled. The wind came in. And so did Mrs Oddie. But the two good ladies took no notice of the new arrival, not so much as by a twitch of the shawl. Were they not Marlingstaffs by marriage and was not Mrs Oddie born a Briggs?

For back in the sixteenth century Cray Point had been practically torn asunder by a feud. And all because Tommas Marlingstaff had poached on Willum Briggs's lobster pots – or so the Briggs claimed. And from time to time the fissure was apt to reaffirm itself.

Be the truth of the matter what it may, to this very day, it didn't do for Briggses and Marlingstaffs to be too familiar. Each side numbered its own.

And that was the reason why, over the way at the Daily Papers and General, run by old Mrs Bossy – ninety-four next neap – Sallie Briggs counted the London Evenings out in silence for Tom Marlingstaff to deliver – in silence, that is, when there was anyone in the shop.

But if not . . .

If not . . .

'Wake up, you two – I'm in a hurry. Can't spend all day long gazing into each other's eyes!' Miss Pinfold's voice had the east wind in it, proper!

Guiltily the young people flushed up. Tom took his bundle of Evenings and bolted. Sal kept her head, hunted for something under the counter, kept Miss Pinfold waiting a good two minutes, all for nothing, and serve the old maid right.

'You'll have to smarten up when the Regatty starts, or whatsom-ever it's going to be they're planning up at Dills's Cottages,' – which was what they were still calling El Cabana, in the Village – observed the pernickety customer, not entirely without reason.

That evening Miss Pinfold called in at No. 3 to pick up the nice crisp crab Sal's Dad had come by. Miss Pinfold kept a guest house, and took a sourish pride in sending her boarders back to London plumper and rosier than when they came to Cray. You'd 've thought she ordered sea-air and sun with the milk, each morning!

'Sal's out, or I'd have sent her over with them, to be sure,' said Mrs Briggs as she wrapped up the crab in the *News of the World*. 'She's gone to the hop at the Village Institute.'

'Dancing,' said Miss Pinfold, 'again.'

'It does young folks none harm to have a little pleasure,' said Sal's Mum.

Miss Pinfold sniffed.

'I notice he pleasure doan't take her to Chapel much, these days.'

'She's shut up in the shop all day long – it's only natural she should want her turn of recreation, to be sure,' said Sal's Mum, stoutly. 'Not that Sal isn't happy in her work – runs across the road to it, singing like a bird.'

'You're quite sure it's work that makes her sing, Mrs Briggs?'

'Whatever do you mean, Miss Pinfold?'

'You're sure it's the work and not the lad she works with?'

'Tom Marlingstaff – Our Sallie?' said the Mother. 'Oh no, Miss Pinfold, Sal would never take up with a Marlingstaff – 'twould break her father's heart, to be sure it would. She'd not do that, our Sallie.' She handed the crab to Miss Pinfold and with an air of finality said, 'That will be two and ten – eight-pence for dressing.'

It was only old maid's talk.

At the Village Institute the three-fishermen band had roo-tootle vo-vodeo-crashed itself to a breather between dances.

'Let's go,' said Tom Marlingstaff urgently.

'But it's early yet,' said Sal.

'Got somethun to tell you – somethun good,' Tom persisted. So they slipped away on the shadowed side of the strict and narrow Village street, though when they came to the churchyard, of course, they lingered.

For the feud had worn a bit thin at the edges, where the younger generation found forbidden fruit more lively than dead sea lobster pots.

But forbidden fruit had to be enjoyed in secret because of the attitude of their elders. For though high seas made strange boat-mates, it was only in the lifeboat that the Briggses and the

Marlingstaffs rowed together, or at a funeral, when all Cray Point followed to the grave.

'Mrs Bradleigh says she'll take me on as chauffeur-odd-job man.'

'At Dills's Cottages?' Sal looked concerned. 'And you're going there?'

'Sure, I'm going. She'll pay me three pun' a week – and there'll be tips when all the strangers come from Lunnon.'

Three pounds was an awful lot of money, when you'd been glad to take home twelve and six of a Saturday.

'Of course it's only for the summer season – the Festival, and that!' admitted Tom. 'But maybe, if I c'n make myself real useful they'll take me back weekends in winter.'

'Maybe they will.'

'What's up with you, Sal? Got a face on you as long as Southend Pier!'

'It's nothing. Nothing, Tom, really. Only . . . I'm going to miss you at the shop.'

'The shop – oh that was only temp'ry, anyway. I was going to make a change when the chance come my way, and now . . . well, it's come.'

'It's come,' agreed Sal, a little drearily.

'So let's have a kiss on it!' And Tom made a grab. Sal fought him off – at first.

'Tom Marlingstaff! And you a Marlingstaff,' she said reproachfully.

'On'y a bit of a cuddle, Sal, to celebrate . . . I wouldn't do you none 'arm.'

And drawing his lips from her forehead to cheek, then to mouth, Tom thought he meant what he said.

Well, that was fully eight weeks before the Festival opened. And a busy eight weeks they were to prove.

For even though Buster had a Duke in the bag there was a great deal of organising to be done. And of course all Cray had to be scrubbed and scoured as never before and painted bright as the flowers in your garden in preparation for the intake of strangers. It was just like Invasion Week all over again, when Cray Point had the honour to be chosen as one of the ports from which the D-Day fleet would not sail forth. And half the British

Army went under canvas on the Marshes, to fool that old fool, 'Itler.

Heidi and Buster had quite agreed – in the beginning – that if anything was a blessing it was not being on the 'phone at El Cabana. But nowadays, having to spend so much time at the Post Office, and never enough pennies for that insatiable and claustrophobic call-box, Heidi had heavy doubts – in fact, in secret, she had filled in a form to get a 'phone installed. She was now waiting for the right moment to break the news to Buster. Buster was busy writing against time, because he had to get *Alexander Triumphant*, his one-act Opera-da-Camera finished – or where would be the Cray Point Music Festival?

This morning she'd been in the musty-fusty call-box for over half an hour, and only two names crossed through. People who were lucky enough to have 'phones at their bedside ought to stay thankfully in them to answer it!

'Good morning, General,' she now cooed into the acrid apparatus. 'I expect you've already heard about our Music Festival.'

'Music?' said the General suspiciously.

'Of course, you wouldn't call what Buster is writing *music*.'

'That's true,' said the General who'd heard a bit of the caterwauling when he and his bewildered lady had tuned in to the Third one Thursday night during the Proms.

'It's just a slice of contemporary thought – a sort of comment in sound – a . . . a way of *living*, really.'

'Well,' said the General, cutting the cackle and coming to the tanks, 'what d'you want *me* to do about it? I warn you, I'm very busy – there's a lot going on in the garden for me to supervise, and I've got to keep an eye on the odd-job man – time doesn't grow on trees like you ladies seem to imagine!'

'One realises, of course, that you're frightfully *affairé* – but the Duchess hoped you'd find time for just one more committee . . . to chair it for us, General.'

'The little Duchess, eh? Well, that's different. As long as I don't have to listen to the stuff . . .'

'Hullo, hullo, is that Lady Dugdale speaking? Well, this is Heidi Bradleigh . . . Lady Dugdale, I know you're the busiest bod in the county, but you see, I'm organising a Festival, and the Duchess . . . .'

And so on, endlessly, cooped in to the point of claustrophobia.

Oh, to be single and acid again, with only one's own career to make a muck of!

Strawberries were good that year – but not at the price Mrs Billicoe was asking at the Greengrocery.

Still, they'd be a treat for Sallie, thought Mrs Briggs, something to tempt her, like. So she opened her leather purse and counted the contents. For Sal had been right off her food a good few days, now . . . nought the peck of a bird.

'Caw-caw-caw,' called a gull, wheeling and dipping and soaring and lording it in the sky above.

Mrs Briggs, her two and six in hand, pored over the baskets.

'. . . A shilling for a cucumber!' Miss Pinfold's voice was shrill.

'They'll be one and nine next week.' Mrs Billicoe's sniff said take it or leave it.

'Everything's up around these parts for the Festival,' said Mrs Briggs, 'and it does seem a shame, to be sure, though they do say it'll mean custom.'

'There's customers and customers,' said Mrs Billicoe, glowering at Miss Pinfold who by now was prodding a marrow she'd never buy.

'Half a crown for a punnet – it do seem a lot,' sighed Mrs Briggs. 'But there – Sall'll enjoy 'em. She's a bit off colour of late, poor sweet.'

'Sallow,' suggested Miss Pinfold hopefully.

'Not herself at all.'

'It's all those late nights, all that gadding and giddying,' Miss Pinfold pointed out.

'It's probably just the spring,' Mrs Billicoe put her oar in.

'The spring,' said Miss Pinfold. 'In mid-July! Of course.'

You could have cut it with a billhook.

It certainly made you think, this rise in prices. The Big Hotel was booked right up for Festival Week and a rush of Bed and Breakfasts sprung to the eye from the cottages.

And only a week to go.

That night Miss Pinfold took her stiff steel pen and scratched out a letter to old Mrs Willis, a regular.

'Miss Miriam Pinfold begs to present her compliments and respectfully suggests that you can't have her first floor front at her usual prices – not at the height of the season . . .'

For the time being, times had changed.

It was a Marlingstaff saw Sallie Briggs slip over to Dr Saye-Smith's surgery as soon as Mrs Bossy had closed next evening.

It could be a bottle of Mrs Bossy's usual.

It could be lumbago again for Her Dad.

Or . . .

But since Marlingstaffs and Briggses bailed out their own boats, it really didn't signify – except, of course, to Sallie.

Sallie hadn't set eyes on Tom this week long. Such a to-do was going on up at Dills's. And Tom in the thick of it all.

And never a minute to spare for his old friends.

But he'd have to find time for what Sal had to tell him.

The Merry Wives of The Thatchings

The six-fifteen from London was rounding the bend. Three parts down Station Hill, and with the yard yet to cover, Mrs Brotherhood broke into a hell-for-leather jog-trot, bursting forth parcels and packages as she lumbered on, which Ivy, her darting daughter, scooped up almost as they touched down, Thursday being Market Day at Leigh-on-the-Edge.

In the padded compartments the usual passengers to Leigh (change here for Upper and Lower Thatchings) were buckling up the usual briefcases; reaching for the usual hats. The ladies were already edging themselves strategically into the corridor.

On the station platform the Market Day crowd, in from the villages, had gathered together their bits and pieces and were advancing cautiously.

All faces turned towards the six-fifteen as it came thundering down. But it went straight through the station in a raucous flash. Then, still without lessening its speed, it dwindled away down the line and was swallowed by the tunnel – a roaring rocket lined with grey-green, absolutely appalled faces.

In short, the six-fifteen had failed to stop at Leigh-on-the-Edge, this evening.

Mrs Brotherhood, clutching her return ticket, had trotted halfway down the platform after it, before the truth finally dawned on her. She would never trust a time-table again; nasty teasing things!

And the consternation on the Down Platform was nothing compared to the helpless fury of the pent-up trundling-on passengers in the train. For the next station lay three and a quarter miles away and there would be nothing for it but to trudge back.

And next morning, there it was in the papers, for all to read.

> 'The driver of the four-twenty-five from Paddington forgot to stop at Leigh-on-the-Edge, last night. Questioned, the driver said he didn't know what can have come over him . . .'

The only occasion Mrs Wintergreen found for leafing through the pages of *Wisdom*, the glossy monthly magazine 'Mainly for Marrieds', was in her dentist's waiting-room. So she put on her plastic rims with that sense of luxury another woman might derive from a well-iced cocktail. And before you could say Mothers' Union Mrs Wintergreen was deep in 'Our August Article'. This had as a sub-heading: 'DO YOU WISH TO KEEP YOUR HUSBAND?'

Now, of course, Harriet Wintergreen wanted to keep fast the affections of the Reverend Arthur Wintergreen. So although her twenty-five-year-old marriage stood in no discernible jeopardy, the good lady read on with close attention.

Not that there had ever been a divorce in The Thatchings, Great or Little; for what with the hard work in the fields and on the farms they never seemed to find the time, the place, and the illicitly loved one, all together, leave alone the energy, enterprise and inclination. In The Thatchings one's neighbour's wife was sacrosanct, if only by default.

As she read on, it became apparent to Harriet Wintergreen that she had left the matter of holding her Arthur dangerously late. He had frequently come home from the Parish to find her looking quite done up (instead, apparently, of all done up). It was years since she had shown an interest in his pet hobby – or, for that matter, since he had, either. And facials and hair-styling cost money.

Mrs Wintergreen sighed. It was fast becoming evident that she had been steering her happy marriage straight for the rocks for the last twenty-three years. But surely among all this helpful and practical advice there must be something she could find to do to stop the rot?

And then she came upon it. A diet sheet with proteins and calories nicely balanced, and starch entirely eliminated. It seemed simple enough to follow, and nice and cheap too;

specially on salad days. And it guaranteed to take off two stone in three weeks.

Mrs Wintergreen took out her shopping list, and noted down the daily menus on the back of it.

And, of course, the rot didn't stop at the vicar's good lady, not by a haystack!

'Who do you think I bumped into in Town today, Hugo?'

'Grrmph!' *The Times* rattled ominously.

'Quite literally bumped, Hugo.'

'R-r-r-h-h!'

'The vicar's wife! She was hurrying past the home-made cake-shop with her eyes tight closed.'

'Tcha!'

'And, Hugo?'

'Ugh!'

'She's on a marvellous diet – simply marvellous – no solids at all for two days and then no liquids, and then every kind of salad and fruit for two days, and then . . .'

But it was no use. Colonel Powderdry wasn't listening.

Birdie Powderdry sighed. She sometimes felt the colonel hadn't heard a word she'd said since Poona.

The Misses Pinfold lived immediately opposite the doctor, in the little house with the plate on the door which read:

THE MISSES ANTOINETTE AND LETITIA PINFOLD
DRESSMAKERS

Miss Nettie did the putting together, and was usually to be found sitting sewing – she had such neat fingers! Miss Lettie did the cutting out and the looking out – she had such sharp eyes.

And so it was this afternoon at Little Thatchings.

'Mrs Wintergreen was in this morning, Lettie, when you went to the Post.'

'Not the navy blue again, Nettie?'

Miss Antoinette nodded. 'To be taken in, this time,' she said.

'Mrs Wintergreen is losing weight.'

'Losing weight?' Miss Lettie sighed. It was all very well for Nettie to weigh twelve stone and like it. She'd had her chance! And mucked him!

'They say,' Miss Nettie dropped her voice intriguingly, 'that Mrs Wintergreen is on a slimming diet.'

Miss Nettie flushed. Somehow it hardly seemed decent in a vicar's wife. She changed the conversation.

'Here comes Mrs – wait a minute – yes, it's Mrs Powderdry,' she said.

'Calling for the colonel's Indigestion, I expect,' Miss Nettie went on stitching placidly.

But the flush was quickening again in Miss Lettie's cheeks.

'It's not the Indigestion, dear,' she said, 'It's us. There's something over her arm.'

'Her mackintosh,' suggested Miss Nettie helpfully.

'In July?' Miss Lettie sounded scornful. 'No, Nettie, it's the second skirt she had made to her grey. She's got the first one on.'

And, sure enough, Miss Lettie was right. Mrs Powderdry had called round to have her skirt taken in.

'You're losing weight,' said Miss Antoinette accusingly.

'Quite a bit,' said Mrs Powderdry, patting her hips.

Miss Lettie could have hit her.

No sooner had the front door closed on the client, than Miss Lettie turned on Miss Nettie.

'Two days liquids,' she said, 'really, the things some fools will do.'

Miss Nettie wiped her specs. 'It's not for us to complain,' she said mildly. 'Taking in or letting out, it all brings in the work, my dear.'

But clearly Miss Lettie, with her twelve stone ten and her sweet tooth, was taking Mrs Powderdry's diminishing silhouette as a personal affront.

'Birdie!' she muttered, bitterly.

Soon slimming started to catch on in The Thatchings.

Isobel Cribbings, the doctor's wife, happening to pass through the hall when Birdie Powderdry had called in to pick up the colonel's Indigestion, was an immediate if secret convert.

'. . . No fats, no sugar, no starch,' she recapitulated, 'and not a word to Christopher! You look simply marvellous, Birdie, and I shall start on Monday.'

'Don't forget, Isobel, you begin with no solids.'

'I shall have to sham a liver,' said Isobel Cribbings cheerfully.

One by one the village took to Makuthin rolls and vitamin pills and the home-made cake-shop started to feel the pinch.

Isobel Cribbings being a doctor-by-marriage as it were, and therefore, morally, at least a medico, kindly copied out a Diet Sheet for Mrs Pestridge to post up in the village shop.

Mrs Brotherhood's Ivy, waiting her turn for a postal order for the Pools copied it out for luck.

And that evening, over high tea, Ivy explained it all, very loud and clear, to Mrs Brotherhood.

'It's ever so easy, Mum! You just balance your calories against your carbohydrates, and . . .'

Carbohydristatics! Nasty teasing things! Whatever would that Ivy be up to next?

Breathing heavily Mrs Brotherhood stretched out a plump pink hand for her nice slice of dripping toast.

Mrs Brotherhood's Ivy obliged on the maid's half-day, up at the House. The House was Leighbeck Manor; where the Squire lived. The Squire was Lady Larkins and no nonsense. Lady Larkins had been Flossie Montgomerie, third from the right in the front row at the Gaiety, before she married Sir Alaric thirty years ago. But there was precious little liveliness up at the House these days, with Sir Alaric dead and in the bosom of Sir Abraham, and neither kith nor kin to live in that old cold mansion with her. Indeed The Thatchings, Great and Little, did not put the bottle past their Squire. After all, what else had the poor old thing to live for but her drop of tiddly and 'The Archers'.

And Lady Larkins was glad enough of a bit of company; so Ivy had fallen into the habit of regaling her with the topic of the hour. Last week it was the Royal Tour. This week it was the Slimming.

Lady Larkins was quick enough to seize the salient point of

the diet: 'Two daysh liquidsh – shay no more, my dear! We'll
shtart to-night,' said Her bibulous Ladyship, affably pushing
the bottle across.

Slimming had become all the rage in The Thatchings. There
was hardly a female abstainer to be found. Even 'The Archers'
took second place on Women's Institute afternoons, and
'General Hospital' was definitely a back number.

Birdie Powderdry's latest loss was stoutly canvassed against
that of Isobel Cribbings and both were accounted insufficiently lacking when Harriet Wintergreen went into Leigh-
on-the-Edge for her weekly weigh and, of course, the market-
ing. Sides – losing sides, that is – were taken. Bets were made –
it was better then the Pools. There was even a move afoot to
organise a raffle, in aid of the Restoration Fund, with prizes for
those lucky enough to draw the first three losers. Mrs
Brotherhood's Ivy undertook to sell the tickets, and dropped in
to tea with Winnie, her married sister, and the kids, en route.

And there was Winn in her usual steamy state – hair a mess.
Figure long lost in fat. A wide gap between her outgrown skirt
and her blouse with the buttons all off and held together with
safety-pins. Winnie had let herself go, and by now was
accustomed to being a slut.

'Look at you!' nagged Ivy, with sisterly candour. 'The state
you're in! And look at the size of you!'

'I know,' admitted Winnie ruefully, 'and I used to be such a
little bit of a thing! It's marriage has done it.'

'Then I'll stay an old maid,' said Ivy.

'Oh no you won't; not if you can help it,' said Winnie.

'I wonder Ernie puts up with it – doesn't he never say anything to you?'

'Ernie, no. 'E's out so much. 'E's never in. And when 'e's in 'e
never has much to say. Comes of working for the Railway. Up
on the one set of rails – down on the other. You do it twice and
you call it a day! Monotonous,' said Winnie, giving her skirt a
hitch.

'I wonder he bothers to come home at all,' said Ivy.

'Sometimes 'e doesn't.'

'Oh, Winn!' Shock made Ivy quite compassionate.

'On change-over nights,' said Winnie, 'if one of the other engine drivers wants to swop a shift.'

'Is that all, Winn? I mean, how can you be sure, with them lady porters la-di-dah-ing it about in uniform? Nothing to do but drink coffee in the refreshments and look the other way when you holler for 'em.'

'Oh, I don't suppose it's as bad as all that. Ernie never was a one to put much stress on beauty.' Automatically, the speaker looked at herself in the mirror, and turned quickly away from her own steamy dishevelment. 'What's looks anyway? It isn't the wrapping that makes the currant cake, dear.'

'All the same, Winn, why don't you fine it down a bit – slim it off – we're all of us slimming in The Thatchings! It's ever so easy, reely it is!' Ivy drew a deep breath and reeled the regimen off: 'Two days liquids, two days proteins, two days meat and two days salads, lots of eggs, no fats, no starchy foods, all the oranges you can eat, and – well, etc.'

After a time it transpired that Slimming had a definite effect on the temper – other people's temper, of course.

For instance Miss Letitia Pinfold on the second of her Two Days Salads could hardly endure to witness Miss Antoinette lingering over her minute but succulent portion of grilled lean meat.

'Really, Nettie, I shall take my meals up to my room in future if you go on making a pig of yourself!'

'Never mind, dear. You'll be on eggs tomorrow!'

'Eggs!' echoed Miss Lettie bitterly.

Even in the Vicarage a certain constraint could be felt at the bow-window end of the breakfast-table as the Reverend Arthur Wintergreen, oblivious to atmosphere, tucked into his splendidly odoriferous eggs and bacon and lashed his coffee with milk.

A constraint that was in no way lessened when Harriet Wintergreen went into town for her weekly weigh and found that in spite of all her sufferings she had only lost five ounces this week.

Of course, dieting was like that. When first you cut out starch down you went, like the Television. But you couldn't keep up

going down – not at that rate. And with her thinking mind
Harriet Wintergreen recognised this. Nevertheless deep in her
secret heart she knew it was that extra fingernail of butter that
she hadn't liked to leave on her plate – such a wicked waste! –
that had done the damage. The claims of conflicting values
weighed heavily upon the vicar's wife. More heavily on than, for
instance, Isobel Cribbings.

Isobel Cribbings had invited Birdie Powderdry to lunch on
Dr Cribbings's Hospital Day, for the doctor did not approve of
slimming without some good and sufficient medical reason for
it, and poor Isobel had been forced to practise many a miser-
able subterfuge.

'What a relief it is,' she had said, 'to be able to lunch off a
lettuce leaf openly!'

'And there was I,' Birdie Powderdry told Harriet Wintergreen, later, 'practically watering at the mouth, only to be given
one sliced tomato and some horrible old grated carrot. And I'd
told her I was on my slice of ham – one *thin* slice of *very lean* ham!
Well, I don't call it *hospitable* of Isobel, do you?'

And Birdie Powderdry was not without her own moments of
domestic difficulty.

'Wazzat – Hh?'

Not for the first time in the last few weeks Colonel Powderdry
prodded the mess on his plate distastefully.

'Steamed cod, dear,' said Birdie Powderdry brightly.

Colonel Powderdry shuddered.

'What's for tiffin, then?'

'St-teamed cod hash – dear,' Birdie added, hoping to make it
sound more palatable.

Colonel Powderdry thumped his fork.

'Either,' he roared at parade ground pitch, 'we have a decent
curry for dinner tonight, or we get a divorce . . .'

'But Hugo – that means rice!'

'. . . and you please yourself which it's to be!'

And, leaving his steamed cod untasted, the colonel flung
down his table-napkin and stumped off to his den.

And then, just as the Slimming had reached its peak and the
Misses Lettie and Nettie were fairly snowed under with
everybody's takings-in and the home-made cake-shop had gone

and sold itself out to a horridly austere and hygienic health store, the craze for counting calories died out in The Thatchings.

Maybe it was because Christmas was now in sight and that old cold weather just around the corner.

Or was it merely another proof that a chain is only as strong as its weakest link? For the day had come when busy Dr Cribbings found time to look up at lunch and discover that his wife was simply playing with her food and not only prescribed a tonic but stood over her to see she took it.

'This'll give you back your appetite, old girl. Soon have you eating like a horse!'

Oh dear!

And once Isobel Cribbings gave up the rot set in. Soon the Misses Lettie and Nettie were fairly snowed under with everybody's lettings-out, for the entire village now proceeded to put on poundage.

The entire village – but not Ivy Brotherhood's married sister, Winnie.

'You wouldn't hardly reckernize our Winn, Mum. Really you wouldn't! She's ever so slender now!'

But Mrs Brotherhood shook a solemn head.

'No good'll come of it, you mark my words,' she said. 'Once you're fat you're fat, and that's the end of it.'

'Not these days it isn't.'

'If fat's what Providence intends, fat's what you ought to be, and it's downright wicked to tamper, Miss!'

'Oh Ma, why be old-fashioned?'

And Ivy wasn't far out, for Winnie Wainwright did look different. For one thing she'd treated herself to a planned outfit – matching twin set and a pencil skirt. And then she'd gone a bust on a hair style. And, best of all, her curves were all in the right place.

One day she left the bedroom door ajar while she was changing into her twin set. The kids had gone to school and Ernie, on his way to the you-know-what before he went on shift, caught sight of the girl he'd married. And it was the first time Ern had really noticed Winn for months.

What's more Winn looked like the girl that Ern had married, once again.

He stood in the doorway, a light in his eye that hadn't been there since his honeymoon weekend. And there stood Winn in her uplift bra, with her tum held in and her tail tucked down, as in her daily dozen, smiling right back at him. And her eyes had that certain look in them as well . . .

But it wasn't a bit of use though the kids were out, for Ernie was already late that morning as it was. And Tide and the British Rail Time-table wait for no man.

But the image of Winn and the way she looked that morning was with Ern all up the Up Line, and right down the Down Line, and all down the Up Line, solid.

And if the morning paper had asked me what had come over the driver of the four-twenty-five on the evening the train failed to stop at Leigh-on-the-Edge I would have said it was, oddly enough, his wife.

Dream Bike

Every time Wilfie Newton thought about his motor-bike his heart raced like an engine – a twin-engine.

It was to be a brand-new 1953 model. It was to arrive on Saturday morning. And thereinafter it would daily whiz him to the works and back like a flash of rip-roaring lightning – bigger, better, and ten miles an hour faster than Syd's old crock. And louder.

Wilfie could see the silver of it; feel the vibrating eagerness of it, handle it, stroke it. He must remember to wave to Grannie as he roared past her sitting-room window at 120 mph three luscious quarters of an hour later than was his present custom each morning – or at least honk, in the early, hanging-on-by-eyelashes stage of drivesmanship. Grannie was giving the gleaming monster to him for his eighteenth birthday.

Pr-r-r! Pr-r-r-r! Pr-r-r-r-rft! What a performance!

Ever since Grannie had announced this handsome intention Wilfie had Pr-r-r! Pr-r-r-r! Pr-r-r-r-rft! himself into ecstasy from which he had never entirely emerged, sleeping or waking and there was room for nothing in his mind but engine noises, backfiring ton-ups and accessories.

Naturally he raided his post office savings to buy a smashing crash helmet – it had a skull and cross-bones on the front, an emblem which in his present frame of mind seemed strongly apposite and indeed highly likely – and round the back a motor-bike at speed. It fitted just above the eyebrows and it hurt like hell. And Mum had given him a pair of super gauntlet gloves – white. You would be able to see his signals in the darkest hours at the deadest of nights.

He tugged them on and held up a line of traffic, just for
practice. Pr-r-r! Pr-r-r-r! Pr-r-r-r-rft!

Then he took them off, laid them tenderly on the bed, put on
his crash helmet, pulled down his goggles, tugged his gloves on
again, bestraddled a hell-for-leather chair in front of his
wardrobe looking-glass, and gave it the lot!

Yip-ee for tomorrow!

Wilfie's dream-bike was due to be delivered at Grannie's little
dream-house around the corner at eleven o'clock that Saturday
morning, and Wilfie, having begged off at the works for a dental
check-up, was round at Grannie's by twenty to, straining every
nerve to hear the distant velvet thunder of the exhaust which
would grow louder and louder as it hurtled through space, till it
subsided in a whee-ee-e at Grannie's front door.

'You're a good son,' said Grannie, in the dull accents of the
partially deaf, for she was going on eighty-four, 'and a good
grandson, and yon ride in the mornings will harden you off.
Always were the puny sort.'

'Wouldn't say that,' muttered Wilfie.

'Oh yes you were,' said the old lady sharply. 'Puny from a
child – don't know how we ever reared you – chesty,' she
reminded him. 'That's why your mother moved out here. But
yon ride to the office every day – that'll do the trick – that'll
harden you off, son – fresh air,' she pointed out.

'Yes, Grannie,' said Wilfie, dutifully. But his mind wasn't on
it. A false alarm purr was fading away and there was Wilfie
back to tensely listening to nothingness again.

But it was true enough that Wilfie needed to toughen up a
bit.

When first Mrs Newton had heard of Uncle Harry's legacy it
seemed like Providence. A little house in Harlingford ever so
snug and easy to run, with a nice stretch of common at the back
and a dream of a duck pond on it. And the air was lovely – well,
better than Grimston, anyway. And it would be nice to have a
little place of your own and no quarter day looming up at you.
In fact it was just like Uncle Harry to die and leave his dream
house to his widowed sister. Ever so considerate. Ever so kindly.

But soon second thoughts set in. There was Wilfie to be

considered. Harlingford was full five miles from the works and Wilfie was inclined to be chesty. Doctor had said he'd grow out of it, but he still had that cough of his all last February.

And there was Grannie, too. It would fair kill the old lady to leave Doverdale, the house she'd gone to as a bride. She was too old to be uprooted from the few friends she'd got left. And it wouldn't do to live at opposite ends of the town – what if she were taken bad in the night?

But it transpired that the old lady was mad to leave the nasty old house she'd been let in for as a green young gal – nasty houses opposite – nothing but nasty curtains – she wanted a new set of nasty houses to look at. What's more she hated the guts of the few friends left to her and couldn't wait to be torn up by the roots and installed in a nice new nasty neighbourhood where she could trot out her memories and flatly contradict a nice new set of nasty but awe-inspired neighbours. In short, Grannie was rarin' to be off.

So old Mrs Higgins was duly installed in the draughty little dream-house around the corner from her widowed daughter's new dream-home.

And there was Wilfie listening to nothingness so hard he'd nearly given himself the earache!

Now at last nothingness congealed into a perceptible purr – perceptible to Wilfie, that is – then a distinct pr-r-pr-r-pr-r that caused the blood to race in his ears and made him nearly swoon with rapture. Then came that blissful, unmistakable rush of air on the end of a veritable tornado that fairly shook the entire double row of little dream-houses. Soon there would be a screeching of brakes in hell accompanied by a satanic back-fire and a satisfying whee-ee-e and Wilfie would die a little rapturous death before marching out to claim his dream-bike and be claimed by it – a true case of love at first pr-r-r!

But the brakes were not applied, the tornado hurriedly subsided, Grannie's little dream-house righted itself having shed a tile or two, and Grannie straightened her shawl.

'There goes that nasty Syd again,' grumbled the old lady, 'always in that old hurry of his – tearing up the road – giving my old stomach a turn – always falling off and coming back by nasty ambulance – one day he'll kill himself, you mark my words!'

Wilfie came back from his other world.

'Syd's all right,' he said sharply. 'A bit prone to prangs, of course – bad for the bike,' he shook his head in condemnation, 'but it doesn't do to worry about things like that,' he finished on a note of hope.

'Mumble, mumble, mumble,' chinnered Grannie. 'Can't hear a word the boy says!'

But oddly enough it was Grannie who heard the dream-bike first.

'Here it is,' she said, as the gate creaked and a firm step on the gravel was heard, even before the front door bell tingled. And she sprang to her feet far more eagerly than the hanging-back Wilfie who was still working out that they must have delivered his virgin dream-bike by six-cylinder, rubber-tyred, semi-silent van.

'Help me on,' said Grannie, producing two coats, galoshes, and furry ear-pads which in no way helped her hearing. The front door bell tinkled again. Wilfie was in a fever lest the van should drive his dream-bike smartly off again.

'Come on, Grannie, *do,*' he urged.

'Hurry-hurry-hurry – what's it all about?' chinnered Grannie from force of habit, but there was a flush of excitement on her cheeks, too.

But when at last Wilfie had dressed the old lady – through a hail of shouted 'Coming right aways', 'Shan't be a minutes' and 'With you right nows' flung over a tortured shoulder at the fast-becoming irascible bell-pusher – levered her out of her arm-chair and tugged her to the gate, there was no van, no virgin dream-bike, no nothing except Mr Baker from the bike-shop and a spindly looking pedal cycle parked thinly at the curb.

'There you are,' panted Grannie, triumphant, 'your dream-bike, eh? That's what you asked for, and that's what you've got. So up on it, son, and let's see you ride!'

'There we are then! Brand-new, up-to-date 1953 model, as h'ordered.' Mr Baker, scenting nothing amiss, beamed.

In the utter silence that followed the sound of an ambulance bell could be heard drawing nearer and nearer.

'That'll be Syd,' said Grannie, cheerfully through her ear-pads. 'Well, Wilfie, don't stand there crying for joy, a great lad like you – aren't you going to thank your old Grannie for giving you such a beautiful present, even if she is a bit hard of hearing?'

Thank his old Grannie? Right then, Wilfie could have killed his old Grannie. He'd never forgive her, never – not even if he lived to be as old as she was. A fine fool his old Grannie had made of him! A beastly push-bike – after all his dreams – it wasn't fair! And the way he'd been cracking it up to Syd! Offering to let him have a spin down the lane in the lunch hour – not in traffic, he had stressed. And now . . .

Well, he wasn't going to take that beastly push-bike to the works, and that was flat, sooner walk. How Syd would jeer – not for a bit, of course, for presumably Syd would be past jeering for quite some days . . .

But a chap felt such a fool riding home on a beastly push-bike in a crash helmet with a motor-bike at speed whizzing around the back of it and his L plate tucked underneath his arm!

By Monday morning, however, reason and the thought of Grannie glued to the window had prevailed. It was a sullen Wilfie who left home at the usual cold grey hour and doggedly pedalled the beastly push-bike down the dream-road, lifting a curt arm in salutation at the Nottingham lace curtains behind which there lurked a pair of beady eyes, as well Wilfie knew.

And the ghastly slow slog to work wasn't the end of Wilfie's humiliation, not by a long pannier bag!

For Wilfie had rather thrown his dream performance about the works; and now, seeing his arrival the hard way, the entire factory, or so it seemed to Wilfie, from jeering groups in the grounds to heads clustering at second, third, fourth and fifth floor windows and hanging from the ferro-conrete rafters, had assembled to give the push-in push-bike the lot!

All of them save young Erne, whose ambition it was to own a push-bike.

Young Erne was just about the lowest form of factory life. Young Erne was the office boy in Accounts. Young Erne was still in the steel-rim specs and spots stage.

'Coo,' he breathed, 'it's smashing!'

'Shut up, you,' said Wilfie; a snub which left young Erne unmoved, for everyone said, 'Shut up, you,' to young Erne. In fact, if young Erne had been in Opera, 'Shut up, you' would have been the young Erne Motif.

'Coo – you didn't oughter leave it thur,' said young Erne, as Wilfie gave the pedal a vicious kick that nearly spun its beastly head off, and propped it up beside the path. 'On'y last week Slater got his'n pinched through leaving it just thur – 'nit wasn't a new'n like your'n!'

. . . Pinched!

Did people actually go around pinching bikes – push-bikes? If only some philanthropist would come and pinch his beastly bike.

So though it seemed highly unlikely to Wilfie that anyone could covet the beastly spidery thing, he left it right there and hoped for the worst.

Soon as the lunch hour sounded Girlie Greenish popped into Accounts where Wilfie worked.

'Hullo,' she husked as thickly as her naturally sparrow-like pipe permitted, 'what about Syd! Won't be back for a fortnight this time, they say . . . Definitely!'

Now Girlie Greenish was Works Pillion Playmate No. 1. She looked her sturdy best belted into plastic. She had the right sort of square-all-the-way-down shape, the right sort of thick-set purple-pink legs, the right sort of trigger-release giggle and – clearly the most important thing of all – an unshakable ability to stay put on a sprung frame. She and Syd were known to be practically A Case and up to now she'd never even noticed Wilfie!

'. . . I shall miss old Syd,' she was saying, 'specially on the way home!' She giggled helpfully. But Wilfie just sat there doodling spokes in wheels – old slow-coach!

'Oh well, back by bus again!' said Girlie. She giggled. 'By the bye, they say you've got a motor-bike, now.'

'Oh, do they?' said Wilfie, through clenched teeth. He doodled a pair of handle-bars with a match-stick Syd taking a header over them.

'An absolutely luscious bike, bigger and better – and faster than Syd's old crock, they say it is. Definitely!'

'Then they say wrong,' said Wilfie.

'Oh well,' said Girlie, 'what-the-hell!' She slid off the table. 'Bye-bye for now – be seein' you! Definitely!'

She popped out.

Yes, Girlie Greenish popped out of Accounts as gaily and completely as she had popped in, but never, from that time forth, out of Wilfie's dream-life.

From now on, deep in his innermost heart, Girlie and his dream-bike were indivisible. He had only to close his eyes and wham! there was Girlie up on the twin-spring-seat belted into her plastic mac with her hair a blown blonde halo . . . Pr-rr-rr-prft!

So Destry rode again – but from now on with a permanent passenger.

But of course when the whistle went at the end of the day, there Wilfie's push-bike still stood, safe as falling off a log, with young Erne mounting guard over it.

'Kept an eye on it fur you,' he said, breathing on the handle-bars and rubbing. 'You don't want nobody to steal a wizard bike like that!'

That's all young Erne knew, thought Wilfie, desperately, but all he said was, 'Shut up, you.'

But there was a touch of tousled glory in the misery of Wilfie's face as he pushed off into the slanting rain.

It had been one of your real fill-dyke summers, ditches and ponds were full to overflowing on the common, back of young Mrs Newton's dream-house. Pedalling fiercely into the wind, with the water streaming down his forehead, Wilfie tore his mind from Girlie's plunging neckline and applied it to practical politics. If young Erne wasn't talking out of the back of his neck as usual, people did steal push-bikes. Old gritty push-bikes. Let alone gleaming silver spiders. And if Grannie's beastly bike got stolen Wilfie would get insurance money. Add to that the further sum his old Grannie could be cajoled into coughing up and Bob was his great-uncle.

Pr-r-r! Pr-r-r-r! Pr-r-r-rft!

Wilfie applied himself to pedalling uphill more hopefully. All he'd need to do was to leave the beastly thing about, then, when he'd got it well and truly pinched, break the news to the old lady – not abruptly enough to have an ill effect on her stummick, but gently . . . mournfully . . . so's to bring out the Fairy God-mother in Grannie.

Here the nice warm bus chugged its steamy, well-lit, cheery

way past Wilfie, and as it overtook him half-way up the hill, Girlie waved. She waved. To him . . . Definitely!

Wilfie felt inspired. His throttle was full to bursting! He resolved to get his bike pinched or perish in the attempt. He owed it to Girlie to offer her a motor-bike made for two with back springing. So no sooner had he gulped his tea when up he got and away on his bike he went.

'We can't keep him off it,' his mother told his gloating Grannie, 'not even *this* weather!'

'Good for him,' croaked Grannie, 'harden 'im off!'

'Over to see Syd before he'd hardly had his second cup – took his slice of dripping toast with him.'

'Did 'e now,' said Grannie enviously. She licked her chops.

'"Visiting the invalid," he said.'

'That Syd!' said Grannie, 'nasty noisy boy! If you ask me, Syd's a pest!'

'Still,' said Mrs Newton, 'it's just like Wilfie to neglect his own tea to go visiting the sick. Ever so sweet-natured!'

'Takes after our side,' said old Mrs Higgins promptly.

But the truth of it was that the dream-street Syd lived in had once harboured an absconding accountant who had incited a bank clerk to crime – or so the papers said. And birds of a feather, thought Wilfie, the ever-hopeful . . .

So he took care to park his silver spider in the dark little off-shoot turning down Syd's road, even though it meant trudging to the house through what had now become a downpour, in spite of which he paused and drew comfort from the gleam of the street lamp – what bicycle thief could resist the time, the place, the opportunity – and the poor street lighting – *and* Grannie's beastly dream gleam!

Syd was even more of a pest, pale and bandaged up with the family flapping fondly round, than hale and hearty and steaming off on that motor-bike of his. Not that he'd ever go steaming off on that old wreck again! For the insurance company had decided to do Syd proud this time. Syd was going to get a new bike – a dream-ike – a bike that would cost a cool three hundred if it cost a penny – megaphone exhaust – prr-prr-rrft and all! Or so Syd said.

It was almost more than poor Wilfie could bear.

But he lingered on, enduring Syd's family's fussing, until

long after his usual hour, ignoring their broad hints to be gone
and leave them to get down to their evening meal in peace, for
where was the point in not locking the stable if you didn't give
the steed time to be flown off with?

At last Syd's Mum took things into her own firm hands.

'High time Sidney went to bed,' she announced. 'Mustn't
overtax what little strength he's got, must we? And as for you,
Wilfie, Mrs Newton will be sending out a search party if you
don't get a move on. You'll find your coat in the hall, where you
left it, and mind and remember to close the front door to, but
don't slam it – Syd's got one of his heads, haven't you, darling?'

The front gate gained, Wilfie strained into the murk as far as
the eye could see for drizzle – and golly – oh golly – the beastly
bike had gone – flown – vamoosed.

Wilfie's heart was pounding like a piston – the beastly bike
had definitely been pinched – stolen – just like he'd prayed it
would be. Definitely!

And now to break the awful news to Fairy Grannie.

With a preternatural self-control Wilfie refrained from
rushing round to tell her there and then. Old people were like a
faulty ignition – timing was the main thing with both. And the
perfect timing for that little dream-bike job would be tomorrow
afternoon on the way home from the works – Grannie would
have had her after-dinner nap – those after-dinner forty winks
that fairly made the dream-house shake.

But that evening when Wilfie had popped round the back
way and let himself in by the scullery door, as usual, and
shouted himself to shreds in the hall so's not to give Grannie a
turn, creeping up behind her like a nasty ole burglar, he became
aware that Grannie had a caller. There were voices in the
parlour – a deeper, firmer bass voice could be heard endeavour-
ing to get in a sentence now and then amid his grannie's
unpredictable combination of dry leaves, cackle and squeak.

Wilfie opened the door a cautious inch and there, sure
enough, was the caller. And that caller was a policeman! And
there, propped up beside the chiffonier was a highly distasteful
object. And that object was Wilfie's beastly bike – and clearly
the one had been brought here by the other. And at the sight of
the two of them Wilfie's stomach turned – just as his old
Grannie's had.

They couldn't gaol him for leaving a bike about in a dark
street – or could they? They couldn't prove he'd done it on
purpose to get it pinched – or had they? Was that what they
called 'inciting to crime', or wasn't it? How long was the stretch
that accountant was serving for exactly what he, Wilfie, had
done – getting someone else to do his stealing for him? Maybe if
he just shut the parlour door quietly and crept away to
Australia or some place . . .

'Come on in, Wilfie, and shut that nasty door, and don't
stand there gawking, a great lad like you, while your old
Grannie catches her death of cold from sitting in a draught . . .'

'Come in, son,' confirmed the policeman.

Well, there it was – Wilfie was well and truly trapped.

'What are you going to say to the kind constable who brought
your bike back, eh? Well . . . what's wrong . . . lost your voice?'

'Caught the thief red-handed,' said the policeman, 'just as
he'd got one leg across the saddle-bar.'

'There, now,' said Grannie with as much satisfaction as
though she'd caught him herself.

'Mind you, son, you never should have left it in the dark road
for so long, unattended – a nice new bike like that . . .'

'Brand-new! Brand-new!' chanted Grannie.

'There's some police officers would take a serious view of
that, I don't mind telling you, but I'm the easy sort – got a
brood of youngsters of my own . . .'

'Got a broody youngster of his own,' corroborated Grannie
eagerly.

'So this time – this time –'

'This time,' repeated Wilfie apprehensively.

'Tea-time,' said Grannie, approvingly, 'crumpets! All my
own teeth!'

'This time,' said the policeman firmly, 'I intend to overlook
the matter.'

'Oh, thank you,' said Wilfie. He sat down suddenly.

'But you'll need to come along with me to the station, just to
make a charge, as I've been trying to explain to your
grandmother, here.,'

'Brand-new! Brand-new! On'y gave it to him yestidy.'

'Satidy,' said Wilfie.

'Satidy *was* yestidy!'

'Oh no it wasn't, yestidy was Mond'y. Satidy was . . .'

'Don't contradict your old grannie. If I say yestidy was Satidy, Satidy was yestidy, see?'

'But . . . ,' said Wilfie.

'Of course,' said the officer, hurriedly, 'you'll have to bring that bike round with you for h'identification purposes.'

'Oh,' said Wilfie.

'But you need have no fear – we'll look after it for you – put it under lock and key as though it were a burglar, eh?'

'Oh,' said Wilfie.

'Well,' said Grannie, 'aren't you going to thank the kind policeman, Wilfie? Speak up, don't mutter! He's all I've got to live for, officer, my grandson and heir. He'll have all I got after I'm gone. And I don't care how soon that is. All my friends gone. Nothing left to live for – *when are they going to bring me my tea . . .*'

The weeks that followed were pretty painful ones to Wilfie. Just one beastly pedal push after another, with young Syd steaming past on his brand-new dream-bike and Girlie Greenish up on the sprung seat behind. Sometimes Girlie waved.

And every morning Wilfie would give his beastly bike a kick on the spidery shins, and leave it with nary a look behind. And every evening the beastly thing was still there.

Thus Wilfie pedalled himself non-stop right through the wettest spring on record and into the rainiest summer ever.

'Harden him off,' chinnered Grannie – it had become her theme song – 'Harden him off – not that he'll make the old bones I've made – look at me – eight-four next birthday and never off me feet but for childbirth. What's for pudding? . . .'

In June they held the Works Dance. The girls had looked forward to this event since the Christmas Concert Party. They made themselves off-shoulder blouses and swing-around coloured skirts and got their hair re-styled.

Syd took Girlie Greenish to the dance, naturally. Wilfie went alone. Not that it mattered. Wilfie went everywhere alone these days.

'Why don't you take D'reen?' asked Syd – he meant well – 'D'reen's broken with Stan Fawley-Smith and this time it's definite – why don't you two team up?'

D'reen was Girlie's best friend. D'reen was quite a dish – curvacious and with all that fair flat hair in one eye, D'reen was the Dizz Works answer to Marilyn Monroe.

But Wilfie only shook his head and sneezed.

On the night of the dance Wilfie cycled in as usual, gave his beastly bike the customary parting kick and prepared himself for an evening of utter frustration. The dance took place in the canteen. There were two bands, one each end and no room to swing a jiving cat between them once the evening got going. And there, right in the centre of the floor, were Syd and D'reen, lost in the shared delirium of a steel-band. From the stove Wilfie looked on.

Girlie wasn't carrying on like D'reen. Girlie wasn't that sort of girlie at all! Girlie was sitting squarely on her chair waiting to be toted neatly round the outer edge. For, let's face it, Girlie wasn't all that hep at bebop.

Wilfie longed to offer her a drink, but how much did a pink gin cost? And by the time he'd found his ten shilling note Les Jones came up and sat down beside him.

'Smashing girl, D'reen,' said Les.

'Think so?' said Wilfie.

'Stan Fawley-Smith must be mad to break with her like that.'

'Oh I dunno . . .'

'Those expectations of his have gone to his head, all right!'

'Expecta . . .'

'Coming in to quite a bit of money, Stan Fawley-Smith is. That's where he gets the Fawley – his aunt is a Miss Fawley, see? And when she dies Stan gets all her bits and pieces.'

'Bits and . . .'

'They say he's borrowed quite a bit on his expectations.'

'Borrowed on his . . . here, I say, how much? . . .'

'Two or three hundred, they say. Definitely!'

Wilfie made a giant effort to master the material facts through the din of the disco.

'D'you mean they give Stan Smith three hundred pounds for his old aunt?'

'Fawley-Smith,' Les Jones corrected him, 'definitely.' He edged himself nearer. 'I say,' he said, 'you couldn't let me have ten shillings – you'll get it back Friday – definitely.'

In a daze Wilfie parted up with his all – it was worth it. For if Stan Smith – Fawley-Smith – could get three hundred pounds from that old aunt of his, Wilfie's old Grannie was money for motor bikes!

Pr-rrrr-ft! Destry was at it again!

And now Girlie Greenish came across, her lips two thin red lines.

'I've had just about enough of this,' she said. 'Let's go.'

The beanless Wilfie blanched.

'Whe – where to?' he faltered.

'Anywhere,' said Girlie. There were tears in her eyes. 'Just anywhere at all!'

It was a dream-opportunity. Our hero cleared his throat.

'Mind if I bring my bike,' he muttered.

Two days later Wilfie took the early lunch hour, gave his beastly bike a parting kick and squared up to the oddly dingy doorway of the almost, well, squalid premises of the Harlingford Finance Corporation.

The information he acquired inside was as smooth as an oily road surface – and just about as deadly. Yes, money was available to Clients with Expectations, able to deposit with the Corporation Written Proof in the form of an Irrevocable Deed signed by the future Benefactor . . .

But this was out of the question! It was as good as asking Grannie to sign her own death warrant! The shock would just about kill the old lady. Besides, could you see Grannie doing it?

And there the beastly bike stood, when he emerged, as safe as push-bikes. And after this it seemed wetter and slower than ever, pedalling home.

The dream of a pond on the common was close on flooding and the bike kept slithering on the muddy path. Small wonder Wilfie sneezed at supper.

'Hope you're not catching a cold, son,' said Mrs Newton anxiously. 'Better not go near Grannie, just in case.'

'Sniffle-snee,' agreed Wilfie, whole-heartedly.

Late that night, when the entire dream-neighbourhood was fast asleep, lulled by the unrelenting rainfall, Wilfie arrived at a desperate decision. If no-one was ever going to do him a favour and steal the beastly bike, he would just have to steal the beastly bike himself. Definitely.

It was the only way. The only way to clear the ground for Destry . . . pprr . . . prrft!

Persuading Grannie that a motor-bike was every bit as hardening-off as a push-bike would be grand-child's play once the beastly bike was out of the way.   And this . . . this was D night. D for Decision. D for Determination. D for, well, D night. Definitely.

Wilfie got into his waterproofs and crept out. Slipping, slithering and sniffling in the dark he pushed the beastly bike through the beastly bleak wet night, over the beastly dream-common to the very edge of the dream-pond, lifted it aloft and flung it from him. It made a satisfying sper-losh. Definitely. Then, shivering, sneezing, sniffling, but elated, he slithered his way back to the toolshed where the beastly bike was customarily kept, unscrewed the padlock and left the door swinging loosely on its hinges.

So much for the Case of the Burgled Bicycle! And they couldn't pin a thing on him. Definitely.

Next morning, Wilfie stayed away from the Works. They didn't thank you for going in with a streaming cold. Mrs Newton brought his breakfast up to him on a tray.

'Wilfie, dear,' she said, 'bad news.'

Wilfie did his best to look startled.

'It's Grannie,' she told him. 'She's been on the nasty old phone – the telephone, I mean. She's had one of her turns.'

'Oh,' said Wilfie, 'is that all?' He laughed hysterically and upset the milk jug.

'*All?*' – Mrs Newton's voice was pregnant with reproof. She did hope Wilfie wasn't going to turn out callous like the other side of the family. She wanted her son to be just like his Uncle Harry – ever so kindly – ever so considerate – in every respect.

Now old Mrs Higgins's indispositions were nothing more lethal than indigestion brought on by eating too much, too soon, too rapidly, dignified by the specification 'Another of my turns'. And she was very proud of them.

That night she phoned for Wilfie and in a gnome-like cackle, peppered with 'Speak ups' and 'Don't shouts', demanded that he go at once to Mr McDoodie's and bring her back a bottle of his Special Strong Peppermint Mixture, nasty stuff.

'At once,' asked Wilfie apprehensively, for Mr McDoodie's chemist shop was three miles away and more.

'At once,' said Grannie. 'Speak up – speak up – and mind, don't shout.'

'But,' said Wilfie, though at heart he knew full well he hadn't an earthly, 'it's raining.'

'Harden you off,' said Grannie. 'And don't waste time talking.'

'But, Grannie, the last bus has gone.'

'What stuff's torn? asked Grannie. 'Speak up, speak up, I can't hear you.'

'The last bus. It's gone.'

'No need to shout,' said old Mrs Higgins, 'even if I am a little hard of hearing. You'd be hard of hearing if you were going on eighty-four.'

'But . . .' said Wilfie.

'I've given you a nice bike, haven't I? So get on with it!'

And old Mrs Higgins hung up.

'Better do what the old lady wants, Wilfie. You'll have to, in the end so you might as well give in now and save time later,' said Mrs Newton sagely.

Three and a half miles there, and three and a half miles back – seven all told – and the last bus gone and the rain coming down in torrents – almost Wilfie regretted that beastly bike.

And then, two days after Wilfie's D day – D for Downpour. D for Drizzle – a D for Dreadful thing happened to Wilfie. A D for Drought set in, and in a matter of a month from being the wettest July for fifty years it looked like becoming the D for Dryest August for eighty.

One fine day the criminal, passing the scene of his crime on his way home from work, was horrified to find the handle-bars of the beastly bike were visible. The water level in the dream of a pond was subsiding rapidly. Two more days and the saddle could be seen too. And before the week was out the whole gaunt frame of the beastly and by now rusty bike would be revealed to the most absent-minded of passers-by.

There was nothing for it but to take his courage in both hands

and make a clean breast of it to Grannie, before someone else
got in before him and brought the beastly thing back.

So that afternoon a very solemn Wilfie popped in the back
door of Grannie's little dream-house to break the news – very
gently – of the loss. He had gone over the scene many a time in
his imagination. How Grannie would cry a little at the shock.
How he would kiss her hand. How she would promise him a
new and better bike – a motor-bike, in fact, and how
thereinafter he would speed through life with Girlie Greenish
on the sprung saddle – Girlie Newton she'd be by then . . .

But from the front room came the sound of voices: Grannie's
mixture of cackle and squeak, and a man's firm voice that he'd
heard somewhere before. And there, by the hall-stand, stood
the bike, horribly whole and every bit as beastly.

And from inside the front parlour Grannie's voice came
shrilly out.

'Wait till I get at 'im,' it threatened, 'I'll give 'im a piece of my
mind, nasty, ungrateful, lying boy! I'll tell 'im what I think of
him. New . . . brand-new . . . his dream-bike . . .'

The man's firm voice tried to edge in an alleviating sentence
to the effect that Boys would be Boys.

'. . . Joys,' cackled Grannie, 'what joys are there left to me?
Shock and worriting – worriting and shock. Worriting and
hungering . . . hungering and . . . *when are they going to get my
tea . . .?*

'Er . . .' said the man's firm voice.

Softly Wilfie tip-toed away.

From down the road the sound of an ambulance in a hell of a
hurry could be heard; its bell was ringing furiously.

It was sure to be Syd.

All that was some years ago. Last month Wilfie really did get
his Dream-Bike. Got it off the Football Pools, what's more!
And it really was bigger – and better – *and* ten miles an hour
faster than Syd's old crock.

And the very first day he took it to work he parked it where
he'd always left his push-bike. Definitely. And when he came
out to stroke it in the lunch hour, well, it just wasn't there any
more.

Gone – stolen – pinched! Now wasn't that Life all over!

'Hi, you!' he called to young Erne, to whom on an impulse he had given his old push-bike, only yesterday. 'You might let me have my bike to go round to the Police Station. Gotta report a loss as soon as possible.'

'Well,' said young Erne, grudgingly, 'if I do – *if* I do – you won't go leaving it about again, will you? I meanter say, some-body might pinch it.'

The Laird Will Provide

Moses Manasseh turned back to the Personal Column. It was still there:

> FOR SALE 1952 DAIMLER LIMOUSINE. Mechanically perfect. As new. Fifty guineas or nearest offer. Inspection invited. Box O/ooo.

It was still there. And suddenly Aunt Ada's meagre legacy, which had heretofore seemed one last masterly insult became the perfect bequest. It was fifty guineas – how those shillings had stung the beneficiary. It was tax-free. It was too much money to fritter and not enough to invest. And you could always sell the Daimler for hard cash which did not figure on the returns. Good old Ada!

But here Mr Manasseh pulled himself together. For of course there was a catch in it somewhere.

If it wasn't a love-call from a burglar to his clippie it was . . . Mechanically perfect – well, you could check up on that . . . Inspection invited – why not?

Mr Manasseh fitted a Turkish cigarette into an amber and ivory holder. It had been Aunt Ada's wicked extravagance thirty years ago the day his liver played him up at Cimiez and she had sneaked off to the shops alone.

He decided to write to the advertiser as soon as he got away from Dr Sharptoe's consulting room. Clearly the family physician was an instrument of Providence. Mr Manasseh was a staunch believer in Providence, particularly when it was manifested in his own ability to recognise a snip when he saw one. And to think that he had been in two minds whether to take his liver to Dr Sharptoe that morning – just a touch of his

old trouble brought on by Aunt Ada's last will and testa-
ment . . . The rest to the Home for Aged Jews – tcha! And it
made no difference that the Home for Aged Jews was one of the
charities to which he himself had been a generous subscriber –
his were donations carefully worked out and noted down
against the income tax, Mr Manasseh's natural foe. Heart as
well as head was included in Mr Manasseh's charitable
instincts. As though he hadn't reminded the old woman the
morning of the afternoon she went off to give herself a heart
attack at the Bluff table that charity begins at home and not in
every seventh kitty. Women, thought Mr Manasseh, should
never be trusted with money. They spent it. He bent forward to
light the spill he had stripped from Dr Sharptoe's *Times* at Dr
Sharptoe's electric fire. Lighters were for spendthrifts, like
Aunt Ada. But money – money was the affair of menfolk. A
sacred responsibility. That Daimler would be worth three
thousand five hundred of anybody's money. It wasn't much,
but it was something he could save from the wreck of Aunt
Ada's impulsive codicil. He must get his hands on that
limousine forthwith. No time to waste on his liver. Time to be
up and doing. Livers were for outrageous old women who ran
up scandalous accounts at the chemist's!   And so Mr
Manasseh tucked in his muffler and left, taking Dr Sharptoe's
Times with him.

    And that was how it was that Moses Manasseh, merchant, of
Aldermanbury Postern, EC, found himself in a train on the
sabbath morning travelling to Pebbles, one of our smaller
Carolean country houses, which is in Norfolk not far from
Sandringham. The sabbath because the address had reached
him only that morning and the city was dead on Saturday
mornings in the summer. And also because it was in the evenings and at the weekends that he missed the mutual recrimina-
tions most. Third class because Mr Manasseh put his purse
before his comfort and only travelled first if he had a lady with
him – a frail and feckless elderly lady who wasted her money on
indiscriminate charities and useless magazines 'to while away
the journey', when a lunch-time edition served to pass his time.
Shiny, extravagant magazines that were only on the market for
the benefit of the advertisers of luxury goods. And Mr
Manasseh would sit there dreading the moment when that

flighty Aunt of his would be through with the beauty hints and
start leafing the luxuries. Putting ideas into women's empty
heads!

A station wagon was waiting at the Halt to transport Mr
Manasseh to Pebbles. For he had sent a wire to herald the
approach of his fifty guineas, lest some nearest offer should
snatch the limousine from him. Putting your faith in
Providence didn't mean letting the job take care of itself.
Pebbles was five and a half miles distant from the Halt, and Mr
Manasseh was glad of this. For the wily old gentleman had a
question or two he wanted to put to the chauffeur. But the
chauffeur was not to be pumped, confound his misplaced
loyalty. Didn't appear to care on which side his bread might get
a little extra butter! His answers were discreet to a fault and no
earthly help to anyone, though no doubt Aunt Ada was enjoying a good laugh up aloft!

Yes, the Daimler was a limousine. Yes, it was a 1952 model.
Yes, the road tax had been paid to the end of the year and the
insurance could be transferred. Yes, it was in perfect
mechanical order. No, he had not driven it himself, but that is
what he had been given to understand.

Mr Manasseh gave up trying to pump the man and surveyed
the green plush countryside with deep foreboding.

At last the chauffeur volunteered a piece of information.

'It's a very pretty colour,' he said. 'Pale blue and doesn't
show the dust.'

As though the colour mattered.

'I've noticed, sir, that ladies like pale colours.'

Mr Manasseh grunted.

Many was the passionate dispute he had waged with Aunt
Ada on the folly of her wearing light colours in the summer that
had to be forever at the cleaners – you'd think they dipped the
things in solid gold – he had long harboured a suspicion that
amounted to a certainty that she disliked pale pink old ladies
every bit as much as he did and only wore the colour to annoy
him. But why? Why did Aunt Ada hanker to annoy him, who,
at heart, would not suffer a butterfly to alight on her absurd,
impractical, outmoded, lacy sunshade – the one Uncle Nat had
brought her back from Paris on the only trip he ever took
without her, except the one that leads to Willesden Lane (for

Jewish women stay at home and weep, and men make hearty noises in the hall so that they may not hear the coffin being carried out). The ivory-handled parasol, that was never from her hand that summer long and smelt of lavender and mothballs. And at the memory of that familiar, muddled scent, and to his chagrin, tears came to the eyes of Mr Manasseh and, though he told himself brusquely that an umbrella would have been a deal more practical in this climate, they all but over-flowed.

The Long Gallery at Pebbles is not so elegant as the Music Room at Harewood, nor so richly ceilinged and encrusted as the Drawing-room at Astley Hall. Nevertheless, in its modest way, it is well worth a visit, and in different circumstances Mr Manasseh would have lingered in the shade taking pleasure in the glowing satins of the Knellers – though he wasn't the painter Rembrandt was, and never would be. But when the butler brought in the sherry he refused it, so impatient was he to see the limousine. After business was another matter. Mr Manasseh intimated as much. At the threshold he paused, however, to take a last look at the cool room where leafy branches tapped the window panes and led the eye past crimson tulips to the cushioned lawn.

The butler shook his head sadly at Mr Manasseh. 'His Lord-ship was very proud of his pictures,' he said. 'And now most of them will have to go to pay the death duties.'

'Too bad, too bad,' said Mr Manasseh. The death duties could be an explanation – but fifty guineas or nearest offer, well it didn't make sense. Not Mr Manasseh's sort of sense.

Mr Manasseh had an allergy to death duties. In their way they were just as bad as income tax, only you were not alive to grin and writhe under them – if you could not wriggle out of them. How often had he urged Aunt Ada to dispose of her estate while still alive so as not to give the government the benefit. But the old lady would only fold her hands and say, 'You'll see, you'll see!' And so he had.

The limousine proved to be all that Mr Manasseh could hope for and more – the very thing to defeat Aunt Ada's ducks and drakes. It was hunched and sleek and shining. It purred like an angel and was as silent as a well-trained servant. In fact it was worth every penny of the fifty guineas that Mr Manasseh was anxious to pay for it – and three thousand four hundred and forty-eight more.

And although the butler assured him that he was the first in the field he was in a fever to get back to the house where he had been told Her Ladyship would be waiting to discuss the price.

For what must have been the first time in his life Mr Manasseh was prepared to pay an asking price. And how surprised Aunt Ada up there must be. For the old lady had dearly loved a haggle – though something made her give up far too soon, which could, of course, have been her breathing trouble, but could equally have been her love of shocking her nephew. When it came to money matters, men were the straight-laced ones, she felt.

On this occasion, however, Mr Manasseh had made up his mind. He would not pull a face about the price. He would not even niggle out of guineas – not so much as hand over the notes and pause and fumble for the silver. A bargain was a bargain and he wasn't going to spoil this one by being too greedy.

Lady Mcgilliefleur was just as Mr Manasseh had envisaged her. Not too young to make him feel an old fool, and not too old to make him feel a cad for taking advantage of what could only be her madness, but a compact, rather bleak and grey-haired woman in a black skirt and a grey knitted twin set – not that Mr Manasseh could have given it a name.

Her Ladyship opened briskly. 'You've seen the car for yourself,' she said. 'Well, is it what you're wanting?'

It was indeed! But of course it wouldn't do to sound too keen in the early stages.

So Mr Manasseh said that he was perfectly willing to pay a returnable deposit subject to inspection by the RAC.

'We'll no be bothering with a deposit,' said Lady Mcgilliefleur. She must be mad. 'I suppose you know it takes a deal of petrol?' She was mad. 'So I thought mebbe to lower the price to pounds.' She had taken leave of her senses. Yet for a female lunatic she spoke quietly enough. 'Well, Mr Manasseh,' she was saying, 'will you take it or leave it?'

'I'll take it,' said Mr Manasseh whose knees had turned to water at her manner of throwing away a deal. Aunt Ada wasn't in it!

'Then you can take the thing home right away, and send me a cheque tomorrow.'

'As – as a matter of fact I – I've got the money with me, the exact amount,' said Mr Manasseh suppressing his emotion, but with difficulty. 'Fifty pounds and,' he fished into his pocket and in his excitement he found himself fumbling after all, 'fifty shillings.'

'I'll no take the shillings, and I'll no take the cash. Fifty pounds or the deal's off.'

'As you wish,' said Mr Manasseh stifflly.

'And by cheque – and let's have a drink on it.'

Was a deal invalidated by the vendor's lunacy? Mr Manasseh wished pasionately that he'd brought his man-of-law with him.

Over the sherry Her Ladyship relaxed.

'You see,' she said, 'it was his car – my late husband's. The station wagon's good enough for me. They're handy little runabouts and cheap on petrol.'

Mr Manasseh winced.

'Angus never drove out in his fine new car – he died before we took delivery.'

'That's sad, that's very sad,' said Mr Manasseh, doing his best to feel the words he spoke.

'Aye, Angus passed away. And left everything he possessed in the world to me.' Lady Mcgilliefleur pushed across the sherry. 'Everything,' she emphasised, 'except the limousine. And that is to be sold and the proceeds to go to somebody else he was expected to provide for.'

'Really?' said Mr Manasseh. He was burning to get away, to phone his lawyer, but too fascinated to rise and leave.

'His mistress,' said the widow, and passed her glass for more sherry.

And up in heaven Aunt Ada gnashed her teeth.

This story of a car and its price for sale happens to be quite true. And yet how few believe me when I say so.

Hear!

The room was too full of furniture. Very good furniture, each antique object a collector's piece. There were flowers in profusion; white flowers – lilies, gardenias, lilac, lilies-of-the-valley, magnolias – a profusion that was gloriously independent of the season.

And there were bills everywhere, too – tucked into bibelots and under Sèvres and Famille Rose; behind the clock – it was a middle period Tompion – and inside the ormolu and latois vases, as though out of sight were out of debt.

In the Italian Renaissance bed Ventura Digbye lay dying. Her fine skin, once magnolia white, was now a creaming alabaster. And the fine hands still, at last, with long lean fingers that had first industriously, purposefully, gathered in the harvest of the ages in the satisfyingly visible form of objets d'art, and then had winnowed and rejected – but only to make room for something better, as her taste refined and affirmed itself.

And beside her, Pearle, her sister, sat and prayed for her.

Upstairs a portable gramophone was playing:

> *The Black Bottom,*
> *You can't beat it!*

Downstairs the portable was playing:

> *Ours is a nice house ours is,*
> *What a nice little house ours is!*
> *The roof's on the top of our jolly little shack,*
> *The front's at the front,*
> *And the back's at the back!*

The two tunes came grinding through the slats of the sun-blind into the windows of the second floor front together with the grit and heat of that summer in London in the mid-thirties.

It made an unexacting background to the Shemah, the Hebrew prayer that Pearle was muttering. The prayer that is said by practising Jews in the morning and at night and which is spoken at their deathbeds.

> 'Hear, O Israel, the Lord thy God, the Lord is one . . .'

On the walls of the room hung a Goya and a Gainsborough, a small Constable, a Flemish primitive, and a Manet. There was the tapestry, too, by Teniers. An Aubusson spread eternal summer on the parquet floor. It was as though all the treasures of this great house in Belgrave Square had sought the sanctuary of this, the only room that had not been let to a lodger.

> *It's sweet, sweet, sweet,*
> *And cheap, cheap, cheap,*
> *It's just like an ice-house, our is!*

ground the gramophone.

The furniture was related to the room and to one another merely by marriage; a marriage of confounded inconvenience. Proximity was all these crowded, unique, aristocratic pieces held in common and they remained aloof and unimplicated in the room, its occupants, their occupations.

> '. . . And these words which I command thee this day shall be in thy heart; and thou shalt talk of them when thou sittest in thine house and when thou walkest by the way; when thou liest down and when thou risest up. And thou shalt write them upon the door-posts of thine house and upon thy gates . . .'

Pearle finished the Shemah but she did not straighten up. Her hands still screened her face.

'Lord God of Israel,' she extemporised, 'I've said the Shemah but it's not for me, it's for Ventura. You know what she is – too proud to say it for herself. But there! You made her, Lord, and so you understand her. She's a Jew all right for all her Christianity. You can't change your race any more than you can change the colour of your eyes. I told her so at the time. But she wouldn't listen then and she won't listen now. Her florist's bill alone! And all this useless furniture! But now the poor soul's time has come. Be with her, Lord. Into thy hand I commend her spirit, and with her spirit her body also. The Lord is with her, she shall not fear . . .'

Ours is a nice house, ours is!

the gramophone re-affirmed.

Mum

Two domestics were standing at the corner of a neo-Georgian Square, in the early dusk, discussing their daily situations.

'I will say this for it,' the woman with a figure like a cottage loaf was speaking, 'it's all-electric.'

'Nice,' said the woman in a head-scarf.

'Labour-saving throughout.'

'Lucky.'

'Oh, but all them parties – and the empties afterwards – and all them gins to be carried out to the dustbins! But there – that's Chelsea for you!'

'Don't Butler give you a hand?'

'Wot 'im?' The cottage loaf was infinitely scornful.

A neat white Jaguar sports car rounded the bend. It had the distinctive number plate PP1.

''Ere we come,' said Cottage Loaf, ''ome early today.'

The two women stood watching the car pull up at the house with the turquoise door. A woman in a dark blue suit swung her slender legs, and was out and on the front step like a flash of dark blue lightning. She paused there, a well-defined arrow with a Hardy Amies' cut, digging in her bag for her key.

'Keeps her figure – I will say that for her,' said Cottage Loaf, 'what there is of it.'

'Trim,' said Head-scarf. She patted her own bony hip.

'Flat-chested I call it. No cleavage.' Cottage loaf checked her own. Both there.

'What's so special about cleavage?' demanded Head-scarf, instantly envious. 'Well, bye-bye.'

'See you!'

They went their separate ways.

In the meantime the woman in the dark blue suit lost patience and pulled the bell. It was an amusing bell with an alarming off-key jangle. Patricia Postern, however, forgot to be amused. She felt a hundred and she feared she looked it as she waited to be eased back into her domestic life by her butler. Patricia Postern had never got used to a butler of her own. She still did not take him for granted, like the bath salts; indeed they carried on a sexless, sempiternal flirtation. Theirs was a Fair Princess and Dagobert the Jester relationship. It all took place in an ivory tower on another plane. It was founded on his professional solicitude and her professional fragility. Both kept to the letter of the cast list.

Patricia Postern enjoyed, too, the recently bestowed title that she shared with her husband. Sir Jeremy Postern . . . Lady Postern . . . Her arrow back reaffirmed its dignity each time those names were spoken. Your Ladyship! It was the best lift she knew. Better then Benzedrine. Better than the fanfare they played for her third act appearance in *The Princess Caroline Story*.

And at an embassy party or at Glyndebourne or on a gala night at Covent Garden, 'Lady Postern's car' not only set the doorman's voice ringing, but all the trumpets sounded for Lady Postern, like they did in *The Pilgrim's Progress,* only well on this side and safely in the bag.

Lady Postern had had luck on her side – and, of course, her adoring husband. She might have remained for ever unnoticed with the amateurs. But one hadn't, thank God! And thank, of course, Jeremy, who had been called in to produce the Ambleside Dramatics. As Patricia Perry she had played Mrs Cheyney in *The Last of Mrs Cheyney,* not, perhaps with as much skill as Gladys Cooper, but with every bit as much assurance. It was 1937 and Patricia Perry was married to Jean-Jacques. Lady Postern preferred to forget that early marriage. She almost never thought of it, these days.

'Sir Jeremy is in the sitting room, My Lady.'

'Thank you, Billings. Oh, Billings?'

'Yes, My Lady?'

'Has Sir Jeremy had his tea?'

'Sir Jeremy wished to wait for you, as usual, My Lady.'

'Ah!'

How soothing one's domestic life had become recently.

Patricia Postern paused before the mirror, touched her hair and flicked her tongue over her lips. Then made her entrance.

The plain girl in the unlikely tartan had a communication to make. A communication she could withhold no longer. She made it to everyone and no-one in the railway carriage. She had been sitting in the window seat of the boat-train to London for some time, and now dusk was falling and Kent no longer held her eager interest.

'I am going to meet my mother. It will be the first time that we meet, my Mum and me.'

The woman sitting opposite took the remark to herself.

'Your step-mother, no?'

'No. My mother. We have never met, we two.'

'Come, come,' the grey-haired man who was, no doubt, the woman's husband protested.

'Never,' declared the girl. 'Never, I assure you. Not since I am a little *bébé*. Not since she ran away with this English *metteur en scène*.

The penny dropped. 'Aha!' said the woman opposite. 'What is his name?'

'But I know all about her,' said the girl with the touching confidence of the very young. She spoke a careful English, tasting each word as though it were a condiment she was adding to the flavour of her meaning.

'She is beautiful, my mother. And very motherly. I have seen her in a film. An American film. It was a very motherly role that she played – oh yes, my mother is a film star and very glamorous. But above all things she is my Mum,' said the daughter with complete conviction.

'Naturally,' said the woman opposite, who had a Siamese cat instead of a daughter. 'And what is her name? Perhaps I know it.'

'You will astonish yourself when you hear it. She is so pretty, this mother, with large eyes,' her own widened until a child could have drawn her white square face, with its two black pools and scarlet gash. 'Lashes like that,' she measured their length between finger and thumb, 'and a first class *coiffeur*. My mother is not the least like me. I take after my father's family. My father is French. Also he is defunct.'

'Oh?' said the man. He seemed a little startled.

'Since last month he is defunct. So me I am on my way to meet my Mum.'

'What did you say her name was?' said the woman.

'Patricia Postern.'

'No!' The man and the woman exchanged a look.

'Postern. You have heard of her?'

'Oh, yes! But . . .'

'She is my Mum,' said the plain girl, almost radiant.

'Then I congratulate her,' said the man.

The girl decided that she did not like him. She turned to the woman. 'I said you would astonish yourself.'

The woman pounced. 'Now that we know each other you must come and dine with us, must she not, David? You must dine with us on Wednesday when Lady Jonas will be there – you would like to meet Lady Jonas, would you not? – she is so amusing.'

'If you ask me she's bogus,' said the man.

The woman frowned at him. But mercifully the remark had made no impact on Patricia Postern's daughter. 'Here is my card,' she said.

The plain girl, rather flushed now, took it.

'"Mrs. D. G. N. Gulliver" – this is you?'

'It is indeed,' said the man.

'Me, I am Martine – Martine Mivraux. I have already sixteen years.'

'Really? . . . And . . . your mother . . . she will be at Victoria to meet you?'

'Oh no! I am not at all waited for.'

'Are we to take it that Lady Postern is due to astonish herself also?' said the man.

Martine ignored him. 'I shall call a taxi,' she told Mrs Gulliver, 'and drive straight to her home – our home – Chelle-sea – you have heard of Chelle-sea? – it is chic, this quartier? – and when I am there, at Numero Trente-et-un, Chelle-sea Square, I shall march straight into the salon – and there will be my Mum with her knitting . . . I stand there drinking in . . . "Mother!" I cry and instantly I fling myself into her arms, and we are weeping, both, a bucket.'

'I wouldn't count on that,' said David Gulliver, 'if I were

you!' He said it not flippantly but in all seriousness.

Poor, ugly, little brat, he thought, whistling in the dark to keep her courage up. For he was not entirely unperceptive.

And indeed, later, in the triumphantly achieved taxi, watching this much-dreamed-of London being drawn past the rattling window – London, not brilliant like Paris, but somehow bright and solid – Martine was not without her misgivings.

Would this Mother – the same Mother who had forsaken one's very perambulator – really be so enchanted now to receive one – to open her life and take one into it – a human Convent to a little Sister? One could only tug one's heart up from one's bootees – one's hungry little heart; one's little Prisunic bootees – and await events; remind oneself that she is one's Mum, and nature is nature, no?

But this close-patterned life of hers – it was already fully occupied, no doubt, with the husband of one's mother – who was not one's father but the father of one's mother's son – who was equally not one's brother.

Martine attempted to find a hopeful answer to the problem her family who, it must be understood, was not her family, was setting her. To have no father of her very own – certainly this was sad – and interesting. Sad, but not so desolating as a Mum who had not cared enough to stay and push one in one's pram. But, she reminded herself, all that was in the past. Now she must think only of the future. They would become such chums, this Mum and this daughter – never was there to be two sisters as close as this Mum and this daughter were to be. Why then this tear upon one's cheek?

'Dear God, give only that my mother does not hate me. Give that I will be welcome – this time – in my mother's life.'

'Don't move, Princess,' Jeremy Postern implored his wife. She was leaning back among the plumping of cushions, her eyes closed to the professionally tasteful, pale green drawing-room.

Theirs was a lifelong romance and it was odd that he should perpetually feel the need of reaffirming it domestically. But there it was.

'Stay – always – just as you are. Curled up – a kitten in a trance on a *chaise-longue*.'

'Prr-prr,' Patricia indulged her doting partner. She did not take the pains to open her eyes.

'Fragile – docile – and so very lovely. In fact, perfection! I wouldn't say that's putting it too high, would you, Dominic?'

Silence.

Patricia's eyes flicked open. An eyebrow arched. Her stepson must be having one of his difficult days. He remained hunched over his book, his spectacles crooked on his pointed nose, his legs everywhere, looking more like his late unlovely Mamma than ever before.

'Dominic,' repeated Jeremy Postern sharply.

The boy looked up. He blinked affectedly. 'Oh . . . hallo, Princess – how long have you been here?'

Maddening boy!

Jeremy rushed in to cover up. 'You know, Princess, I've been needing just this all day . . . the – benefaction – of your head against that cushion – needed it without quite knowing what it was I needed. I know now.'

'Dear Jeremy!' Patricia went through the moves of blowing him a kiss, then closed her eyes and strained every nerve to relax. 'Did you have a dreary afternoon?'

'Without you . . .'

'But you had Dominic to keep you company.'

'So I did. So I did.'

'I bet you had a splendid read, the two of you.'

'Ah, but I've been working out a first-rate plan for you.'

Patricia sat bolt upright, an expectant doll on a hinged back.

'Not Broadway,' she breathed.

'Not quite – not yet, that is.'

'Let's be totally clear. If it's Stratford again it's out – I'm just not strong enough to face those frightful parties.'

'I know. You were heroic. But it isn't Stratford – on Avon or Ontario!'

'If it isn't going to be Broadway I should care where the hell it is! No wait – there wouldn't be a Stratford in Australia? – My God! I knew it – you've booked to Australia!'

'Nothing is settled, Princess.'

'Australia!' It was a wail.

'Think of the lovely suntan on your bod, Princess. And Dominic could fly out to join us for Christmas. You'd like that, wouldn't you, old man?'

'Uh huh,' Dominic vouchsafed.

But the lanky figure huddled itself more closely into its curdle of resentment. He hadn't asked to be born his stepmother's stepson.

'Australia's out,' said Patricia, 'and that goes for Cowes as well.'

'In that case would you like me to have a word with Johnnie Osborne?'

'He could write a splendid angry play for me.'

'Exactly. Or I could have a chat with Harold about that piece Feuillère is doing in Paris. And of course there's always Ayckbourn.'

'Yes,there's always Ayckbourn.'

Dominic came suddenly into their world.

'I think you ought to do a film, Princess,' he said. A film would keep Princess out of the house all day long and in bed all night.

'You're right, Dominic,' she said. 'That lovely lolly and a luscious Charity Gala opening.'

'In the presence of Herself,' said Jeremy.

'Himself,' said Patricia, 'too, – or I won't play.'

'Themselves, then. So that's settled. I'll have a word with Franco tomorrow.'

'Why tomorrow, Poppet? Why not right now?'

'In the beginning was the word,' said Dominic cryptically. 'Like me to dial Italy?'

But before he could get his legs collected the door was flung open by a strange girl in a terrible tartan coat.

'Mother,' she cried in ringing tones, 'my Mum!'

Three Posterns turned to unbelieving stone.

'Mother!' The strange girl hurled herself howling at the stoniest Postern of them all.

Her 'Mum' an arrow of ice, sat there speechlessly being wept over by this tartan monster, and if ever a Princess in an ivory tower needed the ministrations of her butler, this was it.

As though guessing this, he loomed now in the wide-flung door.

'You rang, My Lady?' murmured her butler.

IN COMPANY WITH CHEKHOV

Variations on Themes
Suggested by Sentences
from his Notebooks and
Letters

A writer's notebooks are his way of drawing back from the brink of the exhausting effort of a full creation; a few words jotted down at the incandescent moment of inception which enable him to avoid the labour of the full luminous creation. The milestone, momentarily scanned, before the actual ascent to the mountain top. In these notebooks a single sentence may hold the pith, the heart, and the rueful laughter of a short story or even a play.

To Chekhov, coughing away his swindling scatter of days in what had become the exile of little Yalta, the spa on the Black Sea, the tempting plume of light from a match that called for no greater effort than its striking and merely tended the slower, more demanding glow of creation, had a strong appeal, for if he did not survive to turn up the lamp that glimmered in his notebook, there could yet come some writer in the future who rejoices in the health and strength denied to Chekhov to bring forth a full creation. So should his still-born children, his random jottings, come at last to a kind of foster life.

What Do Young Girls Dream About?

What a lot of foolish geese there are among young ladies. Sensible people have grown so accustomed to the elaborate airs some of them give themselves that they fail even to notice them.

Take Rinka Horosova. She was not precisely beautiful, but then neither was she precisely ugly; but something along the line of a pendulum between these two points according to whether she was passing through an on day or an off day. She had, poor thing, her father the apothecary's nose; a feature which on a prettier face might have been accounted a disaster, and her Aunt Lika's large dark eyes, which would land her in trouble yet – Aunt Lika, whose name was a hole in the family Bible.

When Rinka first caught up her hair in a bun (while still it was apt to break loose in moments of uncontrollable emotion and descend, in a cascade of hairpins, to ripple down to her waist), there came to call on her parents a certain Baron X – the father of one of the girls at the school at which Rinka was soon to become a pupil-teacher. He, after greeting her parents, bowed low over her own hand and kissed it with what the novels from the lending-library call 'a speaking look'. Down came her hair in an uncertain cloud, spangled with falling pins, while the colour drained from her cheeks. Fortunately pallor became her. And from that moment the young girl felt she was another being – no ordinary apothecary's daughter, but a being to whom a Baron had offered homage. And also from the moment of that innocent social kiss, half admiring, half mocking, the young girl became a young lady of some elegance – a high-minded, sensitive, soulful creature (which was something of a trial for her family) for whom the most ordinary conditions took on a special signficance in her mind.

For instance her minor ailments, headaches, colds, heart-burn, that sort of thing, all became calamities charged with possible, if unlikely, fatal consequences; and for them she would tolerate no ordinary medicines out of stock, but the apothecary must send for the newest patent cures from Harkov. And she had no appetite to sit down to the supper-table for honest cabbage soup with the rest of the household, but must nibble at specially prepared delicacies from little trays. She took to her own room more and more, shunning callers and impatient with parental conversation. Instead she read an increasing quantity of books from the library and chose stories about Dukes and Counts and Barons – above all Barons. She loved the passages about love, pure and ideal, not sensual. She skipped descriptions of nature, however beautifully they were written. She went from conversation to conversation with com-plete satisfaction, but while reading the beginning of a book she would break off impatiently and turn to the last pages to assure herself that it ended happily. She took no note of the names of the authors but wrote down her judgements of their writing in careful pencillings in the margin: 'Wonderful!' 'Beautiful!' 'How true!' 'Serve him right!'

And then she could not endure the sons of her parents' friends, the plain Igors and Ivans and Gregors of the neigh-bourhood who, because of her father's solid position, and perhaps a little, too,because of her cloud of hair, but most of all Aunt Lika's eyes, and in spite of the apothecary's nose, would have paid her marked attention on her Saint's Day had not the foolish virgin shown her distaste for them and her preference for Anton, a romantic-looking young actor who drank and sent requests for money in his love-letters, for which reason he enclosed a stamp for prompt reply. This fancy of hers soon passed.

And then, one evening on the way home from the school at which she read aloud from Pushkin to the pupils, and taught embroidery, her friend, Anna Serabskaya, a quite plebian girl with a highly-developed sense of mischief, told her that the Intendant at the establishment at which they both taught, was in love, and meant to lay his fate at Rinka's feet the very next

evening. Down cascaded her hair and the shower of hairpins fell
on the cobblestones in a summer-storm of pings. It was true, it
had to be, for had not the Intendant admired the embroidered
cherries on a piece of needlework she was showing her class?

When the young girl reached home she sat for a long time,
trembling with fear and indecision. She, Rinka, who had considered herself destined to become the wife of an Officer in the
Cavalry at the very least. All night she could not sleep, but lay
awake and towards morning fell in love with the Intendant.

Next morning, flushed and tremulous, she set out for school
with her embroidery tambour and a bunch of cherry-coloured
and green skeins and a book of Pushkin's poems from which she
was to read aloud to her pupils again, while they stitched. All
day she waited for the squeak of the Intendant's shoes in the
corridor and for a turn of the handle of the classroom door. But
no sound came from the corridor and the classroom door
remained closed.

That evening, on the way home, her friend Anna came hurrying along the street to catch up with her, the words bubbling at
her lips, and what with the steam that issued from her breath on
the sharp air as she spoke, she strongly resembled a human
kettle, thought the disconsolate Rinka.

'Such a foolish mistake I made,' she bubbled. 'It seems it was
not you at all the Intendant wishes to marry.'

'Not me?' said the wretched Rinka, with the voice of one who
could not believe her ears.

'No, indeed. But guess – guess who?' The human kettle
bubbled and hissed. And it seemed that it was Anna herself
who was to be the Intendant's bride.

And Rinka? She burst into tears like any ordinary young
woman who had been passed over, and flinging the Pushkin at
the bride-to-be, ran all the way home in the mercifully gather-
ing night.

The next day Rinka ran away to Harkov to try to find her
Aunt Lika andd live out an obscure and sordid existence with
her. To live a lost life. No Baron was ever to kiss her hand again.
And the full shame of it all Rinka was never to know. For the
'Baron' who had kissed her hand in her parents' parlour was

but *soi-disant*. In cold reality he had been the son of a second-hand clothes dealer, who had taken on that style and title to better himself in society. But the bloom on Rinka's life was forever gone.

A Husband of Some Distinction

Rosalie Ossipovna loved her husband Semyon Aromat very much although you could see a dozen Semyons to the quarter-chime sitting outside cafés on Old Cathedral Square; four dozen in New Cathedral Square. You will find one or two of him sipping some ruinous concoction on the terrace of the café with striped awning and the rickety iron tables any noontide in the summer, or gulping honest vodka – who was it called it 'the Cossack's Brandy'? – in the cavern at the back of the tobacconist's shop in the winter. You sat opposite him in the train, or watched him from the window of the Viennese pastry cook's, making heavy weather of dismounting from a hired carriage; puffing, panting and balancing his podgy body with his elbows. And, landfall safely negotiated, quickening his footsteps past the bank as though it were a striped cardboard box and the Manager a puppet on a spring that might jump out at any unwary saunterer. Raising his hat and bowing to the rich merchant's wife; bowing even lower to the rich merchant from whom he hoped to cozen a sizeable investment in his Essence of Aniseed Factory. Pretending not to see his boring brother-in-law to whom he still owed money. Crossing the Square to kiss the hand and be seen with Olga Petrova, the celebrated Petrova that is, in this provincial backwater. Some day St Petersburg should hear her top C, he promised himself. And from there it was but a step to Moscow; and after that Paris, Berlin, Vienna, Rome and who knew, why not New York?

When, some top Cs later, Rosalie Ossipovna learned that her idolised husband had become the lover of la Petrova, she did not speak of it but left humble and loving letters to him on his desk where he would be sure to find them.

'If ever you should be unfaithful to me, let it be with some woman of distinction.' And 'How could I hope to hold you for myself? You who are so intellectual, so sensitive – I who am so dull and stupid, and cannot carry on a conversation or take part in a political discussion, and know nothing of Rimsky-Korsakov.'

She told herself she could serve the man she loved only by dying and so freeing him.

Not by her own hand, for their friends – he had so many friends and all of them people of circumstance – might blame him for neglecting her. But die she must. It was the only way. And to this end she carried the hip-bath to the tap in the yard and filled it with icy spring-water. Before she immersed herself she wrote again:

'If it should so happen that I should die before you, I want you to marry again a woman of some attainment, a woman worthy of you. And I want you never to bath in ice-cold water, nor to wear freshly laundered underclothes while they are damp.'

With that Rosalie Ossipovna offered her comfortable haunches to the comfortless ice-cold water from the spring. But to no purpose. Indeed she died, not elegantly, but choking on a chicken bone. So clumsy.

After his second marriage, Aromat took to going to the Opera every night, wearing his decorations, or rather, to be exact, his decoration – a bronze medal for the census of 1897 – as befitted a man of some distinction – and sitting alone in a prominent box – each time his second wife was giving her high Cs, an attraction for which there was strangely little run on the box-office, his podgy hands immaculate in rather tight white kid gloves, he would sit there, well to the front of the box, beaming; and every time his *diva* hit a high note he would stand up and bow. And it did seem such a pity that the lights were lowered while the performance was on.

The Dinner

Honest Izaak was an honest man: the whole township was agreed about this. 'A saint, a saint!' said the elders, believers to a grandmother. 'As honest as Izaak' became the catchphrase of the businessmen. Theirs was a little town or a large village, according to the worldliness of he who spoke of it, and all who lived there were agreed that old Izaak was honest. 'We will give a dinner in his honour,' they decided. From that moment on husbands lived the life of slaves like their fathers or grandfathers before them; obeying orders from their womenfolk all evening long, with their 'Fetch me this' and 'Bring back that' and 'Do not broach that bottle, it is for the Dinner,' and their everlasting 'What am I going to wear?' – even those who had no choice asked the question, but their more fortunate sisters clucked their husbands, the great geese, into bring home patterns from Diamant, the 'Parisienne' haberdashers from the Junction.

A Committee was formed – not without some nudging and bickering and a private tender or so. The reception room in the town hall was booked. White linen table-cloths to lay end to end along the trestle-tables, were snatched from under samovars, and laundered. Many candles were collected – 'Enough,' said Ivan the Atheist, 'to set fire to all the churches in holy Russia, God forbid!' he ended, out of habit, for Ivan the Atheist was a superstitious man. Scarcely a flagon or a tea-glass in the township that had not been lent to grace the board, and all the village geese and ducks and chickens and turkeys stayed in the corners of their dark coops in fear of their lives. The perpetual fear of small winged things cries aloud to heaven –

that same heaven that Ivan the Atheist had thrown away with
the Ikon – 'God forgive me,' as he would not fail to say, and if
no-one was there to see he would cross himself to make sure – it
was as though the fowls of the earth could foresee that their time
had come to join the ranks of glory as Poultry.

Came the day when the official invitations were taken round
by the Junction wagon. Every family – every family of sub-
stance, that is – received the passport to plenty, from the rich
banker to the poor school-teacher and a fine terra-hee! terra-
ha! there had been about him, for he was considered too poor to
be included by one half of their village, and too rich to be left out
by the other, until it was decided that even though he was as
poor as honest Izaak – God forbid! – a school-teacher was a
school-teacher and could sit at the end of the trestle-table with
unmarried aunts and poor relations. For only in heaven would
the poor be accounted on the infinite abacus of the rich – and a
fine old shiftless place that was going to turn out to be – God
forbid!

On the evening before the Dinner the men kept within doors
in every substantial household in the township, rehearsing the
speeches they would undoubtedly be urged to make at the
Dinner. Wives, their most constant critics, sat for once with
folded hands and nodded as the husbands made their points.
Nor did they forbear from warning with heavily shaking heads
when husbands went on too long, in fact many a hairpin lay on
the floor by the time the rehearsal was over. Marriageable
daughters of rich tradesmen were putting their hair in curl-
papers, preparing to abandon their braided hair for corkscrew
curls for the Dinner, and a strong smell of moth-balls pervaded
the guest-room, where the Master of the House kept his dress-
suit.

'Decorations will be worn,' said the Invitation – it was a con-
dition on which the widow of the late Corporal of the Town
Guard, it numbered three, had insisted – indeed, she had
planned to pin her husband's long service medal on to her own
lovelorn bosom, could she but find the thing, and to this end the
contents of the top left-hand drawer of his bureau (some of
them had surprised her not a little) were lying on the bed she
had shared with him with no noticeable reluctance for sixteen
snow-filled winters, and the parched summers that followed

hard on. 'Aie me!' she sighed. 'Would that all husbands were as honest as Izaak'. But now that alas! her Yacob was dead, better to leave his fidelity in the hands of God. Alongside, her Tuesday Man, Ivan the Atheist, stirred and muttered something in his sleep.

On the night of the Dinner to honest Izaak, a charge of social electricity could be felt throughout the little Town. Fat farmers with their well-fleshed families and sharp-nosed sons-in-law were driving down the principal street – the one with the pavement – and all to the same destination as the Burgomaster, the Government Inspector, the Postmaster, the Prisonmaster, the Stationmaster and Haberdasher from the Junction, and their families right down to the schoolmaster – he walked. For the good old days in Holy Russia were the bad old days for the instructors of Russian youth. Each family brought its own contribution of good things for the general fare, again, save for the schoolmaster. He had only half a pumpkin in his larders, a *ben trovato*, found growing in close-fisted Fyodor's field on which he had gnawed for some days now.

The trestle-tables and the wooden benches were installed already and waiting to groan under their respective weights – for it would undoubtedly be a feast to talk of to one's grandchildren – the coarse crockery and the mugs and beakers were laid out, but not, of course the knives and forks and choicer delicacies; these they could not trust to the drunken caretaker and that doe-eyed daughter of his who was no more virtuous than she should be and would be better working with the nuns, poor things.

Long before all the company were assembled the early-comers had fallen-to on the comestibles, and the wine was flowing, and no sooner had the late-comers edged their way in to the feast then they were totally immersed in the pleasing convention of 'keeping up with Pavlova'. A merry hour or two later, when all had eaten their good fill – save the schoolmaster – and the flow of wine had dwindled to an up-tilt of dregs, Borovanski the Innkeeper (there was, however, another coarser word some used to describe the kind of house that one kept) stood up, swaying but slightly, for he was accustomed to the heady fumes of the grape, to propose the health of the honest man to whose rectitude the repast was being given.

'My friends,' he boomed, 'there falls to me the honour,' he
relished the word, allowed it to roll round the room and
repeated it with considerable pleasure, 'the honour of propos-
ing to you all a toast to honest . . .' he raised his beaker . . . 'to
honest . . .' he squinted up and down and along the depleted
board. But, what with one thing and another, they had quite
forgotten to invite the honest old man.

Next year honest Izaak was marched off to gaol for stealing a
loaf of bread. And the school-teacher, who had to husband his
leaky soles, visited him there every other Sunday.

He Fell Among Thieves

The District Tax-Collector, Botibulov, lived and worked in 'dusty and dishevelled Melikovo'; but for his little son he had aspirations. The district in Melikovo in which Botibulov, a widower, lived with his aged mother and his boy was neglected and unkempt although it housed no Marxists, no Movements, no World-Pessimism and none of the Intelligentsia who, it was well-known, turned towns into pigsties. Instead stagnation, suffocation, and grey mediocrity invaded lives lived in the Tax-Collector's District. 'In this part of town there is not a single musician, not a single orator, not a single prominent citizen,' Botibulov would reflect and sigh.

Botibulov had remained a widower: 'Your mother, may she rest, gave her life that you might live to bring renown to our district,' he told the uncomprehending three-year-old, who wore a black frock-coat, boots and waistcoat, for all the world as though he were a tax-collector, too. They were spoken of by th neighbours as Botibulov the Father and Botibulov the Son, and it was generally conceded by the women of the District, that Botibulov the Father would never marry again for fear a woman younger than his aged mother, a wife with all her feminine fancies, should dilute his influence upon, and strictures to, Botibulov the Son, who clearly was destined from birth to be a man of a different mould.

'Masticate your food twelve times,' Botibulov the Father would instruct little Botibulov the Son, although the child could not, as yet, count

Two years passed. The Son did his best to obey the Father. He masticated. He walked two hours every day. He washed in cold water. And still he remained a lumpen little boy with no discernible talent.

Already, when Botibulov the Son was only five years old, he would accompany the District Tax-Collector on his rounds, carrying a smaller version of Botibulov the Father's bag.

'You saw that man,' said Botibulov the Father of a short, smooth, neat man who employed a lout to answer his front door. 'Success has already given him a lick with its tongue.' And Botibulov the Son, nodded, and noted, and then he spoiled it all by banging his bag against the railings as though he were a common-or-garden little boy. And Botibulov the Father hoisted his son onto his shoulders, for the little lad seemed over-tired, but when they reached home he said the prayer he always prayed before administering a punishment: 'Lord, do not allow me to condemn or speak of what I do not understand,' with which he gave his son a beating for being boy-like. Simple people suffer from mothers-in-law; intellectuals from daughters-in-law, Botibulov the Son suffered from an over-loving father.

Life seemed out of tune with Botibulov the Son. Or was it that he was out of step with life? His father took him to the skating rink when he was seven, strapped on his skates, and skimmed away over the rink of ice as a swallow skims and darts and circles the air. And Botibulov the Son staggered after him, all flailing arms and failing legs. He wanted to overtake his father, to impress him, to overtake life itself and to impress it also – that life, which one cannot bring back, that Father he could not overtake, or catch, just as one cannot catch one's shadow. Poor seven-year-old, he fell and broke his leg. And ever after that he walked with a limp. But what was worse, the limp hampered and vexed Botibulov the Father so much more than ever it afflicted Botibulov the Son. 'We have never had a cripple in the family: we Botibulovs. Do your exercises, Son, and say your prayers. A man is what he believes,' said Botibulov the Father who believed in beating his son.

Botibulov the Son limped on until he was nineteen years old and, for that matter, long after. It was the day of his grandmother's funeral. 'I cannot be said to be handsome,' he told the blurred image in the looking-glass, peering at it myopically, for he had not dared to tell his father that his vision was defective, 'but I am rather pretty.' He tried to meditate on life and death, as was suitable to the occasion, but there seemed to be nothing in his soul except recollections, most of them shameful, of his schooldays.

The day came when news of a balloon, that was plying for passengers on the Ekaterinaslav Square on the other side of the city, came to the ears of the Botibulov Father and Son. 'The very thing,' said Botibulov the Father; 'you shall be the only person from this District to have flown in a balloon high into the sky, and everyone will look up to you.' And humble though he was by this time, it seemed good to Botibulov the Son, for in a balloon he could look down on the world from the height of his baseness.

It was the day when each month the District Tax-Collector took the roubles he had collected to the Town Hall in the centre of the city of Melikhovo. He travelled there by the station cab to guard against thieves. It was dusty and smelled of the horse that pulled it, but on this day, as he saw his son limping off in the opposite direction, Botibulov the Father felt elated, for now he knew that his son belonged to the race of men who will no longer trundle along in dusty cabs, but will fly through the skies in balloons.

But in the course of his long trudge across Melikhovo, Botibulov the Son fell among thieves. And he played vindt with them, and they cheated and he lost the money with which his father had provided him to buy a place in the balloon, for have not half the Russian *petits commerçants,* half the Russian bourgeoisie, run to seed in playing vindt? And Botibulov the Son knew that he could not hold back the sunset and the time was drawing nearer, all the time nearer, when he must tell Botibulov the Father of his fall, and at the thought he turned both hot and cold, and his nose dripped, and he felt the sediment of the dusty future already in his soul.

The Echo and the Tree

The trees in the plantation are dark and heavy; foreboding. They have inherited a green night of their own, pleasant to walk in. Dimly comforting. Outside the sun shines, but in my soul is a darkness to which I am strangely resigned. Why do they thrive and flourish, the great trees, after he who planted them is dead? My father planted them when they were saplings, spindly and delicately green.

And now? My father is a bell that has been tolled; only the echo of an echo and the trees remain. At times it seems there is nothing but the echo and the trees. The soil here is so good that were a man to plant a shaft, in a year's time a cart would grow out of it, my father used to say.

The room that misses my father most is not the room that holds the marriage-bed. All that was over long ago; forgotten by my father. No, the room that always waits for him is lined with the books he lived with; he was a book and tree man. Since his death it has become the room the women speak about but never use. 'Take Tante Sophy's vase – great ugly thing – and put it in the library – it will not be seen in there.' And 'Yes, we have a library. My husband held that "a well-filled mind", and all that. It's a wasted room, really, but what am I to do? Those books . . . those books . . .' And my mother's voice trails off, oppressed by the weight of being a widow with a dower of books.

A vase with no flowers. 'By its flowers a man may know a country,' my father used to say. And flowers have such strange and enchanting names. Crow's Eyes. Warbler. The Little Tears of Our Lady. If I have a daughter I shall call her Little Tear.

But the garden here is coarse and only the sunflowers thrive, like peasant children with heads too large for their rickety legs.

And so, even though I have avoided the library where the books reproach me mutely and the ugly ornaments are sent, I walk in your plantation and I think of you, my father: 'There is never a Monday but it makes way for a Tuesday' – that is what you told me, walking one day under your trees.

And tomorrow I will sit in your library and read your books.

Summer Loving

The Voynitskis' sitting-room was filled with the sound of the bells of the departing horses, drawing the station wagon. It was evening; time for the lamps to be carried in. Little by little, the silver jangle of the bells retreated until they were nothing but a distant shimmer of sound. And after that, strain as he might, Vanya could hear them no more.

They had gone. Vanya turned back to the ledgers which were spread out on the table he was sharing with Sonya, his dead sister's daughter. 'I must work,' he muttered, 'work.' He began to rummage among the bills and letters, picking them up and dropping them down again, making no headway.

'They've gone,' said Sonya. 'We must sit down and work, Uncle Vanya. We have let everything go.' She returned to her abacus. Her hands were red and rough and stumpy, not at all like those of her mother. When there was company she was ashamed of them and tried to hide them by sitting on them.

Astrov, the family doctor, fastened the buckles of his bag. 'They've gone,' he said with something akin to relief: the relief we feel when the dreaded blow has fallen. 'Nothing will tempt the professor back.' He sighed. All that summer, and now, in the late warm autumn, season of exquisite, mournful, late roses, he had been in love with the ailing, querulous old professor's beautiful young wife. How languid, he thought, how languid, and there was an emptiness in him. Now he would spend the remainder of his days with his beloved trees and leave his medicine to God.

He crossed to one of a pair of looking-glasses hanging on the wall. The plump embroidered frames, stitched with gold thread and semi-precious stones, had come in her wooden marriage chest with Sonya's sainted Mamma, and were much admired by Sonya. His face, his face, his driven face, looked lean and even more saturnine than usual, with the drama of the sunset shading it.

And now the old lady, Maria Vassilyevna, hobbled in, the stick without which she dared not launch herself, clenched in her ivory claw. 'They've gone,' she said. She eased herself into her summer armchair, by the window, and returned to the pamphlet she had left open on the ledge. Her back was hunched from a lifetime of pseudo-scholarly pursuits, for she nursed some pretensions to learning though nowadays she had frequently to stop reading, and blink her lids to clear her vision. 'Yes,' she said. 'As I was saying, they've gone.' She settled over her book.

Marina, who had been Uncle Vanya's childhood nurse and did not mean him to forget it, came into the room carrying a lighted lamp. 'They've gone,' she said. She did not sound sorry. Such goings on she had lived through this sultry summer. The professor not stirring, lying in bed till twelve o'clock and the samovar to be kept boiling all the morning waiting for him to ring his bell like the seven devils for his glass of tea. 'Before they came,' she was mumbling, though no-one paid any attention to her, 'we had dinner at one o'clock like other people, but while they were here we didn't have it till six and sometimes seven.' The professor went on all night reading and writing – at his age! – and then all of a sudden ringing his blessed bell at four o'clock in the morning. Goodness me! What now? Tea! People had to be wakened out of their sleep to carry up the samovar. Such behaviour. Man might forget but God would remember.

'Account rendered 2 roubles and 75 kopeks.' Uncle Vanya nodded gloomily causing some ash from his cigarette to fall from his amber holder on to his chest. He did not bother to brush it off. They – she – had gone and his collar was too tight.

Vanya had jibbed violently when the professor had first voiced his plans for the sale:

'My father bought this estate as a dowry for my sainted sister,' Vanya had said, his voice rising with every sentence. 'Until today I have been simple. I thought that to be an honest steward was all that was needed. I did not interpret the laws of inheritance like a Turk. I told myself that my sister's estate would pass to her daughter – intact. And, furthermore, what do you propose to do with your old mother-in-law, and Sonya? What do you propose to do with me? Sonya and I have worked together for ten years – ten years – worked like slaves. We have paid off all the mortgage, have we not, Sonyitchka?'

A farm-worker came in. 'Mihail L'vovitch, your horses are harnessed,' he announced, filled with the importance of his mission.

Sonya ran a red hand across her steamy forehead, brushing away some wisps of hair. 'When shall we see you again, Mihail L'vovitch?' she asked. She asked, but she was quite without expectation of any answer.

'You are not going, Mihail L'vovitch, without your glass of tea?' clucked Marina.

'I don't want any, nurse.'

'Just a drop of vodka, then?'

'Oh, well!' Astrov took the glass and raised it: 'Good luck to you all! Don't come out, there is no need.'

'February the 2nd,' Vanya was writing – his pen needed a new nib. This one caught and scratched. It annoyed him. 'Lenten oil, twenty pounds. February 16th, Lenten oil again. Buck wheat.' There was the sound of departing bells again. 'He has gone,' said Maria Vassilyevna, without looking up from her book. 'He's gone,' said the ancient nurse. She crossed herself. 'He has gone,' said Sonya. With a hasty hand she dashed away the tears that were welling up. The old house settled back on its timeless haunches. They had gone.

But had they? Had they really put the country with its daily walks to the plantation and its tedious weight of boredom behind them for ever? Were they a scatter of autumn leaves floating down from the trees? Or would they return next year, and the year after?

If Vanya could bring off a deal, the slender gains from the sale of the estate might raise, not the wind that blew in from the steppes, as the saying is, but merely a temporary breeze. And another thing, would the questionably halcyon months of a winter in the city alter the Voynitskis in any marked way?

The professor, for instance, would he not be called to his last
account one of those summer dawns, and his young widow be
left to harvest the hay with anyone she fancied?

Yes, one of those early mornings, now that summer had come
round again, before the sun rose, the silence of the sleeping
household would be broken by the clanging and the jangling of
the bell in the best bedroom, for man owes God a death, and
this time the summons would not be for the samovar. But who
was going to believe that?

The beautiful Yelena, at the summons of her dying husband's
bell, yawned. She pulled on her dressing-gown, slipped her rosy
toes into her mules, and crossed automatically to her looking-
glass. It was only Alexandr Vladimirovitch ringing for his tea at
four o'clock in the morning again.

She felt for her hairbrush and, with her eyes still closed,
brushed her heavy hair with languid strokes. She had been
dreaming of last summer. Last summer she had been in love, or
at least on the brink of being in love, with her demonic doctor.
Ah, what a fascinating man! And he has a spark of genius –
genius! Boldness! Freedom of mind! Width of outlook! Of
course, she herself clung so to respectability. She was like that
woman in the play by Ibsen. Heidi, was it? Hedwige? Hedda?
'Well, anyway,' she gazed into the reflection of the two placid
pools that were her eyes. It was true, the thing that she most
loved after her own beauty and the effect it had on men was her
respectability. People were sorry for her – such a beautiful
young woman thrown away on an arid and ageing academic.
'Poor thing! She has got an old husband!' Even Sonya, her
stepdaughter, thought she had married out of prudence. That
as well, of course. But had she not married Alexandr for love?
Or what, at the time she had thought was love, attracted to him
as a learned, most distinguished scholar and man. Was it her
fault that this 'love' was a foolish dream, a story she had made
up in her mind? Her lids covered their accusing image in the
mirror. She gave her, hair another languid stroke with the
brush. What was it that Vanya called her? Indolent: 'You are
too indolent to live! Ah, how indolent!' And he had looked at
her in the way she could not endure. He had eaten her with his

famished – well, hungry – eyes: 'To deceive an old husband whom one can't endure is immoral; but to try to stifle your pitiful youth and living feelings – that's not immoral?' he had mocked.

Even to think of her own beauty thrown away brought the tears welling into Yelena's eyes. One tear hung like a diamond on her eyelash. Pretty.

Her doctor had a weary, sensitive face. But for some reason she had been very shy with him at the beginning of last summer. Sonya was in love with him; that was plain to see. She is in love with him and I pity her. He does not love her, that's evident. She is not good-looking, but she would make a capital wife for a country doctor. In the midst of desperate boredom, poor girl, with nothing but grey shadows wandering about, with only dull commonplaces from people who can do nothing but eat, drink and sleep, he appears on the scene, unlike the rest, handsome, interesting, fascinating, a bright moon rising in the darkness. Even now I am smiling as I think of him! 'The trouble with Astrov,' said Yelena to the image in her looking-glass, 'is that he is in love with trees – trees, I tell you – and perhaps a little with me. His is a very interesting character. Deep, complicated. A wood demon, yet no less a man.'

Sonya, awakened by the bell's jangling summons, was looking at herself in the dressing-table mirror. 'Oh, how awful it is that I am not beautiful! How awful! I know I am not. I know it! I . . . last Sunday, as people were coming out of the church, I heard them talking about me, and one woman said, "She has a sweet and generous nature, but what a pity she is so plain!"' She buried her hot face in her hands, that face of hers, shiny and, she thought, hideous.

Vanya, when the professor's last summer came, was still up, drinking with the doctor.

Dr Astrov was swaying over the professor's medicines assembled on his sitting-room table. 'Medicines,' he said, his speech slurred. 'I have had nothing to eat all day, only,' he laughed – a rare sound coming from this tormented man, 'drink.' He drank. 'Medicines,' he said again. 'Prescriptions,' he tried to say, 'all those – exactly. From Harkov. From Moscow. From . . .' Man was better left to God. Now, had the professor been a tree . . . Astrov lost the thread.

Vanya had been thinking of the recent summer's storm. It had alarmed Yelena. She had been frightened by the thunder, terrified by the lightning. 'I should have held her in my arms,' he told himself. He drank. 'Don't be frightened, I am here.' He nodded owlishly. The doctor nodded back. He did not know why. 'Ten years ago I used to meet her at my sainted sister's. Then she was seventeen and I,' he drank, 'thirty-seven. Why didn't I marry her at that time? By now she would have been my wife.' He sighed profoundly.

'You are in love with the professor's lady,' said the doctor. He drank.

'She is my friend.'

'A woman becomes a man's friend only in the following sequence: First,' he tried to tick it off upon his index finger. He missed. 'First, an agreeable acquaintance, then your mistress, then your friend.'

Sonya hurried in on her way to answer her father's last summons. She took in the two of them. Dishevelled, owlish. 'Uncle Vanya, you have been drinking with the doctor again. Why do you do it? It isn't suitable at your age.'

'I get drunk like this once a month,' the doctor said, quite without shame. 'I don't stick at anything then! I undertake the most difficult operations and do them capitally. I make the most expansive plans for the future. But when I'm sober,' he drank to banish the thought – it would not go. 'Sober,' he repeated, 'at night I lie under the bedclothes in continual terror of being dragged out to a patient.' He mopped his mouth. 'Ugh! What a huge moustache I have grown. A stupid moustache. There is nothing I want. Nothing I care about, no one I am fond of.'

'Except . . .' said Vanya. There was no need to speak the name.

'Except . . .' Dr Astrov agreed.

Vanya became tearful. 'Ever since the professor and his languid wife have been here, our quiet, purposeful existence has been turned topsy . . .' he tried again: 'topsy . . . upside down,' he achieved. 'I sleep at the wrong time, I eat . . . messes . . .'

'What?' asked the doctor. 'What do you eat?'

'Food,' said Vanya. 'Too rich. And I drink wine. Not good for me. Sonya and I used to work in grand style, but now Sonitchka works alone while I eat and drink and . . . and . . .' he waved an expressive arm, 'moon!' He slumped. How lovely she was! How lovely! But she had mermaid's blood in her veins.

The bell in the best bedroom had clamoured for attention for the last time, its rope tugged by a panic-stricken hand. The Voynitski household, unhurried, unaware of finality, gathered to drink nocturnal tea with the peevish invalid, as it thought; the old nurse grumbling as usual; Vanya owlish; his mother, too, awake – for she slept but little – and not averse to a glass of tea, whatever the hour. Sonya was conscious of not looking her honestly shining best. Who would have thought the doctor would be up drinking to all hours of the night with Uncle Vanya? Highly unsuitable in a man so noble, so admirable in every other way.

Last the languid Yelena, totally resigned. And all of them taking the summons for granted, part of the intolerable weight of summer in the country.

At the sight of the figure inert on the bed the doctor came to his semi-sobered senses. In the thrall of silence that had descended on the Family Voynitski he went about his professional routine. 'He's gone,' he said, relieved.

'Gone,' echoed the comatose Vanya. He rummaged in his mind but all it yielded up was a rather ribald couplet from Byron. He decided against voicing it in the circumstances.

'Gone to his sainted wife,' said his mother-in-law, not without a certain grim satisfaction, 'his first wife, my daughter, God took to live with Him.'

'Gone,' said the other old woman, Uncle Vanya's nurse. 'Well, well, well,' she crossed herself.

'Is he . . . is he . . .?' Sonya, unable to finish her question took refuge in childhood and chewed the end of her pig-tail. She ought to be feeling something in the face of the death of her father but she felt only remorse, a childish, unreasoning remorse.

There was a thud. The young widow had fainted. It was expected of her. The Family Voynitski scattered in search of smelling salts.

Once more it was summer. The bells of the approaching horses drawing the station wagon grew from a distant shimmer of sound until it filled the Voynitskis' sitting-room. 'She's come back,' said Vanya, 'she's here!' He even rose to greet Yelena.

'Here to unsettle us all,' said his old nurse. 'Here to turn night into day, God help us!'

She's come back, thought Sonya. Come back to flirt with Doctor Astrov – to marry him, maybe. The thought was a dull ache in her heart. Aloud, she said: 'She's here, Grand'mère.' The old lady looked up from a pamphlet – it had arrived from Petersburg only last month. 'You said something–' she blinked.

The old house seemed just the same – its single virtue in the eyes of Yelena. And the Voynitskis. Her mother-in-law blinking up at her, frowning slightly, as though called from her pamphlet against her will, for was not Yelena *la seconde* and let her not forget it! Vanya, grey and tousled, his suit a monument to the ashes of the cigarettes he had consumed. His old nurse bobbing a stiff-jointed obeisance. The young widow was no chick of her upbringing and must be made to feel this . . . 'Each to her own,' she muttered. Absently, Yelena patted her shoulder.

Sonya, a little awkwardly, kissed Yelena on both cheeks. Then she turned to the old nurse. 'Tell Yacob to carry Yelena Andreyevna's trunks to her usual room – we thought you would feel more at home in your old room. But the best room can be prepared if you . . .'

'By no means, Sonitchka.' Yelena drew off her ridiculously formal widow's veils. They were no longer appropriate. In fact she had only resumed them to stand well in the eyes of the family, since she was forced to return to the country, to economise. A young widow alone had so many calls on her purse, urgent calls. Astrov was not yet here. But he would arrive. Ah yes, he would arrive. It was early in the summer, but already the bees were having their way with the flowers. Soon Astrov would be ardent to have his way with her. He would not understand! He could not understand. Was it her fault that her beauty plagued men's senses?

Indeed, the doctor was driving over to the Voynitskis' even as Sonya and the old nurse unpacked her finery.

'Silk,' clucked the old woman.

'A gown with a Paris label,' breathed Sonya, overawed.

Grimly the old woman stowed away the filmy underwear and elegant *deshabillé*.

For an ardent suitor Astrov was feeling strangely loath. Was it his fault that women lost their heads over him? Head over heels in love, or its equivalent, they tumbled if he held out his little finger. And afterwards it was fetch this, and carry that, and marry me, like as not, and after that you could kiss your hand to your trees. Give a woman an inch and she takes a *verst* as the saying is. But there were fewer and fewer forests. Man could heat his stoves with peat and build his barns with brick. Why destroy the forests? One would be a thoughtless savage to burn its beauty in the stove. When I walk by the woods which I have saved from cutting down, when I hear the rustling of the young copse planted by my own hands, I feel that if, in a thousand years man is to be happy I, too, shall have had some small part in it, the wood demon justified his thoughts. When I plant a birch tree and see it growing, green and swaying in the wind, my soul is filled with pride. How could a woman as idle – as languorous – as Yelena Andreyedna understand that I must be left free as a forest creature to cherish my trees? Ah, but she must understand! Understand that ours must be a summer loving. It will change with the seasons. As for me, my wedding-bells were hung upon a birch tree, as the old song goes.

On the afternoon of the next day, or the day after that – who counts time in the country? – Yelena was sauntering in the plantation with Sonya. They were speaking, when they spoke at all, disjointedly, a lady with a parasol and a girl with a kerchief over her head like a peasant, each following her own train of thought. Each led to Astrov.

Yelena was smiling at her thoughts of him. She had gone back to that scene in the first of the summers in the country.

'You know perfectly well what brings me here,' Astrov had said, and indeed at that time she felt she knew and she had been glad. 'You charming bird of prey, do not look at me like that, I am an old sparrow! Here have I been doing nothing for a whole month. I have dropped everything to seek you greedily. That pleases you. But I am going away today. I won't come back again. How wonderful, how magnificent you are! One kiss,' he had begged, 'if I could only kiss your fragrant hair! Those hands – what hands,' and in spite of her faint struggles he had seized and kissed them.

Ah, what a *frisson* even now as she relived the scene. But that had been the first of the country summers. And then, the oafish look on Vanya's face, as she had settled into Astrov's arms and he had buried his face in her hair, and Vanya had stood there in the doorway, clutching the bunch of late autumn roses that clearly it was now too late to give her. Yelena laughed aloud at the chagrin in his face, the whole posture, of simple-hearted Vanya – a man born out of time, condemned by his own foolishness to live out of time with the essential pendulum of fate. A man of elevated ideas which raised up nobody. A man who could not sleep at night for rage and vexation that he had so foolishly wasted the days when he might have had everything for which his parched heart thirsted now, when it was too late – every Russian family had one such clown in it.

'You are laughing,' said Sonya, bringing her back to the plantation here and now.

'Some foolishness of Astrov's.'

'He is not a foolish man. He is noble, intellectual. And compassionate.' Sonya spoke forcefully. 'Mihail L'vovitch plants fresh trees every year – think of the labour – and already they have sent him a Bronze Medal and a Diploma. He tries to prevent the old forests being destroyed. He says that trees teach man to develop a lofty attitude of mind. And then he says forests temper the severity of the climate. In countries where the climate is mild people are beautiful and sensitive. Art and learning flourish among them and their attitude to women is full of refined courtesy.'

'Refined courtesy,' Yelena pondered, 'so!'

She must return to town, she thought, return as soon as she had gleaned a little money, return to a pair of hungry arms and perhaps, when her lover was secure in her love, which would be lifelong naturally, secure in his marriage to her, he would not squander her money in the merry, feckless manner of last winter. And then they could come back to the country every summer and save – save – or at least replenish her purse. And everything here would be as it was, as it had always been. The

Voynitski estate would still not have found a purchaser, and would be waiting here, a summer haven to them both. Sonya would still be in love with the doctor who would still be in love with her, Yelena, for she could not endure to part with the wood demon's love, even though, married to a young husband she had no further use for it. Uncle Vanya would still be a man of ash and pratfalls – the clown of the family – and on the evening of their arrival the household Voynitski would be filled, like a chime of welcome, with their glad cries: 'They're back! They're back! They're back!'

But Yelena, who loved to see her perfect beauty reflected in men's faces, saw that she must step softly with Astrov and Vanya too, if she wanted to continue to queen it over these summer creatures of hers. Though Vanya, of course, was Two-and-Twenty Misfortunes personified. The way when he shot at her sainted husband he had missed him – twice. Well, that was a foolish thing to do. And highly reprehensible.

And roughly at around the time she was thinking of how gently she would let the change in her affections dawn on the doctor, Astrov was thinking that he must let her see, but with the utmost delicacy, that now she was a widow she must allow her respectability to whistle down the wind – it was a petit-bourgeois tenet anyway – and not insist on marriage, another bourgeois conception; for where was the hand so strong and at the same time so soft, that could break in a wood demon, domesticate him?

And, as the ladies strolled through the dazzle of green, broken by slanting shafts of sunshine, now narrow, now wide, as the blessed breeze gently lifted the leaves on the branches of the sleepy trees, Sonya was dreaming of the future – a future that neither she, nor Uncle Vanya would be here to share, nor Yelena – not even Doctor Astrov.

'We shall work for others, both now and in our old age, and have no rest,' the young girl half-dreamed. It was the eternal half-dream of the Russian Intelligentsia, though in her simplicity she was following her thought slowly and painfully. 'And when our time comes we shall die without a murmur' (that is to say, she thought, that Uncle Vanya would be sure to grumble quite a bit at finding his life had slipped by and he on his deathbed). 'And there, beyond the grave, we shall say that we have suffered and wept. Life has been bitter to us, but God will have pity on us. We shall look back on these troubles of ours with tenderness, with a smile, we shall rest. We shall hear the angels; we shall see all heaven lit with radiance.'

The lovely young widow glanced at the girl. The leaves and the sun cast a shimmering nimbus round her head and for the moment she looked serene as a saint. How terrible it must be not to be beautiful, thought Yelena.

The Black Moth

The night Anton Pavlovitch died there was a storm. It tossed and swung the branches of the trees that grew around the house in a clearing on the edge of the Black Forest. But earlier the sky had been calm, the birds, all living things, were still. The world had been waiting for the rain. Olga, his young wife, was restless. She was always restless in the early evening, the time when the curtain would rise at the theatre, when the play would begin without her. She was beautiful but she was torn. She hated the country, where she could feel her youth, her talent, her friends, and the parties that went on far into the night and at which she felt she was the acknowledged Queen, slipping through her white fingers. The country was a waste of life. But to be away from her husband who was always ill, always dying, would be a waste too. Who would then write parts – true, fulfilling parts for her?

'Man owes God a death.' Although Anton Pavlovitch had been dying all his adult life, for he was tuberculous and coughed his days and nights away, no-one was expecting the good Lord to call and collect that particular evening. Not here in Badenweiler, the Spa to which the specialist had sent the distinguished writer, away from the lifelong love-hate affair he pursued with Russia and the Russians. 'Olga,' he urged, for he knew it was approaching the hard time of day for her, 'why do you not take a turn or so in the air, my sweet little linnet, my dear remarkable little half,' and since she still hesitated, 'my peerless pony.'

When with the first flurry of rain shining on her hair she returned, it was to find him lying in his dressing-gown on the chaise-longue. A few days ago there had been a heart-attack, but tonight he felt a little stronger and very calm. He had written his handful of plays and his armful of short stories. He had watched and noted and been beguiled and at the same time exasperated by the characters he had created. They were his children, his infuriating children, loved as much for their faults as for their virtues, funny, sad and passing away. He had never ceased to warn them of the holocaust that was throwing its dark shadow before it into foreseen history, and would some day sweep them and their kind, their indolent, garrulous, childlike kind, from the face of the earth. As a writer, as a doctor, as a human being, he had earned his moment of calm. The servant would depart in peace. But now his Olga was hovering about the room, his dear wonderful little actress, lost in her need for distraction. He leaned back against his pillows and, to amuse her, retold her favourite among his short stories . . . 'One day, sitting on the terrace of Vernet's restaurant, Gurov saw a young woman walking along the promenade: she was fair, not very tall, and wore a toque. Behind her trotted a white Pomeranian . . .'

Shortly after midnight he roused her. 'Send for the doctor,' he said. It was the first time he had ever asked her to summon help. Four hours later the German doctor arrived – almost he might have been a Russki. The writer sipped the champagne the doctor had ordered, smiled his benignly tolerant smile at his enchantress Olga, and died at the age of forty-four. And from now on it seemed that his pen had plotted his *funérailles*.

Even as his widow was trying to console herself with the reflection that she would be done with his possessive mother and jealous sister for ever, a great black moth flew out of the storm into the room and hurled itself repeatedly against the lamp and walls – the symbol of a writer in conflict with society? Then, in sympathy with the storm that swayed the trees of the forest, as though released by the gales the champagne cork exploded from the bottle – a spirit freed.

And now the funeral took on the features of a farce. The coffin was carried to Moscow in a refrigerated van marked Oysters. It arrived on the platform at the same time as that of a General killed in the Russo-Japanese war. A military band struck up. The two parties of mourners milling about the platform became inextricably mixed. Many of the writer's relatives marched away in the General's procession by mistake. The depleted cortège came to a halt in front of the theatre where the playwright's tragi-comedies were performed. A vast crowd of mourners joined it – for once a prophet was being honoured in his own country. The crowd of mourners did not include his immediate family, for in spite of their mounting hysteria the authorities had refused them standing room on the steps. Crowds attract crowds. By now the pavements on the route were overflowing into the procession.

Angered by the general turmoil, Gorky, the writer, and Chaliapin, the singer with the tolling chest-notes, hurled abuse in the jagged fangs of total disorder. All along the route the swollen cortège plodding on to the Monastery was joined by every kind of jostling onlooker willing to jam by sheer numbers the gateway to the grave, preventing the pall-bearers and sorely tried family from going any farther.

Soon the cemetery was storm-tossed and trampled over by unceremonious guests in a great wave of cracked and broken headstones and the trodden-in remains of flowers.

Can it be doubted that somewhere Chekhov was smiling his patient, tolerant smile?

IN COMPANY ABROAD

Claudie or A State of Soul

Frenchwomen have, on the whole, small bones; small pointed faces; small well-docketed minds. When they are young they have small figures. When they are older they have small meals, long corsets. The general effect, then, remains the same – save from the shoulders up, the ankles down! In France a woman of the world does not grow to be an old woman – just an older woman. Age is a state of soul that only the very poor Frenchwoman can afford.

At any age the Frenchwoman will choose her clothes with care. Her husband, Fate, in the form of her instinctive prudence, chooses for her. Beneath the high-powered lacquer of her Gallic frivolity there is no more serious minded woman than your frivolous Frenchwoman.

An Englishwoman enters a restaurant – a Frenchwoman makes an entrance – the difference is profound. For where your Englishwoman may be self-conscious, your Frenchwoman will be sex-conscious. It helps.

Her name? Well, it could be Madeleine? Germaine? Claudine? . . . Yes, Claudine – or rather Claudie.

So here she is then, this Claudie, a pretty little girl of seven or so, with a pretty little pointed face, potting-out sand-pies on the *plage*, while the Maman, a pretty little woman with a pretty pointed face, too, sits fending off the sun with a practical parasol. Her age? Well, shall we say she's in her twenties? That can mean anything up to thirty, after all.

Her name? Why Claudie . . . yes, *die* – why not? One is still in one's twenties . . .

Little Claudie's voice floats over to us now, light and clear across the sands.

'... *Je m'appelle Claudie ... Claud-die ... die ...* DIE!'

The infant matelot who has been potting-out sand-pies with her says something.

'*Non! Je ne suis pas Claud-dine,*' she stamps her foot. '*Die ... die ...* DIE,' she insists.

The infant matelot nods. It is quite evident to him that she is *die*.

When Claudie becomes Claudine it will indeed be a step.

Maman now rises, clicks-to her parasol:

'*Viens,* Claudie,' she says. There is something in the way she says it that commands instant obedience.

A voice calls after them. It is a man's voice, also authoritative, but rather muffled for it comes from beneath the black cloth, that covers the top of a tripod camera.

The Claudies turn. The Claudies smooth the tartan sashes of their morning muslins.

The Papa bobs from under. He is a little flushed.

'Look at the dickie-bird,' he implores.

Sedately, toothily, the Claudies smile.

Time passes by as unremarkable as a chip of drift-wood floating in on the waves – one wave like another; one year like another. Claudie goes to school – a day school, for the jeune fille's sphere lies well within the Maman's orbit – the Maman takes care of that. Then, on a day like any other day, Claudie has left her school. She stays at home or goes out with the Maman. Claudie has now fulfilled her early promise – her threat the ill-natured would have it – to be a second Madame C. '*On dirait, plutôt, deux soeurs,*' the well-intentioned say. But they say it with diminishing conviction.

For those routine waves upon the shores of time, those days like any other days, have succeeded one another relentlessly and the Maman, she has become thirty – a thing that can happen to any woman of forty which there is no turning back. Soon she must be Claudine – yes, *dine*.

As for Claudie, she is about to take a step, too. For Claudie has met her Fate.

The truth is that they met some paragraphs ago, potting-out sand-pies, Claudie and her Jacquot. Since when, the Maman has never allowed herself, however much provoked, to lose sight

of the social advantages that marriage to an avocat has to offer –
nor has her oppposite number ceased to swallow her pride and
with it the handsome *dot* that Claudie has brought with her. As
simple as this are the workings of Fate.

So now here they are, Claudie and Jacquot, driving clipper-
clopper off in a cloud of confetti, a thoroughly prudent match.

After the honeymoon, also pretty prudent, for Claudie has her
misgivings and Jacquot has been taught to reverence Woman-
hood by his Maman – herself a woman, as she has without
doubt frequently reminded him – after, then, this polite, this
refined, this gentlemanly, this almost maidenly honeymoon,
our married couple return, he to his exigent mistress ('A mistress is not a woman, she is a creature, *voyons!*' – Maxims of la
Maman, Sentiment 27), Claudie to the further tutelage of
Claudine – yes, dine . . . dine . . . *dine* – ah, well, it had to
happen one day, why not now? To the little apartment in the
block next door – a nest for little love-birds in the shade of the
old poplar tree – the Maman has taken care of that, also.

In the second year comes Danger Point.

This is when for the first time Claudie finds out that Jacquot
has been unfaithful.

She packs her bags and unpacks her heart to the Maman.
But Claudine only chides her Claudie tenderly.

'*Mais voyons, ma petite,* it is a man not an angel you have
married. And men . . .'

'It is not a man,' says Claudie, 'it is a monster!'

'It is for you to prove to this "Monster" what a good wife he
has by hearing . . . nothing, seeing . . . nothing. Knowing . . .
nothing.'

Claudie sobs.

'And by not spoiling your pretty looks making a mountain
out of a *maîtresse*. These little Distractions . . . they pass . . . they
pass . . .' says Claudine comfortably. 'They have no importance – once they are safely over.'

'Safely . . .' Claudie sobs a little louder.

'What is important,' Claudine continues, 'what is absolutely indispensable is that it is to you, his little wife, that he returns . . .'

'Never!' says Claudie explosively.

'And also that with it a jewel . . . an automobile . . .'

'He can keep his beastly presents,' says Claudie with conviction. 'No woman of spirit . . .'

'Tt – tt — tt – what a child it is! How do you suppose I got my turquoise necklace, my squirrel coat, and all my diamond rings – real stones – ' says Claudine, flashing them, 'from your father?'

'Then Papa . . .' gasps Claudie, pop-eyed.

'Then Papa . . .' Claudine agrees smoothly.

'And you found out?'

'As to that,' said Claudine, 'I have made my rule to go to quite extraordinary lengths never to hear. Never to see. Never to know – not even to suspect. And always to be around when he returns. This is indispensable.'

'Oh, Maman!'

'It is the least of things,' says Claudine, flashing her real stones.

And this is how Claudie came to acquire her seed pearls.

But not the little gold locket on the charm bracelet – the kind of trinket she might have kept from schoolroom days – the kind of trinket a husband would never question – would not notice. For in the fourth year of the marriage Claudie finds her own Distraction.

And after this? Well to begin with, Claudie comes to tire of her Distraction, finds another – others. Then the Distractions take to tiring of Claudie.

And one day, suddenly, Claudie becomes Claudine, and Claudine? Why she is Grand'mère.

A few years pass and Jacquot's Distractions start to tire of him. The summer finds him entirely undistracted. Hey ho!

And so it is his wife who accompanies him on the trip to the Italian Lakes. Attractive woman, his wife – for her age – men turn to look at her as she passes to her table. Women envy her the solitaire emerald, three-string pearl necklace, diamond clip, ermine wrap and the many fascinating charms on her bracelet.

In fact the trip is quite a second honeymoon.

A Frenchwoman takes a smaller size in shoes than an English, Italian or American woman.

She counts the price before she buys and assures herself of the durability of the article.

A Frenchwoman's best friend is the little dressmaker, shoemaker, coiffeur, around the corner.

And Frenchwomen, sensing that there is a pattern in life, content themselves in living it. The pattern is the same – the colours vary.

And Claudine's daughter?

She is called Claudie – die – *die*, the little creature, skipping about the *plage*, and the Maman, lying in the sun, ignores her.

She will grow up, this skinny little girl, and go to day school. And then come home to help her in the house – unless she becomes Head Vendeuse to a Fashion House – starting in its boutique.

Times change but not people.

The Maman now rises.

'*Viens*, Claudie,' she says. She is nut-brown all over save for the two striped apples of her bra, the striped triangle of her bikini.

A voice calls after her. It is a man's voice.

'Claudine – Eh! – Claudine . . .' he calls. The Maman swings on her hip, one foot carefully placed before the other to give her form allure. One hand on hip – one raised to the horizon as though hailing tomorrow – the one with the bracelet thickly hung with charms.

Click goes the Papa's camera. '*Alors?*' he grunts.

'And now take Claudie with me,' says the Maman.

No, people don't change – it's just their state of soul.

Just Another Party

The Palazzo, when at length it was located, proved to be a vast pile of a proud but needy grandeur, pink in parts.

The Vanderveldts looked small and somehow defenceless, standing before it on the marble steps; and Lally Buchanan felt some compunction at driving off to join her Pa-in-law at his cosy pensione, leaving the poor pets alone with their Palazzo.

The Vanderveldts were the nicest young couple. Jan was Assistant Master at St Jude's, the prep school on the lees with the canary caps, and Hildegarde was the Head's daughter. Marriage was made for them. And now they'd been lent this Palazzo in Arracoelia, the Constantinople of the Adriatic, for the long vacation, a loan they could not have afforded to accept were it not that Lally Buchanan had this new – well, nearly new – car, and was mad to take it on the Continent.

So there they stood, the poppets, almost afraid to enter their dilapidated paradise.

Lally sought for something heartening to say before abandoning her Vanderveldts to their Palazzo. Now that the time to part had come the little rubs and irks that are an inescapable part of human relationships had faded into an over-all rosiness, like the once-bright bricks of the Palazzo.

'You could give a heavenly party here,' said Lally.

'Could we?' said Hildegarde.

'Heavenly,' repeated Lally with her usual firmness, and drove smartly off, feeling pretty peeled-apple without her friendly five-day hairshirt of economising Vanderveldts.

By nightfall Jan and Hildegarde had risen above their amplitude of apartments. They decided to camp out n the coolest of the seven salons. It had a balcony over the azure Adriatic. What more could they want? Except, perhaps, currency . . .

Next morning Hildegarde settled down to write the first of her letters home, sitting at the elaborately gilded, deep blue lapis table, with the breakfast things way over the other end, while Jan went off for a dip.

'. . . The Palazzo is very picturesque,' wrote Hildegarde as Jan splashed and spluttered his way out to an adjacent raft.

The raft was already occupied and the man on it gave Jan a hand up.

'Good heavens!' he said.

'Good heavens!' said Jan. He brushed the trickles from his eyes.

'How many years is it?' they said together.

They lay there looking out over the azure Adriatic and catching up on one another's lives until it was time to race back to shore. They towelled down. They lit up.

'There's the Palazzo,' said Jan. He pointed.

His friend was suitably impressed.

'It's pretty palatial,' he observed.

Jan preened. 'We're thinking of giving a party,' he said. 'You must come to it.'

Lally Buchanan had settled in by this time, too. She and Pa-in-law adored one another. He was so young-at-heart – so readily amusable.

'You'll love the Vanderveldts,' she said. 'They're going to give a marvellous party for us!'

'What fun!' said Pa-in-law. 'I wonder if we could persuade the old Principessa to come. She adores parties.'

'Surely,' said Lally, equally light of heart.

The old Principessa lived in a single room above the tram-tracks of the Via Nerone. It must have been an age since the peeled green shutters had been flung open to admit the noise and dust.

She brightened considerably at the mention of the Vander-eldts' party:

'A Ridotto,' she said, 'at the Palazzo – but it will be sensational! In costume, of course,' she added, for she still possessed a kimono.

'Of course,' said Pa-in-law.

'But why do you invite an old woman like me?' said the Principessa. But she said it from force of habit. Her mind was on more important things.

That afternoon, when the sky had cooled off a little, the Principessa took a drive in the carozza which she usually sent out to ply for hire at this hour, choosing to clipper-clopper not along the coast road where the air was so restoring, but into the huddled town.

She called first at the pastry-cook's to whom in any case she owed some money – by no means her usual practice in such matters.

'Signor Luigi,' she said, 'it may already have reached your ears that my rich friends who have taken the Palazzo are to give a Ridotto.'

'A Ridotto!'

'Everybody who is anybody will be there.'

'Indeed?'

'And it is I who am to make the arrangements.'

'Aha!'

'If I,' said the Principessa, 'persuade my rich friends to place their orders with you, you on your side will add to their bill the usual?'

'Twenty-five per cent,' said Signor Luigi. His grin was at its widest.

'And furthermore,' said the Principessa, 'that small account which has slipped my attention for a month or so . . .'

'A year or so,' Signor Luigi corrected the Principessa – but he made the correction under his breath. 'As to that, Altezza, the sum is trifling and the bill was sent in error. I shall speak sharply to my wife.'

'Do that,' said the Principessa, who did not like her. 'Then it is understood?'

'It is understood,' said Signor Luigi.

And after this the Principessa made herself understood at both the poulterers and all the wine shops, also the perfumerie, and the two silk stores, and finally the entire market-place.

And before long Hildegarde was writing home:

'. . . The tradespeople are most obliging. They call for orders every day. But their prices do seem rather high . . .'

'Well, what can you expect?' said Pa-in-law, called in for confirmation on this point. 'After all, it's the "high" season.'

But only Lally laughed.

Ah, well!

Soon Hildegarde was writing home again:

'. . . Arracoelia is such a friendly place. The people here don't wait to be introduced, but come right up and make themselves known.'

And even as she wrote the words the door-bell jangled.

A leather lady and a plump port-winish gent were waiting on the portico. They looked so much like the Right Kind of Parent that Hildegarde felt homesick instantly.

'We are the Jedburghs,' announced the leather lady. 'This is my husband, Colonel Jedburgh, and . . .'

'And you must be Lady Athene Jedburgh; won't you come in?' said Hildegarde hastily, for even she knew that the Jedburghs were the leaders of the English Colony. 'My husband has gone swimming, but he'll be back quite soon . . .'

The raft, however, had been crowded that morning. Jan's swimming chum had brought along a bunch of buddies. And they'd brought along their Biff-Ball. Jan was jolly good at Biff-Ball. But at last he tore himself away.

'So long,' he called. 'See you at the party!'

'You bet,' they assured him.

Hildegarde told Jan about the Jedburghs over lunch.

'I asked them to the party,' she said, 'and they've promised to drop in for a few minutes.'

'I say,' Jan pushed aside his pizza practically untasted. 'You shouldn't have done that, Hildy. You really cannot go round asking people – just like that! If we're not jolly careful there'll be a crowd.'

'It's my party just as much as yours!' said Hildegarde, and at once felt unworthy.

'Of course it is, darling. But we've got to consider the financial angle, you know. I was adding up on my way home, and I made it eleven not counting us!'

'Or the Jedburghs,' said Hildegarde. 'Oh dear!'

'One thing,' Jan consolded himself, 'Spumante's jolly cheap out here.'

'But, man alive, you can't ask the Principessa to drink Spumante!' Pa-in-law looked quite appalled.

'The Principessa?'

'I'll explain about her later,' said Pa-in-law. 'And anyway, the English Colony is expected to provide champagne.'

'Champagne,' said Hildegarde in a hollow voice.

'Come now, children,' Pa-in-law coaxed, 'it's cheap- enough – if you buy it by the crate.'

That night a newcomer arrived at Pa-in-law's pensione.

He was something to do with the film that was on location at Arracoelia.

'A party, you tell me,' the film executive bellowed, 'why, that'll be great – just great! So who'll I take along? Doan' tell me, folk, doan' Tell me, lemme guess – I got it – none other than Chime Bellfry! Yipee!'

'The film star?' Lally was intrigued. But would she bother, I wonder? I mean, it's just another party!'

The film executive had no need to square his jaw.

'Sure Chime'll bother if I say so – and that goes for her damn lion, too!'

Pa-in-law caught Lally's eye. Pa-in-law winked. Pa-in-law was so amusable.

Still, it was just as well he'd insisted on champagne, as things were turning out.

Next day the printer called at the Palazzo with the invitation cards. He displayed them proudly. He was particularly pleased with his English:

'Mr and Madama Wanderweld rechesdta de pleasiore, etcetera, etcetera . . .' The printer muttered the words devoutly as the Vanderveldts read unbelievingly on.

'But look here, who ordered these things? Did you, Hildy?'

'Jan, are you crazy?'

The printer broke into a babble. The word Principessa bounced out of it several times. Then he dumped the carton of invitations on the lapis table and fled.

Jan shook out the cards and with tight lips he counted:

'Four hundred and forty-nine and one in your hand makes fifty,' he announced. 'Hildy, we don't have to use them all, do we?'

Hildegarde burst into tears.

And that left the Principessa fifty invitations to sell on the black market.

Bravo!

The morning that the Deputation called at the Palazzo, the letter from the bank at home containing the usual unsought information, caught up with Jan. It would!

'Hildy,' he said, 'I fear we'll have to slum it for a bit, when we get home.'

'Okay,' said Hildegarde, comfortably. Slumming it had, so far, only meant the television instead of a cinema on a Thursday night, when Father took Prep.

Then the door bell jangled.

Three wide gents in three wide hats introduced themselves. The Mayor, the Harbour Master and the Fire Chief. They had called, they announced, to finalise arrangements for the water pageant.

'The water pageant?' asked Hildegarde, quite sharply.

'The procession of the fishing boats on the night of the party,' said the Mayor.

'At midnight,' said the Harbour Master.

'With fireworks,' said the Fire Chief.

'But,' said Jan, 'it's just a party – not a coronation.'

'For eleven people – not counting the Jedburghs!' Hildegarde sounded desperate.

'Impossible!' exclaimed the Deputation.

'A private party in the high season at Arracoelia,' the Mayor raised his hands to the heavens, 'and you really think that this will be permitted?' he demanded.

'Without the pageant of the fishing fleet?' queried the Harbour Master.

'All lit up!' tempted the Fire Chief.

'And the blessing of His Eminence the Cardinal,' said the Mayor. 'This is already looked after.'

'By whom?' said Jan. He sounded hostile.

'By His Eminence the Cardinal,' explained the Mayor patiently.

'And the serenade by the massed choirs of the Acadamento,' said the Harbour Master.

'What voices!' breathed the Mayor.

'And the fireworks,' said the Fire Chief.

'The Signora herself shall give away the prizes,' said the mayor, who was of a generous nature.

'The prizes!' gasped Hildegarde.

'Solid silver cups in every class,' said the Harbour Master.

But even then Jan failed to brighten.

'That's all very fine,' he said, 'but who is going to pay the piper?'

Wide-eyed the Deputation stared at him.

'A midnight regatta,' said Pa-in-law ecstatically. 'It's fabulous!'

'I was afraid it would be,' said Jan.

The Vanderveldts, who had been invited to dine ao dine at the pensione, were taking an apéritif in Pa-in-law's bedroom.

'Why ever didn't we think of it before?' said Pa-in-law.

'It'll be such a beautiful sight,' said Lally.

'So will my overdraft,' said Jan.

'The fireworks alone would cost the earth,' said Hildegarde.

'Sure to,' said Pa-in-law placidly. 'The Fire Chief in these parts is by way of being the local agent for a fireworks firm and the insurance company!'

'The thing is out of the question,' snapped Jan.

Pa-in-law rounded on him. 'Man alive,' he protested, 'you can't expect to have a party without paying for it. This is a sterling area, remember!'

'Time we went in to dinner,' said Lally tactfully. 'A lot of people here are just dying to meet you both. You know,' she broke it lightly, 'the entire pensione is simply living for the party!'

Dinner was terrible. So was coffee.

But just as Lally rose to fetch the canasta cards, the film executive came in.

He greeted the Vanderveldts with enthusiasm.

'It sure is good to meet you,' he said. 'And I've news for you – great news! Your little old party's going to hit the headlines and wow the world!'

'Eh!' said Jan.

'His Highness Prince Huzza of Messuparabia has consented to attend! Now, wha'd'ya say to that, little lady?'

'A prince – oh dear!' said Hildegarde. She sat down.

'Confidentially,' said the film executive, 'Huzza is bats about Chime Bellfry.'

'So I hear,' said Lally.

'But what's that got to do with it?' demanded Jan.

'Tell you later,' said Pa-in-law. He winked. He was so young in heart!

'But a prince,' wailed Hildegarde, 'what do I call him? Shall I have to curtsy?' Almost paternally the film executive patted Hildegarde's shoulder.

'Take it easy, honey,' he advised. 'Huzza's a great fella – and he's a great prince – plays the maracas like nobody's business. Just leave him alone with a dance band and His Highness will be as happy as a king!'

'A dance band?' said Jan.

'Sure,' said the film executive. 'You can fly one over from New York;'

'So you can,' said Pa-in-law helpfully.

'Take it from me,' said the film executive, 'it's not the prince that gives the trouble no sir! It's that doggone bodyguard of his. They all got stomach ulcers!'

On the way home Jan said, 'Hildy, would you say that type in the shadows was trailing us?'

For the Vanderveldts had decided to walk back to their Palazzo and save the carozza fare. Poor Principessa!

'I'm sure of it,' said Hildegarde. 'Let's run!'

But at that moment the man who had been hugging such concealment as the bright moon left him, stepped boldly up to them and took from his pocket not the cosh that Hildegarde had envisaged, but some white-backed cards. 'You buy,' he told Jan hopefully.

True to her upbringing Hildegarde averted her gaze. But Jan

took a quick dekko at the things. There was something familiar about those white backs, even by moonlight.

'Good Lord, Hildy – d'you know what he's trying to sell us?'

'I think so,' said Hildy. She blushed.

'Black market invitations to our own party,' said Jan.

'. . . Jan and I are looking forward to our party with mixed feelings,' Hildegarde was writing home a few days later. '. . . Entertaining can be a responsibility as well as a pleasure . . .'

The door bell jangled.

'This way,' said Jan. 'Quick!'

But they were too late. For the beach was brimming with people every bit as curious as the crowd through which the callers had to press their way to the front portico.

The story about Prince Huzza had broken. The Press of two continents had taken up the Vanderveldts' party. And not only the Press. In Paris, in New York, in Rome, even in London the Haute Couture had come out with collections of costumes for the Arracoelia Ridotto. Travel agencies had featured it in their itineraries. And regular trips to the Palazzo were run twice daily by motor coaches from all around the coast.

It had become more than the Vanderveldts dared to do to show their faces in the town and they had taken to living on garden produce sooner than brave the crowds that followed them.

This time the callers proved to be the Chief of Police and his assistant. They had called, they said, to co-operate in arrangements for the Party for the Poor on the Piazza.

'The poor,' said Jan, 'that'll be us – for the rest of our days!'

The police laughed hysterically. But it seemed that this was not just a poor joke in the English taste.

'You could hardly,' said Policeman Primo, 'give a party for the rich at your Palazzo, without also giving one for the Poor on the Piazza.'

'Is that so?' said Jan, savagely.

'Should you attempt it,' the Primo warned them, 'there will be a riot!'

'Surely, surely!' said his Secundo.

'Of course,' said Primo, 'I would do my best to hold them off you.'

'Thanks,' said Jan.

'But soon,' said Primo, 'I shall be outnumbered. And who then will protect you from the fury of the mob?'

'Me, I ask myself?' wondered his Secundo.

'All right, all right,' said Jan.

What did one more party matter when you were ruined anyway?

Arracoelia was deserted. For the night of the party had come and those who were not drinking or offering one another more champagne at the Palazzo, for all the world as though it were spumante, were pressing spumante on one another on the Piazza and grumbling because it was not champagne.

Indeed, the party was at its height. There were more fireworks than there were stars in heaven. And the sweet voices of the massed choirs floated on the warm night air as the Fishing Fleet formed up for the Pageant.

So of course the station was utterly deserted and the two figures huddled on the bench, their collars turned up, their hats pulled well down over their faces, had a place to themselves at last.

The frailer figure of the two was sobbing.

'Don't cry, Hildy,' said the taller one, 'the train'll be in soon, and we'll never see this horrible place again!'

But the frailer figure was not to be consoled.

'I don't suppose they've even noticed we're n-not there.'

'What's it matter? In two days' time we shall be safely home again!' said Jan consolingly.

'And it'll be Father's birthday and we haven't got a thing to g-give him,' wailed the wretched Hildegarde.

'That's bad,' said Jan. He pulled for a bit on his pipe. It was empty, of course, but it still seemed to comfort him. Only the sudden detonation of a skyful of rockets broke the silence.

Then Jan had an inspiration:

'I know,' he said, 'we'll give a party for him!'

There's a Peugeot at the Bottom of
Our Jardin

Repetitious as a nagging woman the clock in the *salle à manger* struck ten. The chime had an acid note.

Le Papa glared at it.

'Late again,' he said. His face twitched. This was a bad sign.

La Maman sighed. 'Ton-ton studies too hard. His light is on till all hours of the morning. One asks oneself how long his constitution can stand it.'

'Reading in the middle of the night!' Le Papa was outraged. 'Early morning is the time for study. My own brain is at its best before seven in the morning.'

La Maman looked at him.

'Or used to be. After seven it's finished for me.'

'Evidently,' said La Maman. 'But Ton-ton is different. He is like me. He comes to life at night.'

Le Papa sighed.

'And then he has the artistic temperament. My temperament.' She patted a curl. 'And you know, my dear, when one has the Temperament . . . No, you wouldn't understand.'

For Le Papa was not impressed by the Temperament.

'Three minutes past,' was all he said. He checked the ormolu by his hunter. 'Disgusting.'

'But, Robert, Ton-ton is a barrister – or will be, when he has concluded his studies.'

'Oh,' said Le Papa, 'and when will that be? Let me know, I'm strangely interested . . .'

It was into a frigid silence that Gaston at length descended.

The dark circles under his eyes would not have put to shame an elderly roué with a troubled present.

'Bonjour, Ton-ton! T'a bien dormi?' piped La Maman, bright as the robin she strongly resembled.

'Suivez-moi,' snapped Le Papa, without further ado. His face twitched.

'Robert, don't be harsh with him,' implored La Maman as the door of her husband's sanctum snapped behind her menfolk.

The paternal harangue followed the usual pattern, highlighting Gaston's bone idleness, his insensate extravagance, his revolting ingratitude and his unnatural habit of purloining his father's car without first obtaining permission; and all this in contrast to Le Papa's own thrift, industry, selflessness and saintly patience.

' . . . Once and for all, Gaston,' Le Papa banged his fist, 'I will not be ruined by my son's electric light bill.'

'Agreed,' said Ton-ton. He suppressed a yawn. 'Can I go back to my books now? It is broad daylight,' he pointed out.

'You can go back to the devil,' said Le Papa, violently.

That reminded Gaston of something.

'And can I borrow the car tonight?'

'No,' said Le Papa. His faced twitched. 'And that is my last word on the subject.'

So that night Ton-ton remembered to switch off the light in his bedroom before tip-toeing in stockinged feet past his parents' room.

Stealthily, like a thief in the daylight, he opened the salon window (the one that gave on to the *balcon*), lowered himself from the balustrade, slithered down on to Le Papa's favourite flower bed (the one with the rarer orchids) and, fresh as a somewhat jaded lark, legged it down the drive to the garage.

A shadow detached itself from the wall of the cave as Gaston padded up.

'C'est toi, Georges?'

'Tu es en retard, mon cher.'

'Don't blame me. Blame the fellow who invented canasta – for matches.'

'You disgust me.'

Ton-ton shrugged. 'La Maman has the Temperament – she comes to life at night. Whereas Le Papa . . . ,' he shrugged again.

In silence the two young men applied their shoulders to the sliding door. The panel wheezed, rattled, groaned and refused.

'I meant to grease the idiotic thing,' said Gaston.

'Ah, ça!' Georges shrugged off his friend's threadbare intention.

A few more bumps and bruises and the surly panel slid back to reveal Le Papa's brand new Peugeot. Even in the dark it gleamed with a delicate lacquered lavender grey – the colour of La Maman's eyes.

In silence Gaston got in. In silence Georges pushed.

Slowly, silently, with Georges pushing and Gaston guiding, the car moved down the road until it gathered sufficient speed for Gaston to slip in the gear. The engine purred, as a cat purrs, first hesitantly, then in an even, inner, muffled rumble of contentment. Georges hopped in. They were off.

Soon the sleepbound little scatter of roofs called Marchez-la-Colline had tilted into the skyline behind them and before long Marchez-la-Platte – equally sleepily, had also dwindled into the velvet folds of the sweet Arlesian night.

Ahead, the lights of Marly-les-Bains beckoned.

Now Marly-les-Bains may not be much of a high spot, if you have ever hit Paris, New York, Buenos Aires. But it was the Bright Lights to the unfledged Gaston. Marly made the dull slow hours of the day worth crawling through, cracking headaches and all, and the small hours of the night worth living in – Marly and the Temperament.

But you could not get from Marchez-la-Colline to Marly-les-Bains without a car.

'Well, and where do we go from here?' enquired Georges, as Le Papa's Peugeot bumped itself about the earliest cobbles of Marly and slithered down the tram-track. 'La Martinique? Le Perroquet?'

'Chez Jo,' Gaston was quite decided on this point. 'We've got some serious drinking to do before I can face the hooch they sell at those flash joints of yours.' It was clear that in the matter of sophistication Gaston took the lead.

He pulled up, now, beside a grimy bistro, leapt out and dived through the dusty rattle of beaded curtains, his friend hot at his heels.

The night followed the established pattern of Gaston's nights. Chez Jo, Chez Max, Le Mardi Gras. In Le Jardin de ma Mère they tagged themselves on to a bunch of boys from the USAAF. At La Bouillabaisse Gaston changed a small cheque. At La Martinique he changed a larger cheque. The Yanks footed the bill at Le Perroquet while Georges and Gaston frankly fumbled.

Outside, in the shrill light of day, they parted somewhat unsteady company. The American boys beat it back to camp hooting their jeep through the early traffic of the already hiving market.

From the middle of the crowded street Georges clutched his throbbing brow while barrows whizzed past him.

'Formidable!' he announced admiringly, as the jeep missed a dray by a miracle.

'Formidable,' agreed the great Gaston.

Then it was that, for the first time, they noticed Le Papa's brand-new off-side wings. Not to put too high a polish on the matter, they no longer looked brand-new.

Sometime, somewhere, something had brushed against them.

Ruefully, the two friends inspected the damage. It swayed a little. They shook their aching heads. And they without a sou between them! The barman came out for a breather. He seemed to be swaying too.

But as luck would have it the barman had a pal who worked at Marly's only all-night garage.

It took a little while to entreat the barman's friend off the opulent streamlined dollar job he was engaged upon and to plead him on to Le Papa's modest middle-class Peugeot. But an hour later, there it was – straightened out and gleaming with a good coat of fast-enamel wing-paint. By the time they made Marchez-la-Platte it was as dry as an American throat at sundown.

At Marchez-la-Colline Gaston switched off his engine.

Georges jumped out and pushed. Le Papa's Peugeot entered La
Papa's garage more or less silently. The garage door groaned
to.
'A demain soir, Gaston!'
'A demain, mon vieux.'
Another night was over.

That morning Ton-ton was late again. Le Papa did not fail to
comment on the fact. La Maman rushed to his defence.
'And you, Robert, I suppose you yourself have never been
late for anything in your life. I suppose you did not, for
example, allow the chocolate to grow quite cold while you
prowled about the garden before breakfast.'
'I left the garden-twine in the car. A spray of my favourite
orchids was broken off entirely.'
He laid it gallantly upon La Maman's plate.
'The mistral,' suggested La Maman, placidly. She speared
the spray to the napkin at her bosom.
'A two-legged mistral, in my opinion,' observed Le Papa
grimly.
The clock in the living-room struck the hour. Le Papa rapped
it out with mounting impatience, on the table. But La Maman
ignored the chimes. Hers was a spirit above mere time-pieces,
one gathered.
Into the unnatural silence their son descended. His face was
the colour of unripe corn and he wore dark glasses.
'So,' snarled Le Papa, ominously.
'Now, Robert, don't be harsh with the boy. Can't you see his
head is hurting him. Sit down with your back to the light, Ton-
ton, while Maman infuses a good tisane . . .'
She bustled happily away, dropping her spray of orchids as
she went.
Ton-ton looked hesitantly at Le Papa. His face was
twitching, a bad sign.
He tried to stoop to pick up La Maman's fallen spray. But the
floor revolved about him and he groaned and gave it up.
'Do as La Maman bids you, son.' Le Papa spoke with lethal
sweetness. 'Sit down. Sit down, I say.' He retrieved the spray of
orchids from the hearth rug, and looking at it his face twitched

again. 'And while you are awaiting her tender ministrations, no doubt you will wish to explain to me how it happens that the off-wings of my Peugeot are as smooth as a lick of new paint, though I remember distinctly – I repeat, distinctly – putting it away last night with both wings badly scraped and dented – owing entirely to a grave miscalculation on the part of the driver of the other car – a jeep . . .'

Gaston groaned.

'And now, sir, I await your explanation. What have you to say to me?'

Gaston groaned again while in his agitation Le Papa was holding the spray of orchids as though it were the switch which clearly he had used too sparingly earlier in life.

High Wind in New York

Walter was a reasoning and, on the whole, a reasonable man; patient with his widowed mother with whom he lived, and daily functioning largely as part of the office wallpaper. At forty-seven he had but three overwhelming hates: a woman – any woman – parking a droopy cigarette at the corner of her mouth; a high wind that twanged his tri-gemind neuralgia; and any reminder at any hour of the day, of the sweet-tasting confections forbidden to him but for which his whole being craved, for he was a diabetic.

If life was passing Walter by, he scarcely noticed it, swallowed daily, as he was, Monday through Friday with its sleepwalking office routines from which he awoke every evening to listen to his mother tangling with the cost of living.

And then, one night, he met her. It was the night of the office party. No one would have recognised the old place as the serious house of business it was on the other days of the year. The young ladies had presided over its transformation with energy if not inspiration.

They had closed the doors to customers immediately after what on every other weekday would have been lunch-break and set about titivating everything within reach all afternoon with many a squeal and giggle, adding their touch of frivolity with holly, here, there, and glitter-frost everywhere; stringing the outer office wall-to-wall with large tinsel cardboard letters which spelled out the unlikely – life being life – sentiment that all who bought or sold at Baron, Berg and Rumplemeyer's should have a Merry Festive Season, said season being tactfully unspecified that no man be outraged in his beliefs – not even those, if any, of Hermie, the Go-For boy.

Already Hermie had Gone For the beers, cokes and V8s and the snow-white beard that had been affixed beneath the photogravured chin of Clarry Rumplemeyer I, the well-loved founder of the firm – God rest his soul – not to be confused with his young brother, Meshuganer Mowshay who went to Wall Street in the Depression to shoot himself but forgot to bring the bullets with the gun – and a jolly little red-hooded, red-cheeked, red-nosed, snowy-bearded Santa Claus that some office wit had affixed to the bookkeeping door, the bookkeeper being Clarry Rumplymeyer III, the young man who flashed his rolled-gold jewellery and was considered flighty and probably light-fingered by the second generation Barons and Bergs who sent sons Manny and Sid to keep alternate watch over his figures, his flightiness being equated with his extreme youth at thirty-eight. But, light-fingered with the firm's figures, that was something different again, which could never happen here.

Such was the background to Walter's meeting with Linda, the love of his life.

Her given name had been Lilly after her mother's real mean sister. So when it was made plain that she would have nothing to gain from stingy Aunt Lill, she called herself Linda, a name she had always coveted. Linda had been taken along to the office party by Daiz, *née* Daisy, the switchboard girl, who only emerged from her adenoidal boredom when young Clarry Rumplemeyer was the caller – it was the gold tooth that did it. Linda and Daiz were sisters. Linda had large grey eyes and a mean mouth: her Aunt Lill's mean mouth. But Walter concentrated on her eyes and fell in love with her. Oh, those office parties! So they married to her mother's relief and his mother's disgust. They married, so why didn't they live happy ever after? It happened this way.

The morning after a tentative – on his side – wedding night and an unforgiveable bout of bad temper on hers, she emerged from the shower feeling fatally glib.

'Honey,' she said. The diabetic in him winced.

'Honey,' she repeated. This did nothing to help. She shifted the cigarette, her third that morning, to the corner of her mouth. 'Be sure to wear that muffler your mother half-knitted for you and my poor mother had to finish. It's a cruel east wind today and we don't want you home with your neuralgia tonight, do we?'

Whereupon Walter's trigeminal nerve felt a twang like someone had taken a sword to his head and sliced it in two.

Small wonder he dashed blindly into the street and ran – he would have been hard put to it to explain why – and kept right on running until he reached the Empire State Building where the wind blew him in with never a let-up.

The 102nd floor had an observation post. So did the 86th, which did not concern him at this moment. Walter, half-blinded with the burning in his head, got into the right lift – there are eighteen of them in the Empire State – and stumbled out. The observation post on the 102nd was swaying – so was the rest of the steel and crystal tower. Walter hurled himself over the brink and into the wind. It was the point of no return. Or should have been. But the wind upheld him and blew him right back to the Empire State and on to the observation post on the 86th floor.

With a thumping heart and a throbbing head Walter battled his way through the relentless wind back to his rancorous marriage and prepared to sit it out, till death, or divorce. Whichever came the sooner. Only once did he stop to glare at the slightly swaying summit. 'Oh well,' he thought, resigned, and would have shrugged but for the pain in all his muscles.

Walter's story is true enough. It must be. It was printed in the *New York Times* in the first week in January, 1978, so it had to be true. And it seemed that Walter was not even the first man to jump from the Empire State Building in one of those high winds in New York and be deposited right back by the wind into *The Guinness Book of Records*. Oh well.

Pal Grisha

Grisha is a great guy. A good friend. A first rate human being.

Grisha has an endless supply of inexhaustible energy. When he's at the end of his he uses up yours.

Grisha is American – one hundred per cent naturalized American blood runs in Grisha's veins. Grisha's a character. A crazy guy. Grisha's an impresario.

So there you have it! A big guy with a great big heart. And what an intellect! Each time Izzak Ben Saloman scrapes his bow across his Strad, or the Grand Ballet de Corsica goes into a spin, that means money in Grisha's overdraft. Money and Headaches – that's what Art is to Grisha.

Grisha is a man of action – immediate, headlong, whizz-wham action – taken by telephone – a tangle of telephones – to New York, Paris, Belgrade, separately or all together if necessary – which it always seems – to Grisha, that is – and to every airport mid-flight, as simultaneously as circumstances permit. If the Devil hadn't invented the telephone, man would have had to do it – to get Grisha in instant global communication with his contacts.

So I'm not all that surprised when I learn that Paris calls me at four in the morning. I am in bed in Yugoslavia at the time. But I don't sing Boris so good any more, and I keep a civil tongue in my head when a coo from a hacksaw husks into my share of the pillow:

'That you, Sergei? Here's Grisha. How's things?'

'They were fine – just fine,' I say, a little sadly.

'Then get up and take the next plane to Paris,' said Grisha. 'It leaves the airport in forty minutes' time. I checked.'

'You did?'

'Sure. You got exactly ten – no, nine minutes to dress and pack your bag.'

'I'll never make it.'

'You'll make it. I got somepun for you here. Somepun good.'

'Not Ivan?'

'You said it . . .'

'My Ivan's pretty Terrible these days.'

'. . . But somepun ve-e-ry attractive. And it's little Grisha telling you.'

'But Grisha – it's the middle of the night, these parts. I'm in bed . . . well, hell! I'm in bed.'

'What's so new about bed?' says Grisha heartlessly. 'That's seven minutes you got, now. You better beat it or you'll never make it.'

So it's Paris in spring, this morning. Only you don't notice the season so much in Grisha's office.

Grisha is all tied up with telephones, just like the doodle in the spider's web. But he frees a hand to stub out his cigarette. Grisha doesn't smoke like other people – with him it's whff-whff-whff . . . and a cigarette's a dead man.

'Siddown, siddown – take a fauteuil,' he says between a hailstorm of 'Ullo-'ullos.

I look around.

The fauteuils are filled with world-wide bottoms. That's normal. So the world-wide bottoms on the sofa snake up a bit to take me in. But my frozen hand is not so tiny these days! So I cause them to snake up some more.

'Too bad I gotta leave you folk right now,' Grisha is saying between hook-ups and wrong numbers. 'You've come a long, long way to please an old man!'

And the way Grisha says it would bring a lump to your world-wide throat.

'Right now, I have to be on my way,' quavers Grisha . . . 'No, not Havannah, Miss,' he bellows, 'Suvannah – S like in Chaliapin . . . So little Grisha's sure gotta beat it. Elsa's flying

in from Nassau – her plane's due right now. 'Niff a guy doan
meet his wife at the airport some other guy'll sure do it for him,
uh? But I'll be right back, so wait here the bunch of you . . . I
daren't be late for Elsa.'

There is a world-wide groan.

'And who does he think he is,' demands a world-wide Gloria,
tartly, 'Lohengrin?'

And this wasn't so smart because her Gloria is by no means
so Glorious as it was. In fact it's only good for Sadler's Wells
these days.

Grisha vanishes. That is to say he takes the wrong homburg
off the hat-peg, checks with the mirror, gives himself a well-
pleased frown and goes right back to his telephones. He picks
them up the way the guy does the handbells in *The Bluebells of
Scotland,* only transglobally.

The world-wide bottoms sigh and settle themselves for a
sitteroo.

Grisha always goes by air. So do Grisha's clients and his
family. Grisha's clients *are* his family, between wives. Grisha
did once travel by train. He had his reasons. And they all
turned up at the airport with their writs. That's normal.

Grisha's time is money – other people's money.

But other people's time, that's different. And hell! what's
other people's time for, if not for waiting for Grisha? So Grisha
is never on time – not Greenwich Mean Time, that is. But
there's other sorts of time besides Greenwich Mean Time, and
Double Grisha Time, which is just about two hours late. And as
Grisha says, you can take it or you can take it!

When Grisha has greeted the new arrivals, and gone right
back into the past with them, and had a teensy argument with
the printers on two telephones, and checked over last night's
takings, and given the Opera the Or-Else, and wolfed a plate of
caviare sandwiches and a glass of lemon tea, Grisha gets down
to the gimmick.

'My friends,' says Grisha, 'you're my own people. My little
family,' and but for the telephones Grisha would gather his
little world-wide family into his two loving world-wide arms –
Grisha's arms being loose and hairy like a gorilla, but right now
he's still in his shirt sleeves, though his collar has eased up on
him.

'I love you,' says Grisha, and the tears well up in his own eyes, 'I love you like you was my own children . . .'

Here his world-wide family look grim. It seems like they know their little Grisha.

'And I loved your fathers and mothers like they were my own . . . *better,*' Grisha reminds himself. 'And now I've got somepun for you . . .'

'Covent Garden,' breathed a Salome, who seemed to have brought her seven veils with her and was wearing them.

'Hush-up, honey,' says a world-wide Negro singer. 'All God's chillen gotta shoosh!'

'And that somepun is a hoise,' announces Grisha.

'A horse?' said the world-wide family, faintly.

*They know Grisha's horses.

'Sure a hoise, a good hoise this time,' and Grisha bangs a fist to silence protests. 'And whaddya think this hoise is called – Impresario . . . Impresario!' and Grisha leans back and beams all over.

'I guess that makes it a natural for the photo-finish,' sighs a cellist, easing the legs a little.

'It sure does,' says a Pagliacco, raring to put his Motley on it.

'It's gonna win all right this time. You'll see!' says Grisha confidently. 'And we're going right over to Longchamps to see it leave them other tramps behind. And it's little Grisha says so!'

'Okay, Grisha,' says the world-wide bunch, resigned.

'So long, kids, see you at the Tote! Sergei, stick around!'

Sticking around Grisha means a number of things and all take plenty of time. But that's okay with me. My Tristan's purty Triste, these days.

First, Grisha has to have a drink. I figure Grisha needs that drink real bad – and so do I!

And Grisha has to have his drink some little joint downtown of no place, where the Barman is a Russki. And that takes time. But I guess Grisha needs that drink – and so do I! And Grisha says his doctor says to walk it. And that takes time.

And Grisha wants to do the Barman a favour on account of he's a Russki. So he gives him Impresario. And he tips him good money to put on it. And he borrows it – cash – from me. And that takes genius!

Then Grisha has to call in at the Boy's Beauty Shop. 'Want me to let you into a little secret?' shouts Grisha above the vibro.

'Cheddar-chudder-chudder,' says the local Figaro – at least that's all you can hear above the apparatus.

'IMPRESARIO!' yells Grisha.

'Chudder?' mouths the Figaro politely. That Barber sure is *Civil*, uh?

'IMPRESARIO!' Grisha roars above the vibro. 'Like me!' he thumps his chest.

Figaro stops the vibro and gest busy with the lather bowl.

'Cain't lose,' bawls Grisha into the hush.

And Figaro slaps on the suds and grins. They put a noo complexion on the matter.

And all this time I stick aroundaroo.

Not that sticking around Grisha doesn't have its bad moments.

'Next,' he says, 'we go tell Elsa all about it.'

'All about what?'

'All about what I don't do,' says Grisha. 'You see, I don't do gambling.'

'Huh?'

Grisha grins. 'Elsa don't like it none too good when I come home cleaned out. She's crazy, that girl! Gets real mad at me each time I lose my shirt.'

'Time I was getting along,' I say.

'You stick around with me, Sergei.'

My Merry Wives of Windsor have lost their girlish laughter, these days, so I do as Grisha says. It's normal!

Telling Elsa how we had to visit a sick relative in the kinda country she wouldn't care to drive through, takes time. So does listening to the things she wishes us while we tell her.

So does getting stuck in the lift at the ancient dump where Grisha lives when he's in Paris on account of its being run by a Russki, too. But Grisha gives the Impresario to the Concierge's husband when he gets us out, and it cheers him up a lot – Grisha, I mean.

On the way to Longchamps Grisha stops by at his office – 'to see what don't go on!' his shoemaker and the florist. And every

place he calls he telephones. That's Grisha.
  'Sure, sure!'
  'This ain't no ordinary flower-dump, neither,' Grisha says.
'The guy who owns it used to be in the ballet.'
  'You don't say!'
  'Ain't life crazy?' Grisha says.
He should know.

So what with this and that for Elsa, and the fortune teller and
the Madame Butterfly, and the goddam telephone, I'm not all
that surprised we make the race-course on the late side. In fact
the three-thirty is already put away and there's a lot of high-
class toilettes streaming out. And among them are some
characters with strictly local faces, and I seen them some place,
and it could be Grisha's office – especially when I come to see
the tops of the writs that are bulging out their pockets.
  So I point them out to Grisha who says, 'Step aside, Sergei,'
and makes for where the crowd is thickest.
  And soon he is surrounded by his world-wide family, the
Barber, the Concierge, the Switchboard Operator, and the
Barman, all smiles, all kiss-the-hand, all winners.
  'Thanks a lot, Grisha.'
  'You should have seen it run.'
  'Like the cops was after it.'
  'Too bad you missed it, Grisha!'
  And so on, through the Hallelujah Chorus.
  'What did little Grisha tell you?' crows Grisha into the
ecstasy. 'An Impresario cain't lose!'
  'If only you'd got here earlier,' mourns a Swan who takes a
long time dying.
  'As to that,' says Grisha, 'I promise I give up backing hoises.
And my gentleman's agreement is always worth the paper it
ain't written on. And I figure out not getting here on time saved
me a packet.' And he points to where the last writ trudges sadly
through the exit.
  But the world-wide family don't get it, and they go on
sympathising, and offering fifty-fifty. So do the Concierge, the
Barber, the Switchboard Operator and the Barman.
  And Grisha, he takes them up on that.

'Stick around, Sergei,' he says 'and collect. And tell-you-what – I promise Elsa I doan put a cent on a hoise – gentleman's agreement! But I doan give no undertaking about you, Sergei.'

'Uh?'

'So just you take the lot and place it on a certain numero in the four-thirty I fancy.' And he points to number seven on someone else's card.

My Boris ain't quite Godunov these days, so I grin and back it. And so does Grisha's little world-wide family.

And that horse is called Elsa's Prayer, and we lose our little world-wide shirts.

It's normal!

Possibilities

'Good?' The enthusiastic but virgin play-rite – virgin, to be fair, only in the sense that all his plays were intact – pouted, 'I mean, it's great! And the title – *First Spank Your Faggot* – I mean, it's just great! It's gotta take off.'

'It's got possibilities,' said the man in the T-shirt. He pushed away his chair.

'Sure, it's got possibilities,' said the virgin play-rite. 'I mean . . .'

But they by no means meant the same possibilities. A failure of communication.

A week later the man in the T-shirt – it was, of necessity, the same T-shirt – was saying to the manager of the only out-of-town bank left without a computer, 'It has . . .' – the pause was mouth-watering – 'possibilities.'

The bank manager, a new man with stars in his eyes about such images as backstage, chorines, fully frontal, and New York, New York, nodded sagely. Again a lack of communication. 'How much?'

'Off Broadway, for starters say, $1000. When we transfer . . .' The man in the T-shirt was wary of the word 'if', as becomes a man with dreams that his fare back to Manhattan depends on not admitting 'if' to his sales-pitch.

'Why not?' thought the new manager at the out-of-town bank. 'Granted,' he said.

The man in the once off-Broadway T-shirt knew his subway

fare back to Manhattan was assured. He departed jauntily, humming 'He's a dreamer, aren't we all?' From this time forth he was to smoke nothing but cheap, opulent-looking cigars. That was until he could afford an opulent cigar for real, just around the corner. Where else?

Two months filled with activity for the dreamer-activist in accession of increasingly sexy and expensive T-shirts and emptied of any kind of opening date on the part of the off-Broadway, off any-stage, virgin. I mean, they were back at Joe Allen's, on 46th between 9th and 8th, sharing a scarlet-chequered table-cloth. The virgin was picking up the check.

'Nothin' fixed?' he said, palming a valium. 'I mean, nothin'?'

'Nothin',' said the operator, in his newest, sexiest, costliest – there was no way that Gucci would ever be a main-drag Woolworth's. No way! 'But I'll be driving down to speak to my out-of-town Source of Finance next month – or the month after.' He puffed cherubically from within his cloud of smoke. The next-best Havana cloud.

'No way?' protested the virgin, still in the wings. 'I mean, no way? Tomorrow at latest, or else . . . ?'

'Tomorrow,' the financial wiz in the cloud of smoke capitulated. He watched the virgin pick up the check and leave a week's main meals for the sinuous waiter. Four weeks, twenty-eight days, 632 phone calls and one cable later – all from the virgin still waiting in the wings for the off-Broadway theatre – the hustler in the fur-lined coat called on the out-of-town bank manager. No longer new. No longer a dreamer. No longer without a computer.

'But you don't understand,' the operator in the sable-type-lined coat came close to bleating. 'First, I have run out of money.' The bank manager looked at the client's new overcoat carefully flung open to reveal a careless fold of sable-type lining. His managerial look was bloodcurdling.

'Then you must find a new investor to pay back your loan.' The bank manager had no soul. No dreams. He was a monster.

'But you don't understand.'

'I do,' said the monster. 'I understand all too clearly.'

'I mean,' said the sable-type-coated client, 'to attract talent

and money I must dress the part. I mean, that makes sense.
And to attract the money I must eat at the right places. Up-
town restaurants where the French champagne comes from
France. And what does my future investor say? He wants to see
the theatre he invests in. So I have to take an option on a building. And I can't ask a backer to an empty building. I mean, first
I must buy a coat of paint. But that is not convincing if I have
not got wall-to-wall carpeting. And where is the conviction if I
cannot offer a prospect a chair? And how can I bargain with
him if I am not sitting behind a desk, a goddam desk to put the
fear of the Lord in him? I mean, there is an old Israeli folk-song.
It goes, "For the lack of a match, the fire wouldn't burn."

But this time the bankrupt operator left the bank singing that
song – in a minor key.

And the virgin is still a virgin.

Big Like a Toboggan

Not that the village was anywhere near the sea. It clung like a
limpet to rock three parts up the summit that towered over
Innsbruch and it was called Bibls. And from it came a constant
tap-tap-tap of hammering.

For the Puppa Rothberrien was building a ship.

Not, again, that the Puppa Rothberrien had ever seen the
sea, as Anna, his good wife, frequently reminded him. But the
Puppa was no fool. He knew just how a ship should be – big like
a giant's toboggan. And when it was done, anchor, mast and
propellor – and a little cabin for the Anna and her naughty
children – the family Rothberrien would put out to sea and sail
to America. Already the Puppa had charged himself with many
messages to the Great Aunt of Herr Schneider, the best tailor in
Bibls – in fact the only tailor in Bibls – who had married a
tourist – the only tourist in Bibls – and the Tante Schneider –
now Mrs Taylor – if still alive, was surely to be found in Kansas
City. The Mrs Taylor had held much the same views on the
village as the Puppa. It was just another village, wasn't it,
lacking scope, breadth, vision. Also the Puppa had spent fifty
years in it.

For some time, now, he had been restless – sick of celestial
slopes from serrated horizons. Sick of snow. Sick of spiked pines
under an Austrian heaven.

A man must see something of the world that lay beyond the
Tyrol while he was young – well, fairly young – and strong –
yah! strong like a bull – for one morning he would wake to find
that he was eighty and then it would be over. And at this

thought, the Puppa hammered even more energetically in the cowshed.

Each morning early, before he went to work carting logs and coke and fetching letters and the midwife and anything else that a village could need by a good little goat, the Puppa took himself off to his cowshed and there he would hammer away at the good ship – by common consent named Anna – supported by Sepi, his little son; his first-born and favourite, who helped the Puppa by upsetting the pot of varnish, throwing the nails around, and so on. And each evening, when the cow's work was done, the sound of the hammer would sharply pierce the gentle rumble of the distant, ever-present, thunder, deep like a giant's laughter. And this morning as on other mornings.

'Good day, Herr Rothberrien,' called the merry voice of Herta, swinging her way down to prepare the early breakfasts at the Family Freiburg, Baker and Guesthouse. 'How is the ship?' She stopped by to kibitz.

'Great God! Goes well, goes well!' said the Puppa. He patted a plank.

'Goes well,' Herta confirmed. 'And you will really sail to the America?'

'Naturally,' said the Puppa. 'Starting from Venice.'

'The Venice – to marvel!'

'We follow the course of the Kon Tiki, naturally. You have heard of this Kon Tiki, no?'

'No,' said the Herta. She ran a stubby finger along the boat's broad bow.

'There will be cheers, crowds – the gondolas will line the Grand Canal to give us God-speed!'

'It takes a smart fellow to get to the America!' said Herta with conviction.

The beaming Puppa did his best to look a trifle modest. Then picked up his hammer and went to it with a will. Smart fellows off to the America had no time to waste on women.

But after the Herta had swung her hearty hips around the bend the shower of blows ceased. The Puppa had gone to work with a pot of gold paint and there, where it had been taken for granted the name 'Anna' should be inscribed, he painted 'Herta' in good, archaic, curly, unreadable script right across the ship, big like a toboggan.

The Puppa stood back to admire the effect. The cow viewed it with less favour.

'Jakob . . . Jakob . . .!' the voice of Anna rang roundly out to the shed. She followed it.

The Puppa, delicate to a degree, laid aside the pot of paint and took up the hammer.

'Ach! Here you are then,' she could hardly have been surprised. It was just polite pretence. 'Little Schneider wants to come also to the America.'

'That one,' said the Puppa.

'And why not?' demanded Anna. 'She is big, the *Anna*, no?' She regarded the Puppa's ship. If she saw the name Herta, she made no sign. 'Why not? There is plenty room in the *Anna*, no? And I shall need a good jacket to wear when we go to visit the Tante Taylor, no?'

'No,' said the Puppa.

'And little boy Sepi must have strong trousers to his seat, no?'

'Yes,' said the Puppa.

'Already Little Schneider has taken away the sails to sew,' said Anna. 'Me, I have enough to do with the children, without all this stitch . . . stitch . . . stitch!'

And that was how the wizened but chirrupy Little Schneider came to be a member of the crew, with his one foot longer than the other, and his face lined like a rock.

Blow by blow and beam by beam the *Herta* grew. So did the crew.

Never can a village have given birth to so many sons with the urge to leave it. The villagers were sick of their village, like whooping cough.

It was indeed an oddly assorted crew that collected itself around the Puppa. Baker, wine-maker, cobbler, cowherd – in all twelve men, not counting little boy Sepi, who never ceased to help the Puppa by clambering all over the ship while the varnish was still wet, and hammering his thumb by accident. A fine little fellow, that Sepi, and the very image of that father!

Came the day when the two fine masts were hoisted into position – this took the entire future crew and sundry grumbling grandmothers. Came the day when the propellor was slotted home. Came the day when the blacksmith finished the anchor. Even Anna stroked it.

Came at last . . . at last . . . the early morning when the *Herta*
was lashed to a low wheeled truck and the truck hitched on to
the good little goat.

'And we lend hand up hill and push,' ordained the Puppa.
The crew nodded – especially Little wizened Schneider.

'And down the hills you all pull back,' said Anna, the
practical. The men ignored her.

It was raining when the ship, big as a toboggan, left Bibls by
goat.

'It will get wet, the ship,' mourned little boy Sepi.

'Boats *are* for getting wet,' comforted the Puppa.

'Blow the nose,' said Anna, 'we go now.'

Thus the goat cavalcade took leave of Bibls, alternately
pushing upwards and pulling back and generally winding its
way down and along and up and between the mountains, with
the Puppa and his crew encouraging one another, themselves,
the goat and stopping for Anna to milk it and give to her
naughty children – one big happy family.

These were the early days. Everyone was happy, everyone
eager to do his share. Each had been allowed to contribute in
cash or kind to the expedition – golden America lay ahead.
What more could a Tyrolean want? Ten pounds a head per
crew the Puppa had folded into his leather purse – to be repaid
in salaries after the expenses of the journey had been defrayed.
The Puppa had been officially appointed Skipper to the expedition. Had he not given his ship, his goat, his all? Early days.
Energetic days. Hopeful, happy days. The good little goat was
the first to club them. She dropped dead. This was at the
Brenner Pass. Dead as mutton. But thoughtful mutton – for
there, at hand, was a railway station.

What to do? The crew turned to their skipper.

'So! We go home,' said the Anna.

Back to Bibls – it was out of the question.

The Skipper spoke.

'We go on,' he said. 'Naturally! To the sea. To Venice. By
railway train.'

The crew breathed again.

'But this costs money,' said the Anna.

'Naturally to travel by railway train costs money,' said the
Puppa. 'And you,' he told the crew, 'must find work in the

villages, each according to his trade . . .'

'And if there is no work?' asked the Anna.

'Must make work,' said the Puppa.

The crew nodded. They understood.

'And in the evening we gather together here, where come the tourists, and we sing Tyrolean songs and the little boy Sepi,' he beamed at his son, 'shall take around the hat.'

'But we do not sing so good,' said Herr Schumann, the cobbler.

'It is enough for the tourist that we sing at all,' said the Puppa firmly. 'And the Anna, she shall sell the goat for butcher's meat.'

'Was thin, the goat,' mourned little boy Sepi, 'thin as Herr Schneider,' and he pointed to the tailor already loping happily off to ply his needle and thread to the beautifying of the Brenner. The Anna slapped the pointing down. Sepi howled.

And so it was.

By the end of the week each had earned his ticket to Venice, which, once achieved, would be the end of the Skipper's troubles. Naturally.

So the crew went to work with a will, dismembering the boat and loading it piece by piece into a piled-up luggage van. And the Anna kept a count on her children and her deep suspicion of the railway to herself.

It was already late when the *Herta* and her crew reached Venice. And it was raining. But even in Venice the Family Freiburg (Baker and Guesthouse) had a means of their own for acquiring accommodation for Anna and her brood for nothing from the Italian branch of Tyrolean Family, Freiburgioni (Baker and Albergo). As to the *Herta*'s crew, no sleep for them.

The ship big like a toboggan had to be carried piece by piece and there and then to the port to be reassembled and – oh, moment of moments – launched!

All through the night the Skipper and his crew worked like beavers.

And then it was daylight and the ship stood stoutly on the quay, a little scratched but altogether whole. The Skipper checked it over . . . Despair! . . . a mast was missing! Left behind in the van without doubt.

'And the railway train has gone,' mourned little boy Sepi.

That's right,' said Anna. 'So now we go, too.' And she looked back over her shoulder in the direction where she fondly fancied Bibls perched. 'You,' she told the Puppa, 'should count your pieces like me I count my littles.' She sniffed self-righteously.

The crew looked at their Skipper.

'I have it!' cried Little lined Schneider, happily. 'I will go stitch, stitch, stitch around the city, so we can buy the wood and the Puppa can build the Anna another mast. For a tailor – good tailor,' he made a point, 'there is always to stitch in this world.'

And so it was.

Three days it took to earn and buy and build the mast. Then came the ceremony of the hoisting. There was quite a crowd to watch, but not one shoulder to help.

'It is like this in cities,' said Little Schneider wisely.

'How you know, Tyrolean?' asked Anna, crudely.

'I know.'

'So now, men,' said the Puppa, 'we push the ship onto the water with a one – two – three . . .'

But even as the crew prepared to heave, Authority, in gold braid and a sword, descended on the *Herta*. It was the Harbour Master, hungering for papers.

'But,' said the Puppa, 'we have no papers. Only a ship.'

'Big like a toboggan,' pointed little boy Sepi.

'Without papers,' said the Harbour Master, horrified. 'Impossible to sail.'

The crew looked at the Skipper. What to do?

'These papers,' said the Puppa, 'what must be written on them?' 'Permission from the government,' said the Harbour Master, 'to export this old junk. You people cannot sail off to America just like that,' he snapped a white gloved finger.

'Your government or my government?'

'Both governments,' said the harbour Master, 'and the American government – permission that you land there.'

'Permission?' said the Puppa. He looked dazed. How did a Tyrolean get this permission?

The Harbour Master guessed his thought. 'It is a matter for a lawyer. A good lawyer. You know a good man of law here, in Venice, without doubt?'

There was a heavy silence. The crew looked at their Skipper.

'I . . . I . . . ,' began the Puppa.

'Speak up, speak up,' said the Harbour Master. 'Well?'

Then Little Schneider, who had been bobbing about trying to catch the Puppa's eye for some time, now spoke.

'Leave this man of law to me,' he said. 'I know a tailor – with an establishment – and where there is a tailor, must be a lawyer. How else should the client pay the bill?' He scuttled off.

It took the Little Schneider's tailor's lawyer two full weeks to come by the permissions. Weeks during which the Family Freiburgioni became less and less hospitable and finally quite curt to Anna and her naughty children.

And each day the crew went to work in order to eat. And each evening they assembled at the harbour to feast their eyes on the *Herta*.

'The *Anna* craves the water – she starts to crack in the sun,' said Anna. The men ignored her.

At last, at last the day when, armed with his precious papers, the Puppa presented himself at the Harbour Master's Bureau.

'Let's see,' said the Harbour Master, detaching the papers from the clam-like Puppa. He put on an enormous pair of tortoise-shell spectacles. He read them clause by clause. 'Will do – will do,' he admitted grudgingly. 'So now, there is only to ask you for the fifty pounds – in lire . . .'

'Fifty pounds?' faltered the Puppa.

'Harbour dues for eighteen days – it is eighteen, is it not, that the ship has been lying there rotting, taking up good space on my quayside?'

'It is – it is,' agreed the Puppa, none too amiably.

'Very well, then,' said the Harbour Master. 'But my expenses, my emergencies, my salaries . . .' The Puppa was near to tears. But the Harbour Master was a man of stone. 'If you are not off by noon, it will cost you a thousand more.'

The Puppa paid up.

Came now the moment of the launching. The launching of the ship big like a toboggan had been a dream in the Puppa's mind – glorious like a vision – a feast to be tasted and retasted during those happy hours of hammering and hoping back home in Bibls. The launching was nothing like the dream.

There was a crowd all right but it was apathetic and rude in turns. And anything but helpful all the time.

'Jealous,' said Little Schneider, who could not push and so

had time to talk where others could only grunt and wipe the sweat from the brow.

'And one . . . two . . . three . . .'

Bump, bump, bump had gone the boat.

And when at length the *Herta* touched the water, all breathless as they were, her crew gave a great cheer – a cheer echoed by the ironic crowd on the quayside.

It was a sweet moment for the Puppa. His ship was on the sea at last. She floated, the *Herta*. Naturally. And even his good wife Anna looked less grim – a very little.

'The *Anna* rides the sea like schlagsahne on the Kaffee,' said Anna. And the crew gave three great cheers for the good ship *Herta*. And now they crowded round the all-sufficient Puppa, hugging him, slapping him between the shoulders, cheering him.

'The ship,' cried little boy Sepi, 'it moves by itself. See . . .'

Only Little Schneider, who lacked the brawn to force his way into the heart of the melée, and had been bobbing wistfully about on the edge, heard the boy. He turned his head. There, sure enough, the *Herta* was already a goat-leap from the quay. Together they leaped, the Schneider and the Sepi. Together they converged upon the anchor. Joyously they heaved it overboard. It sank.

'No matter,' said Herr Putzenhoff, the blacksmith, when the weeping Sepi broke the news. 'Iron is cheap, and I will forge another next time we put in shore.'

'Next time will be the America,' said the Puppa.

'We shall have need, then' said Herr Putzenhoff, with a comfortable certainty.

The ship big like a toboggan was floating, fair and very square on the sea. The Puppa's troubles were over. To navigate the course of the Kon Tiki would be play for kitty katz after navigating the affair of the Harbour Master!

'And now,' said Herr Putzenhoff, 'the pay day!'

'Pay?' the Puppa paled.

'Yes, pay,' said Herr Freiburg. 'The *Herta* now is launched, she rides the water. We have worked hard and patiently. Now pay . . .'

'Now, pay,' agreed the crew.

The Puppa swallowed.

'My friends,' he said. 'Together we have come through many adventures. And many lie ahead. Let us hold on to our resources.'

'Eh? what's that? No pay? But it is our money – our own money.'

The Puppa looked appealingly round the ring of faces, formerly so friendly, now clenched against his scrutiny.

'There is the anchor – this I must make good – and who knows what more?'

'Who indeed?' said Anna. They ignored her.

'We are at sea – we stay at sea for many weeks – yes, months – we have to eat, to sleep, in our good *Herta* – all this I find – naturally – so what need you have of money till we land?'

'If we land,' said Anna. They ignored her.

'You've spent it! You have spent our savings – all we have in the world. On what?' the crew demanded.

'There was the Harbour Master,' said the Puppa miserably. 'And then a skipper must keep a little something in hand, a reserve against a bad day! And we Tyroleans know well how storms come sudden like a seven-month child.'

The crew muttered among themselves. They went on looking ugly. Even Little Schneider had stopped smiling.

Then Anna spoke.

'The sea,' she said, 'it comes into our ship. Soon she will sink. You shall see . . .'

They followed her pointing finger to the floorboards. There, sure enough, water had started to seep through.

'Is rude to point,' said little boy Sepi, gleefully. 'Is rude to point.'

She hit him. Rather hard.

A back-breaking day and night the crew spent thereinafter, bailing out and caulking the *Herta*. A day and night, non-stop. And the family Freiburgioni were out and out rude when once again the exhausted Anna and her naughty children turned up on their trattoria-step, just like the proverbial bad lira.

But though by noon the *Herta* was ready for her re-launching, and the Puppa's 'and one . . . two . . . three...' were as stout of heart as ever, there was something awfully hollow about the cheers of his crew.

However, it was under blue skies and with the lightest of

forward breezes that the *Herta* skimmed – well, perhaps not
skimmed, precisely, but remained afloat upon the water.

'Is not bad, the *Anna*,' said Anna with near-approval, and
straightway plunged into her washing-day.

Slow like a procession – a funeral procession – the *Herta*
sailed from harbour to the accompaniment of storm cones and
yacht's sirens, all of which the Skipper took as compliments.

'You hear?' said Little Schneider, sunnily. 'We are at sea!'

And the Puppa stood contentedly at his admittedly blunted
helm and gave a couple of orders, and saw that it was good.

The Skipper had never been to sea, but he had seen Lake
Como, once, in cloudless weather, and it had been just like this
but choppier – naturally.

'This' was before blew up from nowhere a great storm,
sudden like in Tyrol, and made the *Herta* rock like she was little
like a slice of Apfelstrudl. The wind blew and whistled her
about the waves and the sea jumped up – and this was on their
very first night.

What next? The green-faced, staggering, drenched and –
who knew – drowning crew looked at their Skipper.

Next was half a lifetime later when the *Herta*, by a miracle,
limped to landfall without a rudder and with both her tall masts
stumps, having gone with the waves for full two days like this.

The Skipper and the crew turned ravaged faces to the sun
and thanked The Great God for San Marino. Here was no
harbour neatly defined on concrete, no ships' stores and
probably no tailor, as the Little Schneider, wry like an unripe
apple, observed, but:

'Here stands still,' said Anna.

'And here is no Harbour Master,' said the Puppa, and fell
straightway to sleep.

Sleep.

And so it was the Mayor of San Marino, all tarnished braid
and creaking sword, came upon the wreck of the *Herta* and her
sleeping crew.

'Wake up! Get out! At once!' He shook the Puppa firmly by
the shoulder. 'Ships can't land here. They never have. It is too
shallow,' he shouted.

'But the *Anna*, she has landed here,' said Anna simply. The
Skipper and the crew slept on. They were impervious to buffet-

ing. Slept on like sea-green children, out like a candle-flame.
While the sea-green children, from the safe shelter of her
familiar skirts, eyed the Mayor's sword with bleary-eyed
approval.

'No ship has ever landed here before,' the Mayor repeated.
'And you must put to sea at once, or you will cause a lot . . . a lot
. . . of trouble for me. Why, they'll be coming here all day, all
night, with their noisy fog-horns and their drunken crews. Next
thing you know we'll have the neighbourhood teeming with
bastards, and . . .'

'One thing leads to another,' said Anna grimly, taking a
lunge at little boy Sepi, for luck. 'And always the same thing,'
she finished glumly. 'But who is going to pay the train fares
back?'

'Back?' asked the Mayor of San Marino.

'Home,' said Anna. 'Back . . . Back to Bibls.' And her brave
eyes filled with tears. The lullabies and slappings and the sea
had claimed their toll.

So now the odd tourist passing through Bibls on his way from
somewhere else to Innsbruch may well take shelter in the
Puppa's home. A quiet man, the Puppa; says little, thinks the
more, no doubt. And if the storm has blown up after school
hours the tourist may well hear through the roll of the retreat-
ing thunder the tap-tap-tap of a hammer coming from the
former cowshed.

'Little boy Sepi,' explains Anna. 'He is building a ship, the
Anna, big like a toboggan. Some day, some day,' she tells the
tourist dreamily, 'he will sail his ship to the America and visit
with Mrs Taylor.'

'Nice place, America,' the tourist says, 'and nice place,
Bibls . . .'

And the Puppa?

Maybe he winces. Maybe it's because he feels the iron
turning in his soul.

What Shall We Call the Baby?

All day long it had been stifling. Flowers fairly wilted before you could carry them home from the market. Horses were falling down in the streets. Sensible people stayed at home behind the jalousies.

But with the cool of the evening, they too ventured forth and were to be seen sitting at the café tables fanning themselves.

On his way home from the office, young Monsieur Gustave had dropped in to the Grand Café de l'Univers et de la Gare as usual, and was sitting at a table with his friend, Monsieur Michel. The Café de l'Univers et de la Gare had been opened only a couple of years before in 1893 and was still the sensation of Dijon.

'And you seriously mean to tell me that Monsieur Durand broke into your house in the dead of night to steal your Maidenhair Fern? I can hardly credit it!'

'It was a very fine fern,' Monsieur Michel sounded almost defensive. 'The salon doesn't look the same without it. I tell you, that fern had character!'

Young Monsieur Gustave consulted his watch, siffléd the waiter for his check, collected his hat and gloves. 'And you're quite sure the intruder was Monsieur Durand?'

'I got a good look at his face before he turned down the gas in the vestibule. I tell you, my Old, there is no possibility of a mistake.'

His Old clicked a shocked tongue. 'Really,' he said, 'the things people do!'

At the gaunt lodging-house where he rented his modest and suitably inaccessible room, Monsieur Gustave stopped to speak to the concierge. As usual, she was sitting knitting in her office, a dark little cave at the foot of the stairs. It was mostly taken up by dog. But on the sill of the hatch stood a Maidenhair Fern that was clearly the pride of her heart.

'Ah, Madame la Concierge, what news of your daughter?'

Madame la Concierge beamed. Monsieur Gustave was such a gentle gentleman. Ever a kind inquiry on his lips!

'Ah, Monsieur Gustave, with these first *accouchements* you never know where you are! And then, she lives so far away. I wanted them up in my second floor back, but my son-in-law, he wouldn't hear of it!'

Monsieur Gustave did his best to look surprised.

'But I'm expecting a summons to go to her at any minute – any minute, Monsieur Gustave – and I want you to take care of my fern till I come back.'

'Your fern?'

'To you, it's just a fern like any other, but I assure you, Monsieur Gustave, this fern has character. I'd know it in a thousand!'

'You would?'

'I would,' said Madame la Concierge firmly. 'Take it up now, and mind you don't forget it. And remember, these Maidenhairs need watering every day.'

'Every day, Madame la Concierge?'

'Every day, Monsieur Gustave.'

Scarcely had Monsieur Gustave reached his room and put his burden on the wash-stand, when the apparatus buzzed. Monsieur Gustave décrocheted it from the wall. 'Allo, allo?'

The frog at the other end turned out to be his rich Aunt Mignonnette – his only *tante à héritage*. 'You have not forgotten tomorrow, Nephew?'

'Tante Mignonnette!' Monsieur Gustave played reproachfully for time. 'Tomorrow' – he thought furiously – 'that's Saturday, isn't it?'

'The *conseil de famille* takes place in the afternoon. A weekend in the country with the Family will do you a world of good, this weather.'

'The Family?'

'Now, Gustave, listen to me . . .'

Monsieur Gustave listened to his Tante.

Monsieur Gustave looked at his plant.

Monsieur Gustave's natural prudence dictated his decision: 'I shall be there,' he said.

Numéro onze, rue du Congrès was just a house like any other. But not to Monsieur Gustave, standing on the doorstep with his fern. To him, the sun, the moon, and the stars appeared to have taken up their habitation there.

For here lived Mademoiselle Sophie.

Their *fiançailles* had been under haggle for several Sundays already, and the lovers had little doubt that in the end a settlement would be arrived at to their mutual benefit, by Mademoiselle Sophie's Papa and Monsieur Gustave's Tante.

Now it so happened that this day, Friday the 13th of September, was Mademoiselle Sophie's Maman's birthday, and the champagne was in the bucket. But Monsieur Gustave knew nothing of this, and great was his surprise upon finding himself embosomed – the wrong bosom – embraced, and his fern taken from him.

Impossible to explain that he only meant to leave his fern in Mademoiselle Sophie's care while he visited his Tante, when here was her Maman calling on heaven to witness her gratitude to it for sending the little Sophie such a kind, thoughtful, noble, generous possible-future-husband.

Mademoiselle Sophie's Maman was an exuberant lady. But she was also a vigilant chaperone.

'See, my Little,' she cooed, taking Mademoiselle Sophie by the well-puffed shoulders and prudently increasing the distance between the young girl and the impetuous suitor by giving the girl a sharp shove in the direction of the salon, 'does not our salon look handsome with Monsieur Gustave's distinguished gift upon the piano?'

'Yes, Maman,' said the Little dutifully, and straightaway started edging herself back to the thrilling danger zone of Monsieur Gustave's ardent proximity.

Toasts had been proposed. Healths had been drunk, compliments paid – *'On dirait, plutôt, deux soeurs!'* – and the champagne finished.

Yet it was a sober Monsieur Gustave who stopped, on his

way home, to look in at the lighted window of Madame Clotilde's flower-shop: 'Ses Fleurs – Sa Couronne Mortuaire'.

And then, in a flash, his face brightened.

For there, in the very centre of the window, between the musty Immortelles and the dusty Honesty stood a Maidenhair Fern – the last one left. It was just like any other maidenhair fern, so far as Monsieur Gustave could see. *Prix:* 50 frs.

Should he acquire it? Monsieur Gustave lingered outside the flower-shop, pondering the point. Madame la Concierge had declared that she would know her own fern among a thousand like it. But would she . . .? Would she . . .?

Monsieur Gustave felt for his purse. A single coin, by great good luck a fifty-franc piece, was in it.

Slowly Monsieur Gustave raised himself onto his toes, slowly sank back on to his heels, and thus tittupping, toe to heel, heel to toe, broke into a *siffle.*

Monsieur Gustave was saved!

But scarce had he siffléd a stave when Monsieur Gustave's tittupping came to a slow halt, and his *siffle* withered at his lips. For the firm figure of Madame Clotilde appeared at the window, and the last fern left disappeared from it.

She had taken his fern away. She was showing it off to the Widow Grimaldi. The Widow Grimaldi was opening her chain purse . . .

In his agitation Monsieur Gustave dropped his fifty-franc piece, and by the time he had dodged between the passers-by, groped in the gutter, been stumbled over and sworn at, and finally found his coin and rushed into the shop with it, the Widow Grimaldi had acquired the only fern left.

'And I must water it every day?' the Widow Grimaldi was saying.

'Every day. Without fail,' Madame Clotilde advised her. 'Above all in this weather.'

Speechless with despair Monsieur Gustave held out his fifty-franc piece to the Widow Grimaldi. Misunderstanding his meaning, the Widow Grimaldi gave Monsieur Gustave a *gifle.* What kind of a widow did he think she was – grass?

With smarting cheek and a heavy heart, Monsieur Gustave went on his way.

In the hall Madame la Concierge put her head round the

corner of her cave: 'You won't forget to water it every day?' she urged.

'Every day,' responded Monsieur Gustave, falsely.

And from that moment Monsieur Gustave stood committed to his Maidenhair Fern.

In the dead of night, when even Madame la Concierge was asleep, Monsieur Gustave stole forth on a desperate venture. He had determined to break into the house of Mademoiselle Sophie's parents to retrieve his fern.

The streets of Dijon were deserted. Numéro onze, rue du Congrès was as dark as a witches' sabbath. There was not so much as a glimmer of gas showing through the fanlight in the hall. But at the back a flight of stone steps led obligingly to the salon.

Even if the noise of breaking glass were to rouse one of the sleepers, Monsieur Gustave would be up, off, and away with his fern before you could cry poker!

Monsieur Gustave possessed himself of a nice sharp flint from a handy grotto. But as he was about to fling it, Monsieur Gustave paused. The sound of a voice – his own voice – came to him from what seemed to be a lifetime away: '. . . And you seriously mean to tell me,' Monsieur Gustave's voice was saying, 'that Monsieur Durand broke into your house in the dead of night to steal your Maidenhair Fern? I can hardly credit it! . . . Really, the things people do!'

How shocked the voice sounded.

'Prig!' said Monsieur Gustave, and flung.

Crash! The good sharp flint had done its work. Monsieur Gustave dived into the salon.

'Poker!' cried out a startled, a girlish voice.

It was not the salon. It was Mademoiselle Sophie's room.

Who would have the heart to dwell upon the painful scene that follows? The wild accusations of the fearful girl, the wild reproaches of her frightful parents. Their night attire. The violent manner in which they shake their pokers at the incontinent villain. His unlistened-to denials. The instant breaking-off of possible future nuptials. Mademoiselle Sophie in a swoon. Her Maman in a swoon. Angélique, the *bonne à tout faire,* in hysterics.

The Door! It was the end!

Monsieur Gustave's Tante Mignonnette was seated at the head of the dining-room table. Her near relatives were polka-dotted down both sides. They were looking determined rather than hopeful. He himself was installed at the foot of the table. And on the puce plush-and-bobble expanse between Monsieur Gustave and his *tante à héritage* stood a noble Maidenhair Fern.

The *conseil de famille* had been going on for some time now, and looked like going on for some time longer. For it had been summoned to consult on certain new dispositions in the latest codicil to Tante Mignonnette's will.

'And the jewellery,' Gustave's Tante Marie-Rose was saying. 'surely you would not wish your turquoise parure to go to the ignoble Maximilien, now that he no longer agrees to marry the young lady of your choice?'

Tante Mignonnette bestowed upon Tante Marie-Rose the kind of cold regard a suggestion from a mère-in-law deserved. 'As to that,' she said, 'I am fully decided my turquoises go to my dear nephew Gustave, who is on the point of affiancing himself to the charming young lady I have chosen for him.'

She beamed at Monsieur Gustave, who was gazing fixedly at the Maidenhair Fern.

'And the pedigree cows?' asked his Oncle Prosper.

'They go to Gustave, too.'

'And the three-odd acres?'

'What good would the cows be to my favourite nephew, without the grazing?'

Tante Mignonnette tap-tapped a tattoo on the puce plush – always her habit when becoming vexed.

But Oncle Prosper was in a mood to press his point: 'So,' he finalized, 'our nephew Gustave gets your stocks' – he ticked an irate finger – 'your shares, your rents, this house, the furniture, the pedigrees, the paddocks, the jewellery, the lot!'

'The lot,' agreed Tante Mignonnette, 'if he is prudent. Mademoiselle Sophie is a very charming young lady, well brought up, domesticated, dutiful, and of a loving disposition. And also she has a *dot* which is not to be sneezed at!'

'Atchoo,' said Monsieur Gustave. And even as he felt for his bandanna his eyes remained riveted on the Maidenhair Fern in the centre of the table.

Tante Mignonnette tap-tapped.

Meanwhile, in torrid Dijon, Monsieur Gustave's concierge, still waiting for the summons to her daughter, was entertaining a guest – and a guest who had not called to see her empty-handed. This was Angélique, Mademoiselle Sophie's Maman's *bonne à tout faire*.

She had brought with her a handsome Maidenhair Fern. Would Madame la Concierge be so kind as to take care of it for her, while she went for her annual holiday?

For only that morning Mademoiselle Sophie's Maman had sent for the *bonne à tout faire* in the salon. 'You see that kind of a cabbage there?' she had pointed to Monsieur Gustave's fern. 'Take it out of my sight this minute. I never wish to set eyes on it again. It was given me by a monster!'

When her friend had taken her departure, Madame la Concierge peered at the plant and sniffed. It was not to be compared to the noble specimen that Monsieur Gustave was looking after for her.

Truly, it is a wise housewife who knows her own aspidistra!

How noisy a night spent in the quiet of the country seems to one accustomed to ignoring the clip-clop of hoofs and the rumble of carts on cobbles in a busy town like Dijon.

Monsieur Gustave, tossing and turning under his mosquito-netting, was unable to close an eye for the hooting of the owls, the lowing of the cows, the braying of the ass, the scratching and scampering of the mice, and the snoring of his relatives, rising and falling in a somnolent symphony.

Of what use counting sheep jumping over a hurdle? They only multiplied a thousandfold and melted into the fronds of a Maidenhair Fern . . . Monsieur Gustave blinked himself bolt upright. He arrived at a desperate decision. He would dress, pack, and purloin Tante Mignonnette's Maidenhair Fern. A note pinned to the little cushion on the dressing-table, explaining that he had been recalled suddenly to Dijon, would suffice to allay Tante Mignonnette's alarm. He would be as quiet as a mouse . . . No, quieter!

His toilet made, suitcase packed, his note speared to the pincushion, Monsieur Gustave, at great pains to make no sound, descended to the salon, negotiating the staircase, snore by snore.

It was dark in the *salle à manger* and Monsieur Gustave had some trouble getting the paraffin-oil lamp going. But at last he achieved a fairish flame, turned to the table, fell over the footstool, clutched at the plush-and-bobble table-cover in an effort to save himself, failed to – and the Maidenhair Fern came crashing down with him.

'Poker!' Tante Mignonnette's voice, firm rather than frightened, gave the alarm.

Monsieur Gustave fought furiously to free himself of plush-and-bobbles.

The ass brayed.

The train to Dijon was not uncomfortably crowded. Monsieur Gustave found a corner seat without difficulty. The only other passenger to join him was a plump little woman, like a pigeon. Monsieur Gustave, who was staring moodily at the window, did not even notice her arrival. The porter carried in her luggage, placed a wicker picnic-basket beside her.

'Be careful of the plant,' entreated the woman. 'Put it in the corner, opposite – then it can come to no harm.'

The train moved off. The little woman opened the lid of her basket, drew from it a luscious morsel of cold chicken, glanced uneasily at Monsieur Gustave, and ate it in as delicate a manner as possible. But she need not have bothered to be so nice. For Monsieur Gustave was still gazing out of his steamy window, rapt in some vision of his own.

And Monsieur Gustave's vision was clear enough, for all the smoke and steam on the window in which it was mirrored.

For Monsieur Gustave was seeing the *salle à manger* of his Tante Mignonnette, who was sitting tap-tapping at the head of the table, with her near relatives grouped along both sides and an empty place at the foot . . .

The little woman produced a bottle of wine. She poured a glass and held it out hospitably. But Monsieur Gustave did not notice. He was listening to a very painful conversation.

'And the jewellery,' Tante Marie-Rose was urging, 'surely you cannot still wish the ignoble Gustave to have your turquoise parure?'

'My turquoises to that villain – are you mad? They are for my dear niece Rose-Marie.'

In the steam of the window Tante Marie-Rose relaxed. 'She is a dear, good girl, if I do say it of my own daughter!'

By now the little woman with the picnic-basket had thrown all pretence of polite concealment to the steam. She particularly enjoyed the drumstick, and this she ate without troubling to disguise her relish, licking each separate plump little fingertip when she had done.

Then she arose, brushed off the crumbs from her travelling-costume, and went down the corridor to wash her hands, leaving Monsieur Gustave alone with the Maidenhair Fern.

But Monsieur Gustave was listening to his voices.

'Then,' his Oncle Prosper was finalizing, 'our daughter Rose-Marie gets your stocks, your shares, your rents, this house, the furniture, the pedigree, the paddocks, the jewellery, the lot!'

'The lot,' agreed Tante Mignonnette placidly.

Somewhere in the world that is, an engine whistled. The train passed through a tunnel. Monsieur Gustave's vision was blotted out.

But by this time the little woman had returned to the carriage and was refreshing her fern with a bottle of Evian. 'You have to water it every day,' she explained.

Monsieur Gustave blinked.

It was a leaden-hearted Monsieur Gustave who, with hang-dog head and heavy tread, approached the entrance to his lodging-house, some hours later, although the Day of Judge-ment was still in the comfortable distance of the future, for Madame la Concierge was certainly still with her daughter and by now should have a grandchild on her mind instead of a Maidenhair Fern, for assuredly the summons must have come.

So Monsieur Gustave cheered himself up and came striding quite buoyantly through the hall where, from the concierge's cave, came a well-known voice: 'Monsieur Gustave! Monsieur Gustave!'

The summons hadn't come!

With the Day of Judgement here and now and right in the cave on his doorstep, Monsieur Gustave turned tail and fled. And Madame La Concierge, carrying Mademoiselle Sophie's

Maman's *bonne à tout faire's* Maidenhair Fern – much inferior to
her own fine specimen in Monsieur Gustave's care, of course,
but still quite tolerable in an impoverished sort of way – went
hurrying after him. She wanted to leave this one in his care also,
while she was away.

It is, indeed, a wise washerwoman who knows her own
mangle!

It was still very warm that evening. All fashionable Dijon
seemed to have crammed itself into the Café de l'Univers et de
la Gare, and was fanning itself. It had been a sweltering Sunday
and tempers were more than a little frayed.

At his customary table, Monsieur Michel was drinking an
apéritif with his wife.

'Look,' she said, 'there goes Monsieur Gustave. I wonder
where he's off to in such a hurry on a hot night like this? And
look, there goes Madame la Concierge – and she's in a hurry,
too. There, now – he's running. And so is she. Now he's turning
round and coming back.'

'Must have forgotten something,' said Monsieur Michel
comfortably.

'Madame la Concierge has turned, too. She's carrying something – it must be her new baby.'

'Or her old fern.'

'I'm almost sure it's the baby.'

'If I know Madame la Concierge, it's the fern.'

'There, now – they're crossing over – I suppose we shall never
know.'

'I know,' said Monsieur Michel smugly. 'There's nothing
wrong with my eyesight!'

'And there's nothing the matter with mine,' riposted his wife
strongly. 'And I tell you it was the baby she was carrying.'

'And I say it was the fern!'

'It was the baby!'

'It was the fern!'

'The baby!'

'The fern!'

'Baby!'

'Fern!'

Just then Monsieur Gustave doubled back again with his concierge coming after him! And now even Monsieur Michel's wife could see that it was not a baby.

This was too much. Monsieur Michel's wife made a grab at the first object to hand – the Maidenhair Fern that stood upon their table. In a fury she flung it at her husband. He ducked. It felled the doubling-back Monsieur Gustave.

While they are binding up Monsieur Gustave's poor head with strips of table-cloth and taking him home in a fiacre, a very different scene has been taking place in the *salle à manger* of Monsieur Gustave's Tante Mignonnette from the one at which he had gazed so dismally in the steamy surface of the window of the train earlier in the day.

For, it being Sunday, Mademoiselle Sophie's parents had called upon Monsieur Gustave's Tante for the formal breaking-off of the no-longer possible future *fiançailles*.

It is true that, from the outset, Tante Mignonnette had been tap-tapping on the curiously bare and exposed table. But this was the sole outward sign that her inner composure was in the least, troubled. She herself might be harbouring the gravest doubts as to her nephew Gustave's sanity after his latest exploit, but before strangers she would defend him to the last cow and acre – family feeling demanded it. Was not blood thicker than *vin du pays*?

It was Tante Mignonnette's dearest wish to see her favourite nephew married to the right young girl – the young girl of Tante Mignonnette's choice – with the right *dot* – the *dot* that Tante Mignonnette had haggled out of her parents – safely settled down with a dear little Mignonnette of their own, who closely resembled Tante Mignonnette. Opposition to this cherished plan served but to stiffen la Tante's resolve.

'So you wish to break off the match?' Tante Mignonnette fixed Mademoiselle Sophie's Maman with a firm, undaunted regard. 'No doubt, Madame, you know what is best for your own daughter – such pretty hair! Is the wave natural? – But, as I said to my nephew – my favourite nephew,' – here Tante Mignonnette switched her firm regard to Mademoiselle Sophie's Papa – '"Gustave," I said, "we must be prudent. We must consider carefully, is Mademoiselle Sophie – oh, a pretty enough little thing, I grant you – but is she quite up to running the solid establishment I intend to provide you with?"''

'Intend, Madame?' Mademoiselle Sophie's Papa was quick to follow up a point, even if it were only from force of habit.

'Intend, Monsieur. And my nephew – well, Gustave is so hot-blooded.' The regard switched back to Mademoiselle Sophie's Maman – 'particularly in this weather! But we, Madame, are women of the world, and understand how it is with men in these affairs! And with young girls, too, for that matter!'

Mademoiselle Sophie's Maman winced.

'Gustave, as I was saying, cared nothing that the girl is a green little goose . . .'

'A goose, Madame?' la Maman took her up sharply.

'A goose,' repeated Tante Mignonnette playfully. 'You must teach her to manage our six-room house as you do, Madame!'

'Eight rooms,' said le Papa, automatically.

The regard switched. Then: 'Eight rooms,' agreed la Tante amiably. 'The dear boy is so much in love – and who can wonder at it? – for they would have made the handsomest pair in the village.'

'In Dijon, Madame, in a house in the next street but one to our own?' La Maman must have noticed an *A Vendre* board.

'In Dijon,' acquiesced Tante Mignonnette.

'And by way of jewellery?'

'The little Sophie would look very well in corals.'

'Very well,' agreed the proud Papa, a little too quickly.

'She would look even better in turquoises,' said la Maman, only just in time.

'As to that,' la Tante said, smoothly, 'I had always intended to give la Petite my turquoise *parure* on her wedding-day.' La Tante gazed straight at the ceiling as though directly daring it to challenge this statement.

La Maman relaxed.

'And now,' said Monsieur Gustave's Tante, 'what sum do you propose to allow the young couple, annually, towards the upkeep of this ambitious establishment?'

By almost imperceptible *démarches* the battle had gone to the strong. Both sides were victors. The matchmaking was on again.

The following morning Monsieur Gustave remained in bed. It was the doctor's orders. Indeed, he had given Monsieur Gustave quite a lecture on not overdoing it.

'The human mechanism,' he explained, 'is like that of a delicate plant . . . or shall I say a fern with many fronds?'

'No,' said Monsieur Gustave.

Soon after lunch Monsieur Michel dropped in to see how the invalid was doing. 'My wife would have come with me, but she is quite prostrate – it was the shock,' he explained.

Monsieur Gustave shook a sympathetic head – it hurt him.

'But she has charged me to bring you this little present, with her best wishes for your rapid recovery.'

And Monsieur Michel tore off the wrappings to reveal a Maidenhair Fern.

A little later Monsieur Gustave had another caller. His Tante Mignonnette had come post-haste from the country to see for herself that her favourite nephew was being looked after properly.

'You must have had it on you all the weekend,' she opined.

'Oh no! Indeed, that was the point!' Monsieur Gustave endeavoured to explain.

Tante Mignonnette felt his bandages. Still feverish, she decided. 'I have brought you something from the country – something to make your room look brighter. You may be having some important visitors soon,' she told him playfully – playfully for Tante Mignonnette, that is. And she took up the object she had set down.

It was a Maidenhair Fern.

Scarcely had Tante Mignonnette departed when two more guests appeared for Monsieur Gustave. They were Mademoiselle Sophie's parents, who, hearing of his mis-adventure, had hurried over to assure themselves that all was not ruined.

'Bygones are bygones,' said le Papa.

'And turquoises, turquoises,' said la Maman unaccountably.

Monsieur Gustave blinked. But la Maman was speaking again: 'Outside waits one who has a gift for you – a simple enough object, but then, we know you have a liking for such things. Open the door, Vercingétorix – the Little can enter now!'

And there, on the threshold of this miscreant's room stood an angel straight from heaven, a Maidenhair Fern in her hands.

And this was not all. For scarce had Monsieur Gustave's temperature jumped a point when there was yet another knock at the door. Madame la Concierge's summons had come. In fact the baby was already there – a sweet little girl who resembled her father not at all. And would Monsieur Gustave be kind enough to take her friend's Maidenhair Fern also into his keeping?

It was not as grandiose a specimen as the one she had already left in his charge – and here the concierge looked round for it, failed to see it, and supposed that it was standing on the window-sill behind the curtains drawn to shield Monsieur Gustave's suffering eyes from the glare of the sun. But poor as was the fern that her friend had left with her, it still had far more character than any of the so-called Maidenhairs here! Madame la Concierge sniffed.

It is indeed a wise cook who knows her own onions!

And that reminded Madame la Concierge . . . The christening was taking place next month.

Would Monsieur Gustave be kind enough to look after her dog?

Under the Juniper Tree

Early one morning, before the sun had sailed itself clear of the far Sierras, a small boy crouched crying before the shrine in the sun-baked square of a timeless village in Spain.

Timeless because remote – one century being strictly like another in High Sierra.

The square looked rather as though the small boy had drawn it – the sun-baked houses with their balconies scrawled across them, the plain oblong church, the sullen gaol, the inn, the well, the nine and seventy steps that led up to the bridge that spanned the millstream; the lot of them tilted against the sky.

The shrine was erected to the Glory of God and Our Lady of Showers, by public subscription some centuries ago, to give High Sierra proprietary rights on an occasional downpour. And the boy had been told never to touch the beautiful blue-cloaked, crowned and smiling Madonna that stood behind the gilded grille of the shrine. He was sobbing because he had. And there was Our Lady of Showers in two irrevocable pieces, a catastrophe that would outrage the whole of High Sierra, when tomorrow, the first Sunday of the month, and not a cloud in sight, the villagers were due to assemble at noon and formally indent for rain.

So the boy was beside himself with terror and remorse. Not only would he, for a variety of reasons of which this was certainly the gravest so far, burn in hell eventually, which was a long way off and so hardly counted, but also he would be thrashed to within an inch of his life, practically at once. Aie! Though less, of course, for the wrath of God than for the fury of High Sierra!

'Carlo!'

Peremptorily his name came floating down from a window in the hard dry voice of the Widow Alborado. The boy trembled and paled. It was well known that the rich old woman had one eye more than ordinary people – set in the back of her head.

What had she seen? What did she know, already?

'Carlo!' rasped the voice impatiently. The boy held his breath and closed his eyes. He wished the Widow Alborado would drop dead, like Miguel Money-bags. He wished the whole of High Sierra would do the same. Passionately the boy prayed that the world might come to an end before the village could find out.

Soon the sun had sailed into the clear and the bright hot day had begun. High Sierra came, unwillingly, to life. Lattices were thrown wide, carpets were flung out, and from the windows voices scolded, sang snatches, exchanged the gossip or the insults of the day and commented on life as it passed in the square below.

A sprawling figure collected itself into one piece and wavered over to the inn. Ignatius, the village loafer, thirsty already, rapped on the door and holla'd for wine. The landlord, the meanest man in High Sierra, including even the late Miguel Money-bags, snarled and slammed the door in the loafer's face. The loafer shrugged and pulled his hat over his eyes and twanged a phrase on his guitar, while the enwindowed ladies laughed at his discomforture.

'Work, work, you lazy wretch! Leave thirsting to your betters,' rasped the Widow Alborado, just as though she did have an eye set in the back of her head.

On the balcony of the inn, Concepcion, the flashing young wife of the angry innkeeper, was holding a red rose in her white, white teeth, but it is not the thought of her husband that brings the blood up to her cheeks and makes her glance so melting. She is waiting for the gay young miller, who will come across the bridge. The neighbours hurled coarse words at her, but inwardly how envious – how envious!

Soon the roofed-in well-trough was lined with doubled-over women who had brought their linen to wash. Among them merry Marika, the Corregidor's love child. How could Alonzo, the village lecher, resist stealing up and pinching merry Marika. Marika's shrill high-pitched giggle floated across the square.

'Slap him on the face, you slut,' enjoined the Widow Alborado. She must indeed have had an eye set in the back of her head. For had not the rich old woman been bedridden these fourteen droughts and three downpours? At the store a fine old haggle was in progress, where Andreas had been caught short-weighting Granny Alcazuna.

'Thief! Thief! Thief!' rasped the Widow Alborado from her bed. And as Andreas and Alcazuna looked fearfully up to the rich one's window, Innocente, the village pilferer, dumb but crafty, grabbed an aubergine from the counter and went beetling off with it, one leg dragging behind. If the Widow Alborado could have clawed that far she would have torn his tongue out.

The Widow Alborado was the richest woman in High Sierra. For a quarter of a century she had ruled the village by disinheritance. All day long she sat bolt upright in her bed, wrapped in a black shawl, issuing orders, and scolding, even when they had been carried out; her eyes were small black beads, her fingers jewelled claws, and she made her ward's life a misery.

Elvira was in love. But all that Pedro the Penniless could hope to inherit, now that the Corregidor had cheated him out of the farm his dying father had left in his charge, was the love of God, which was nothing like enough in the three eyes of the Widow Alborado, so she never gave her ward a minute's peace.

'Pauper! A pauper! That's what you will be if you marry the penniless Peon, for not a peseta of my money will you see! I shall leave it all to the holy sisters – unless of course they vex me! You shall see!'

'But, Tia, we love one another,' said her ward and niece. What did anything else matter?

'Ninny,' snapped the Widow Alborado.

'And Pedro has such a wonderful voice – you ought to hear him serenading,' pursued Elvira, glowing.

'I do,' said the Widow Alborado, grim. 'And if he comes caterwauling here again, I'll pour cold water on him if I have to leave my bed to do it!'

But Elvira failed to tremble at this terrible threat.

She was looking longingly out of the window where Pedro the Penniless had joined Ignatius and his guitar at the flagonless table.

Thrum!

The last man to come reluctantly to life under the glare of the brazen sun was the man in the village gaol, the Inglés, who was going to die tomorrow for the murder of Miguel Money-bags. Outside it was a regular scorcher as usual, but the man who would die tomorrow was not concerned with the weather today. Partly because, as it so happened, the gaol was quite the coolest place in the whole of the village. Nor was he haunted by remorse for the killing of Miguel Money-bags. Better men than Miguel got killed by accident in hold-ups, and Miguel had been a pompous old fool, as swollen up with self-importance as his saddle had been with the money that had eased the Inglés' last inglorious days.

The Inglés, gazing out and down to the only part of the square he could see through the high barred windows of the gaol, a glimpse which, ironically enough, took in the table outside the inn at which so many of his years of living in the sun on what remittance came early in the month – that very table at which so many of the pennies from – no, not Heaven, though that is what they seemed like every time – had been squandered.

From the high barred window, the Inglés could just see the shadow of a man with a guitar. That would be Ignatius, the village loafer, his friend, and José the hot-head, father of little Carlo, the poor little half-starved devil of a Spanish kid and brother of Luisita, his little love, who, for all her Spanish fire, had been too cold and proud – or too shy and afraid – to let him come to her. This the Inglés regretted far more than the fatal mishap to Miguel Money-bags; for there had been a moment when it seemed that it must be either Miguel or him. Unlucky, that as things turn out, it had to be both! But then, of course, that was death all over!

But even stronger than his regret over the fierce virginity of Luisita, was a strong sense of frustration which was hag-riding

him in these, his last hours on earth, that since his death was to
be untimely, he had not met it more heroically in the war he had
stayed away from fighting.

The Inglés sighed and turned away from the pair of legs that
had just added themselves to the shadow of the arm and the
guitar. The key was grinding home in the ancient lock. It was
Luisita, who came each day to keep house for the Corregidor,
with a flask of red wine in her hand. The Inglés' last breakfast.
Just like all those other breakfasts.

Luisita turned her grave look on him. 'It is sad,' she said,
'that the holy priest is still abroad in Málaga.'

The Inglés grinned. 'I shan't miss his holiness while you are
here, I promise you!'

'But,' persisted Luisita, 'if the priest is not back by dawn
tomorrow, you will burn in hell forever.'

'*That* in any case,' said the Inglés.

'But I am serious,' said Luisita.

'Me too,' said the Inglés. But he was teasing her as usual.

The tears welled up in Luisita's eyes. 'Why did you have to
kill Miguel Money-bags?' she mourned. 'Why did it have to be
you who killed him?'

The Inglés shrugged. 'One of us had to,' he said, 'or he'd
have had one of us.' The girl nodded gravely.

'Sooner me than José the hot-head,' said the Inglés. 'José has
a son.'

'Little Carlo,' said Luisita fondly. Almost she was smiling for
a minute. Then she remembered: 'José wants to see you,' she
said.

'Well, I don't want to see him,' said the Inglés shortly.

'But . . .' began Luisita.

'I tell you I'm not seeing anyone. And if you let him in, I
shan't have you to sit with me in the night watch. Mind,
Luisita, I mean it,' he warned.

Luisita held back her tears. Time and enough for weeping
them in all those sad, sad tomorrows. Some devil must have
entered into the Inglés to make him hold up Miguel Money-
bags, and not wish to bid his friends farewell. She picked up the
empty flask.

'I will bring you more wine,' she promised, 'after the siesta.'

Siesta-time in High Sierra. From every window came the sound of snores. Only little Carlo was awake in all the sun-baked square. His sin was heavy on him. All morning he had hung about the scene of his enormity, afraid, lest someone should open the grille to enlist the sweet intercession of Our Lady of Showers, when he would be undone indeed!

Now, although at siesta-time the village was deserted beyond the wildest dreams of the poet, it was the hour of the daily descent of the Wise One.

The Wise One lived a life of contemplation in the cave by the Juniper Tree at the foot of an even Higher Sierra. The Wise One knew all – it was well known. Besides, he could read. Indeed, drudging along in the narrow ravine between the third eye of the Widow Alborado and the uncanny foresight of the Wise One, the path of High Sierra should have been one of extreme rectitude. Nevertheless, High Sierra back-slid, as villages the world over will.

The Wise One lived his life of contemplation on whatever, of its plentitude, High Sierra put out in his food bowl, which stood at the foot of the shrine. They took it in turn to placate the Wise One, filling his bowl with delicate white fowl and good rosy rice, lest his second sight should turn into the evil eye.

Today it was the turn of Luisita.

But today, as we have seen, Luisita had a great deal else on her mind. There was this matter of her virginity.

With her love about to die tomorrow for killing Miguel Money-bags, could virginity be anything like so important as bearing the Inglés a son to pray for his soul in eternal torment? The Inglés who used soap for washing with; the Inglés who could make her heart flutter like an oleander leaf. But if she bore the Inglés a son, what would the Widow Alborado say? Or rather, what, indeed, would the Widow Alborado not say? Aie!

Here was a problem that not even the Wise One could hope to solve. Small wonder that, lying wide-eyed on her truckle bed, Luisita should have forgotten to fill the Wise One's food bowl.

Down in the sun-baked square, little Carlo's ears pricked for danger, and he hid behind the covered well-trough. But it was only the Wise One, come down from his hill to fetch his food bowl.

Above his bowl the Wise One went into his daily routine of delicious procrastination. First he closed his eyes. Then he snuffled thrice. Then he picked up the bowl and prodded. Then looked to see what the good High Sierra had provided . . . Aie!

Today, confronted by an empty bowl, the Wise One flew into a rage to make the rocks shake. In a frenzy of fury he rang the bell on the cord at his waist, crying woe to the waking-up village, a lived Elijah from an El Greco canvas.

Soon all High Sierra, with the exception of the rich old woman in her bed and the poor young Inglés in his cell, had assembled in various stages of anxious awareness before him.

'Woe! Woe! Woe!' intoned the Wise One.

High Sierra shivered. Clearly some terrible thing had befallen. Maybe the Widow Alborado was dead at last.

Certainly it was not the Widow; for here came her accustomed comment, floating down from the window, dry as a cactus:

'Well, what is it?' she demanded crisply. 'Speak up, man, and don't stand there mumbling.'

The Wise One cleared his throat.

'It has been revealed to me,' he announced, 'by certain manifestations,' he glared at his empty food bowl, 'that the world is about to come to an end.'

A gasp arose from the village.

'Tomorrow at dawn, the earth will stop revolving and all living things thereon will perish,' proclaimed the Wise One. 'Perish,' he repeated petulantly.

'Aie!' mourned High Sierra from seventy throats. The end of the world had come!

'Tomorrow,' the Wise One told them, 'at dawn, the sun will fail to rise. Woe! Woe! Woe!' he intoned with some satisfaction.

'Aie! Aie! Aie!' agreed the village. It threw its shawls over its heads. It was the end!

The Wise One pulled his girdle more tightly in. He turned to stalk off, and in turning caught sight of Little Carlo standing before the well. Little Carlo turned to stone; fear and remorse reflected in his countenance. For see what his wickedness had brought on High Sierra; on Spain; on the whole world!

The Wise One, majestic and very empty, stalked up the hill. High Sierra stood there helplessly, watching the gaunt frame dwindle.

Then all High Sierra lamented together. All High Sierra advised at once. High Sierra turned with sixty-nine voices on the Mayor and ordered him to use his influence with Providence, but it soon transpired that this was the one direction in which there was not one near-relation of the Mayor's to be found.

High Sierra turned to the Corregidor. Was he not as twisty as a tendril? Could he not find some way in law to stop the ending of the established order? But crafty as he was, the Corregidor could not find a single clause to make the world keep turning.

Desperate, High Sierra steeled itself to disturb the Widow Alborado and called upon her to buy them out of total extinction. But money cuts no Spanish onions in Heaven, and for once the Widow's third eye could see no way out.

The sun was going to fail to rise tomorrow, and nothing and nobody could bring on the dawn. It was written in the stars. And it would mean the end of the world!

Even Little Carlo had found his voice and was using it to make sure of something: 'Before the prayer for rain?' he asked almost with hope.

'Yes, yes, poor little innocent,' said High Sierra, and it wept anew, and quite failed to notice that Little Carlo was looking, on the whole, relieved.

High Sierra set about preparing itself to meet the end of the world with clean, or at least with cleaner, hands.

Innocente, the village pilferer, whose wits were not blunted by the wear and tear of finding words to cloak them with, was the first to apply them to the squaring of the hereafter. Having, in the hubbub, filched, from force of habit, the handkerchief out of the apron-pocket of Concepcion, the innkeeper's suddenly less flashing young wife, now bethought himself and replaced it. But being less skilled in restoring than extracting, she caught him at it, and was about to box his ears, when she remembered her end, and with tears in her eyes, pressed it back into his astonished hand. And he, every bit as anxious to stand well in the sight of Heaven, pressed it back again. And the whole thing looked like developing into a nasty brawl, and there could be no shade of doubt that it was as well that there was going to be no giving and taking of handkerchiefs in the hereafter.

As for her husband, the innkeeper, he was engaged in a curious new kind of moral barter with, of all men, the young miller. Indeed, had not High Sierra had quite so much on its conscience at that moment, it would have been agog at this fascinating haggle.

'Take her, my friend, she's yours,' the innkeeper was saying emphatically.

'No, no, old friend,' the miller protested. 'I am resigned. I have restored Concepcion to her loving husband's arms.' He folded his own.

'And I,' said the innkeeper, 'decline to deprive you of her.'

They glared at one another.

Concepcion, who had solved the problem of the handkerchief by ripping it in two pieces, was glaring too.

Meanwhile, the Corregidors had flung a fatherly arm about Pedro the Penniless and was bestowing upon him the deeds of the farm he had so cleverly tricked him out of. In fact, everyone who had anything to give away, gave it, as hastily as a suddenly developed reluctance to receive, quite different from High Sierra's normal attitude to the property of other people, per-mitted.

Bolt upright in her bed, the Widow Alborado was banging unbelievingly on her floor with her ebony stick, her customary method of summoning her household to her. No-one had come hurrying in. No-one. Gradually it dawned on the rich old woman that her reign was over. Money could do nothing for her now that poverty held no terrors for other people. She would have to fall back upon natural affection.

'Ninny,' she shrilled. 'Elvira! Ninny! – where are you, hussy? Where are you, slut? Where are you, child . . .'

But her niece was out in the sun-baked square, hand in hand with Pedro the Penniless.

Even Ignatius, the village loafer, had arrived at a stern deci-sion and gone to work at last. There he was, scrubbing down the tables outside the inn. Luisita, hurrying past on her way to bear the tidings of the ending of the world to the Inglés who was to die tomorrow, nearly paused to take in the unaccustomed sight.

In his cell the Inglés awaited the advent of his little love with some amusement.

Here she came, as he knew she must, flying into his arms and babbling about the end of the world, bless her. He buried his face in her hair. She was trembling like a frightened child.

'Oh, Inglés,' she sobbed, 'Oh, Inglés, tomorrow we are to die after all together!'

'And would that be so very terrible, my little love?' he whispered.

And he was thinking, 'Perhaps tonight!' Perhaps . . .

Night had fallen in High Sierra – such a night as you never did know.

For the innkeeper had thrown open his cellars and the carousal was on the house. High Sierra, having made what terms it could with eternity, was now in a mood to enjoy its last night on earth.

Husbands and wives, for years estranged, sought one another out. Young lovers urged their mistresses to yield now, while there was still time. And there was to be a midnight wedding – or the next best thing.

For the Widow Alborado had consented to the marriage of her neice and ward, Elvira, to Pedro the Penniless. 'If you are determined to starve, Ninny, at least it will be only till tomorrow,' she rasped.

So though, with the priest away, Elvira and Pedro the Penniless could not be married in the church, they were to be wed by the Ceremony of the Candles – that ancient rite which High Sierra had inherited from those unenlightened centuries when it had still been nothing but a gipsy encampment.

And so, as the church clock creaked into the third quarter, the nine and seventy steps that lead down to the square became a glimmer of candle-shine, as from every house young people trooped to join the bride's procession.

And when they had gathered in the square, Elvira came down to her Pedro. She was all in white – a creamed and crackling white, for the gown had been the wedding dress of the Widow Alborado.

And there, in the presence of God and man, and well within

the vision of the third eye of the Widow Alborado, bolt upright in bed, bride and groom solemnly promised to cleave to one another till their last day should come. And together they paced the solemn measure of the dance of the candles, while rustic voices changed, and with here and there a hiccough. Until the village clock chimed twelve. And then, slowly, inexorably, the death bell tolled.

It was tolling for the village. For Spain. And for the whole world. And with its tolling the rustic voices ceased their wedding chant and sang together a threnody – it was the village death song, that they sang for the death of the village.

And when they had finished the threnody, High Sierra went its ways, some to cleave to one another. Some just to sleep. But most went back to the inn and drank themselves into a stupor.

In an olive-orchard, at the foot of the even higher Sierra, not a gourd's throw away from the Wise One's cave, the Inglés was lying under an oleander tree with his little love. For since he was to die tomorrow like everyone else in the world, of what avail to lock him up tonight? This was logic.

Yet he lacked the happy air of a man with his love beside him. Once again, love had failed to bring peace.

For the Inglés knew well that freedom lay ahead, yet was he impelled to stay here. Escape was not for him.

Luisita, by his side, gave a little sigh. She was coming back to a world of woe. But which woe? For the moment she'd got her sorrows mixed and it was the older one which possessed her spirit. 'Why did you have to kill?' she asked. 'Why you?'

So the Inglés lit a cigarette and tried to explain this thing that he could not understand himself.

'No man wants to kill another,' he told her, 'not if he has time to think. There are other ways . . . But maybe a man has need to kill. It can happen that way. Maybe there's a war and it's his duty to do it. And maybe he runs away and leaves other people to do his killing for him. We owe God a death,' said the Inglés. 'Shakespeare,' he added, 'and you can read it both ways.'

But his little love ceased listening. She was burying her face against his shoulder. How white and tender Ingléses were – and they smelt of soap – how strange!

Came the dawn. Or very nearly. To the sound of the tolling bell High Sierra blinked itself awake. Was it in Heaven already? If so, it looked strangely like its own village. And wherever it was its head was bursting. Aie!

The bell tolled.

High Sierra came suddenly to its scattered senses. The last sleep was upon it and here it was, asleep.

As one village, it betook itself to the rise of the hill. As one it turned its face to the East, waiting for the sun that would never rise and shine again in this world. And High Sierra trembled.

The bell tolled.

Up the hill came an unlooked-for sight. The Widow Alborado had left her bed. She advanced stiffly, for it was a quarter of a century since she had admitted to nether limbs. She advanced proudly, for high Spanish pride was hers by heritage. She advanced in company, for Innocente, the village pilferer, who dragged one foot behind, came whimpering with her, and together they wavered and dragged up the hill to die with all the village.

The bell tolled.

In the olive-orchard Luisita awoke. A succession of stubbed-out cigarettes proved that the Inglés had long been wakeful.

'Hark,' she said.

'Seek not to know for whom the bell tolls, for it tolls for you,' he misquoted. Luisita felt for her rosary.

The bell tolled, and the village sank upon its knees.

The bell tolled again. And again!

'Now,' thought High Sierra and it held its breath.

And as the bell gathered its sound the Wise One came out from his cave and stalked down the slope to the village. And as he stalked he rang the bell on the girdle at his waist.

'Attend! Attend!' he intoned. 'For Providence has relented.' The village attended. 'Seeing how well you have mended your way of life, the world will not come to an end . . . yet.'

The bell tolled again.

And even as he looked meaningly at his food bowl, the sun sailed out from behind the highest of the Sierras and touched the world to life.

Overwrought, the village turned and hugged its neighbour.

Little Carlo burst into tears. And all the time the great bell tolled.

Beside itself with joy, High Sierra ran down to the square to bring the tidings to Fernando, the bell-ringer.

So High Sierra, redeemed, looked at the world with new eyes. How good the blue sky looked today! How good their homes.

And that reminded them – whose turn was it to fill the Wise One's food bowl? For with the end of the world over, or at least postponed indefinitely, the threads of life must at once be resumed.

Straightaway Elvira hastened to the Widow Alborado's larder and filled the Wise One's bowl to overflowing with good rich goose and rosy rice and to spare – Elvira, the new bride.

Aie! For by now the village had had time to look the future in the face – and it did not care at all for certain of its features.

A pretty pass their good behaviour had brought them to!

Here was the Widow Alborado, denuded of her third eye, but in full possession of her legs. Aie!

And here was her ward and niece, Elvira, indisputably the wife of Pedro the Penniless, though not as penniless as he might have been, now that he had got his farm back from the Corregidor.

And here was the Corregidor, who had rashly given away all that he had stolen from the village, about to go into a huddle with his law-books to see how he could quibble it back again.

And, cruellest of all, here was Ignatius the loafer, stranded with a job on his hands, and already someone was bawling him out for not doing it!

The innkeeper and the miller were in angry conclave.

'And I demand that you, you give me back my wife.'

'And I demand that you return my mistress.' They glared . . .

The snap of a finger in their faces recalled their livid looks and focused them upon Concepcion, the flashing bone of their contention. Through with the pair of them, she was swinging her hips for the benefit of Alonzo, the village lecher.

And Little Carlo was running a temperature.

A pretty Spanish pass High Sierra had come to.

And who was the cause of it all?

As one village they turned to run the Wise One out of town.

But, as though by divination, already he had reached the seventy-ninth step and was about to dwindle over the bridge.

Triumphantly, gloriously, briskly the bell tolled on, for Fernando the bell-ringer was a man of habits not easily broken.

And up the nine and seventy steps, over the bridge, keeping to the shadow of the even higher Sierra, Dulcinea the Shrew betook her secret way to the Wise One's Juniper Tree. So now the day of judgment had turned out to be nothing but a misjudgment of the Wise One, the old fool. And that made it necessary to collect the Widow Alborado's mended rosary immediately.

Dulcinea had but one eye, and that evil, according to High Sierra. From force of habit Dulcinea's Evil Eye darted here and there as she crept up the slopes.

Aha! Carmen the cow, who belonged to Pedro the Penniless – for the moment – was about to calve. Aha!

And was that the mule of the village Contrabandista tethered outside merry Marika's cottage? Interesting, indeed!

And what was that beneath the oleander tree in the olive-orchard? The Evil Eye of Dulcinea the Shrew crept up behind a boulder the better to inform itself.

'So,' said Luisita, under the oleander, 'the bell was not for us today, after all,' and she laughed for the very joy of living.

Tenderly, gravely, the Inglés took her face between his hands.

'No, Luisita, the bell was not for you,' he said.

Luisita's eyes went wide. 'You,' she said. She covered her mouth with her hand. She had completely forgotten this earlier woe.

'Me?' The Inglés shrugged. And he laughed. But his laughter rang falsely. It cut straight to Luisita's heart.

'They couldn't kill you now,' she said.

'Why not?' said the Inglés grimly. 'Miguel Money-bags is dead. Nothing changes that.'

'Then you must go now. Now. At once!' Luisita's little hands began to push him, desperately, unavailingly. The Inglés caught them and kissed them.

'No, Luisita,' he said. 'Man owes God a death. And death is a debt I could have paid in the war if I had gone back to my country. Instead I stayed here; and instead I shall die here. And,' said the Inglés, 'that is all there is to it.'

The Evil Eye of Dulcinea the Shrew saw the rightness of this.

'Go, go, at once. Go quickly,' urged Luisita, 'and if you will not save your own life for your own sake, save it for mine.'

'No,' said the Inglés, 'no, my little love. I must stay.'

'But why?' she demanded. 'Why?'

'I will tell you why,' said a man's voice behind them.

The Evil Eye of Dulcinea the Shrew jumped.

It was José, the village hot-head.

The Inglés took a step towards him, and made to speak.

José ignored him. 'I will tell you why the Inglés will not go, little sister. It is because if he goes I must die.'

'You,' said Luisita. She did not seem surprised. But the boulder gave a gasp.

'I killed Miguel Money-bags,' said José the hot-head. 'Miguel Money-bags, pfui!'

'Yes,' said Luisita dully, 'it was you, José, I see that.'

The Evil Eye of Dulcinea the Shrew popped.

'He did it to save my life,' said the Inglés. 'And so it's only fair that I should save his. I shall do it by dying.'

'Dying,' said José the hot-head with scorn. 'What is it to die? Yesterday we were all going to die together. Today I die alone instead. Pfui!'

'Exactly,' said the Inglés. 'Only it is I who will do the technical act.'

'Thief!' cried José the hot-head. 'So now you plot to steal my honourable death from me!'

'Have you forgotten Little Carlo?' said the Inglés. 'Poor little Spanish Carlo?' Little Carlo. Brother and sister looked at one another. The boulder wriggled with delight.

'The Inglés is right, José. The one who dies must not be you,' said Luisita. 'For if you die there will be no one to care for Little Carlo.'

'There will be you. Nothing changes that.'

'No, José,' said Luisita, 'for I shall be in hiding with the Inglés. I, too, have a life,' she told them proudly.

'But I shall have none, this time tomorrow,' said the Inglés, 'for it was I who killed Miguel Money-bags, morally. When

José sprang at the gun it was being pointed not at him but at me. Only it went off in the body of Miguel Money-bags. So you see your brother saved my life, and now – let us say for no better reason than to save Little Carlo from the scolding of the Widow Alborado, I will be the one to die.'

'You are a brave man, Inglés,' said José the hot-head, 'but we Spaniards die our own deaths. Pfui!'

'And Little Carlo?' asked Luisita, 'shall he be left to the mercies of Dulcinea the Shrew?'

The boulder hissed.

'Shall the little innocent no longer walk before the priest at Mass?' She wept.

a'Little Carlo walks in the shadow of the family honour. In Spain this is an honour,' said José the hot-head.

'Poppycock,' said the Inglés.

'Pssst!' said Luisita.

For two figures had emerged from the Wise One's cave and had planted themselves in the shade of the Juniper Tree.

'But, my friend,' the priest was protesting under the Juniper Tree, 'that impulsive and singularly ill-founded prophecy of yours has sent my village back into the dark ages.' He tapped with his fingers on his stomach and he shook an admonishing head at the Wise One, who had surrounded himself with the village *objets d'art*, most of them in a minimum of three pieces.

'Oho!' said the Wise One, 'professional jealousy, eh?' He picked up half a china pitcher that belonged to Concepcion and dabbed it with juniper sap.

'Nevertheless, you have to admit,' he pointed out, 'that High Sierra had mended its ways.' He picked up the other half of the pitcher and set the two pieces together.

'Poof!' said the Priest. He was not impressed. 'As to that, I saw Innocente making off with a fine fat aubergine, as I passed through the square, which argues small improvement.'

The Wise One was searching round for the appropriate handle. There now! Concepcion's pitcher was all in one piece again, and ready for narrowly missing the innkeeper all over again.

'Backslider!' growled the Wise One. 'And that reminds me of a problem I have to pose.'

'Pose away, my friend,' said the priest.

'Let us suppose,' said the Wise One, speaking a little more loudly, 'let us suppose that a man is about to die for his friend.'

'To suppose costs no pesetas,' quoted the priest.

'Let us suppose,' the Wise One postulated, 'that these two friends have waylaid a traveller to – um – arbitrarily borrow gold.'

'Arbitrarily borrow,' said the priest, 'snff – snff – snff – that was well defined, my friend. Beautifully defined.' He closed his eyes and took a pinch of snuff.

'Let us suppose that this borrowing leads to a struggle,' said the Wise One, 'and in the struggle a gun goes off.'

'Pointed guns have hasty habits,' granted the priest.

'Let us suppose that the man who is willing to die for his friend, who in turn would have been dead, but for the struggle that ended in killing Mig . . . the traveller . . . has, by some miracle, been granted a chance to escape and live . . .'

'God is good,' said the priest. He looked approving.

'And some of His children are not without wisdom,' said the Wise One smugly. He smirked. 'However,' he continued, 'let us suppose that his man is now free to go with the little Luisita where they can live out their lives together.'

'Yes, my friend,' said the priest, 'let us suppose that.'

'But,' said the Wise One, 'let us also suppose that he is not willing to seize this chance of life, our innocent man, because the friend, who killed old Money-bags in his defence, has here a little son, who would be delivered up to the uncharitable.'

'Uncharitable folk in High Sierra,' said the Priest. 'Ttt – ttt - ttt!' He managed to sound shocked.

'My – um – my slight miscalculation over the end of the world,' admitted the Wise One, 'while it is a matter for general rejoicing, has left these three people with a problem that it is beyond even my powers to solve.'

'Oho!' said the priest.

'The man who did not kill holds that he has a right to die his own death.' The Wise One ticked off another finger.

'And the little Luisita?' asked the priest.

'She thinks of Little Carlo and she weeps.'

From under the oleander, a stifled sob floated across to the Juniper Tree. The two old gentlemen wiped their own eyes.

'And who can wonder,' said the Wise One, 'for is she not

sister to the man who killed and – um – betrothed – to the other?'

'Betrothed,' said the priest, well pleased. 'Well, well, it seems only the other day I was christening the little Luisita!'

'To the point,' chided the Wise One. He reached for more juniper juice. 'What is the view of the Church on this three-cornered predicament?'

The priest took a pinch more snuff. Then he said, thoughtfully, 'For a man to take the life of another is mortal sin. But for the man to save the life of another, this is accounted unto him for virtue . . . And since intention must rank, in the golden ledger of the blessed recording angel, as high as the achievement, the act, after some temporal atonement, will be cancelled out.'

'Ah!' said the Wise One. He had counted on this. 'Therefore I take it that you would take your purse and fill it with the paltry pesetas that the Widow Alborado donated so hastily to the poor box yesterday . . .'

The priest held a leather money-bag aloft and smiled gently at his friend.

'. . . and place it for – um – safety under the Juniper Tree . . .'

'For safety,' said the priest, 'that was well bethought.'

'And you would leave it there and forget to take it with you.'

'The memory of man,' sighed the priest, 'is full of holes.'

'So that the Inglés, happening upon it, may have the means to escape and take with the little Luisita.'

'And even put a little away for a sunny day,' said the Priest.

'Quite, quite, quite, quite! And you, my friend,' he ordered, 'will take your food bowl . . .'

'Wazzat?' said the Wise One.

'Filled to overflowing with rosy rice and good rich goose . . .'

'Blessed if I will,' said the Wise One, showing fight.

'And you will place it,' said the priest, quite unperturbed, 'beside my money-bag, and you will lose your appetite . . .'

'Never!' said the Wise One hotly.

'You will lose your appetite,' ordered the priest sternly.

'Oh, very well,' said the Wise One, 'but don't forget what happened last time I missed my meal.'

'And you will leave it behind where the little Luisita can find it, that they may not starve before they reach the border.' He pointed and the Wise One crossly complied.

'To starve at our age,' said the priest light-heartedly, 'is better than to pay an insurance premium.' It was not for nothing that he had been nicknamed Pius the Practical at his seminary.

'And what of the man who killed?' asked the Wise One.

'That one,' said the priest, 'must give himself up – as an act of expiation.'

The oleander tree sobbed anew.

'But,' he added hastily, 'since the gun went off in self-defence and the death of the man was accidental, they will only send him to gaol for a time.'

'Pfui!' said the oleander.

'And there,' went on the priest, more loudly, 'he will atone for the – um – arbitrary borrowing of Miguel's money-bags, and one or two other little matters, for he is a hot headed young man.'

The oleander tree said something rude but the priest failed to hear it.

'And after that?' enquired the Wise One, eyeing his food bowl hungrily.

'And thereinafter,' said the priest with a twinkle, 'I would invite a foolish friend of mine to dine with me.'

'Let's go,' said the Wise One. He rose.

So did the boulder.

'A pretty pair of plotters,' screeched Dulcinea the Shrew, and she picked up her petticoats and ran, while the two old gentlemen picked up their skirts and came running after her.

And as she ran, Dulcinea flung verbal stilettos of living venom over her shoulder at them. She was going to tell the village that the Inglés who had held up Miguel Money-bags was on the run. And that José the hot-head, his killer, was in their midst. And she was going to brand Little Carlo as a son of a gunman. And – clearly this was the worst threat of all – she was going to tell her mistress, the Widow Alborado, just what had been done with her poor-box pesetas! And all at the top of her voice.

Till the Wise One was forced to drown her upbraiding with a great ringing of his bell; and thus, helter-skelter and hugger-mugger, they came clattering over the bridge and down the nine and seventy steps.

From the sun-baked square High Sierra gazed at its livid Greek chorus with sullen disapproval.

Was the end of the world coming after all? High Sierra hoped not. Right now it was busy laying its garlands of flowers at the foot of the shrine of Our Lady of Showers, ready for that monthly act of optimism, the prayer for rain.

'Neighbours! Neighbours! To me! To me!' screeched Dulcinea. 'Aie!'

On an impulse the Wise One had picked up a dwarf cactus and thrown it at her. He missed. Unlucky!

To High Sierra, suffering from reaction, spiritual and spirituous, this was more than too much. As one village it hurled everything it happened to have with it, on it, or near it, rapturously into the air. Soon the square was full of flying marrows, pomegranates, hats, boots and china – preferably other people's. Tables and chairs rained down light-hearted as confetti.

Dulcinea made to mount a table to address the populace. Wham! a well-aimed melon struck her amidships. On second thoughts she crept beneath the table. This did not stop her from screeching. Vengeance was hers! 'In the name of Miguel Money-bags, he who has died the death, I call upon you, good neighbours, to avenge yourselves upon his assassin! Assassin! Ass . . .' What was that she could just define, as she peered out from the table with her one eye? A familiar shape, undeniably rotund, effulgently protruberant – it was the pot-belly of Miguel Money-bags.

From the porch of the church the priest smiled happily. He had known all along. For had he not come upon Miguel at the cross-roads with scarce a breath in his body, and had him cared for at the monastery, which was why he had been absent from his overwrought parish for longer than had been anticipated.

And as for High Sierra, it stopped throwing things and began to laugh. And there it staggered, laughing wildly, hysterically and with tears running down its cheeks, at the sight of Dulcinea crouching under her table, confronted by her dead man, and hardly able to credit the evidence of her own one eye.

Ha! Ha! Ha! Ha!

Ho! Ho! Ho! Ho!

Hee! Hee! Hee! Hee!
High Sierra, tickled to death, was killing itself with laughter.

And now, out of the church and down thirty-three of the nine and seventy steps and into the laughing sun-baked square wound the solemn processional for the prayer for rain, with Little Carlo at its head swinging a censor. His eyes were black beads of terror, and his face was like a ghost. Nothing could save him now.

Inexorably the processional advanced on the shrine of Our lady of Showers, their voices raised in ancient chant. More soberly the village stood around with here and there a hiccough. It was time for the golden grille to be opened.

Little Carlo lifted a hand to it that trembled. Now all was lost indeed.

A great hush had fallen on the village. Slowly the golden grille swung open. Little Carlo dared not to breathe. But forlornly, and very bravely, he fixed his gaze upon the open shrine. And there, smiling down at him, and out to all High Sierra, stood Our Lady of Showers, kind and gentle and infinitely whole.

And only the Wise One knew that just above the girdle of her beautiful blue cloak was a juniper stain.

And even as Little Carlo wondered, and High Sierra adored, there fell the first, the unexpected, the most welcome miracle – a great plop of rain.